Unraveled

Books by Reavis Z. Wortham

The Red River Mysteries
The Rock Hole
Burrows
The Right Side of Wrong
Vengeance is Mine
Dark Places
Unraveled

Unraveled

A Red River Mystery

Reavis Z. Wortham

Poisoned Pen Press

First Edition 2016

10 9 8 7 6 5 4 3 2 1

Library of Congress Catalog Card Number: 2016933731

ISBN: 9781464207099   Hardcover
      9781464207112   Trade Paperback

Poisoned Pen Press
6962 E. First Ave., Ste. 103
Scottsdale, AZ 85251
www.poisonedpenpress.com
info@poisonedpenpress.com

Printed in the United States of America

This book is dedicated to The Hunting Club, a loose, unofficial group of outdoorsmen I've camped, fished, and hunted with for the last thirty years. Thanks to the original core group—Larry Williams, Jerry Halpin, Dr. Gary Reeves, and Pat Chumley—for providing the fun, laughs, and inspiration that created the syndicated newspaper column, which morphed into the gang from Doreen's 24 HR Eat Gas Now Café, and eventually provided the author's voice that led to the Red River series.

Acknowledgments

Many people have supported my work by reading early manuscripts, offering suggestions, and spreading the word about my novels. Thanks to my mentor and good friend John Gilstrap (I'll never be able to repay my debt), C.J. Box, Craig Johnson, Sandra Brannan, Jeffery Deaver, Joe Lansdale, T. Jefferson Parker, Michael Morris, Owen Laukkanen, and Jan Reid, to name only a few authors who have supported my work. The same goes for Sharon Reynolds, Mike Miller, and Steve Knagg (for reading the manuscripts). Ronda Wise is my go-to gal for all things medical. Things wouldn't be the same around here without my English teacher daughter, Chelsea Hamilton, for offering academic insights and our youngest daughter, Megan Bidelman, for the jacket photo. Thanks also to my agent Anne Hawkins, and Poisoned Pen Press editors, Annette Rogers and Barbara Peters. You gals are great.

All this rides on one foundation, the love of my life, my wife, Shana, who is always at my side (good luck in your new adventure)! You all offer more faith than I deserve.

And thanks to you, the Readers out there who support my work. It is humbling.

Frisco, Texas

Chapter One

Grandpa Ned always said our quiet little country community in northeast Texas was like a stock pond, calm and smooth on the surface so there's not much to look at, but full of life and death down below.

Center Springs wasn't much to see back in 1968. I guess what you'd call the hub of our community was an unpainted domino hall squatting between two clapboard country stores at the intersection of Farm to Market Road 197 that ran east and west, and FM 906 that started there and crossed the Lamar County Dam.

A skinny county oil road angled to the northwest behind the domino hall and past the Ordway place, a fine two-story house full of ghosts and bad memories.

Mostly all you ever saw up at the stores were a few farmers loafing either on Uncle Neal's porch, where we did most of our trading, or under the overhang at Oak Peterson's competing store that carried the same staples, plus gas.

Houses were scattered beside pastures full of fat cattle everywhere along Sanders Creek and the Red River bottoms. Those small scratch farms that survived the Great Depression and hung on tight to the land had been in the same families for generations.

A lot of folks lived way back in the woods off dirt and gravel roads. Most waved when they saw you, except for a few old soreheads who turned away so they wouldn't have to wave back.

Since he was constable of Precinct 3, Grandpa got called out both night and day for more than you'd expect for such a small place. There were family fights, reports of whiskey stills, misunderstandings, cattle on the roads, fistfights, farm accidents, or car wrecks.

Because of a cluster of cinderblock beer joints called Juarez across the river in Oklahoma not five miles away, drunks came weaving through our little community most every week.

Most of the time Grandpa pulled 'em over and hauled 'em to jail in nearby Chisum, the county seat. But sometimes he came along to find cars all tore to pieces and bodies on the road, or in a ditch, or slammed into trees. The ones that made Grandpa the maddest was them that took other good folks with 'em.

It was a car wreck only a few weeks after Reverend King had been laid to rest that tangled Grandpa Ned up in what folks started calling the Lamar County Accident.

Oh, and I'm Top Parker, and this is how we wound up in the middle of all that trouble....

Chapter Two

The scruffy man slipped out of the house in his stocking feet. The eastern sky would soon brighten, but he'd be long gone by then. He'd stood in the shadows for a long time, watching the sleeping couple tangled in the damp sheets and listening to their soft breathing. He sat on the edge of the porch as if he owned the place, pulled on his shoes, and walked in the open until he reached the woods, not caring that he left a trail in the wet grass. It might make it more fun if they noticed.

The Motorola mounted under the Plymouth's dash squawked. Deputy Anna Sloan's soft voice cut through the static. "Ned, you there?"

The slender deputy was on desk duty, working dispatch after nearly dying from a gunshot wound early in the fall. It always startled Ned to hear Deputy Sloan on the radio instead of Martha Wells. Martha had worked the day shift on dispatch for thirty years.

Without taking his eyes off the road, Constable Ned Parker leaned over and turned the volume up to drown out the stock report coming through the dash radio. His grandkids in the back seat sat forward to hear. Fifteen-year-old cousins Top and Pepper were so similar in appearance that strangers thought they were twins, though Top was unusually short for his age.

Ned plucked the microphone off the bracket. "Right 'chere."

"There's been a bad wreck on the Lake Lamar Dam. Somebody missed the curve and went off the backside."

"Oh, my God!" In the passenger seat, Ned's Choctaw wife, Miss Becky, covered her mouth and closed her eyes, saying a quick prayer for those in the car.

Ned stomped the foot-feed and the Plymouth Fury's big engine roared. They were on Highway 271 and had to loop through Powderly to come in from the east side. "I'm on the way, and don't you try to come out here. You ain't healed up enough yet."

"I won't."

Miss Becky patted the big purse in her lap, as if that would emphasize her words. "Drive careful, Ned. Don't forget them kids in the back."

Top frowned in exasperation. "I'm not afraid of going fast."

Ned ignored the boy's comment as warm, humid air blowing through the open window threatened to snatch the hat off his head. "I knew somebody'd go off that dam, but I didn't think it would happen so quick."

"They got reflectors there." Top's near-twin Pepper could never sit back and not be a part of any adult conversation. She held her long brown hair in the slipstream, adjusting the headband with one hand and holding an eagle feather in place. An Indian boy gave it to her in New Mexico and she wore it attached to a headband almost all the time.

"It don't make no difference. That curve sneaks up on you if y'ain't payin' no attention to it."

She wouldn't quit. "You expected somebody to drown, first."

The Lake Lamar Dam wasn't a year old, and the lake itself not quite full. Ned nearly worried himself sick from the time he heard they were going to build it only a mile from his house. His baby brother drowned when they were kids, and Ned never got over his fear of water. It was the thirty-degree bend near the midpoint of the dam that scared him the most, because he was always afraid someone would miss the shallow angle.

"Y'all hush." He keyed the mike as he made a U-turn on the highway. "John. You get that?"

Deputy John Washington's rich, deep voice cut through the static. The huge, almost mythical black deputy was always at Ned's side. "On the way, Mr. Ned."

The familiar voice of Sheriff Cody Parker came through. "This is Cody, Ned. I'm almost to Deport. It'll take me a while to finish up and get back there."

"All right, then." Ned slowed to make the left hand turn onto the winding road lined with pine and hardwood trees. Talking softly to himself, he alternately slowed and accelerated, depending on the whim of the two-lane. The lake broke into view. When they passed the recently constructed overlook point cut into the woods, he saw two pickups parked several yards away from the curve at the midpoint in the mile-long dam.

A knot of locals stood in the middle of the road, making no effort to do anything but stare downward off the backside toward the spillway.

That's when Ned knew it was bad.

Chapter Three

Grandpa braked to a stop about twenty yards from the ragged hole in the guardrail. Several posts were sheared off at the ground, and the mangled rails bent outward over the steep drop. He angled the car to block both lanes and yanked the door handle. "Y'all stay here."

Miss Becky folded both hands on top of the purse in her lap. "My stars."

"It's too hot to sit in here." Pepper rolled her window down and we watched Grandpa join the two men I recognized as Uncle Neal Box and Jimmy Dale Warner. I believe it was the first time I'd ever seen Uncle Neal out of his store, and for some reason he didn't look as big as he did behind the counter.

Pepper was right, the humidity hung heavy over the bottoms. The men milling on the road already had sweat stains under their arms and it was barely nine in the morning.

"I need some air." In two seconds Pepper was out of the car with me right after.

"You kids don't get underfoot! Stay close to the car and don't be looking over there." Miss Becky closed her eyes again and I figured she was praying. She spent a lot of time doing that, especially for Pepper.

"Yes ma'am!" I called over my shoulder, because I knew my dumb girl cousin wouldn't answer.

Grandpa was talking to Uncle Neal when we came up behind

him, trying to stay out of his sight as long as possible. "Either of y'all been down there?"

"My knees won't let me." Uncle Neal ran his hand through wavy white hair that stood straight up. I almost laughed at the thought of the big, soft, barrel-shaped man huffing and puffing down and back up the steep slope.

Miss Becky's eyes were still closed, so I peeked over the guardrail and saw what was left of a red car not far from the spillway at the bottom of the earth dam. It looked like it had been through the wringer because every square inch was scraped or dented. The hood and a fender lay in the dirt halfway down a long swipe through the dew that showed the car's path. A set of tracks angled down in the soft ground where someone had already worked their way down to the car.

Jimmy Dale shook his head at Grandpa's question. I knew him from the store, but he lived on Bodark Creek, not far from Telephone. "I did. There's a woman inside, and a man's body under the car. I think he was throwed out right there at the end and the car rolled over on him."

Grandpa blew his lips out like he did when he was thinking. Sometimes he talked to himself, but there were enough men so he didn't have to. "I don't recognize the car, what there is left of it."

Uncle Neal rattled the change in his pants pocket. "Well, it's a Pontiac Bonneville convertible and it belongs to Maggie Mayfield."

"She's that high yeller gal from Slate Shoals."

"She is."

"Wonder what she was doing out this way?"

"That's the *other* piece of the puzzle. It's Frank Clay under the car."

Grandpa studied the car, both hands in his pockets. "*Mayor* Frank Clay?"

"Yep."

"Oh, hell. That ain't no puzzle. It's a problem."

Jimmy Dale pulled at his ear. "What do you mean?"

"I don't know if you remember, you were probably too young, but the Mayfields and Clays got crossways during the war right after Pearl Harbor. Before it was over, more than half a dozen people were dead, some on both sides. I like to never got all that sorted out, and wouldn't have done it if Old Man Mayfield hadn't died of a heart attack one day while he was drawing water from their well.

"Somebody would have said he was murdered, if his wife and a couple of kids weren't right there in the yard when he dropped the water bucket and fell over dead as a doornail. He's the one kept it going for so long, and things settled down a few months later. Now here they are all tangled up again."

"Maybe nothing'll happen." Jimmy Dale stared across the lake. "Do you reckon?"

Grandpa grunted. It was answer enough.

"Nobody else in the car?"

Jimmy Dale looked like he was more interested in the lake itself than the mangled car on the other side of the dam. "Nope. Her and Frank was the only two."

Grandpa followed his gaze and studied the calm water like the answers were floating out there on the surface. Drowning trees with shimmering green leaves fringed the edges. "She's separated from her old man. I heard she was living with her daddy-in-law, Hollis Mayfield, instead of her mama's people."

"I don't know nothing about what niggers do."

"Well, Jimmy Dale, her mama's white, so I reckon you ought not call her that."

"Don't matter. Her daddy's black as…"

"So's John Washington, but that don't make him any less a man." He jerked a thumb toward me and Pepper. "Them's my grandkids, so watch what you call people."

It was a shock to realize he knew we were there, even though he still had his back to us and we'd moved side to side like two of The Three Stooges to stay behind him. I always figured he had eyes in the back of his bald head, and he sure proved it to me that time.

Jimmy Dale wouldn't leave it alone. "Why? She didn't have no business riding around with Frank Clay. They're married to different people."

"She might have give him a ride." Grandpa rubbed the back of his sweaty neck. "I do that all the time with Mrs. Peters."

"It ain't the same."

I always thought Mrs. Peters was the sweetest old woman I ever met, besides my Miss Becky. Though Mr. Peters had a truck just like every other man in Center Springs, Mrs. Peters walked everywhere she went, hoofing it in her old sensible shoes. She even walked from their unpainted house up behind the cotton gin to the Assembly of God church across the pasture from our house, no matter if it was Sunday or for night services, rain or shine, cold or hot.

Grandpa looked a little aggravated. "Everybody gives her a ride, if she'll take it, and she usually does. They pick up Cliff Vanderberg, too. Folks still help others."

Uncle Cliff walked just as much because he didn't have a car, only it was mostly from his house to the store and back.

Mr. John Washington's highway patrol cruiser rounded the bend and came past the overlook to slow down and squeeze past Grandpa's Plymouth. He crept past us to the other side and used his car to block the highway from that direction, putting us in a safe pen on top of the dam.

Jimmy Dale turned so he didn't face Mr. John straight on when he walked up. I guess it was better than turning his back on him, but not by much.

Mr. John winked at us. "Mr. Ned. You was right. This old lake is already tied to death and it ain't a year old." As usual, he was chewing on a toothpick. "Who is it this time?"

"Maggie Mayfield."

He sucked in his breath and sidled over to the steep drop-off to see the car below. "I reckon somebody's done made sure she ain't hurtin' down there."

"I did." Jimmy Dale didn't take his eyes off the lake.

Pepper whispered close and the eagle feather in her hair tickled when it brushed my neck. "He was worried they didn't go down and check on somebody who's colored."

Her comment shook me, because I couldn't believe anyone would leave a person alive and hurting in such a bad wreck. "How do you know that?"

She didn't answer, because she wanted to hear the men's conversation.

"Was Tylee in the car with her?" Mr. John directed his question toward Grandpa, because he could already see that Jimmy Dale didn't think much of him.

"Said Frank Clay's underneath."

"Ohhhhhh." He trailed off.

Grandpa didn't look at Mr. John. He studied the torn up slope of the dam. "What'n hell's a big wheel in a small town doing out running around with a colored girl? They were just asking for trouble."

Pepper whispered in my ear again. "Frank Clay's the mayor and Tylee's that woman's husband."

"How do you know all this?"

She rolled her eyes and we leaned again. I bet it looked like one of those *Wild Kingdom* shows in TV where birds bob their heads around to one another. "I listen."

"Well, I listen too, but I don't hear these kinds of things." A car pulled up and two men got out. I recognized them both.

"That's 'cause you tune people out when they're not talking about hunting and fishing. You ought to get your nose out of them books of yours and you'll hear a lot more than you do."

She was probably right. I spent a lot of time reading when adults were around, because they usually talked about things I didn't have any use for. I stood there wishing I'd paid more attention.

The two new arrivals hadn't said a word. One was Chester Davis, who farmed in the bottoms, and the other was Rod Post, the community's shade tree mechanic who worked on everything from cars to tractors.

Mr. Rod let out with a low whistle. "That roll beat the *hound* out of that Bonneville."

Beyond them, I saw Mr. Ike Reader's green GMC pickup coming our way from Center Springs. Grandpa saw it too. He reached around, grabbed my shoulder and pulled me to his side. "Go get your grandmother and tell her Ike Reader's gonna take y'all home."

"We're not going to town after all?" That's where we were headed when Grandpa got the call. Going to town was a big deal for me. Miss Becky bought groceries while me and Pepper went to the show. We usually made a stop at the Woolworths so I could get either a comic, a book, or a model car. Pepper always bought 45s that she played on her red and white portable record player.

He gripped tighter without looking at me.

"Yessir." When he turned me loose, I walked to the car. "Grandpa says Mr. Ike's gonna take us back to the house."

Miss Becky gathered her purse like she'd been expecting it. "That'll be just fine. We can get groceries later."

Pepper fell in beside me and didn't say a word as Miss Becky led us past the men who all said hello but really wanted to get back to talking about the wreck. I knew Pepper was planning something, though. I just couldn't figure it out.

We passed through the men and the hole torn in the guardrail. There was a really short set of skid marks that led to the gap. I could imagine the shriek of rubber as the car went through the rail.

Grandpa met Mr. Ike before he could get to the knot of men. The jerky little farmer was talking long before he got to Grandpa and it aggravated that old bald man to no end.

"Ned, listen, you need for me to do anything?"

Grandpa took off his straw hat. "Sure do." He rubbed the sweat off his head and replaced it. "I need you to take Becky and these kids home."

Mr. Ike's face fell, and I could tell he'd rather do anything than drive us to the house.

"Thank you, Ike." Miss Becky gave his skinny arm a pat through his gray shirt sleeve and led the way to the truck, with us marching along behind like baby ducks.

Mr. Ike stuttered a little. "Well, all right then. Listen, listen Ned, I'll be right back once I drop 'em off."

"That'll be fine, Ike. Thank-yee."

With Miss Becky in the cab, and us kids riding on the tailgate with our feet dangling into space, Mr. Ike carefully turned his truck around. When he was backing up, I looked across the creek bottom from that high point like I always did to see our house, over a mile away. Behind it was the barn, sitting on the hill above *our* hill. Down and to the left, I could barely see the roof of Uncle Cody and Aunt Norma Faye's house that Mr. Tom Bell willed to them after he disappeared down in Mexico.

Mr. Ike stopped and as he ground the gears into first, I looked down between my feet and saw a two-foot skid mark shaped in a crescent moon over the solid yellow lines in the middle of the highway.

Mr. Ike accelerated as a wrecker pulled up from the far side of the dam, followed by two ambulances. One of them was a sprung Cadillac from the funeral home the colored people used.

It was a good thing, because the other one wouldn't have transported a high-yellow woman for love nor money.

Chapter Four

The Wraith wiped sweat from his forehead with an oily rag. It was easy for him to get away from his job for an hour or two. As long as he did his work, no one said much. But the best time was before dawn when he could come and go without anyone knowing. He tightened the loose nut on a pivot pin, straightened, and waved to an associate that he was finished.

Ike Reader hadn't completely finished his three-point turn when Phil Bates arrived from Powderly. His wrecker barely had enough room to pass Ned's car, squeezing by with only inches to spare. He stopped close to the men gathered beside the missing rail.

Ned stepped to Phil's open window. "We can't move it yet, not 'til Buck gets here. We got two dead down there."

"I'm in no hurry. I'll wait. Who is it?"

"Frank Clay and Maggie Mayfield."

Phil grunted. "*Mayor* Clay?'"

"Yep."

"Jesus. How far down are they?"

"All the way."

"I may not have enough cable." He pointed in the direction of the highway that wound past Ned's house, knowing that once he crossed the Sanders Creek bridge, a dirt road skirted a pasture of alfalfa nor far from the creek. "Can I go around and get to it from down there?"

Ned thought for a moment. "No. They cut a road when they were working, but it warshed out with all the rain back in the fall."

Buck Johnson was the county Justice of the Peace and it was his job to pronounce the victims dead before the bodies could be moved. He arrived twenty minutes later to join a growing crowd in the middle of the dam. "Well hell, Ned. I'm getting tired of death exams around this lake, and around here in general."

"I don't blame you." Ned jerked his head toward the nearly unrecognizable car. "You're not gonna like this one a'tall. There's two bodies down there and one of 'em's Frank Clay. It's a steep climb, but John'll go with you and take the cable down with y'all. You can hold onto that to help you back up."

"Oh, hell." Buck thought for a moment. "You been down?"

Ned unconsciously rubbed the scar on his stomach from a recently healed bullet wound. "Naw. I ain't in any shape for that."

Big John led the way down the steep slope with two folded quilts under one arm, digging his boot heels into the soft soil to remain upright. Buck followed, using those same deep impressions as steps all the way to the bottom.

Standing with his shins against the undamaged rail, Ned saw Buck stop beside the woman's arm hanging out the window. He took her wrist to check for a pulse. He lowered it, pressed her neck, then moved around to the other side where he and John knelt and disappeared behind the battered car.

Seconds later John stood and cupped both hands around his mouth. "Have Phil bring a chain down with that spare cable he carries! That'll be enough to reach, and we can get the car off Frank!"

Phil backed the wrecker to the edge of the pavement and leaving the engine running, worked his way down with a chain and cables. Buck helped him attach the rig and he puffed his way back up the steep slope with Phil while John stayed below to make sure the chain didn't slip off once they took up the slack.

At the top, Buck caught his breath. Phil climbed into the cab and the engine idle increased.

"Is it really Frank Clay down there with that colored gal?"

"Rod, let the man blow for a minute." Ned stepped back as the winch tightened the cable. The wrecker settled, trembled, and the cable vibrated like a guitar string before the car finally moved.

Ned took Buck's arm and moved him out of earshot. "It was Frank for sure?"

"Yep."

More local farmers arrived. One was Ross Dyer, a man with hairy ears and the sour stink of armpit sweat. Ned never cared for him because he was eating candy every time Ned saw him at the store, but the man never took any home to his kids. Dyer pulled Rod's shirtsleeve between a thumb and forefinger. "That's the mayor down there?"

"Yep."

"I thought he had better sense than to run around with another woman. I guess they *are* town people."

Aggravated that Dyer was asking questions, Ned rubbed his chin. "He moved to town and the rest of that Clay bunch stayed out 'chere, farming, raising kids, and cooking a little moonshine every now and then. I catch 'em when I can and run 'em in for it."

Frank Clay's family had lived in Center Springs for generations. They were sullen and clannish for the most part, but Frank always had more ambition than the rest. He wanted to leave Center Springs for state politics.

The questions piqued Buck's interest. "He never was as mean as them others."

"You're right about that. Frank broke away from the rest of that sorry pack and worked hard to earn enough money for college. He came back to Chisum, did pretty good in land, and went on and made a politician. Got on the city council and then got hisself elected mayor. I hear he throwed his hat into the ring for state representative. He's been running with the bigwigs down in Austin." Ned tilted his straw hat back. "Thissun'll make the front page of the paper."

"It'll be on the TV, too." Buck cut off a hunk of Days Work chewing tobacco and tucked it into his cheek.

"He almost made it, didn't he?" Despite Frank being a Clay, Ned had been following his rise and had voted for him in every election.

"Don't mean nothin'. He was just another man." Ross Dyer spat over the rail and walked away, digging in his ear.

Buck watched him go. "It's a damned shame, that's for sure."

"I bet the county'll want to put up a monument to him."

Buck closed his knife and settled the chew into his cheek. "That don't usually happen to dead politicians that ain't got to going yet."

Ned watched a sheriff's car pass the lookout and slow. "It will this one. He was different."

Sheriff Cody Parker pulled around a long line of vehicles waiting for the accident to be cleared. On the Center Springs side of the lake, an even longer line of trucks waited. Most had driven out to see the wreck, while a few were simply trying to cross the dam.

Sheriff Cody Parker left his door open, settled the Colt 1911 on his hip, and worked his way through the gathering crowd. He stopped beside Ned and watched the car containing Maggie's draped body top the crest.

The old constable waved toward the car as Buck gently placed her bare arm under the quilt made from flour sacks. "Cody, That's Maggie Mayfield. I reckon you know her from your joint." He almost spat the word as if it had a nasty taste. Cody still owned The Sportsman, a rough cinderblock honky-tonk in a cluster of mean clubs on the shallow Oklahoma bank of the Red River. Folks called it Juarez, referring to the joints south of the Rio Grande, in Mexico. Ned had been after him to sell what he called the gun and knife honky-tonk after Cody was elected sheriff, but he was disinclined to do it.

Cody ignored the comment and peered over the rail at John who waited with Frank's covered body "This ain't good, Ned."

The old constable sighed. "I'm afraid this is as good as it's gonna get."

Chapter Five

Mr. Ike let us out at the house and left to get back to the wreck before we were even on the porch. The phone was ringing and Miss Becky hurried in to join the local grapevine. I followed Pepper around to the north side of the house where we could barely see the top of the dam through a gap in the trees across the road.

She stepped up on the porch to get a better view overlooking the highway that wound around our hill like a stream around a rock. "I still can't see much. You know, we can walk to it from here. It ain't that far down to the wreck."

"It's on the other side of what was the creek."

The engineers had dredged and straightened Sander's Creek at the spillway, I reckon so water could get away from the dam pretty fast when the lake was high. It stayed straight for a quarter mile until reaching the woods they hadn't knocked down, and then turned back into a wiggly creek. The bridge was a mile and a half from there.

"Top, you beat all. We can walk down to the bridge and after we cross, it won't take us no time to get there."

"They'll all be gone by then."

"Right. That's the idea. They didn't want us there in the first place, but I want to see where the car landed."

"It'll just be a big old gouge." I wasn't sure about going back. I figured it would be a lot like seeing the highway after a car wreck, some scuff marks and maybe a piece of chrome or two.

"Well dammit. I'm going alone, then."

She was always like that, coming up with ideas that usually got us in trouble.

We waited an hour before drifting off the porch and across the yard to the corner fence post behind the house where we played in a deep sand cut when we were little. The cut overlooked the highway and we got in trouble one time for throwing clods at the cars passing below. Even when we missed they hit the road and grass with an explosion of sand and dust.

Most folks never noticed because our aim was so bad, but I got hold of a good solid clod one day and led a truck just right. It hit square on the hood of an International and Mr. Floyd Cass slammed on the brakes so hard he almost threw Mrs. Cass through the windshield. He pulled right up our drive and when Miss Becky stepped out on the porch to see who it was, he told her what happened.

We got in pretty bad trouble over that, but didn't get a whippin', mostly because she didn't tell Grandpa. He found out a couple of days later up at the store, but by then it was too late. He was pretty mad, but she'd already made us cut the yard and clean out the chicken house as our punishment.

I think I'd rather have had the whippin', because it would have been over a lot quicker and chicken houses stink like butt.

Grass had spread over most of our play pile in the past couple of years and it was almost grown over. I kicked at the loose sand for a minute, thinking. When I glanced back up, Pepper'd started down the slope. "Hey. We're gonna get covered in sandburs."

I knew that for a fact, because when we were about eight, we decided to roll all the way down that same hill. We'd only made about two turns when we both jerked up from the sharp pain of hundreds of sandburs stuck in our clothes. My dad and Uncle James laughed loud and long while we cried and they picked the stickers out one at a time.

"I guess you'll learn to think before you act," Dad said. I recalled his voice that day, but was surprised when I realized that many of those details were already starting to fade. The sound of his voice was getting away from me since he and Mama died.

Pepper led the way. Gravity grabbed us both and we jumped a couple of times to the bottom of the hill to keep our balance. She darted across the highway without looking, but that was okay, because you could always hear cars hissing down the pavement long before they arrived. Instead of following the road like she said, she cut down a deer trail through the woods.

I saw the cuffs of her jeans were full of stickers. Mine had just as many. "Hey, this won't take us to the other side."

"I know a way. We're gonna have to cross that big ol' foot log over Center Springs Branch, though. C'mon!"

"Watch for snakes."

She slowed down some. Folks in Center Springs were killing snakes left and right since the lake started filling up. We'd seen more rattlers and water moccasins than usual when they started clearing the creek bottoms, but the rising water ran 'em out in numbers the old folks were talking about up at the store.

One week before, someone ran over a big old timber rattler close to the house. Uncle Cody called us down to see it. He cut its head off, then gave the tail a shake so we'd know what a rattler sounded like. It had thirteen rattles and a button, and I hoped I'd never run across one without having a hoe close by.

Pepper jogged through the trees and I had to hurry to keep up. Minutes later we came out in an open pasture. Hot as it was, we still loped through the deep grass until we came to the woods bordering the branch.

The clear spring water of Center Springs Branch ran across both sand and gravel bars. Grandpa said the Indians used to come out of the Oklahoma Territory and camp there before he was born. The sites were somewhere nearby and the Indians traded with the white settlers who started our community. We were always finding arrowheads and old rusty pieces of metal, and once I found a spear point that saved my life.

Uncle Cody and Grandpa liked to hunt quail and squirrels along the branch, too. I'd been down there often enough to know the land, and where the big old red oak tree Pepper was headed for had fallen across the branch. The last time we hunted down there, Uncle Cody and I used the foot log to cross to the other side.

That was the day we sat on that log and he told me some things about my mama that I'd never heard. She and Daddy died in a car wreck right before I came to live with Grandpa and Miss Becky, and there was a lot I didn't know.

Uncle Cody pointed toward the deep branch. "See that foot log there?"

The steep bank fell off to the trickle of water far below.

"It's a long way down."

"Yep. That tree's been there before you was even thought of. I crossed it with your mama and daddy the year before you were born, on the way to catch some crappie out of the creek. I've always been a little skittish over footlogs, especially them that are so far above the water, but your daddy walked across like it was a sidewalk. I don't believe I ever saw him afraid of anything.

"That's when your mama surprised me. She was in a dress, but she took off her shoes and went barefoot across right behind him. I was shocked to see her do that and I asked her, 'When did you learn *that*?' She whispered something to your daddy and they laughed, arms around each other on the far side. She said 'You'd be surprised at what I can do.'"

Uncle Cody shook his head and grinned. "Until then, it hadn't occurred to me that the young girls I knew would someday grow up to be mothers, and she looked completely different to me all of a sudden."

At that moment, thinking about what Uncle Cody had told me, I had something happen that I'd never experienced. I saw Mama standing there in a blue print dress, clear as day and as solid as the woods around us. She was twisting her wedding ring like she did when she was thinking or worried. She shook her head and watched over her shoulder toward the dam. Then she faded away and there was nothing left but the woods.

Every hair on my body stood up and I knew what Miss Becky called the Poisoned Gift was working again, but it had never actually brought *ghosts* in front of me. Uncle Cody saw one once, and I wished he was there beside me right then. My heart skipped a beat and I could feel my jaw moving with me trying to talk but nothing coming out but the sounds I make when I have an asthma attack.

"What are you doing?"

Pepper's voice jolted me back from wherever I'd been and I realized for only the second time in my that life I'd experienced the Gift while I was awake.

It scared the pee-waddlin' out of me.

I finally snapped back to Pepper. "I just saw Mama."

She knew I saw things in my dreams that came true, but they were always mixed up and we couldn't figure out what was going to happen, until after the event. That near-'bout drove us crazy.

Pepper's eyes widened and she looked around as if Mama might be hiding behind a buckeye bush or something. "What was she doing?"

"Nothing. Standing there and worrying at her wedding ring."

"Far out! Did she say anything?"

"No." I imagine adults would spend some time talking about the vision, or what might be coming, but we shared so much over the years that we didn't need to say hardly a thing. "She's gone now."

Pepper shrugged and led the way like she always does. "Then what are we standing here for?"

The log was solid, but scary. We were log-walkers from way back, but we still eased across like it was a thousand miles to the bottom. Even if we'd fallen, the ten-foot drop into soft mud and water wouldn't have been bad, but it'd be a mess and we might have broke an arm like Kevin McDaniel did last year. What was worse, I heard about a cousin who fell off one and broke his neck.

Pepper crossed with her arms out like a tightrope walker. I didn't want to look like that, so I tucked my own arms close and kept my eyes on the far side instead of the log. The rotting bark crunched underfoot, but the bridge held steady. My tennis shoe caught on a stob and I caught my balance just in time to skip and dance the last couple of feet with a lump of fear as big as a horse apple in my throat.

Back on solid ground we followed a game trail winding around trees and tangles of berry vines. A squirrel scolded us all the way, running from limb to limb and chattering like we'd stole his nuts. I wished I'd brought my BB gun to sting him and shut him up.

Pepper was looking around for a rock to throw at him when she stepped in a thick stand of tall grass. The world exploded around her as a big covey of quail whirred into the air, scaring her so bad she jumped and screamed. The birds scattered and sailed through the trees.

"Shit!"

I laughed and pointed a finger "Pow! Pow!"

"It ain't funny. I think I peed myself a little."

That made me laugh even more.

"I wish *you'd* stepped in 'em, then I could laugh at *you*."

"They're only tee-tiny birds. Come on."

We finally broke out of the woods at the base of the dam. I stopped at a barbed-wire fence and peeked through the cedars growing thick and tall. We could see the broken rail high above at the top of the dam, and the long gouge in the dirt where they'd dragged the car back to the top.

"They're gone." Pepper put her foot on the second strand of barbed-wire where it was stapled to a bodark post and crawled over the fence. "Shit! Look at this." She pointed at a thick pool of blood.

We're no strangers to blood. We kill and eat our own cows and pigs, and hunt and fish, but I'd never seen so much in one big, thick puddle. It had already started to dry on the dirt and what little grass there was, and it looked like strawberry jelly to me.

It was a *person's* blood and it made me queasy.

I couldn't take my eyes off it, but Pepper stepped around the damp patch and kicked through the young Johnson grass.

"Here's her makeup." She pointed up the slope. "There's a pair of sunglasses up there."

It looked like someone had dumped a load of trash down the slope. Tissues, pens, papers, maps, and a dozen other things were mixed with dirt clods, torn-up grass, and scattered chrome trim. I imagined the woman screaming while the spinning car tore itself apart on the long way down.

I noticed a man's shoe nearby. My head spun. "They lost their shoes. Why would they lose their shoes?"

Pepper was unfazed by it all. "There's stuff everywhere."

"Don't touch it."

"Why not?"

"It ain't ours. It belongs to that poor lady and Frank Clay." I didn't know her, but I'd seen him a time or two up at the store after I came to live with Miss Becky and Grandpa Ned. He was a nice guy, the kind who always winked and grinned at a kid, whether he knew them or not. He had three kids of his own, but they were all younger than me.

Pepper was holding a lipstick that she dropped back on the ground. "I've never seen anything like this."

A car slowed as it passed high overhead. I was sure the driver was looking at the rail, but he couldn't see us from his side.

We were trespassing where we shouldn't have been and I felt bad for the folks who'd died there. It was suddenly personal. It reminded me of Mama and Daddy's wreck, even though I hadn't seen it and all of a sudden I felt like crying. "We need to go."

My eyes stung and I turned so Pepper couldn't see. She bit her lip and I could tell she was watching me, but she wouldn't let it go. "Do you think they suffered?"

"Probably not." I hoped my parents hadn't suffered, either.

Quiet for once, Pepper took one more glance around us.

The lady's shiny high-heeled shoe looked so out of place in the dirt that I felt swimmy-headed. I dropped to my knees thinking that it might help. "Should we get their shoes for them?"

"No. What we do with them? They don't have any use for shoes anymore."

"They're good shoes."

"There's only one of each." She drew a deep breath and headed for the fence.

I started to leave and noticed a tissue that looked like a big white Hershey Kiss. It was sitting up, with a rubber band around the top. Wanting to get my mind off the shoes, I picked it up. There was something hard inside and I started to tear it open when we heard a branch break on the other side of the spillway. Something grunted.

You couldn't tell if it was some*one* or some*thing*, but it was enough to spook us. I stuck the Kleenex in my pocket and we skinned on out of there so we wouldn't get caught.

Chapter Six

The scruffy man once heard a story about something called a wraith. He looked it up in a dictionary. "A ghost or ghostlike image of someone, especially one seen shortly before or after their death" sounded exactly like him. He liked the dark sound of the word so much he memorized the definition, and The Wraith came alive. It was time for a reckoning.

Harriet Clay, now a widow, sent word to Ned that she needed to see him at her house, if that was possible. It was the least he could do for her, and in his opinion, it was his job to give her the bad news in person.

Ned drove to the Clay house half an hour after the ambulances took Frank and Maggie away. Set half a mile off Highway 79 toward Hopewell, the Queen-Anne style farmhouse was barely inside the Chisum City limits and surrounded by tall burr oak trees. Folks up on the river tended not to move into new houses if they could stay where they were raised, but in order to run for mayor, Frank Clay had to live in town.

Shade was thick and solid around the house built back in the late 1800s. Ned parked under a tree with a hitch ring grown into the trunk. Sheriff Cody Parker pulled up and killed his engine. They met at the house.

Cody rubbed his chin. "They live in town, so I guess I'll tell her."

"Nope." Ned absently touched his small constable's bade with one finger. "They're really Center Springs folks. I'll do the telling."

Cody's response was cut off when Wes Clay stepped outside. Tough and strapped with corded muscle, Wes had packed a lot of life into fifty years, spending more than a few of them in prison down in Huntsville. Most people said Wes would fight a buzzsaw.

He scratched his flat belly through a dingy white tee shirt. "Well?"

The two lawmen walked closer to the porch. Ned stopped and looked up from under his brim. "Harriet sent for us."

"You gonna tell her my baby brother's dead?"

Cody thumbed his hat back. "We need to talk to Harriet."

"You can talk to me. I'll tell her."

Ned felt his face flush. "Is she in there?"

"She is."

Cody jerked his head toward the house. "The kids close by?"

"Naw. I took 'em over to Andy's house. They don't need to be here for a while."

Ned knew Andy and most of the huge Clay family. "You gonna invite us in?"

Wes planted his feet as if they were about to lunge.

The tense situation evaporated in an instant when Harriet's weak voice came through the screen door. "Howdy, Ned, Cody. Wes, it's all right."

Her brother-in-law refused to move, but Ned and Cody climbed the steps and parted around him. Harriet held the door and gave a vague wave to come in. Every window in the house was open to catch any available breeze on that still, humid morning. The air was thick and fragrant with the odor of bacon.

"Y'all sit." Harriet's dark hair was messed, as if she'd been running her fingers through it. Her eyes were red from crying.

Neither lawman sat. Instead, they backed up to the couch, holding their hats.

Harriet dropped heavily into a blue chair. "He's dead for sure, ain't he?"

Ned nodded. "I'm sorry."

Instead of dissolving into tears, she ducked her head as if thinking. Her Baptist raising prompted the next question. "Had he been drinking?"

Ned took the conversation. "We don't know."

"Was he driving?"

"We don't know for sure."

"I heard someone else was driving." It was a statement. "That his car's across the river in Juarez."

"We don't know that for a fact, yet. Frank was in the car with Maggie Mayfield. She was still behind the wheel, so I believe she was driving, though I don't know how she stayed in." Ned hesitated after realizing he was talking too much. "They went off the bend in the Lake Lamar Dam. There was some skid marks. She might have been going too fast for the curve, or maybe she tried to miss a deer or something on the dam."

"She is…was, Frank's secretary." Harriet dried her eyes with a damp handkerchief. "He hired her here-while back. She may have been bringing him home. He's worked late a lot lately, 'cause of the job. Maybe his car wouldn't start or something."

The tightness in Ned's stomach released now that he had an answer to his questions. "Well, that explains a lot."

She worried at a button on her blue print dress. "He's been getting ready for the election in the fall. It takes a lot of time to lay groundwork. He's been doing so much on his own, and even though he has what he calls his staff, he needed someone to handle the little day to day things. Maggie was supposed to take some of the pressure off and now she's taken him with her." She broke down in sobs.

"I bet you're right." Cody fiddled with the brim of his hat. "They worked late last night and she was bringing him home."

Ned didn't believe that, because evidence pointed toward the west, away from where they would have been going. He also hated giving the information piecemeal, but he didn't seem to be able to stay in charge of the conversation. He wiped a film of sweat from his bald head.

They waited in awkward silence until she composed herself. "Did he suffer much?"

"I don't know for sure." Ned tapped his hat against his leg, a sure sign that he was ready to go. "We'll never know."

"My poor babies don't have a daddy anymore."

Wes used a forefinger and pulled the screen door open. "That's enough now."

Ned agreed with him. "I reckon you're right."

Cody surveyed the bright, airy room that was neat as a pin. A cluster of pictures on the wall showed Frank with a Texas senator, a member of the Texas House of Representatives, and the former Chisum mayor. "Harriet, I'm sorry."

The lawmen exchanged looks and Ned wiped his head again, ready to get outside where at least a little air was moving. "All right, then. That's all we know. You holler if we can do anything for you."

She buried her face in the handkerchief again. A black woman Ned didn't recognize came in from the kitchen and put her arms around the grieving widow. Neither looked up as Wes held the screen open.

The lawmen filed through and were in the yard when Wes' soft voice stopped them. "She's a Mayfield."

Ned stopped and sighed. "Yes."

"No Mayfield had oughta work for a Clay. Frank shoulda known better, but he'd hired one already." He jerked his thumb toward the house. "Did you check to see if there were tire marks other'n hers? Whoever run 'em off the road got two birds with one stone, 'cause he was in the car with that high-yeller woman that was married. I heard them Mayfields didn't like it that she'd been seen across the river in Frogtown since her old man run off. They'll pay for that."

"No they won't." Cody's face reddened. "We don't know it was intentional. It was an accident until we find out something different. Stay out of it."

"I hope y'all are going over to that nigger slut's house to see what she was up to. I think there's more to it than you're lettin' on."

Ned leveled his gaze at Wes who was working himself up. "We'll do what we do. That's none of your business."

"It *is* our business. He's kinfolk. Them Mayfields are some sneakin', fightin' sonsabitches and they took Frank with 'em when they got rid of that slut. I'm gonna find out for sure what happened. When I do, I'll take care of it."

Cody clamped his jaw. "He's already told you to keep your nose clean. It's law business."

Wes lit a cigarette, flicked the match at Cody, spat onto the boards between his feet. "It's *family* business, now. It just came clear to me. A Mayfield killed a Clay. There'll be blood over it."

Chapter Seven

The Wraith thought about crossing the river for a beer, but recognition was too dangerous. Instead, he drove to the lake overlook and stayed in his truck, sipping from a half pint of whiskey and thinking about how close he'd come to being run over the night before because he'd been drunk and not paying attention. He thought about the two who died with little interest other than their names. Mayfield and Clay. An idea was born. He chuckled and tilted the bottle toward two houses barely visible in the distance opposite the glistening body of water.

Late Saturday afternoon Ned and Judge O.C. Rains were drinking coffee in the back booth of Frenchie's Café, only a block north of the Lamar County Courthouse. Boyhood friends, they argued like an old married couple most of the time.

Judge Rains blew over the surface of his coffee and took a tentative sip. "Say she picked Frank up and gave him a lift?"

"That's what I think happened. He hired her for a secretary last week. I went by his office here in town, and some of the young folks who volunteer for his campaign say they'd been there late in the night and were the last ones to leave."

"So did his car not start? Is that what happened?"

Oklahoma Sheriff Clayton Matthews had located Frank's Ford in the parking lot of The Black Cat, one of the many honky-tonks just across the Red River. No one had seen Frank in the club, nor Maggie either.

Ned picked at a rough edge of one fingernail. "Can't say yet."

"It's a mystery. That's a fact." O.C. knitted his white eyebrows together. "I can think of one or two reasons a man might be with a woman."

"Not one that's high-yellow, and not Frank Clay. They're... they were both married and he's one of the best men I ever knew. He was a good husband and doted on them kids of his. The problem is that the wreck's done relit the fire between them two families. You know of that Mayfield bunch Maggie was married into. John Washington says every one of them boys are mean as snakes an'll kill you for your hat if he decides he's partial to it, and the Clays are just as bad. Hell, O.C. you sent Monte Clay up for shooting his own brother's business off two years ago when Monte thought he was messin' with his wife."

O.C.'s eyes flicked over Ned's shoulder when the bell over the door jangled and followed the customer down the counter to watch Frenchie pour coffee. "Hell, if you're part of that Clay bunch, you're either sorry as the day is long and belong under the jail, or you're such a teetotaler that you won't admit that you like a beer ever now and then."

"Cody went over and asked around too, and said nobody saw Frank in any of them joints last night. Somebody woulda recognized the mayor, if he'd been in there."

"I figured you'd be the first to suspicion something." O.C. leaned forward and laced his fingers. "Especially since Maggie's been spending more time across the river than usual."

"If you knew that, why didn't you tell me?"

"You didn't ask." O.C. grinned and let him off the hook. "John told me this morning."

Ned grinned. "She's been seen around them gun and knife clubs out by Frogtown. They'll let anyone come in and drink over there, white, colored, high yeller, or red."

Despite how badly Ned despised the cluster of beer joints just across the river from his precinct, the joints backed into the deep woods several miles farther east were nothing but a deeper level of hell. The dregs of Oklahoma lived there, earning a living in mysterious, and usually illegal ways. It was a dark place of cuttings, fights, and unspoken atrocities. Not a man given to fantasies, he wished the whole collection of warped shacks would catch fire and burn clean.

Frenchie came by with a plate and headed for the booth closest to the door. O.C. gave her a grin when she passed and she winked at them.

"Careful, you old coot," Ned chuckled. "One little dose of that'll kill you."

"I'm too old to even think about it these days." It was Judge Rains' way of saying things were still same at his house. His wife, Catherine, had been bad sick for years and the only relief for her was the white light at the far end of the tunnel.

O.C. tapped at the scarred table with a thick fingernail. "You talk to Tylee yet?"

"Ain't laid eyes on him. John asked around and says he went off visiting his woods children out toward New Boston. He got in a scrape and wound up in jail. Still there as far as I know."

"Knowing how he is, that's the best place for him right now."

"There'll be a killin' over this when he gets out."

Ned shook a few grains of salt into his coffee to cut the bitter. "Maybe not. I hope they all learned their lessons after the war. Killin' one another don't solve a thing."

"I hope you're right, but folks don't always pay attention to the lessons of their elders."

There wasn't anything to say to both truths.

They sipped for a few moments, surrounded by the smells of fried food, coffee, and the constant underlying odor of bacon and grilled onions. The backbeat of customer's voices and the tinkling of dishes from both the booths and the kitchen was as comforting as a soft quilt to the two old lawmen who'd been eating there for decades.

Frenchie came around with a fresh pot and filled their thick mugs to the brim. "Y'all need anything else, O.C.?"

"You have any peach pie back there?"

"Nope. Cherry and apple."

"I'd rather have peach."

"You'll get either cherry or apple today. That's all I got to offer."

"Why don't you ever have peach?"

"We do. But not *today*. Cherry or apple?"

O.C. frowned in disappointment. "I'll have to study on it."

"Fine." She popped her gum, smiled at Ned, and stopped by another booth to check on the customers there.

A ghost of a thought flicked through Ned's mind. Their ongoing discussion of pie, especially *peach* pie, made him think of Frank and Maggie, but it was lost before he could get a good grasp on what it was.

O.C. burned his lips on the coffee and hissed. "I knew good and well that was hot."

"I've done the same thing myself. Stings, don't it?"

"It'll feel better when it quits hurtin'. Say Frank and Maggie came over the dam and went off the backside?" They were back on the subject at hand.

"Yep. Right where it curves."

"Which way were they going?"

"Toward Center Springs."

"That don't make no sense." O.C. shook his head. "They didn't have any business being over there."

"It's a free country, last time I looked."

"Have you talked to any of Tylee's people yet?"

Ned studied O.C. for a long moment. "This is bothering you, ain't it?"

"That whole damn *family* bothers me. I've had members of both sides before my bench in the past. You know as well as I do what happened after the war before it all settled down. We're lucky more people weren't killed in that little feud. Hell, we don't even know for sure who killed who, and only two of 'em were sent to the pen."

"Well, I'll get over there to talk to 'em directly." He paused and picked a callus on his thumb. "I been thinkin' on it and can't rightly remember exactly how all this started to begin with."

O.C. drank some coffee. "It was a silly disagreement. Frank Clay's uncle Randall Clay sold Old Man Mayfield a lame blue-nosed mule one Saturday in the Chisum wagon yard. Randall said the mule was fine when they traded, and that Mayfield'd lamed it on the way home.

"The next Saturday Old Man Mayfield was back in the wagon yard with the mule and told Randall he wanted his money back. They took to arguin' and before you know it, they almost went to fighting. A couple of cooler heads kept 'em apart, and it was a good thing they did. A black man hitting a white back then was cause enough for a lynchin'. Anyway, Mayfield finally shot the lame mule right between the eyes at a cutbank by the road, not far from the army camp and let it lay where it fell."

"I remember now. Randall's own mule was found dead in his barn a few days later. Somebody'd cut its throat and Randall accused the Mayfields."

"That's right. The whole thing spun out of control after that. Archie Mayfield's old truck had a flat on a high-bank gravel road a couple of miles from his house and he was changing it when William Clay came by in his car. Archie couldn't pull far enough off that skinny little road, and William Clay couldn't get past. It made him mad that a Mayfield was blocking his way, and he got out to give him a cussin'. When William looked in the back of Mayfield's truck, he saw half a bushel of pears and said Archie stole 'em from a tree on his property.

"He backed around and headed straight for town where he swore out a complaint with Sheriff Poole. Well, you know Poole was crooked as a dog's hind leg and didn't need much excuse to arrest Archie. He'd arrest a colored fellow for breathing air, so he caught Archie at the wagon yard in town and worked him over for what he said was resisting arrest, and then took him in to spend a month in jail before they let him out. Archie drove straight to the bottoms and caught William having lunch under a tree by a cotton field he was plowing and beat the hell out of him. Archie went back to jail after that and woke up dead in his cell. Nobody knew how it happened. Old Judge J.W. Haynes ruled it a suicide and before you know it, it was one thing after another."

The stories took Ned back for a long minute. "Well, things has changed over the years, even though there's still hard feelings. Both families have long memories, but at least a couple of 'em turned out all right, like Frank. He was a good man. The rest of them Clays are rough as cobs. I'll speak to a few of the Clays and have John talk to the Mayfields, and warn 'em off, but that's all I can do."

"Better let Cody tell John."

"Why?"

"He's sheriff. I don't believe you oughta be tellin' John who to talk to. He ain't *your* deputy, you know. Times are changing, and you better not be giving him orders no more, no matter how long y'all've been working together."

"'I god, you're right. I'm just so used to working with him, it's got to be a habit."

The bell above the door jangled and Ned's eyes lit up when he recognized Graham Harwell. Ned waved him over and pointed at a stool at the counter beside their booth. Their hats rested upside down on the counter, the usual way of reserving the stools so customers couldn't hear their conversations.

"Graham, sit there and tell O.C. what happened out by that damned lake the other day."

O.C.'s expressive eyebrows rose at the unusual offer.

Graham took the stool with a sheepish look on his face. "Mr. Ned, that story's embarrassing."

"Why come?" O.C. noticed Graham's arm was in a cast. "Your busted wing have something to do with it?"

Graham sighed. "I'm gonna get this out of the way and tell it one time. After that, I don't want to hear one question or one word."

Ned chuckled. "Fine, then."

"Well, Ned knows I bought me one of them used Airstream campers and have been itching to use it. Anyway, they opened the new campgrounds up out at Lake Lamar, and I pulled it over there and set it up. Some friends decided they wanted to see the trailer, so they came out and we had a big old time. We built a fire outside, and before you know it, more folks showed up and camped out, too.

"Anyway, a lot of beer came with 'em, and it was after midnight before we finally got tired. Some folks crawled in their own tents, and one or two drove back home, but a few stayed around the fire to talk. Linda and I went into the trailer and I decided to take a shower before going to bed. I was standing there, in a stream of nice hot water, when I heard her scream from the living room. She'd seen a snake crawl under the sofa."

O.C. shuddered. He's always been afraid of snakes, especially since Ned threw one on him when they were kids.

"Buck-nekked and dripping water, I came running in there and she hollered that a snake was under the couch. I didn't believe her, but I got down on all fours to look."

Ned's imagination got the best of him and he shuddered at the mental image.

"Linda's little Dachshund was passing through about that time and when he saw me on all fours, he cold-nosed me somewhere that we aren't going to discuss."

Graham had to wait until the two old men regained control of themselves.

"What did you do, fall and break your arm?" O.C. had forgotten his coffee.

"I wish. I jumped forward and cracked my head against the table and passed out for a minute. Linda didn't see what happened and thought the snake bit me and caused me to have a heart attack, so she ran to the door and called for help.

"The guys hurried in to get me and take me to the emergency room. They made a stretcher out of a blanket and were carrying me out the door, still nekked as the day I was born, when Winston Moore got tickled about the whole thing and lost his grip on one corner of the blanket and dropped me half in and out the door. That's how my arm broke."

Frenchie returned with the coffee pot and refilled their mugs and they realized she'd been listening from behind the counter. "Did y'all kill the snake?"

"You've only heard half of it," Graham said. "While they were gone with me to the hospital, Hubert Stillwell stayed behind to do just that. He looked the trailer over and couldn't find the stinking thing, so he told Linda he believed it was gone. She was worried sick and sat down on the couch and when one of those little throw pillows fell over, there that damned snake was and she fainted dead away."

Graham smiled to himself on that one.

"Hubert killed it and seeing Linda passed out, he thought *she'd* had a heart attack and laid her on the couch. Anyway, he's had some training because he's a volunteer fireman, so he leaned over and blew in her mouth. Now, remember, they'd all been drinking some, so when Hubert's wife walked in right about then to check on Linda and saw them like that with his mouth on Linda's, she picked a cast iron skillet off the stove and laid him out.

"Anyway, Linda woke up with Hubert across her chest, bleeding from the scalp. She screamed bloody murder. That's when Hubert's wife saw the dead snake on the floor commenced to beating it 'til the skillet's handle broke off and the pan slapped Linda in the side of the head, causing *it* to bleed.

"About that time Ned here rolled up to check on everyone after he got a call there was a disturbance. He knew we'd all been drinking, 'cause he saw Hubert come back from across the river earlier in the day."

When Graham paused to take a breath, Ned picked up the story. "That's when I heard the commotion in the trailer and when I pushed through, I saw Linda screaming on the floor with Hubert laying across her and his wife standing there with that broke handle in her hand. There was blood everywhere, so I spent the next two hours sortin' out what happened."

"So now you've heard the story and I ain't telling it again."

O.C. had been laughing so hard his sides were hurting. "What kind of snake was it?"

Graham looked embarrassed. "Just an ol' rat snake. Anyway, I'm trying to sell the trailer, if anybody wants one. It has a hole in the floor, though."

O.C. leaned forward, knowing something good was coming down the pike. "How'd it get a hole in the floor?"

Graham shrugged. "You know how snakes are, they'll still move or twitch or curl even when they're dead. Well, my cousin Benny came in and thought it was still alive and shot that dead snake with his .410."

Graham paused. "I'll sell it cheap."

"I bet you will," O.C. grunted, waved to Frenchie for more coffee.

"Oh, I remember why I came in here in the first place. Ned, some carnival folks asked me if they could set up in that pasture I have out near the army camp on Highway 271. They can't get the fairgrounds for some reason, so I told them yeah."

O.C. grunted and tasted his coffee. "They can't get on the fairgrounds because they run crooked games." Ned and Graham raised their eyebrows at the same time. O.C. waited a beat before continuing. "They were talking about it after the city council meeting here while back. They say the games are rigged, so they've been uninvited since the last time they were here."

Ned sighed. "That means they'll be fleecing folks in my precinct. I hope you get paid good for all this trouble."

Graham brightened. "The feller I talked to said they'd give me ten percent of the gate."

"You get that in writing?"

"Sure enough."

"Well, it probably won't be enough, because they sure saw you coming."

"Why come?"

"Carnies don't make their money at the gate. They make it from the games."

Graham's face fell. "I thought it was a good deal."

"It is for them. I reckon I'll have to go over there and have a talk with 'em. When do they plan to open?"

"Tonight."

"Fine then." Ned gathered up his hat. "That'll be all right. I'll run over there and check on them."

"Well, I just wanted you to know."

Ned shrugged. "There shouldn't be any problems with that."

Chapter Eight

The Wraith had arms made of whipcord and sinew. He cracked the knuckles of his leathery hands and waited in the hot, still woods, remembering. He was back in his hometown of Center Springs for the first time in four years.

Ned turned off Texas Route 271, the main highway from Chisum to Oklahoma, as the sun sank toward the trees. He pulled into Graham Booth's pasture not far from the decommissioned Camp Maxey army camp.

It was once a bustling facility during World War II, training nearly 50,000 troops. By the time the carnival arrived, the army camp was only a shadow of what it had been, with a few offices and a building that most locals referred to as the powder magazine.

Booth's barbed-wire fence was down, and the crooked bodark posts they'd pulled from the ground were stacked a hundred yards away to provide access to the open area swarming with cars and trucks. Ned pulled off the highway and across the culvert to the impromptu parking lot already identified by cars lined up in rows.

A wide banner stretched across the newly erected entrance read: The One and Only Patterson and Bates Dreamland Exposition!

Tents sprouted from the grass trampled by a small army of rough-looking men and women who were putting the finishing touches on rides and game booths. Ned threaded his way through tangles of ropes and cables, passing the Tilt-a-Whirl, the Skydiver, a sign for "Oddities of the World," and a cotton candy stand. There were already a few curious patrons drifting through the bustle.

"Can I help you?" A long-haired young woman in patched jeans balanced a toddler on her cocked hip. A cigarette dangled from her lips and Ned noticed her sneakers were filthy. Dried mud flaked off her bell bottom cuffs.

"I 'magine you can. Who's running things here?"

"Delmar Hopkins."

"You know where I can find him?"

She reset the snotty-nosed toddler to a more comfortable position. The little girl watched him with wide, unimpressed eyes. "I saw him by the Ring Toss a few minutes ago."

"Thanks." Ned left her and walked down the growing midway that was five times larger than any traveling carnival he'd ever seen. A man with wavy gray hair curling over his collar held a clipboard and issued orders to a pair of ragged middle-aged carnies. Ned hadn't seen anyone dressed so shabby since the Depression.

The silver-haired man's eyes flicked to the stranger and the small gold badge on his shirt. "Howdy Sheriff."

"Constable. Constable Ned Parker."

They shook. "Name's Delmar Hopkins. Help you?"

"Naw, I just dropped by to say howdy. This is my precinct and I like to keep an eye on whatever's coming or going around here."

"Glad to have you."

"When are you firing all this up?"

"Tonight."

Ned nodded like he hadn't already known the answer to his question. "And you'll be here how long?"

"Until the crowds fall off. Usually a week or ten days."

"I'd have expected y'all to be at the fairgrounds in town."

Delmar's eyes flickered. "They want too much of the gate in Chisum. We'll make more here."

"Um hum." Ned's comment told Delmar that he didn't believe him, and the carnie boss saw it.

"You want a tour?"

"Naw." Ned paused. "Just wanted to know who was running things. You make a lot of money off these games going up here?"

"Enough to put groceries on the table. Folks love the games."

"They win very much?"

"Sure do. See all these prizes they're unloading? We'll go through most of 'em before we leave."

"I bet you will." Ned studied the cheap dolls and even cheaper plastic toys and stuffed animals that local boys would try to win for their girlfriends and wives. A cluster of giant colored hippos hung from the game's roof and down the sides. He pointed to shelf of transistor radios, low-end binoculars, and a tin spyglass. "Some of those look expensive."

"Those are the *big* prizes, but a lot of them will walk out the gate with the rube...the customers."

"Rubes. Marks. Chump. Mooch. Clems..."

"All right." Delmar's face fell. "You know the lingo."

"I know quite a bit. I know the ring on that Basketball Toss is barely bigger'n the ball, and that it has so much air it'll bounce to China if they throw it hard enough. I know the bottles are weighted in the Milk Bottle Toss."

Delmar scowled and shrugged the dingy coat back on his shoulders as the men beside him faded away.

"Here's the deal. Folks'll come out to have fun, but I want them treated right. Don't stack the milk bottles against the back wall, and don't use them that's weighted so heavy. I know how this works even down to the Duck Pond. I expect you mostly give more than ninety-five percent slum prizes for these...rubes, but I'll tolerate say, sixty-five or seventy percent."

Delmar flinched. Slum prizes, the cheapest plastic toys cost little to give away and kept the rubes interested, because they got at least *something* for their money and it gave them hope, urging them to play again. But if his gamers had to increase the distribution of their better prizes like the large stuffed animals or even the transistor radios displayed at the forefront of their booths, the amount of take-home for the carnies would be dramatically less.

Scowling, Delmar hunched his shoulders and listened as Ned continued.

"If I hear of anything crooked, I'll come out here with a dozen deputies and we'll start looking real hard at the rest of the games and the folks working here. There's a few I saw ducking around corners who's liable to have warrants.

"Now, I'm going home in a little bit and after supper, I intend to get out all my wanted posters and go through 'em one by one. If I see anybody that looks familiar when I come back, we're gonna have a talk about aiding and abetting. You get me?"

"I got you." Delmar's flat voice matched the look in his eyes. He reached in his pocket. "How much will it take...?"

"Get that hand out of your pocket. I ain't taking no bribes. You run this straight or you can pack it up and string Graham's fence back together."

Delmar's hand came out empty and he smoothed his oiled hair. "Fine, then."

"Good. Let these folks have a good time and win some."

They stood in silence for a long moment while Delmar waited for more. When nothing else came, he sighed loud and long. "Were you a carney?"

"Nope, but I've been at this a long time."

"I expect you'll be here every night?"

"Most likely."

The carney studied his worn out shoes. "You want some tickets?"

"Naw. I won't need a ticket to get in."

The man's faint smile faded.

"Oh, by the way, make sure them rides are safe, too. I don't want nobody hurt around here."

Ned left, passing the young woman with the baby. His demeanor changed and he stopped to let the toddler grab his finger. He handed the woman a folded bill with his other hand.

"This is for you to get this baby some clothes. She looks like she could use some shoes and something for that runny nose. What's her name?"

She spoke around the cigarette bobbing in the corner of her mouth. "Amanda."

"Yours?"

She raised an eyebrow. "You asking for professional reasons, or personal?"

"I like to know who's in my county."

"Did you ask the rest of these carneys around here?"

"Nope, but none of them others' got a baby on their hip, neither."

She studied on his answer for a second. "Connie."

"Howdy Connie. Don't you blow that money on cigarettes. They're gonna kill you, you know."

"If they don't something else will." The woman blew smoke from her nostrils without taking the toonie from her lips. "Thanks Sheriff."

Ned sighed, "Constable," and left.

Chapter Nine

A wheezing International pickup pulled off the highway and up our drive, trailing a cloud of blue smoke. It was after breakfast on Sunday and I was in the hay barn with Grandpa, helping him put out some nuggets for the cows. Neither he nor Miss Becky considered that work, no more'n her cooking breakfast or the dinner already simmering on the stove.

He slapped a lid on the 55-gallon barrel and walked to the front of the truck backed halfway into the pole barn's hall. "You recognize that truck?"

I hopped into the bed and leaned over the top of the cab. The pickup pulled up the slight incline and parked behind Grandpa's Plymouth. "Nossir."

Half a dozen black-haired kids rode in the back, and the cab looked to be full of people. You could squeeze four folks into those Internationals, if they were kinfolk and didn't mind rubbing shoulders, but it looked to me like they'd packed in at least seven, four adults with little kids on their laps. That explained why the driver's whole arm and shoulder was out the window.

I could tell he was Indian right off, most likely Choctaw, 'cause that's what we had the most of around our part of the state. The truck idled while Hootie gave it a good barkin'. Miss Becky came out on the porch. We couldn't hear what she was saying, but she talked to someone through the window. Grandpa left the front fender and took a step toward the house.

The passenger door opened. My breath caught when Miss Becky threw up her hands, the dish towel flying overhead.

Grandpa jolted when her scream drug us. He reached in the front pocket of his overalls, pulled out his pistol, and started downhill. "Mama!"

I jumped up on the cab. The biggest kid in the back threw something over the side of the truck. I'd been watching *The Rat Patrol* on TV the night before and expected it to blow up like one of those satchel charges. He followed it and run at Miss Becky. I shouted and waved my hands, hoping to attract their attention so she could get away.

The guy's long black hair was flying every which-a-way as he charged up on the porch and grabbed Miss Becky. She shrieked and started beating him on the back.

Grandpa raised his pistol, but couldn't shoot because the truck was directly in line between him and the front porch.

I came off the cab, running downhill until my momentum threw me off balance and I knew I was gonna fall. Instead of landing flat on my face, I tucked a shoulder and rolled with it, coming back onto my feet and passing Grandpa in an instant.

He had his pistol pointed and was hollerin' for Miss Becky to run. "Top! Stay out of the way!" I heard his feet pounding behind me, but much slower and heavier.

I was through the open gate when Miss Becky shoved the guy away, but she didn't run, and she didn't let go, neither. That's when I saw she wasn't fighting, but hugging somebody. I slid to a stop and waved my hands. "Grandpa! Don't shoot!"

He heard me and lowered the .38, his face was white as a sheet. "What?"

"They ain't fighting! They're huggin'!"

"Well, who is it then?"

The guy looked our way and I started hollering too.

It was my best friend, Mark Lightfoot.

Chapter Ten

The Wraith couldn't help it. It was dangerous, but he rode past Ned Parker's house and glanced up the drive to see a truck backed into the barn and a ratty-assed International pickup parked near the house. The glimpse didn't last long and he was past. Less than a hundred yards down the road, he squinted toward Cody Parker's house and felt a familiar ache.

One day Mark Lightfoot was living in an unpainted house tucked in the woods not far from Grant, Oklahoma, eating beans and greens when they had them, and sleeping in the same full-size bed with four other cousins. The next day he found himself standing in front of Ned Parker's house.

He'd lived there before. Ned and Miss Becky took him in after his mother, brothers, and sisters were murdered in a sharecropper's shack not far from the Parkers' farmhouse. Until that night when his crazy daddy burst in with an axe, his life had been one bad patch after the other.

His dad was eventually captured, charged, and convicted of the horrific murders. Mark stayed with the family for the next several weeks and came to understand the Parkers were his dream family. When Ned and Miss Becky offered to let him live with them, he thought his life had finally taken a turn for the better.

It was the time of the Skinner, when folks locked their doors at night and slept with guns next to the bed in case the lunatic that roamed the darkness decided it was their time to bleed. Even then, Mark felt safe, because his informally adopted grandfather, Constable Ned Parker, could take care of anything.

The dream disappeared in an instant when relatives Mark didn't know he had, showed up one day in a ragged sedan to tell him who they were and that he was going to live with them in Oklahoma. There wasn't anything Ned and Miss Becky could do about it. The law was on his Aunt Tillie's side.

She looked like his mama, but of course sisters always favored. She lived with a shiftless sharecropper named Grover and it was like living with his mother all over again. Grover didn't do much more than loaf around the house smoking or chewing cotton bowl twist, and working only when Tillie drove him away from their leaning shack of a house to earn a few dollars for beans, beer, and more cigarettes.

Eleven kids lived under one roof and Mark fell exactly in the middle of his new family. They pretty much ignored the youngster most of the time. Every child had a job. The older kids worked the fields in season, or hauled hay, or did odd jobs whenever they came available. The younger kids had chores around the hard-scrabble farm, from hoeing, to feeding chickens and gathering eggs, to cutting wood for the stove. There was no electricity in the house, and the only light at night came from coal oil lamps.

Mark found he had a knack for milking. It was their sharp-boned Guernsey cow that kept the least ones alive. The older kids had already grown tired of getting up first thing in the morning, rain or shine, cold or hot, to milk. It had to be done again in the evening. Even though he couldn't stand the taste, Grover went into a rage and beat anyone who spilled the milk on the way back to the house for straining, so they gladly gave the chore to Mark.

It was the only time he had to himself and the boy grew to enjoy it. That confounded cow and those younger kids became his life. He'd lost count of how many times there wasn't any food in the house and it became a source of pride that at least they had milk.

Through necessity, he gained experience at sneaking into other folks' corn cribs, smokehouses, or barns, and filling a 'toe sack with whatever food he could steal. Sometimes it was only potatoes and onions from cribs. On a chilly night after a nearby family killed hogs, he got away with a few hocks and the cheeks, because those parts tended to be overlooked and their disappearance blamed on dogs or rats.

One winter he was able to steal a few ears of feed corn from a barn on a weekly basis without getting caught. The yellow dent was so hard it had to be soaked for a day before they could cook it. They lived on mostly boiled corn and hand-ground cornbread for months.

The Oklahoma law came by the house a time or two, sniffing around to see what they could find out about petty theft reports, but Grover always convinced them he knew nothing of the pilfering. The gaunt looks of the Choctaw family usually told the sheriff or constable that the folks were barely alive as it was, and even if someone did bring home a few ears of corn intended as chicken feed, it wasn't much of a crime.

He went to school, though. That was the one thing he insisted on, and it was there he excelled. The small rural schoolhouse built by the WPA housed both Indian and white kids from their part of rural southeast Oklahoma. Mark stood out, making good grades and showing he had an aptitude for numbers.

Then one morning three-and-a-half years after his Aunt Tillie and Grover showed up out of nowhere, she called him off the porch. "Mark, you need to get in the truck."

"Where are we going?"

Grover came out of the house with a rat-chewed cardboard suitcase. He pitched it into the truck bed amid a collection of hoes, bailing wire, loose hay, and empty feed sacks. "Get in, like she said."

"I've told you you ain't my daddy. You're not the boss of me."

Grover shrugged. "Don't make no difference nohow. You're going and good riddance."

"Where?"

"Where Tillie told me."

Mark watched the kids scramble into the bed over the sides and tailgate, excited to go somewhere. Martha and Brock, two other kinfolk who weren't blood but insisted on being called aunt and uncle climbed in the cab, setting the smallest kids on their laps.

Mark shrugged and joined them, hoping they were heading to Hugo and he could loaf around town for a while. At least it was something to do besides work.

He was shocked when they passed over the bridge and into Texas. He hadn't been across the Red River since Tillie and Grover came to get him. He knew for sure where they were going when Grover steered right and onto westbound 197.

They weren't going to the fields, because it was too early to work. There were no crops yet.

Mark watched the woods flash by as they cruised down the two-lane highway with excitement growing in his chest. One of the boys, Carl, rode with his arm over the edge of the truck bed. The wind blew his shaggy hair into his face. "Where we going, Mark?"

"I don't know."

"We don't never work this side of the river. They don't much like Indians over here."

"Some folks do."

"I want to pick next to you."

"It's too early in the year. We ain't picking nothin'."

"Then what?"

They crossed the Sanders Creek bridge and Mark instinctively knew what was happening. "I think I'm going somewhere for a while."

"What do you mean?"

Mark pulled his whipping hair back. "I'm going to be gone for a while, so you need to take over my chores for me."

Carl looked down at his ragged tennis shoes. He was only one year younger than Mark. "I don't like to milk."

"That's all right. You need to do it anyway to feed the lil'uns."

"Where you gonna be?"

"I believe I'll be gone for a while."

Herschel, three years younger, raised up on his knees to look through the cab and out the windshield. "I don't want you to go anywhere, Mark."

The fourteen-year-old was torn between sadness and excitement. "I don't have a choice."

The truck slowed below the white house on the hill. Grover turned up the drive and gravel popped under the nearly bald tires. He stopped in the yard at the same time Miss Becky came out onto the porch. Hootie ran up, barking. Mark thought she hadn't changed at all in nearly four years. She didn't notice him in the middle of the kids riding in back.

Tillie leaned out the window. "Miss Becky."

She was drying her hands on a dishtowel. "Yes?"

"We done brought him back."

"Who?"

"Mark. We can't take care of him no more."

"Mark? Lightfoot?" She stepped closer to the edge of the porch.

"Yep. It was a mistake to come get him. We got too many mouths to feed and my own come first."

"And mine," Grover said.

Tillie didn't comment. She stuck her head out the door. "Mark. Get out."

Miss Becky was rooted to the boards. "Y'all come and took him without a word, and now you're a-bringin' him back the same way. He ain't no dog you can give away and come get later."

"I know it. We ain't comin' back."

Mark had heard enough. He pulled Carl close and hugged Herschel. A small girl named Kate watched with wide eyes. He gave her a kiss on the nose. "Y'all take care of one another. I won't be back too soon, but I'll come help y'all directly. All y'all be good and remember I love you."

Kate's eyes welled and they were the last thing Mark saw before he threw the little suitcase over the side and jumped over the rotting sideboard. "You kids do what you're told and be careful. I done told you I'll come back someday and get you. Don't forget it."

"No you won't." Grover said over his shoulder after he spat into the yard.

Mark spoke to the back of the man's head. "And I'll be growed and bigger'n you and you'll pay the price when I get there."

Miss Becky flapped her towel in excitement when she saw Mark rushing up the steps. "Praise the Lord!"

Eyes suddenly full of happy tears, and for Kate's wide-eyed look of sadness, Mark ran into her arms.

Someone shouted from the direction of the barn, but Miss Becky's hug filled his senses and he couldn't look up right then.

Chapter Eleven

Sunday dinner was louder than usual. The excitement over Mark's return bubbled over like it was Christmas Eve. Grandpa'd already called Judge O.C. Rains at home and he promised to start working on the paperwork first thing in the morning to give Grandpa and Miss Becky full custody.

As usual, us kids were eating in the living room because the kitchen table wasn't big enough for everybody. We didn't mind for once, because we could talk all we wanted. The conversation in the kitchen came through loud and clear, and we kept it low with an ear out in case they said something about us.

I was barely halfway through my first chicken leg when Uncle Cody caught my attention.

"Ned, I don't mean this to sound bad, but y'all are getting a little old to take on another kid."

"I said the same thing." Uncle James was in my line of sight, and I saw him throw a glance in our direction. "We thought about letting Mark come live with *us.*"

Aunt Ida Belle chimed in. "You brought it up and I told you that was a bad idea in a lot of ways. Ned and Miss Becky didn't think it would be a good neither, especially with all the puppy love those two are passing back and forth."

Pepper slapped her TV tray, almost knocking her tea over. "We're sitting right *here.*"

Miss Becky twisted around to take a pan of biscuits off the table without getting up. She gave me a smile and waved. "All right. James, y'all don't have no more room in that little house of yours anyway. It ain't no bigger'n this one."

Uncle James made an announcement that surprised us all. "We'd have room. We're buying the Ordway place."

"Well, my lands." Miss Becky's hands fluttered over her plate. "I thought Dr. Dangerfield was living there."

The doctor was a retired veterinarian who bought the Ordway place the year before, but only lived there a few months.

"He was, but he's moving to Dallas so he can be close to his daughter." Uncle James sat straight and leveled his shoulders. "When I found out, I contacted a realtor in Chisum and got the ball rolling."

"Shit." Pepper leaned toward Mark, nearly sticking her nose in his long black hair. She took a lot longer than she should have to whisper in his ear. "That place is haunted. I don't want to live in no haunted house again."

"You believe in ghosts?"

"Do you believe Top has dreams that come true?"

"Sure do. I've seen it."

"Then believe in ghosts, too."

Mark's sober face took the news as if she'd said the sun was bright. "Didn't y'all live in that house once already?"

I spoke up to make sure they hadn't forgotten I was there. They'd already started conversations that left me shut out. "Uncle James and them rented it when I first came to live with Grandpa and Miss Becky."

Grandpa's voice came through loud and clear since he was facing us from the head of the table. "That place left a bad taste in my mouth. You oughta buy the land, push the house over, and build a new one."

Aunt Ida Belle didn't like that idea at all. "It's a good house, and I've loved it since I was a kid. I didn't want to move in the first place back when we rented it a few years ago."

"Well, I wish y'all'd find someplace else to live." Grandpa buttered another biscuit.

"The sale has almost gone through. We didn't want to say anything until we were sure. We wanted to surprise you."

Uncle Cody finally spoke up. "It'll be good to have you so close. That'll put us all within a mile of one another. That makes me feel pretty good. We can keep an eye on each other."

"That's the way it was in the thirties," Miss Becky recalled. "I 'magine we had twenty or more of our own families living within two miles of one another. It was good then. We could help each other when we needed it."

"We do anyway." Grandpa took a spoon full of red beans from the bowl in front of him. "It don't matter how far off folks are, but that's all right. Family helps family."

"I'm gonna put some money into it and clean the place up." Uncle James owned a hardware store in Chisum.

"It was shot full of holes." I filled Mark in on the history of the Ordway house, since he'd been gone. "Some folks from Vegas rented it and we liked them a lot, but the guy worked for some gangsters. They came after him and there was a shootout one night a year or so ago that almost got us all killed."

Mark jerked his head to get the hair out of his eyes. "I heard about that. Sheriff Griffin died that night."

Pepper shuddered. "I hate that house, and they haven't told me a damn thing about it until just now."

Mark grinned. "What makes *you* think it's haunted? I remember hearing Uncle Cody say he saw spirits one night when he was a kid, but I thought he was just trying to scare us."

"Me and Top heard ghosts in there not long before Anthony and Miss Samantha moved in."

"Who?"

"The gangster and his girlfriend."

"How'd you hear the spirits?"

She peeked into the kitchen. "Me and Top snuck in through a hole in the floor. We were in the living room and heard someone walking around upstairs. It had to be a ghost, because the house was empty and the doors were locked."

"Somebody could have snuck in just like y'all did."

"Maybe." I thought about it for a second. "But I don't think so."

Pepper brightened. "You want to sneak back in after dinner and see if we hear something?"

Mark shook his head. "Nope. I don't intend to get in trouble with anybody. I just want to go to sleep in this nice house and eat when I'm hungry."

Pepper's eyes welled, an unnatural act for her. "Was it rough where you were?"

"Yeah. My aunt and Grover don't have any money, and there were too many of us to feed regular. He worked ever now and then, but a dollar or two a day don't buy much after they smoked up a lot of it and drank the other half. He expected us kids to bring in the rest."

"Whose idea was it for you to move back here? Grandpa would have come and got you any time you wanted."

"I knew he would, but they weren't gonna let me go until they got good and ready. It was Grover's idea to get rid of me. He hit one of the little'uns one too many times and I busted him in the nose for it. He knocked me in the head and kicked me out for a couple of days. I stayed in the barn at night, and that wasn't too bad. The weather's been nice and I had a quilt to lay on.

"Then he came out this morning after I was through milking and said they were bringing me here 'cause I ate too much, and that was that. I didn't eat that much, really, but now the little ones will have my share of the food.

"And now my cousin will have to stand up to Grover. He'll be my size next year and he can take care of 'em. When I get out of school and get a job, I'll go back and get every one of 'em that's left." He looked down at the full plate on the TV tray and spoke as soft as if he were in church. "There one minute and here the next. Damn that happened fast."

They must have got to talking about adult stuff in the kitchen. Norma Faye came into the living room and turned the volume up on the television, a sure sign they didn't want us listening in.

Miss Becky's voice came through loud and clear. "Praise the Lord, we're all back together again!"

Norma Faye shook her red hair, gave us a grin and a wink, and went back to the table. The baseball announcer's voice made it hard to hear them after that.

Pepper got up and turned the television back down when the action stalled and the adults wouldn't know she'd done it. It didn't help, though, because they were talking quiet and we finally finished eating and went outside.

Chapter Twelve

Nerves jangling, The Wraith walked through the dew-soaked grass around the empty farmhouse where he lived before his wife left him for another man. He peered into the windows and studied the bare floors, remembering and feeding on the anger that was a steady ache in his chest. The odor of death found his nostrils and he peered inside a bucket sitting on the porch to find it half full of water with a rotting rat carcass floating on top. The Wraith had an idea and built a real smile for the first time in days.

Ned steered his Plymouth down the dirt road between high cut banks. A hardwood canopy laced overhead, cooling the thick, wet evening air.

Deputy John Washington rode in the passenger seat with his big arm hanging out the open window. The sleeve rolled above his elbow looked as if it would split at the seams from the pressure of his biceps. "I cain't believe that boy's back with y'all."

"I wouldn't have believed it, neither. Them kinfolk of his decided they were tired of feedin' him."

"Y'all gonna raise him?"

"Yep. O.C. said he'd draw up the papers so nobody can take him again."

"Mr. Ned, you're gonna have a houseful of young'uns, and at your age."

"Don't I know it. They'll be the death of me before they're grown."

John's wide smile split his face. "That'll be good for Top. He needs a boy around to put some bark on 'im."

"I'm more worried about Pepper than anything else. She's got eyes for Mark, so I don't know what's gonna happen."

"They're gonna be kids."

"That's what worries me. Listen, if these Mayfields swell up, you step in and cool 'em off."

"They'll most likely not say much. They're grieving right now. The only ones that might give us trouble are a couple of the younger folks, but I expect their elders'll calm 'em down."

The .38 on his belt, the sap in his back pocket, and the pump shotgun on the seat between them didn't help Ned's unease as they turned off the dirt road and rolled slowly down a two-lane track to the Mayfield house that was in direct contrast to the Clay place. "Here we are."

The unpainted, rambling house had seen better days. It squatted in a clearing surrounded by thick woods on three sides and a pasture on the other. Two tall sycamores shaded the dirt yard. A tire swing hung still in the dead air. Rusting screens, their holes stuffed with rags, barely kept bugs and critters out.

Two dozen cars and trucks were parked haphazardly in the dirt yard. The front porch was full of people. An elderly black couple carried foil-covered dishes across the yard and into the house.

John got out first and threw a hand up in a wave. Most waved back. Several faces closed up when Ned appeared from behind the wheel. He threaded his way between the cars, watching a mixed pack of dogs rush up to smell his pants legs.

They stopped short of the steps. Tilting the straw hat back on his head, Ned found Hollis Mayfield sitting in a tired rocking chair to the right of the door. "Hollis. I'm sorry for your loss."

The old white-haired man rocked slowly in the shade. Two women who appeared to be in their twenties moved closer to him, as if for protection. He plucked at the galluses on his soft, faded duckins. "Constable. John. How y'all doin'?"

Big John propped one foot on a lower step and leaned on

his knee. "Fair to middlin'. I sure am sorry about Maggie. She was some punkin'."

Hollis gave him a weak smile. "She was a ring-tailed tooter, all right."

A thick middle-aged woman in her Sunday clothes came outside and handed him a sweating mason jar full of sweet tea. "Here Daddy. Supper'll be ready in a little bit."

"Thank you, baby." Chipped ice tinkled against the glass as Hollis drained half the quart jar in one long draught. "You gentlemen care for some sweet tea?"

"No thanks." Ned shook his head.

John wiped sweat that trickled down his cheek in the still air. "Nossir, but thankyee. Just came by to see y'all for a minute and tell you we're lookin' into the wreck."

"It was murder, John." Those around the old man nodded. "We done heard there's rubber thick on the road where someone run our girl through the guardrail. You need to be out looking for a car or truck with creases down the sides."

"Cain't say that yet, Hollis. All we know is they went over the dam."

His eyes grew moist. "I dearly loved that gal. Bringing her into this family was the only good thing Tylee ever done. Them Clays'll be mad about it, sure as shootin'. I already heard they're sayin' we had something to do with it. They'll be laying for us."

Ned shook his head. "I thought y'all buried that hatchet years ago."

Hollis stared off into the trees. "Some did."

John studied the raw, dusty boards at his feet.

A thick man in unbuttoned overalls thumped the legs of his chair to the floor. "There's gonna be *trouble*, all right." He sounded like a fire and brimstone preacher.

"What makes you say that?" Ned tried to place the man but came up empty. "You know something the rest of us don't?"

A middle-aged man in suit pants and a white shirt spoke up. "We never had no business with any of them since the Trouble, but when her and Rubye went to work for him, it all came back."

"Now don't go bringing the past up, Willie." John frowned at the big man. "Let it lay. Have they done anything to any of y'all yet?"

A younger man with thick forearms spoke up. "I done seen cars I don't know driving slow up and down the road last night. You need to do something about it, John."

The big deputy wiped sweat from his eyebrow. Ned and John were baking in the direct sun. "Nothin' to do yet, Bryce. It looks like a pure accident when she didn't make the turn over the dam. If we learn something different, we'll let you know."

A woman holding a hip baby spoke up. "White law won't help us find out what happened. You're gonna have to do it for us, John."

"That ain't true." Ned shook his head. "I'll do everything I can."

She raised an eyebrow. "Everything?"

"Yep."

"Then why you here now, a day and a half after she was killed? A full day and a half after you already went to them white people's house?"

The truth was that Ned couldn't bear to talk with two grieving families on the same day, and then with Mark showing up, it had slipped his mind. He realized how it looked and was ashamed.

John took the focus back on himself. "Avon, that was my fault. Him and Sheriff Parker talked to the Clays first, but I couldn't get over here 'til now and Mr. Ned wanted to come with me. You know I woulda been by yesterday if I could and Mr. Ned here, well, he had some family business to take care of this mornin'," he waved a hand toward the cars behind him and the house full of grieving people, "and y'all *know* about family."

She backed off and Hollis sighed. "Well, I appreciate y'all checking on us."

John tilted his straw hat up on his forehead and wiped at the sweat again. "Bury your dead, and I'll do everything I can to find out what happened. Just y'all don't take it on yourselves, no matter what. Stay away from the Clays."

"If they'll stay away from us." Hollis rocked and sipped at the sweating jar.

Ned didn't like that comment at all. "I'll come by and check on you, too. Y'all call me if there's trouble."

"Ain't got no phone."

Ned wasn't surprised. "Well, somebody close by does."

"I do." Avon shifted the baby to her other hip. "But I'm on the other side of the pasture. Daddy cain't run over to tell me every time sum'm happens."

"You'll know if there's trouble." Hollis finished his tea.

"How, Daddy?"

"You'll know."

Ned worried at that statement all the way home.

Chapter Thirteen

Mark and I were finishing breakfast Monday morning when a car pulled up our gravel drive. Miss Becky was washing dishes and humming her favorite sacred song, "In The Garden." The wooden kitchen door was open and the candy-apple red '67 Impala I saw through the screen almost took my breath away. Hootie barked a couple of times before slipping under the porch.

"Uh oh." Grandpa took one last sip of coffee from his saucer and rose from the table.

Miss Becky dried her hands on a flour sack dish towel. "Who is it?"

"Frank Clay's brother, Donald Ray." Grandpa took his hat from the rack beside the door and set it just so on his head. He stepped onto the porch. "Shut up, Hootie! Get out Donald Ray."

"Does he bite?"

"Naw. The worst he'll do is histe his leg on you."

"My lands." Miss Becky cleared the table around me. "He don't have to talk like that."

Mark and I snickered 'cause we'd heard worse up at the store. Miss Becky raised an eyebrow. "*You* watch what *you* say when you get older, Mister Terrence Orrin Parker, and you too, Mr. Lightfoot. Hurry and brush your teeth. The school bus'll be here any minute."

Grandpa and Donald Ray were talking in front of the Impala when we came out, spitting Pepsodent. We sat on the porch to wait for the bus.

Mr. Donald Ray was about half mad. His horn-rimmed glasses had slipped down on his nose and he pushed them up with a finger. His voice rose. "What are you gonna do about it?"

"I don't see much *to* do, Donald Ray. It was a car wreck and we're looking into it."

"Shouldn't you be trying to find out why he was in the car with a nigger gal?"

Grandpa flicked his eyes at us, and I pretended to be interested in the ink scribbles on the brown paper cover on my math book. I probably should have been paying attention to the contents, because I was lost as a goose in "new math." I'd been pretty good at arithmetic, but all those sets and unions got past me on the first day and I was still having trouble catching up.

Mark didn't have any books because he wasn't even enrolled yet, so he just studied his feet. Grandpa promised to come up to the school before classes took up so he could sign the papers.

"I don't believe there was any laws broke, him riding with her." Grandpa's hands were in the pockets of his overalls. "We're thinking she was giving him a ride home and lost control and went off the dam, or maybe somebody might have strayed into her lane."

"He was in the car with a jigaboo and somebody got mad about it and ran 'em off the road. It's clear as the nose on your face." His glasses slipped again, and this time he looked over the top of them.

"We don't know any such thing."

"You should be investigatin' or something instead of hanging around here at the house."

I figured that was one of the worst things anyone could say to Grandpa. He hated for people to tell him his job, the one he'd been doing since World War II. He was good at it, too, catching moonshiners, drunks, and even a murderer or two.

"Tend to your own business, Donald Ray, and don't tell me what I *oughta* do."

I knew more about the Clay family than the Mayfields. It was a pretty good sized family, and all of them were used to giving orders. A couple of 'em were the most well-to-do folks in Chisum with money earned from cattle and crops raised by sharecroppers. Grandpa said others always operated right on the edge between good and bad, and they'd skin their hands for two bits on a wagonload of cotton if they saw a chance.

Grandpa sighed. "Cody has a deputy working on it. But she hasn't found anything yet."

"She? He got some secretary making phone calls?"

"Did you hear me? I said a deputy. He hired a woman deputy."

"Good God. You got that Washington feller on it and he ain't doing nothing 'cause that Mayfield gal was half nigger, and now a split-tail workin' on Frank's case. I want somebody who'll take it serious and find out who did the killin'."

Grandpa's ears were getting red, a sure sign he was mad.

"I'm getting tired of saying this. There weren't no killing, as far as I know right now. It was an accident until we find out otherwise, and if you have trouble with that, you need to take it up with Cody's *deputy* handling the case. Her name's Anna Sloan and she's as good a hand as anybody else I know. Do you have anything that'll help us, or are you here to just yap and not listen to me?"

"You better be glad it's me here instead of Royal. You know how he is."

Grandpa rubbed his neck, telling me he was doing everything he could to hold back. Listening to Donald Ray, it was like telling a two-year-old to quit being nosey. "That's enough of that. I don't want to hear you call nobody that word no more. Now, murder's a hard thing to prove."

"I'll take Royal and Wes over there with me to Slate Shoals and they'll beat the goddamn truth out of Hollis Mayfield. I bet he knows."

I'd heard of Royal Clay ever since I came to Center Springs. I wasn't sure how they were all kin, whether they were brothers, cousins, or uncles, or even how old they were, but everything I'd ever heard about him told me he was tough as boot leather and mean as a snake. The adults talked about him in soft voices that always sounded full of fear, like they were talking about the Boogie-man.

Grandpa took his hands from his pockets and closed the distance between him and Donald Ray, who jerked for a second like he was about to jump back in the car. I didn't have to see Grandpa's ice-blue eyes to know they were flashing. He lowered his voice, but the wet air was so still we could hear him clear as a bell.

"You keep on and I'll haul you in for being a public nuisance and interfering with an investigation, and maybe even trespassing, if I think it'll stick. You better settle yourself down, hoss, and stay out of my *business*. All you're gonna do is start trouble."

"You can't tell us where we can go and where we can't. Royal's done said what needs doing." Donald Ray poked at Grandpa's chest with a forefinger. "He don't want to wait."

"You better fold that finger in if you want to keep it!"

They were both breathing hard, like they'd been throwing sacks of feed into the back of the truck when Miss Becky's voice floated through the screen. "Ned, your eggs are ready, if y'all are finished talking."

She cut through his mad with just a few words. I knew there weren't any eggs on the table. It was her way of cooling things off.

Donald Ray's hand dropped.

Grandpa's voice was still chilly. "If I's you, I'd back off for a while and let me alone."

I was disappointed when the school bus made the corner in front of the church and headed towards us. I sighed, picked up my books, and we headed down the drive, looking back over our shoulders a time or two to see if they were still going at it.

Donald Ray was back in his car by the time me and Mark got halfway to school, and that red Impala was nothing but a blur that disappeared toward Forest Chapel.

Chapter Fourteen

We were eating supper when Grandpa pushed back from his plate. Pepper was with us, because Uncle James and Aunt Ida Belle were in town, signing some paperwork on the Ordway place. "Did I hear y'all are going fishing this weekend?"

Pepper stopped, holding her fork in the air and twisting her hair around one finger on her other hand. "Uncle Cody says he's gonna try."

She was acting like her old self now that she'd gotten that California hippie phase out of her system and Mark was back. One day a few months earlier she went stringing off toward San Francisco to find out that the hippies weren't as colorful and cool as they looked on television.

During that week she run off, Pepper learned that even though they wore bright tie-dyed and beads with their bell bottoms, fringed vests, and peace signs, the Counter Culture Revolution was just a bunch of inexperienced kids with big ideas and empty pockets.

She hadn't said much about California since she got back, and I figured that little jaunt took some of the starch out of her. She whispered one night that the thing that soured her the most was their ideas of what the kids called "free love." The love we felt from our family was one thing, but some of the boys she ran into wanted a lot more. She teared up when she told me about it, and promised that someday I'd hear the rest.

The whole thought gave me a sick feeling in my stomach, because I had a good idea what'd happened.

Grandpa drained the last of his sweet tea. "I thought you'd growed out of fishing."

"I thought I had too, but when Uncle Cody said the white bass were running, I remembered how much fun it is to catch them."

"You gotta clean 'em, too." Mark grinned down at his plate. "And I bet you won't like that part."

"Top can do it. He's faster than I am."

"Hey! I'm not cleaning all those fish. The last time you only gutted two and then said you were sick or something and I had to help Uncle Martin 'til it was nearly midnight. I'm not doing that again."

"It was kinda like being sick. I got my period."

"Pepper!" Grandpa and Miss Becky both hollered at the same time, but they weren't mad, they just wanted her to hush.

Mark lowered his head even farther, hiding his grin behind a curtain of black hair. Miss Becky rolled her eyes toward Heaven. "My stars, girl."

Grandpa studied his own plate for a minute. "You kids want to go to the carnival tonight?"

Our heads snapped toward the head of the table. "What carnival?"

"There's one set up down from the army camp. I need to go out there and look around, and figured y'all might want some cotton candy or ride a ride or something. Mama, you want to come with us?"

"Lands no. They have those gambling games and I don't want to be anywhere around that kind of sin. I'll stay right here. This is a school night, remember."

"I know, but John's taking Rachel and the kids, so I figgered these urchins can go too."

"Well, they don't need to be out late."

"It's just a carnival and not the fair. They can see everything in an hour or two and we'll be back around their usual bedtime."

Grandpa sounded like one of us trying to talk *him* into letting us have some fun. It gave me a little peek of what Grandpa was like when he was our age. "I bet James'll go with us. They oughta be back in a little bit."

Pepper's face fell at the thought of her daddy going along, though she tolerated him a lot more than she used to. Grandpa noticed. "It'll be fine. I 'magine your mama'll come over here instead of going with us."

I felt better when I heard that. I love Aunt Ida Belle, but she was always a drag when we wanted to have fun.

We came over the hill an hour later. The glow of bright colored lights not far from Camp Maxey was a base for two spotlights at the carnival gate. Grandpa was surprised. "Well this is a bigger outfit than it looked when I was here a while ago."

We joined a line of cars waiting their turn to get into the pasture. Grandpa parked at the end of a long, wavy line of dusty cars and mud-caked pickups. Far from the carnival lights, it was dark and shadowy.

I thought Grandpa was going to take us straight back home when Pepper stepped out and said, "Well, shit."

Uncle James' blue eyes flashed. "What did you just say?"

"Shit. Cowshit. I just stepped in cowshit."

Grandpa chuckled as he slammed the door. "Well, this *was* a cow pasture last week, and it will be again the next. Watch where you're walking."

"And watch your language, young lady." Uncle James wrinkled his nose like he didn't like the smell of cow flop, which we were around all the time. "There's nicer ways of saying what comes out of the south end of a cow."

I couldn't help but laugh at her as we joined a stream of people walking toward the entrance gate. Pepper kept dragging her foot like the Mummy in that Boris Karloff movie.

Mark held back to walk with her. He made a sound like the Mummy. "Mmmmmmmmgh."

"Shut up!" She drug her foot again, trying to scrape the last of it off, but she wasn't mad like she would have been with me. She gave him a funny little grin and ducked her head. "Or I'll knock your damn head off."

Mark stuck his arms out and walked like Frankenstein, but she still didn't get as aggravated at him. I didn't understand a thing about he'ing and she'ing, and wondered if she'd *ever* get mad at him.

Grandpa was at the ticket booth when we caught up. The woman behind the glass looked like she didn't know what to do. "I have a note here that says to let you in, but it don't say nothing about anyone else."

I wasn't paying much attention, looking instead at all the bright lights that turned the night into day. I bet the ticket booth had five hundred lights bulbs all by itself.

"I ain't asking for them to get in free." Grandpa pulled a few limp bills from his wallet and passed them through the slot.

We breathed in the thick odor of fried foods, cotton candy, gas fumes, and hot grease. At the same time we were blasted with a wall of noise, flashing lights, loud music, shouts from the carnies manning the game booths, and screams from kids on the most exciting rides.

The Octopus was the first attraction inside the gate and we felt the air whooshing past from the spinning arms. The long midway was lined with game booths like the Shooting Gallery, Darts, Ring Toss, and Basketball Throw. Short trailers sold corny dogs and hot dogs beside a gypsy fortune teller. In the distance I saw a line of tents with painted canvas signs advertising freak shows. If I squinted hard enough there were other tents and signs beyond that. One said, Girls! Girls! Girls! Featuring the Latest Go-Go Dances.

I was immediately overwhelmed with the whole thing and just stopped.

Pepper's eyes were bright. "Let's ride it!"

That Octopus thing scared me to death. Grandpa and Uncle James were talking to someone they knew and weren't paying

any attention to us. "Let's look around first." I wanted to get
an idea of what we could do before committing our money to
a ride I really didn't want to get on.

"Grandpa, we're gonna walk around."

He reached into his pocket handed us each three dollars in
quarters. "Y'all stay together. I want you back right here in an
hour and not a minute more." He returned to their conversation
before we even walked away.

It seemed like everybody in northeast Texas was there, and
we were careful not to get separated, even though I felt like I
knew half of them and was probably related to the rest in some
way. That's what they always say about small towns, don't talk
about anyone, 'cause they're probably kinfolk.

The rest of the crowd was a mix of farmers and town people,
and the families passing through were almost as interesting as
the carnival itself. Some of them looked as if they hadn't seen
civilization in years, and many of them reminded me of the West
Virginia coal miners I saw in our history book.

When he thought I wasn't within hearing distance, Grandpa
called them river rats.

He didn't have anything against poor folks. He always said
they come in all colors and a lot of them can't help it. Him and
Miss Becky grew up dirt poor, but that didn't stop them from
working hard to get what they had.

Miss Becky always made sure of a few basics when Mama
and Uncle James came along during the Depression. They were
fed, had clean clothes, even though they might be homemade
or patched over and over again, had their hair washed and cut,
and the men always shaved.

His complaint about river rats wasn't usually due to how they
looked, even though that carried a lot of weight, but it was about
how they acted. That went for everyone, including the Negros.

I was a little surprised at the number of colored folks there,
too. I was used to seeing mostly white people. They liked fun
just as much as us and a carnival was cheap entertainment, if
they were careful and stayed away from the games.

There were even a few Indians that I figured were from over in Oklahoma and more than one person slowed down to look at Pepper and Mark in their headbands she'd made of old material. Her eagle feather hung on one side and glowed in the lights.

And there I was in my Boy's Regular haircut, sneakers, jeans, and a button-up shirt.

I found myself looking for Mr. John Washington and Miss Rachel. It'd be easy to find them what with his size and the number of their family and all. Mr. John didn't have any kids when they got together, but Miss Rachel had two of her own, Bubba and Belle, and they were raising her dead sister's kids, too, so there were fifteen of them total.

I knew Jere and Daisy the best, because they were closest to my own age. Their stair-step brothers and sisters, Betsy, Frederick, Christian, Josephine, Bessie, Myrlie, Florynce, and baby Bass Reeves, all hung together pretty close. I figured it was because their mama was killed after their daddy run off, and that drew them tight to one another.

The game operators were yelling and waving for us to come over, but we passed without stopping. I wanted to find the Funhouse, if they had one, or the Spook House. I real quick saw what I wanted to ride for sure and stepped onto the metal landing for the Ferris wheel.

Pepper grabbed my arm. "I don't want to ride that!"

"Don't then." I jerked loose and paid for a ticket. It felt good to be in charge and not follow her. "The state fair's is bigger, but I like the feeling when you go over the top and down the front side. Y'all can wait here."

"I'm going with you," Mark said.

The ragged-looking guy running the wheel held up, waiting to see what Pepper would do. She grumbled, bought a ticket and sat down hard in the seat between us to let me know that she wasn't happy about riding it. I just grinned while we swung back and forth. I'd won a small battle with her and it made me feel good.

It took forever to get the Ferris wheel going. We finally got high enough to see the parking lot and off in the distance, the glow from the lights of Chisum. Stars glittered overhead and the lights below were bright and colorful. Off in the distance, cars passed on the highway going to and from Oklahoma.

Remembering I wanted to see the Funhouse, I scanned the booths and rides below until I found it. I was grinning like an idiot when I saw a face down in the crowd looking up at us. It was like I had a pair of binoculars, suddenly drawing the face close and clear, but I couldn't place him from that distance. Someone passed between us and he disappeared.

It was one of those things that I knew would drive me crazy if I couldn't figure out who he was. I pointed "Did you see that guy down there? Who was that?"

Pepper watched the crowd milling below. "There's a few hundred folks I can see."

Mark leaned over the side to look and the car rocked. I thought Pepper was gonna suck all the air out of the world. "Shit!" She grabbed him around the neck and pulled him back. "Sit back before you kill us all."

He laughed at the stars. "Don't worry. I'm not afraid of heights."

"Well I am!" She shifted her grip and held his arm. "Stay still."

The moving mass of people down below reminded me of busy ants. "There he goes, see? He just went out past them trailers toward the parking lot. Where do I know him from?"

"What difference does it make?" Pepper started to say something else when she jumped and screamed like the ol' Devil hisself had aholt of her. She started slapping at her head and shaking her hair. I thought she was having a fit until something slapped against the back of *my* head and then grabbed everything grabbable on the way down my shirt.

Mark jumped. "Oh!"

Another *thing* with pinchers landed on my neck and Pepper she screamed again. "Shit! Shit! Shit!"

I believe I'da flown out of that seat if we hadn't had that bar across our laps. But it caught me at the hips and jerked me back and that's when I realized big old hard-shelled June bugs were attracted to the lights. The one in my shirt crunched when I leaned back.

I knocked another June bug out of Pepper's hair and then Mark started laughing like a loon. "This is probably good medicine!"

"Get me off this damned thing." Pepper was furious. "It's bugs, not Indian medicine."

The wheel started turning and before you know it, we were going straight down, past the landing, and then back up again. The bugs didn't land on us while we were moving, and that was a relief. Pepper settled down and snuggled up against Mark on the second revolution and quit griping.

I knew they were getting lovey dovey, so I ignored 'em and looked for that feller again every time we got to the top. I thought I mighta seen him once, going between some cars in the makeshift lot when a pair of headlights caught him, but after that he was gone.

We were back on the ground a few minutes later, with Pepper cussin' a blue streak. "That's the last time you're gonna pick the rides tonight. The next one is mine and it sure as hell ain't gonna be buggy."

She led off, pulling at Mark's hand and I followed. I was eyeing the bright red candy apples in a free-standing booth when a really greasy guy behind the counter of the Balloon Dart game waved to catch our attention. "Hey, little girl! Come try your luck, sweetheart!"

"Kiss my ass." Pepper said it loud enough for them to hear it. "I ain't your sweetheart." She stopped, as if someone had thrown a switch.

"What?"

"Look at the prizes there."

They looked like baby toys to me. "I see a bunch of stuffed animals."

"No, behind and to the right."

I saw a display of pocket-size transistor radios tucked between the cheap prizes that caught her eye.

Mark shook his head. "You'll never win one of those."

"Bet I do." She was already digging in her jeans for the quarters Grandpa gave us.

The carney behind the counter held a handful of darts. "C'mon, young lady. Give it a shot. Five darts for a quarter. Pop them all and win!"

"I want one of those radios."

She had a transistor radio up until just before she ran off for California. She broke it and had been wanting another one ever since. I tried to explain that the adults were enjoying the silence, because they didn't like the Rolling Stones or the Beatles. They wanted country music when it was soft and low, but she kept on aggravating them by playing rock 'n' roll on the black plastic GE in the living room. Miss Becky kept it tuned to the local Chisum station so they could listen to the weather and ag reports during dinner, when Grandpa came in from the field. They always got irritated when they found it on a different station.

The man took Pepper's money and handed her the darts. "Get them all and you win the grand prize."

Her confident smile was a mile wide. She threw the first dart and it stuck in the soft, pitted cork between a red and yellow balloon. Disgusted that she'd already lost, she pitched the rest without a care. One bounced off a red balloon, and the other hit the tied end, poking a hole that slowly whistled the yellow balloon flat.

"Good try." The carney handed her a plastic doll that probably cost three cents.

"I want another go at it." She handed him some more money and lost when she popped only two balloons.

I was watching pretty close and started to get the idea that something was wrong.

"Let me try." Mark traded money for the darts and had the same bad luck.

Ten minutes later, Pepper was out of Grandpa's money and digging for the folding allowance she had in her back pocket.

The carney clapped his hands. "That's the way, gal, get mad and win one of those big prizes."

I didn't like the look in the greasy man's eyes. "Hey, we need to go do something else."

She had her back up by then. "I *said* I want one of those radios."

"You're not gonna get it." Mark took her arm and glared at the carney. "Let's go ride something. How about the Octopus?"

Her blood was up. "No. I'm gonna win at this game."

"Look. Did you check those darts?" I was watching the man's hands. "There's something wrong."

He gave me a smirk that I'd seen before on other people when they thought they knew something I didn't. "Hey, kid. You're wrong. Watch this." He threw a dart, popping a blue balloon. He threw another, and this time a yellow one popped. "That's all there is to it." He popped a third.

"See?" Pepper gave him another dollar and the carney made change. He handed her five more darts. "Good luck."

"Why don't you give her the ones *you* used?" I'd finally figured out what was going on. I turned to tell Mark, but he wasn't there.

The carney's face changed, the way a person's will do if you start to worry on their last nerve. "She *has* darts."

"Not those. Pull yours out of the board there and let her throw *them*."

"I don't want to get in the way of her throwing."

Pepper ignored us and popped three. "See. I'm getting the hang of this."

The carney handed Pepper a cheap stuffed monkey and flashed her a grin with yellow teeth that needed brushing. "I bet you can do it this time, gal."

"Hey, let me throw." I was sure the game was rigged.

I paid and he handed me the darts. I ran my finger across the tips to find one was sharp, and the others were dull as a worn pencil lead. I rolled one in my hand and realized it was lighter than the others, and they were bent. I threw the first and missed. The second glanced off a balloon and stuck in the corkboard.

"You need to throw harder kid."

"No I don't." The next popped a balloon. The last was one looked different from the others and the point was sharp. One side of the balloon board was thicker with more targets than the middle. I flicked the sharp dart toward the top without putting any effort into the throw. It hit the board and fell, popping three balloons on the way down.

"Sorry, kid. Falling dart. You lose."

"No, he don't."

Grandpa's voice was clear as a bell over my shoulder. Mark was right beside him and I knew where he'd gone.

"It's a disqualified throw. They have to stick."

"Where does it say that? All I see is pop five for the prize."

The carney's eyes hooded. "Them's the rules."

Grandpa put his hand on my shoulder and pulled me back with the other two. He stepped close to the booth. "You want me to look real close at those darts? I bet they need sharpening. How about them balloons? They might look like they're full, but I bet they ain't hardly got no air in them at all."

I moved a little, and the man saw Grandpa's gun on his hip, then he noticed the badge. In that second, he deflated like the limp balloons on the board. "Fine then." He reached up to unhook a giant stuffed bear that was hanging overhead.

"Not that." I pointed. "She wants the radio over there."

It looked like someone had stole his soul. His shoulders slumped and he reached for one on the shelf.

"Nope." Grandpa's voice was soft, but it seemed to cut through all the noise and music. "Give her one of them you have hid under the counter."

With a pained look, the carney fetched a radio still in the box. Pepper took it like the guy was gonna grab her. Grandpa nodded his head. "Take it out and turn it on."

We waited while she did, and it flickered to life with static.

Grandpa was satisfied. He took Pepper's shoulder and turned her away from the game. Now, young lady..."

He was interrupted when a guy with silver hair rushed up to Grandpa. "Constable, we got trouble."

"We had trouble right here with one of your people, Delmar."

The carnival owner looked surprised when saw the radio in Pepper's hand. "We'll talk about that in a little bit. I just got word there's a man dead in the parking lot."

Grandpa stiffened. "You kids find James and stay with him, and keep away from these games." He took off after the carnival owner.

"I think I saw Daddy by the gate." Pepper headed toward the entrance.

I followed, knowing what was on her mind. "You didn't neither."

"It's a good place to start looking."

Mark hung back. "I know you. You're gonna get us all in trouble."

"Daddy may be at the car. That's the best place to meet up with him. Why, you scared?"

I saw something in Mark's eyes I'd never seen in my own. It was a look of complete confidence. "I'm not afraid of anything anymore."

"We can't get in trouble doing what we're *supposed* to do." She batted her eyes and pulled a strand of hair from her mouth. Her eyes widened. "Oh, I'm *scayered*." She stretched the word into two long syllables. "I heard something about a dead man. I need my *Daddy*."

There was no use arguing, so Mark and I followed her out the gate.

Chapter Fifteen

The Wraith stood at the back of the crowd, watching from under a slouch hat that hid his features. Not even his own cousin nearby recognized him. It was good to be back in Lamar County, where he intended to settle up before leaving to earn a living in Alaska. He'd be safe there, far away from Texas. At least he wouldn't have to put up with the humidity there, where the government would give 160 acres to any man who wanted to homestead.

Ned followed the silver-haired carnival owner through the haphazard parking lot, dreading what he might find. As usual, bad news traveled fast and a crowd had already converged on a point farthest from the brightly lit grounds.

A crooked column of cars was parked close to a strip of woods bordering the pasture, some with their headlights on, illuminating the nearest trees and casting harsh shadows into the woods.

Onlookers milled in the beams. A still body lay facedown in the trampled grass.

"Step aside, men." Ned rounded a bumper and pushed toward the still figure. "Y'all don't get in my light. Anybody see what happened?" Heads shook as Ned knelt and shook the colored man's shoulder. "Feller, you all right?"

"I believe he's dead, Ned."

He looked up, squinting at a backlit figure. "Who're you?"

"It's me. Rick Patterson."

"Oh, Rick." Ned had known him since the man was a kid. His daddy owned the Chisum feed store. Ned felt for a pulse. "You didn't see what happened, neither?"

"Naw. I swung in to park and the lights caught him laying there. We left 'em on for you."

"You didn't see anybody leaving?"

"Nary."

Ned rolled the body over and felt a chill down his spine. "Well, if that don't beat all."

"Who is it?"

"Merle Mayfield."

"I don't know him."

"I do." Ned rose, picking up the silver Cross pen that had fallen from his pocket. Merle Mayfield was one of Hollis' younger brothers. Ned frowned at the sight of Top and Pepper pushing through men lining the area. James stepped up behind them, put his hands on their shoulders, and turned them away, back toward the car.

Ned felt empty, standing in the harsh headlights. With Merle Mayfield dead, he was sure the long-standing feud between the Mayfields and Clays was back with a vengeance.

"'I god, this is just getting started."

Someone handed Ned a flashlight. He glanced up to see the frightened eyes of Isaac Reader. Most of the gathering crowd kept a respectful distance, but the twitchy little sun-browned farmer stayed close by. It seemed that Ike was a magnet for death and trouble, which kept him rattled most of the time.

"Ike, what'n hell are you doing? Don't you know they have clowns in there?"

Reader was deathly afraid of clowns and often slept with a shotgun close at hand when the bigger Carson and Barnes Circus folks came through town on their way to the winter grounds across the river in Hugo, Oklahoma. Ike admitted to worrying that someone dressed as a clown would show up at his door, asking to borrow a gallon of gas for a dead car or something.

"Listen, listen, I know they do, but this ain't the circus. The only clowns in there are selling balloons, and you can tell where they are by watching over folks' heads." He lowered his voice. "I came to see that tattooed lady I heard about. They say she don't wear much, 'cause she's all covered in pictures…"

"I get what you're sayin'." Ned snapped on the light to examine the body and surrounding area. "Good Lord. He's been beat to pieces. Y'all stay back. I don't want no one tramping through this grass and maybe destroying evidence."

"He's right. Give him some room." The deep voice of Deputy John Washington filled the night air, clear as a bell over the cacophony behind them. Dressed in black slacks, his khaki shirt with the deputy sheriff patches and badge, and his ever-present Stetson, the giant of a man towered over the crowd.

"Glad you're here, John. You get a call?"

"Nawsir. We was already inside when I heard there was trouble with one of my people out here. You know who that is?"

"Merle Mayfield. He's been beat plumb to death." Ned directed his flashlight through the crushed grass, realizing he'd been smelling it since he walked up. "It wasn't with no fists, though. His skull's busted in. Somebody used something on him." He glanced around. "I want everybody back behind that next row of cars over there. Nobody pick anything up, neither."

"Back y'all, back!" Ike waved his arms as if moving a herd of cattle. "You heard the man."

Ned would have grinned if the situation hadn't been so horrific. He saw a silver Rayovac in John's hand. "Shine your light around these cars and trucks and see if you can find anything. I'm gonna talk to that feller over there that found Merle." He rose on popping knees and turned to the carnival owner. "Delmar, you know anything about this?"

"Nope. We don't have trouble inside. I have people watching all the time, and when trouble starts, we come get one of y'all, or whatever deputy is close by. The problems are always past the gate and the lights, where they get to drinking and arguing in the dark. I've had folks robbed before, too."

"Well, this wasn't a robbery. It was a killin', and I suspect I know why."

"Um humm." John returned with a bloody axe handle ten minutes later. "This was in the bed of that pickup over there. The blood's still wet."

The rough handle was aged by the weather and Ned knew it wouldn't contain fingerprints. "Hold it for evidence, then."

Ike Reader visibly shivered at the sight of John holding the bloody axe handle. "I swan."

Delmar seemed unsure of what to do. "What about me?"

Ned shrugged. "I don't see no reason you can't go back inside. There'll be lots going on out here for a while, ambulances and such."

"You want me to shut it down for the night?"

Ned caught a glimpse of John's girlfriend, Rachel Lea, standing with her kids near the cars. They were grouped around her like chicks around a hen, but the two oldest, Bubba and Belle, stood a little off. Belle had the toddler on her hip.

"Nope. Let them kids have fun." Ned caught John's eye. "I need to see you over by the car a minute…alone."

They wound their way through the cars and trucks parked in ragged formation. "What is it?"

Ned's face was a stone mask when he reached into his pocket. "I found this in the grass by Merle's body. Thought it was mine, but mine's in my pocket."

It was a chrome Cross pen with the initials C.P. etched into the body.

They'd seen Sheriff Cody Parker sign with it dozens of times.

Chapter Sixteen

The Wraith slipped between the thin sheets and with his hands behind his head, stared through darkness at the ceiling. It had been a good night's work and things were coming together right nice. Of course they should, he'd been planning for years.

The dirt and grass parking lot of the Forest Chapel Methodist Church was full by nine-thirty Tuesday morning, a full half hour before Frank Clay's funeral. The overflow lined up on both shoulders of the two-lane highway, a testimony to the mayor's reputation.

Ned and a dozen men visited in the thick shade cast by large burr oaks that were older than the church that was built in 1920. Ned watched groups assemble and dissolve into new clusters. Miss Becky stood nearby with a number of other farm wives.

Several members of the city council had already filed inside the little white church, joined by representatives from Austin. Highway Patrol cars were scattered up and down the highway, some to help move traffic, others there to pay their respects to a man who'd almost made it to the capital.

Ike Reader ran a finger around his loose collar, more out of habit than anything else. "Listen, I swear. I didn't expect this many folks."

"Most everybody liked old Frank." Neal Box watched the people file down the highway in twos and threes. His store was closed so he could attend the funeral. "When you're the mayor and you pass away young, there's bound to be a big turnout."

"Who's that?"

They followed Floyd Cass' point to see a well-dressed man accompanied by two young men in dark suits. They'd parked beyond the adjoining cemetery and were walking along the fence, avoiding the ditch. Ned recognized him at once and was surprised to see him so far from the state capital. "That's Senator John Tower."

"You reckon you oughta go over there and escort him in?"

Ned shook his head at Ike's question. "Naw, I ain't much of an ass-kisser. He might be a senator, but that don't mean I gotta do any more for him than anyone else."

The senator stopped to visit with a knot of farmers in sport coats and overalls. Ned watched a young man with slicked-back hair pass close to Miss Becky. She reached out to take Terrence Clay's arm. She'd always been partial to the soft-spoken young man who also wanted to make something of himself. "You come here and hug my neck."

"Howdy Miss Becky."

He bent and gave her an awkward hug. She wrapped her arms around him for a moment and then pulled back. She patted the outside of his coat, near the small of his back.

"Is that what I think it is?"

He cut a startled look at Ned who figured out right quick what she was talking about.

Terrence hung his head. "Yes ma'am."

Ned moved away from the group of men and stopped by Miss Becky. She shook her head. "Hon, this is a church. You don't need to go in there with a pistol."

"Miss Becky, them Mayfields is trying to kill us."

Ned joined in. "Not here they won't."

"Mr. Ned, you know as well as I do what they're up to."

"Son, do you see any colored folks here?"

He looked around. "Yessir, a couple. There's John Washington over there, and Missy Lee Davis, and..."

"Are any of them Mayfields?"

"Nossir. Not that I can see."

"Then why don't you go put that pistol back in the car? You don't need to have it hanging outside your khakis."

"Is that an order, sir?"

"It's a real strong suggestion."

Miss Becky squeezed Terrence's arm. "You go put it back in the car and come back and walk me in."

"Yes ma'am."

Terrence left. Ned cleared his voice and spoke loud enough to carry across the churchyard. "All y'all! This ain't no place for guns. If you're carryin' a pistol, go put it up right now, and pass the word inside."

Several men broke away and drifted from the churchyard to their cars and trucks. Miss Becky went inside with Terrence and soon more than a dozen others came out of the church and headed for their vehicles. Judge Rains arrived in a new silverbelly hat, fresh from the box. His clothes were the same as usual, all black.

He raised his eyebrow at those returning to their vehicles. "I know I'm getting old and my mind's not what it used to be, but they appear to be going in the wrong direction."

The corner of Ned's mouth twitched. "Disarming themselves. Where've you been? We expected you to come by the house."

"Stopped by Frenchie's for some pie." O.C. jerked a thumb toward Tower. "You gonna go escort the senator inside?"

"Hell no." Ned snorted, knowing O.C. was trying to get his goat. "He can see the door as well as I can."

As is often the case at country funerals, the men seemed reluctant to enter the building until the skinny funeral attendant with a large Adam's apple waved them inside. Ned nodded. "Well, all right boys. Let's get old Frank laid down proper."

They climbed the church house steps once again for still another funeral.

Chapter Seventeen

The Wraith moved through the darkness, familiar with everything he touched, every turn and every dead end. He almost giggled when someone brushed his arm and screamed, but that was all right. It was part of the game, though he'd intentionally touched the young woman's breast. It wasn't his fault. They put him there, but it was a long way from working in the hot hay and cotton fields right there in Lamar County.

Maggie's funeral was set for two in the afternoon at the Mt. Zion Church on the south side of Chisum. A large number of Mayfields were in attendance. Funeral services tended to be longer affairs at the colored Baptist church, but after a long struggle with himself, Ned decided to stay the entire time.

Ned rode with John Washington and took a back row seat on the aisle while John continued to the front to view Maggie in her casket. Ned quickly saw he was the only white face in the small crowd. Hat in his lap and staring straight ahead, he sat on the back row and ignored the angry looks of several congregation members who twisted in their pews to glare.

The little church was like an oven and almost every woman there cooled herself with paper fans supplied by the funeral home. Ned wanted to use his straw hat to do the same, but decided it might look disrespectful, so he sat still, simmering.

Bryce Mayfield stopped beside him. "We don't need you here."

"I'm sorry you feel thataway."

Bryce's father, Willie, knelt in the aisle and spoke softly. His short hair was peppered gray. "Mr. Ned, it might be better if you go."

"Why's that?"

"You know what I'm talkin' about."

Ned watched the man's face. "I know what you think you've heard. But what you hear ain't always the truth, now is it? I'm here because it's the right thing to do. And y'all need to let me alone because I'm looking into Maggie's death, just like I'm looking into Merle's now."

John glanced down the aisle and saw them talking. The expression of Ned's face brought him to the rear of the church. "Y'all all right?"

Willie stood. "Just talking to Mr. Ned about being here."

"I invited him."

"Well, you might want to *un*invite him."

"I won't do no such of a thing. Bryce, you better get yourself in a pew and bow your head."

"All right, I's just sayin'."

Ned held up a hand. "Willie, you and Bryce need to know we're doing what we can. You pass the word that the law'll handle it."

Willie's eyebrows met in the middle as he rose. "The law don't care about colored folks."

"That lawman standing beside you does, and he'll vouch for me that I do too."

Bryce wouldn't leave it alone, and Ned saw the glassy look in his eyes. "Ned, don't you come back here for Merle's funeral, neither."

"He will if I bring him." John's deep voice rumbled with anger.

The preacher stepped into the pulpit behind the simple wooden casket. The skinny spray of roses looked pitiful to Ned. The men surrounding him faded back to their pews and he slid down a little on the polished wood so John could sit.

Ned realized the preacher was the thick man with the deep voice who was on Hollis' front porch Sunday afternoon. "The family sure is proud to see all y'all here on this glorious day when one of our own is settin' beside Jesus. Let us pray."

Chapter Eighteen

It was uncomfortably warm and humid after school when I accidentally killed Miss Becky's mean ol' red rooster. He'd get out of the chicken yard no matter what she did to keep the gate closed or the fence tight to the ground, so she just gave up and left him to fend for himself.

I watched him make a run at her that same morning before we left and she had to kick him away from her bare legs, else he would have spurred her. "You devil you!"

He glared at her.

She scattered her pail of potato peelings and scraps over the fence and into the pasture for the hens. "You're gonna be supper for a wolf one night."

He darted back under the smokehouse where he decided he'd live.

I doubted there was anything tough enough to eat a bird that old and mean. He'd been wild when he came up to the house a few months earlier and took up with Miss Becky's hens. Living like that gave him an attitude and he got so he'd fight anyone or anything that came across what he considered his territory.

He chased Hootie away from the smokehouse two or three times and once he made a run at Grandpa. That little stunt cost him a few feathers when Grandpa kicked him a good one. It kinda addled the rooster for a while and he limped around for a week before he finally got to feeling better.

I was always afraid he'd cut me with those spurs of his. It wasn't anything for him to run up to one of us and try to jump on our legs. I was showing out for Pepper, because I'd suddenly become the third wheel since Mark showed up, and that's what got everything started. "Miss Becky's rooster's mean."

Pepper wasn't paying me no mind. She was dialing in a station on her new transistor radio. The three of us loafed on the porch, enjoying the sunshine. Our countdown had already started and end of school was days away. Summer fun was on our minds and it would be the first full summer for me to have someone to pal around with. I was looking forward to it, if I could pry Mark away from Pepper.

He was leaning against a porch post. "He'll spur you if he gets the chance."

"Shit." Pepper found a station and worked hard at dialing it in clear. "He better not make no run at me. We'll be eating fried chicken an hour later."

"You talk big for a girl," I laughed at her. "Miss Becky'll give you a whipping if you kill her rooster. You just have to get your bluff in on him."

"I don't need to bluff no damn chicken." She tuned her radio sharp enough to get the Chisum station. "We're the bosses here, not him."

She cranked up the volume and the announcer sounded like he'd had too much coffee. "This is the greatest song I've heard in *years*! I have an early press of a yet-to-be-released album by a new band called Steppenwolf. I don't know what that means, but this song is so far out you won't come back for a month! The lines are open. Let's give 'er a spin and see what you think if you were 'Born to be Wild'!!!"

The sound that came out of that little speaker was something like I'd never heard before. At the first notes, Pepper leaped to her feet. "My *God!*" She started dancing, throwing her hair around and acting like she had ants in her pants.

"What was that?" Miss Becky appeared at the screen door.

Pepper quit dancing for a moment. "Did you say something?"

"No missy. What did *you* say?"

The loud music filled the air as Pepper struggled to think of an answer.

"That's what I thought. There's a revival coming next week. We're all going. Maybe that'll help you understand that it's a sin to take the Lord's name in vain."

She disappeared back into the kitchen and Pepper shrieked, "Far *out!*" Holding her head, she started dancing like crazy again. This time her hair came loose from her headband. "That sound's an *acid trip!*"

Mark ran both hands through his own hair and pulled it away from his face. "Wow!" He had a grin a mile wide, but I couldn't understand what was so cool about the song.

The DJ came back on, laughing like a lunatic. "Next, come with me while the Beatles explain about what it's like to be a walrus!"

"I Am the Walrus" came on at the same second Miss Becky's old red rooster ducked under the barbed-wire fence and headed in our direction.

Pepper was back to slinging her head and flopping around. "*Psychedelic!*"

Mark joined her and they danced in the yard like they do on *American Bandstand.* I ignored their hippie talk and flopping around, watching the rooster slip under the barbed-wire fence. He crossed the yard, bobbing his head and looking for grasshoppers. "I'll show him who's boss."

They weren't listening, but I didn't care. I'd seen an axe handle on the back floorboard through the open window on Grandpa's Fury. I figured he'd bought it that morning to replace the one I'd broken chopping wood. I was getting the hang of swinging an axe, but for some reason I kept missing my mark and hitting the handle right short of the head. After about a hundred blows, the hickory splintered and the axe head threatened to fly off.

I took the handle out of the floorboard, noticing it wasn't new. There was dirt and dark stains up and down its length. That figured. Grandpa never bought anything new if he could find it used. Cars, furniture, feed troughs, lumber, even the swamp coolers we used to stay comfortable in the summer had all been near 'bout used up before we ever got them. None of the water pumps worked to keep the straw wet, because they'd given up the ghost and that's why the folks sold the coolers in the first place.

I swaggered into the yard, swinging the handle back and forth singing with the Beatles. "I am the eggman, koo koo cajoo, and you and nothin' but an old rooster, you!"

The music was loud and the rooster fluffed up and hissed. He cocked his head sideways and watched me with one black beady eye. I could see the meanness in it. I walked toward him like gunslingers do in the movies, pretending it was a showdown.

"Be careful." Pepper and Mark stopped dancing, suddenly realizing the rooster was serious about his territory.

"I ain't afraid of him." I took a one-hand practice swing like there was a golf ball on the ground. "Koo koo ca…"

Instead of scaring the rooster, it made him mad. He spread his wings, puffed up twice his size, and charged so fast it took me by surprise. My breath caught and for second I thought about running, but in the back of my mind I knew I'd never live it down.

That stupid old bird jumped and tried to spur me. I swung harder than I intended to. The flat of the handle caught him full in the chest with a soft "puff" sound. The blow lifted him off the ground like a line drive over the fence. I believe it was really the top strand of barbed-wire that killed him, and not the swing, because his neck wrapped around it as he flipped over. He rolled once a couple of feet inside the pasture and was still.

"Shitfire!" Pepper looked over her shoulder at the house. "Now you've done it. You swung that thing like Mickey Mantle. You've killed Miss Becky's rooster and that little Choctaw woman is gonna whip your ass!"

"I didn't mean to." I held the handle out to her like she'd asked for it. "What are we gonna do?"

"*We* ain't gonna do nothin'." She snapped the radio off and backed away like I was trying to give her a live snake. "I didn't kill him, but you'd better come up with a good story."

Mark shook off his shock and started laughing. "Man, that was the funniest thing I've seen in a long time."

I didn't have long to think. The kitchen door opened and Miss Becky popped out with a pan of table scraps for Hootie. She knew something was wrong when she saw the three of us standing there with guilty looks on our faces and me with the axe handle in my hand.

"What did you do?" She immediately got to the meat of the situation.

"He killed your red rooster," Pepper tattled.

"I didn't intend to." I thought about tearing up, but I didn't want to do it in front of Mark.

"What fer?"

"He tried to spur me." I figured honesty was going to be the best policy.

"That why that axe handle's in your hand?"

"Yessum."

"I believe he was afraid." Pepper put the radio it in her pocket. I wasn't sure if she intended to help me or hang me.

Mark stepped in front of her. "Miss Becky, he didn't have no choice. That rooster was gonna cut him, sure as shootin'."

Miss Becky stared at Mark long and hard, then turned to me. "Where'd you get that handle?"

"Out of Grandpa's car."

The shocked look on her face told me I'd made another mistake.

"Put it back, right now. You'll need to tell your Grandpa about it." She handed Pepper the pan of scraps. "Go throw this out for the dog."

"Yessum."

Miss Becky opened the screen door and paused before going back into the kitchen. "Top, go get the rooster and bring him up here. Since you killed him, you're gonna have to clean him. It's about time you kids learned how to scald a chicken anyway." She returned to the kitchen.

Mark had a disgusted look on his face. "Aw *man*. I already know how, and I hate it. I'd just as soon take a whoopin' as to scald one of them stinkin' things."

Pepper put one palm against her lower abdomen. "Miss Becky, I think I'm getting cramps."

Her voice came through the screen. "You didn't have them a minute ago when you was throwin' your arms around like you was havin' a fit. I believe you'll be all right, besides, young ladies need to learn how to work through the cramps anyway. And don't be talking about such things around these boys. It ain't ladylike."

We learned all right, but I decided after that I'd let Miss Becky do the chicken killing and cleaning from then on. It was a smelly, nasty job that didn't appeal to me at all. Miss Becky showed us how to dip the bird in scalding water to loosen the feathers so they'd come off easier and we almost gagged at the smell of wet feathers. She took over once we had him plucked and seared off the last of the tiny hair-like pinfeathers. Then we watched as she cut him up for the pot.

Grandpa pulled up in the yard an hour later and slammed his truck door. "That smells good. What are we having for dinner?"

"Chicken and dumplin's."

The happy look on his face made me feel worse, because I knew what I had to tell him.

Pepper jerked her thumb at me. "He killed her rooster dead-ern' a doornail."

Grandpa studied me, then his grin widened. He tilted his hat back. "I swear. I leave you alone at the *house* for five minutes and y'all still get in trouble."

I wanted to grin with him, but wasn't sure it was the right time. "She didn't say much."

"Well, let's eat. Then y'all're going to town with me, Top. You boys don't need to be underfoot anymore today, and Pepper, your mama wants you home in a little bit to help clean house. I'll drop you off after the dishes are done."

Her face fell. "Well, Top has something else to tell you."

I wanted to strangle her. "Uh, Miss Becky told me to tell you that I used the axe handle in the backseat of your car on that rooster."

His shoulders slumped and the expression on his face made me think he wanted to ring my neck. He glanced into the car, and turned those cold blue eyes of his on me. I shivered, thinking of the bad men who'd also been on the receiving end of that stare.

"Well, you may have screwed the pooch, son."

Without another word, he climbed the steps and the screen door slap-pop-popped behind him. I knew he was mad, because adults never let the screen slam.

Chapter Nineteen

The Wraith bided his time waiting until he could step once again into the dark of night to do what needed to be done. He chuckled. The Clays were in for a rich surprise when his little deceased friend started to do his work.

The sun was still high above the treetops when John Washington steered his cruiser down the dirt road leading to Wes Clay's house. Tree branches met overhead and formed a shady tunnel that instantly cooled the juicy air.

Ned rode in the passenger seat, his elbow hanging out the open window. "Why didn't you call me out to the house fire last night?"

"It weren't nothing but a fire and it was late. I went out there, but it was pretty much gone by then. Horace Mayfield lived in a two-room shack not far from Camp Maxie, right on the tracks. I carried him to his sister's. He'll be fine. He's been burned out before, but we didn't know this one was set until this morning. I'da called you before if I'd found out that. Wouldn't have known it was arson if Horace hadn't come back this morning and found a gas can that wasn't his."

"That's exactly how the Clays and Mayfields fought the last time, killing one another and burning their houses down around them." Ned blew out his lips for a moment. "I swear, I don't know what it is about burnin' that they like so much. These folks are all stirred up, so watch what you say."

"I don't intend to say much of nothing. How come we're out here?"

"Wes told me at Frank's house there'd be blood between them and the Mayfields. Looks like somebody made good on it. He's our first stop."

A two-lane dirt track led off to the right. Woods crowded close. A jay called and the sound echoed through the trees. A house soon came into view, the yard full of cars. It was hard for Ned to tell which ones ran or just provided a place for mice to nest.

It was an unusually hilly area for Lamar County. A long rise led up past the house, while a slope behind it dropped off to a sharp, sun-dappled gully that climbed back up to a little ridge on the opposite side. The front porch overlooked a wooded slope to the west.

A pack of skinny mongrel dogs barked at the newcomers as Washington killed the engine. They waited until a dishwater-blond woman stepped onto the porch, wiping her hands on a dingy dishtowel. She tilted her head. "Help you?"

Ned spoke over the dogs. "Need to talk to Wes."

"Hush up! Git!" The pack quit barking and gave the car some room. "Y'all get out. They're over by the well." She waved an arm toward a well shack beside a leaning power pole and disappeared back inside.

Ned opened the door, eyeing the nearest Heinz 57 mix of whatever breeds happened to be in the yard in previous generations. A red-haired dog that looked to be part coyote lowered its head and came close. Ned held out a hand for a moment before scratching behind the animal's chewed up ears.

John gently closed his door and stood still so the dogs on his side could get a good sniff. A cluster of men beside the well a hundred yards away watched the lawmen head in their direction, threading their way along the winding, uphill path.

Ned stopped, hands in the pockets of his black slacks. "Men."

The electric pump was disconnected and set atop the plywood housing. Shirtless, Wes stood on the well's plank curb, a rope in his hands. A rawhide tough Korean War veteran, he had only recently returned from working as a roughneck in the Midland oilfields and a short stint in their jail.

Wes nodded hello and returned to his business at hand. Four other Clays were scattered nearby, watching. It was obvious that Andy, Martin, Wilbur, and the youngest, Cecil, favored so close they could have been quadruplets. They shared a hooked beak that identified them as much as their last name. While they watched, Wes pulled up a galvanized three-foot well-bucket full of water and emptied it onto the muddy ground. The sweetish odor of decay rose as the water funneled away.

He dropped the bucket back into the well and waited for it to fill up. A spring of oily hair fell over his forehead. "Help you?"

Instead of getting right to business after such an abrupt welcome, Ned chose to engage them for a moment. "Something wrong with your well?"

"Rat drowned in it. Nothing smells like a rotten rat."

Andy Clay spoke up. "I thought you said you suspicioned somebody put it in there."

The look on Wes' face shut his cousin up in a hurry, but Ned picked up on it right quick.

"How long's it been?"

"Long enough to smell when we went to drink the water."

"It's still in there, then."

"Yep, I'm trying to catch it in this bucket."

Though Ned had a rock-hard disposition, his weak stomach turned on him when it came to certain things. It rolled at the thought of drinking water from that nasty well. He choked down a gag and used the velum in the back of his nose to close off his sinuses so he couldn't smell the odor of decay any longer.

The weathered boards beneath Wes' shoes were soaked and dark, and a stream of water ran between the men toward a nearby ditch full of bottles and trash. Ned glanced down at the muddy rivulet to take his mind off what was happening and noticed a small mat of short charcoal hairs caught against the leaves and yard trash from bucket after bucket of water.

His stomach heaved again, but he met Wes' gaze and swallowed it down. "Got a few questions."

"Go ahead on, if you have to."

"It's about Frank." The Clays around Ned shifted like reeds pushed by the wind at the name. "You want to talk about this somewhere else, just the two of us?"

The bucket rattled back down the well. "Nope. I ain't got nothin' to hide."

"Fine, then. There was a colored man killed the other night at that big carnival across from Camp Maxie after Frank and Maggie died."

"I heard."

"Were you there?"

"Nope."

"Where were you?"

"Across the river."

"In one of them honky-tonks?"

"Yep."

"Which one?"

"The Dew Drop."

"Will anybody over there vouch for you?"

"Half a dozen."

"I'm gonna go check."

Wes tugged on the rope to see if the bucket was full. "I don't give a shit what you do. You said you wanted to talk to me about Frank. What does that have to do with him?"

Ned studied the warped boards around the well and wondered how they were supporting Wes' weight. They looked to be completely rotten. He switched topics. "Was Frank much of a drinker?"

Wes stopped and glared. "He weren't a teetotaler."

"Was he a hard drinker?"

"What difference does that make? As far as his wife knows, he didn't take a drop, and it better stay that way."

Ned shrugged. "Frank was a good family man. He loved his wife and kids, and he was gonna make something of hisself. I figured someday he'd be governor. From what I hear, Maggie was working hard too. I don't believe she wanted to spend her whole life in an unpainted shack in the bottoms."

"Frank had ideas, all right. But they didn't work out and I don't give a shit what *Maggie* wanted, neither. What'n hell you doing here? I don't s'pect you spend a lot of time on other car wrecks."

"I'm here 'cause your brother come by and demanded that I do something. I swear, you Clays need to get together on this. Either you want me to investigate the wreck and everything that might be associated with it, or not."

"Us Clays take care of each other, just like you Parkers..." Wes paused and broke off eye contact as he raised still another bucket of rancid water. He dumped it out. Besides Andy, the other cousins still hadn't said a word, as if Wes had told them to remain silent.

The metal bucket rattled back to the bottom. They waited for it to refill.

Ned drew them back into the conversation. "Where were you the night Frank died?"

"I's across the river."

"Drunk?"

Wes smirked. "As Cooter Brown. In Cody's joint. And I believe I still got a headache over it." His kinfolk chuckled.

The words cut Ned as deep as a razor. He felt the heat rise in his face, but didn't take the bait. "Horace Mayfield's house burned last night."

"Say it did?"

"Somebody set it."

"How you to know that?"

"'cause I know somebody poured coal oil on the outside kitchen wall and lit it. Funny thing is, some of the oil got spilled when he set the can on the woodpile to light the fire. It was some of that new coal oil they have out now that has coloring that'll start to stain your fingernails after a couple of days if you get it on you."

Ned grinned and rolled his eyes. "They're putting color into everything now. I saw a gas station in Dallas here while back that advertise pink air to go in your tires. I never heard of such a thing."

Wes held out both hands without blinking an eye. He flipped them over. "So that's why you're here. See? Nothin'. You need to get off my back and let me alone, unless you have better evidence than that. You ain't lookin' into Frank's death. You don't need to be over here suspecting me or any of us over a house fire or killing a nig…." His eyes skipped over John. "Uh, a colored feller." He pulled on the rope hand over hand.

Ned watched him raise the bucket. "I didn't say it was you. I come to tell all y'all that this little war that I believe's sparked up between you and the Mayfields again is gonna stop, or I'll throw every one of you in jail and let you fight it out in a cell."

"You won't do no such of a thing, because there ain't no war between us. That ended years ago." The bucket reached the top and Wes whooped. "I got the rat!"

The cousins came to life and crowded toward the well. Wes carefully lifted the long metal bucket over the curb boards to expose the blanched blue-white body of the largest rat Ned had ever seen. The hairless carcass hung over the lip and immediately filled the air with a reek of decomposition.

Wes dumped the bucket and the rat splashed out to flow in the stream toward the ditch. He climbed off. "Wilbur, put that pump back on and draw as much water you can without running the well dry. Keep at it 'til it don't stink no more."

Without another word Wes hopped off the curb and stalked toward the house. He shouldered past John, bumping him hard. The mountain of a deputy didn't move, or even acknowledge the challenge from the wiry man.

Ned watched him walk away. "Let's go, John."

The big deputy followed, but kept an eye on the youngest cousin, Cecil, who put both hands deep in the pockets of his overalls after the mention of the coal oil and kept them there.

Chapter Twenty

Another job completed, The Wraith lay on his filthy bed and studied the photo of his ex-wife. It was the only thing he had left, other than the hate he tended like a bank of coals for her and the man she left him for. His girlfriend came to bed, glanced at the photo in his hand, and rolled over to get some sleep before the baby woke up.

Judge O.C. Rains stopped rocking in his wooden desk chair. "He did what?"

"He killed a damn rooster with the handle."

"The axe handle you had in the car for evidence?"

"That's the one."

"Well hell. That's not gonna help anything."

"I know it. I turned it in to the evidence room. I didn't say anything about the chicken, though."

O.C. grunted. "I hope you picked the feathers off of it."

"There weren't none. Besides, Merle Mayfield was beat to death and the handle was wet when John found it. We both know that's what the killer used."

"But legally we can't use it in court."

"We sure use that word a lot around here lately."

"Killer? I know it." The flat statement hung in the room like a dark cloud. "I got something else to tell you, too."

O.C. peered over the tops of his glasses. "I'm a-waitin'."

Ned reached into the inside pocket of his dress jacket and

pulled out a white envelope containing the Cross pen he found in the grass. He handed it across to O.C. "You might not want to touch it."

Frowning, Judge Rains opened the flap and slid the silver pen onto his desk.

"So?"

"It's Cody's."

"Where'd you find it?"

"Right beside Merle's body not twenty minutes after he was beat to death."

The judge sighed deep. "Was Cody there?"

"Nope. We handled it and he never came by."

"There could be a lot of folks with the same initials."

"Yep."

"What do you think this means?"

"Well, I think it means there was a pen with those initials there."

They studied the instrument as if it were about to move of its own accord. O.C. pursed his lips. "Anyone else know about this?"

"John."

"Okay, maybe he went by earlier that day and lost it when he got in or out of the car."

"I asked if he'd been out there. He hadn't."

"This puts a wrinkle in things."

"It could."

"I reckon you're gonna have it dusted for fingerprints."

"Can't. I thought it was mine when it fell out of my shirt pocket. I held it for a minute or two before I put it back and saw mine was still there." He paused, thinking. "I believe I'll just leave it right there for a while. Folks will ask questions if we start that mess."

"Well, you know as well as I do...."

"I know, but that pen being in the wrong place at the wrong time won't look good."

O.C. laced his fingers across his stomach. "Do I need to say it?"

"Nope. I'll deal with it when the time comes."

"I hope you don't have to."

Instead of answering, Ned sighed, set his hat, and left.

Chapter Twenty-one

The Wraith came into the yard, carrying the shotgun over his shoulder like a casual hunter. The old man stepped out on the porch and stopped, a butcher knife in one hand and an apple that he was peeling in the other. He frowned in recognition. He hadn't expected to see The Wraith on his land, and hadn't thought about the man since he was a boy raiding his watermelon patch. He stopped in fear.

The Wraith smiled. "Howdy."

Sheriff Cody Parker knocked on the door of a sprawling ranch-style house in east Chisum. He didn't often get to that upscale section of town. It was late in the day and he dropped by to get a personal check from the acting mayor for the upcoming Sheriff Department's fundraising ball.

One of his deputies usually handled the job, and he'd considered sending Deputy Anna Sloan, but changed his mind when he saw her earlier that afternoon. Though Anna was well on the way to recuperation from a shotgun blast before Christmas, he saw that she still looked awfully tired by three in the afternoon.

Since Mayor Frank Clay's death, Joe Bill Haynes was acting in the mayor's position until the swearing-in ceremony at the next city council meeting. Joe Bill was already overwhelmed with the duties of mayor pro tem. It would also be good to stop by and give him a few words of encouragement.

The new mayor's car was parked in front and there wasn't a person on the street as Sheriff Parker knocked on the door a second time. When there was still no answer, he circled the house, noting the well-manicured lawn and shrubbery.

The gate was propped open, and when he looked into the back, he found the mayor and his wife beside an in-ground swimming pool with his hands in his pockets.

"Joe Bill."

The man even looked like a politician. Short dark hair graying at the temples, his skin was smooth since he seldom saw the sun. "C'mon in. I been expecting you."

Maybelle kissed her husband's cheek. "Hello Cody. Good to see you. I'll go in and leave y'all to your work."

"You don't have to run off."

"I have a cake in the oven. Come in and get a piece when y'all finish."

"I won't have time, but I'll take a raincheck." She crossed the yard, patting her perm into place.

Cody shook Joe Bill's hand and followed his gaze to the dark, murky water of the swimming pool. "You look like you lost your best friend." Not too many people in Chisum had pools, and the only ones Cody had seen were sparkling clear. "Dang, that water looks like a stock tank."

Joe Bill sighed. "Yeah, I haven't messed with it much because the kids are grown up and gone. Then the ground shifted. There's a crack down there somewhere and the water leaks out. Now I for sure don't have the time to fool with it."

The water line was three-quarters of the way to the coping. There was no visible crack above the waterline.

"It doesn't look too bad, though I don't know much about concrete pools." Cody glanced upward at the thick trees lining a shallow stream at the bottom of a slope behind the house. A bright jaybird flickered through the limbs, raising the ire of a squirrel that sat up and chattered in anger. "Think it'll be expensive to get it fixed?"

"Probably." Joe Bill shook his head. "It'll kill the fish, though."

Cody studied the document in his hand. "Funniest thing. It sounded like you said it would kill the fish."

"It would."

Cody watched a slight breeze ripple the water's surface. "There's fish in there? I never heard of fish in a swimming pool."

"It wasn't always like that. I went fishing with Hill Lawrence back in the fall," Joe Bill called the game warden's name. "We caught a mess of crappie, and didn't get in 'til late that night and I told Hill I'd clean 'em and we'd have a fish fry. Well, I was so tired that night I dumped 'em here in the pool, figuring I'd drain it in the next few days so I could get it fixed. I wouldn't have to do anything but pick them up when it was empty. Well, that didn't pan out. They've been there ever since."

"What do they eat?"

"I've been feeding them a few dozen minnows every week, and they're fine."

"So how are you gonna get them out?"

"That's what I've been trying to decide. I don't want to completely drain the water until the pool company takes a look at it."

Cody grinned. "I could bring you Ned's minnow seine, and Top. I figure he'd enjoy seining a swimming pool."

"It probably wouldn't work." Joe Bill toed at a dandelion coming up through a crack in the decking. "I think the catfish are too big now. They'd probably tear a hole in your net."

Cody shook his head in disbelief. Before he could ask the obvious question, Joe Bill held up a hand. "I had some channel cats I didn't want to clean back in September, so...well...I dumped *them* in, too. I feed 'em crawdads ever so often."

The surface of the water suddenly boiled in the shallow end. "What the heck was that?"

"Sunfish. I had a friend bring a bucket full to put in here, so the other fish wouldn't get hungry."

Two neighborhood kids about eight years old appeared from the woods, carrying cane poles. They looked annoyed to see the adults standing there.

The youngest gave Cody a long, slow appraisal. "Mr. Joe Bill said we could fish here, Sheriff."

Joe Bill raised his eyebrows. "He ain't here for that, and it'd be the game warden you need to worry about." He gave them a big wink. "Catch a big 'un."

Not wanting to stand in the way of dedicated fishermen and their favorite fishing spot, Joe Bill pulled out his checkbook. "I need to borrow your pen."

Cody reached toward his shirt pocket for the Cross pen Norma Faye bought for him when he took the sheriff's job, forgetting it had disappeared within the last couple of days. They searched the house over, but couldn't find the pen.

"I've lost it somewheres." He patted his pockets. "I forgot to pick one up at the office. That'un run dry?"

Joe Bill plucked one from his own shirt pocket and unscrewed the cap. "Naw, but it's a real ink pen and it smears if you're not careful. I started carrying it for signing official documents when I have to wear my new mayor's hat." He wrote the check and waved it in the air for a minute. "That should be dry enough. I'd appreciate it if you wouldn't say anything about this. It's kinda embarrassing, having a concrete swimming pool and it being in this condition. I oughta be ashamed of myself."

"Don't worry." Cody took the check and gave him a grin. "As long as I can come over here with a pole and a can of worms when things get too rough. I'll see you at the café for breakfast sometime this week."

"Maybe so." Joe Bill turned back to his pool.

Chapter Twenty-two

"There's a lion up on the river."

Ty Cobb Wilson made that statement at the same time I walked in the door of Uncle Neal Box's store. Mark and Pepper went over to the Ordway place after classes let out, but I wanted a cold drink, and to get away from their moony eyes for a few minutes.

I stopped just inside to eavesdrop. The men in the Spit and Whittle club loafing on the porch probably wouldn't mind me listening, but they'd watch their language and maybe even leave out some details.

"You see it?" That was Floyd Cass. He always reminded me of someone who should be in movies, what with his pencil-thin mustache and slicked-back hair.

"Naw."

Jimmy Foxx, Ty Cobb's brother, had a higher voice of the two. They spent most of their spare time hunting and fishing the Lamar County bottoms. I never knew how they made their money, because they didn't farm much, or raise crops. Neither was married and they wore knee-high rubber boots year round.

"We was settin' some nets…uh, trotlines where Sanders Creek hits the river and saw tracks in the mud. I bet it's a big tom panther."

I could see Floyd from where I stood beside the red drink cooler. I had the lid up and the cool air rising from the interior was refreshing in the heat. Coke, Dr Pepper, Orange Crush, Tab, Diet Rite, RC Cola, Yoo-Hoo, Mountain Dew, and a collection of Nehis in grape, orange, peach, and strawberry were tempting, but I pulled a Pommac, because it tasted like what I thought champagne would be like.

Miss Becky didn't want me to drink them and thought Pommac was a sin, even though it was a soft drink made from fermented fruit and berries just like wine or champagne, but it didn't have alcohol. She really didn't want me to play board games with dice, or to go to the movies, either, because it was against her religion.

I popped the cap and put a dime on the counter. Uncle Neal was in back, loading blocks of salt and bags of feed in a truck. Sipping my drink, I drifted back to the door to listen.

Floyd was sitting with both hands on the 2x6 rail. He leaned forward to take some of the pressure off his rear end. Their conversation shifted and it was a heckuva lot more interesting than mountain lions. "They say the carnival has one of them girly tent shows. They won't let 'em have those at the regular fair in town, 'cause them gals strip down near nekked."

They chuckled and I figured they'd already forgot me again. Mr. Floyd shook his head. "Old Ike's been talking about that show ever since they heard the carnival was coming. He's gonna slip off over there to see it and I'm thinking about tagging along just to watch his face."

He noticed me again and smoothed his pencil mustache, returning to the earlier conversation. "I swear I heard a lion scream a while back when I was on the porch after dark. It sounded like a woman a-screaming and I almost called Ned before I figured out what it was."

A truck passed and pulled off on the oil road running behind the domino hall, engine growling as the driver downshifted. They watched it go by and I settled onto a wooden box beside the door.

"Remember, we trapped those two a few years ago," Ty Cobb said. "I figured they were a couple of young littermates working their way through the country, but now we're thinkin' different."

Mitt Harris shook his head, as if he'd heard someone died. "I hope y'all get 'em all. They'll kill stock before a deer. Cows is easier."

"I like the idea of having 'em back." Jimmy Foxx twisted around to spit off the porch. "We come across bear tracks a few months ago. I believe the lake filling up's running them out of the creek bottoms. It was so rough back up in there that they've raised for years without most of us knowing it."

"Bears and lions were pretty thick back before I was born." Mr. Floyd nodded his head toward me. "I remember hearing Daddy tell about Top's great aunt who barely outran a panther one night. You ever hear that story, Top?"

I shook my head.

"Well, you had a Great-Aunt Calpurnia who was coming home on horseback one night under a full moon. It was way too late for her to be out. She was riding bareback by the moonlight and her horse kept acting spooky. Her daddy was sittin' on the porch smokin' his pipe when he saw her coming down the lane. He saw a shadow move behind the horse and realized it was a lion.

"He high-tailed it in the house to get his rifle and Calpurnia's mama knew something was wrong. About the time he came back outside, the horse smelled the lion and Calpurnia saw it coming. She kicked that horse in high gear and the lion chased 'em, jumping at the horses' haunches and running to catch up again. Her daddy came off the porch with the rifle to get an angle and her mama was hollerin', 'Ride, Calpurnia, *ride!*'"

They chuckled at the imitation of a woman hollering.

I couldn't stand it. "Did the lion get her, or did her daddy get the lion?"

Floyd leaned forward again, his skinny arms like ropes when he took the strain. I tried to get a good look at his faded navy tattoos, but they'd spread so much I couldn't tell what they were. "Why, he missed and the lion ate Calpurnia, then her mama and daddy."

The men tried to keep straight faces for a minute, then they laughed and I knew they were kidding me. I let 'em go for a second. "Was the rest of that story true?"

Mr. Floyd nodded. "I was pullin' your leg, but the story's true. The old man missed and the lion disappeared. As far as I know, no one ever saw it again."

Grandpa's truck rolled into the parking lot. He looked tired when he got out. I was surprised to see him out of the field that time of the day. He walked up with heavy steps. "What are you doing up here?"

"I wanted a cold drink after school."

He climbed the porch and dropped into a cane-bottom chair with his back against the wall. "You know she don't want you drinking that near-beer stuff."

"Yessir." I started to take a sip right then, but decided not to. "There's a lion on the river."

He knew good and well I was changing the subject, but it was enough to get the conversation started again, taking the heat off me. I finished my Pommac by the time they got back around to the end for a second time.

"Ned, you out there?" Uncle Neal came to the door at the same time. "Well, there you are, after all."

"What does that mean?"

"John Washington's on the phone. He thought you might be here."

I could tell that announcement bothered Grandpa. If Mr. John was calling up to the store to find him, something was wrong.

Grandpa grunted up and went inside. He wasn't gone but just a little bit, and the look in his blue eyes when he came back out was enough to make a feller back up a step. He walked down the steps. "Get on home, boy."

I knew better than to say a word right then. Grandpa hurried down the steps and jumped in his truck. Gravel and bottle caps popped under the tires until he hit the pavement, then on the pavement as he took off.

Uncle Neal stood in the door and watched the Chevrolet disappear down the highway.

Ty Cobb slapped both hands on his knees. "What was that all about, Neal?"

"Somebody cut Hollis Mayfield in two with a shotgun."

Chapter Twenty-three

The Wraith took his dressing down without a word. It was the best way to deal with a boss, so he let the cussing roll off his shoulders and promised not to slip up again. It wasn't his fault that Cody Parker'd passed by. He couldn't help but follow him up to the new mayor's house where dumb luck turned into one more chance for a little revenge. The Wraith returned to his job when the boss finished, painted a smile on his face to satisfy the customers, and earned his meager paycheck thinking all the while how he'd outmaneuvered everybody he came into contact with.

Cody met Ned in his usual booth on the left side of Frenchie's café. Since O.C. wasn't with them, Ned took the seat facing the screen door after resting his hat crown down on the counter beside them.

Frenchie saw the sheriff come in and poured him a mug of coffee as he worked his way through the café, slapping shoulders and shaking the hands of customers seated at the counter and in the other booths.

He slipped a finger through the handle and Frenchie gave him a wink. He slid in across from Ned. "Where's O.C.?"

"Court date."

"The doctor know you're eating pie?"

"He would if he was here, but he ain't." Ned cut a bite and chewed. "My stomach's fine now."

Cody sipped the coffee, then shook a few grains of salt into the mug to cut the bitterness. "Well, you nearly died from that infected bullet wound back before Christmas." He sipped again. "You need to be careful."

Ned chewed. "Here's how careful I am. I ain't never going back to Mexico again. How's that? Have you heard anything else about Hollis' murder?"

"Some. John went by and found out one of Hollis' gals dropped by the house to take him something to eat and found him dead, half in and out his front door."

"Anyone see a Clay nearabouts?"

Cody shrugged. "That's all I know. I talked to some other folks, but that didn't help one little bit." The bell over the door rang when a customer came in. Cody glanced over his shoulder to see who it was. "I remember that feud from years ago, but don't recall why they got crossways with one another."

Ned told him about the mules, the truck with a flat, the pears, and the killings that ranged from shootings, to cuttings, to one lynching in the dead of night. All those dirty deeds were done in the dark, or on lonely roads with no witnesses.

"Everyone knowed who done what, but evidence was hard to come by in those days. I'd have a better chance at it today.

"So no one ever proved anything?"

"Naw. That's how those things work. People get mad at one another for good reason, or no reason at all, and then their mad takes over." Ned shook his head. "Folks died over a damn lame mule."

"How many?"

"More than I'd like to remember. I think there was a dozen in all, maybe more, scattered over about ten years. And now the same's happening over a car wreck."

"Did any of the killers get caught back then?"

"Like I said, some was brought in, but remember this was back over twenty years ago. Most of them old lawmen are gone now. I remember there was a trial for one of the Clays. The jury sent him to the pen over the killing, and that's only because he lit a Mayfield house afire and a woman burned to death. He was bragging about it, and that's what got his goat."

"Any of the *Mayfields* get caught at it?"

Ned studied the thick white mug between his hands. "They's colored, son. The law didn't catch them, officially. They usually found bodies, and that's all."

The weight of what happened so long ago, and the badge pinned to Cody's shirt, settled on the sheriff's shoulders. "Now it's flamed back up."

"Yep. Folks in both of them families have long memories." Cody drained his cup. "I gotta go."

Ned's eyes flicked to Cody's empty shirt pocket. He thought about bringing up the pen, but decided it wasn't the right time. He once suspected Cody of a series of murders in their community, and still felt embarrassed when it turned out to be someone else. He hadn't said anything then, and he sure wasn't going to make those kinds of allegations now.

The sheriff left, and Ned stayed where he was, worrying.

Chapter Twenty-four

The Wraith was once a deer hunter. He knew how to stalk, and that's what he did best.

The phone on Cody Parker's desk rang. He was downstairs with Judge O.C. Rains. Deputy Anna Sloan answered it. "Sheriff's Office."

"Can I talk to Cody?"

"Sorry, ma'am. He isn't here right now. Can I help you?"

"My husband's missing."

Still standing by the desk, Anna picked up a pencil. "What's his name?"

"Joe Bill Haynes."

"The acting mayor?"

The voice on the other end broke. "Yes. He got up before daylight this morning and took his coffee outside. He never came back in."

"Maybe he walked over to somebody's house."

"No. He don't do that."

"And your name is?"

"Maybelle Haynes."

Cody came in while Anne was writing. "The sheriff just came in the door. I'm gonna hand you over to him. Give me your phone number before I get off so I can have it and we'll start looking."

She wrote the information down and handed the phone to Cody. "The acting mayor's missing."

"Joe Bill?" He frowned and they exchanged places. "Maybelle, is that you?"

Anna left to put together a missing person's report. She came back as Cody hung up. He didn't look good and she stepped closer to his desk. "You all right?"

"Yeah, just thinking." He leaned back in his chair.

"Did you get any more information?"

"Probably not much more than you did. What'd she tell you?"

"Nothing much. He was there this morning and then wasn't."

The phone rang again and Cody answered. Anna heard a woman's hysterical voice through the receiver. "I found him! He's dead! He drowned in that damned swimming pool!"

"I'm on the way." Cody slammed the receiver down, snatched his hat off the rack, and slapped it on his head. Anna grabbed her own Bailey's straw that replaced the traditional deputy pillbox hat she wore when she first came to Chisum.

Bypassing the slow elevator, they rushed down the stairs and into the parking lot. Cody jammed the key into the ignition, started the big engine, and called dispatch before they rolled out of the parking lot. "Martha."

"Go ahead, Cody."

"Send an ambulance out to Joe Bill Hayne's house."

"I was gonna do just that. Your desk phone rolled over to my desk. It was Maybelle again. She thought she called the fire department number. I did it for her."

Lights flashing and siren shrieking, they pulled up at the house ten minutes later. Jittering with nerves, Cody led the way around to back, expecting to find people milling by the pool. Instead, the yard was empty. He walked to the coping and looked down to see a body just under the surface of the scummy water.

"Oh, Lordy." A deep voice startled him.

"Didn't hear you come up, John. I'm getting jumpy." Rubbing a hand across his mouth, Cody studied the body. "Let's get him out. Then you can call Buck to come pronounce him."

"Can't stay but a few minutes. I was on my way out to Hollis Mayfield's house when I got this call."

"Trouble?"

"Naw, Miss Anna. Goin' to talk to some of his family and see if they can tell me anything. Figured I'd see what you needed here first 'fore I go."

Cody knelt and motioned for John to join him. The body was within John's longer reach. He dropped to one knee, got a good hold on Joe Bill's collar, and pulled him closer until he could and grabbed the corpse's arm. Cody took a leg and counted. On three, they pulled. There was nothing gracious about dragging Joe Bill's already stiffening body out of the pool and onto the concrete deck.

Cody's nerves jangled and it felt like everything was getting away from him and spinning out of control. "I'm going inside to talk to Maybelle. I need to wash my hands."

"You go ahead on." Always calm, John headed for the outside faucet. "I'll use the hose."

John's comment meant that he didn't want to go inside. It wasn't because he didn't want to clean up, but mostly it was because black folks in white homes often made the owners uncomfortable and he was well aware of that. He was already rubbing his hands under the streaming hose when Cody and Anna stepped through the open sliding glass door to find Maybelle at her kitchen table.

She turned anguished eyes on the deputies. "I should have started looking sooner."

"Don't blame yourself." Cody laid his hat on the kitchen counter. "I doubt it would have done any good."

Anna took a chair beside her at the gray Formica table and rubbed Maybelle's arm. It was the only thing she could do. "It's not your fault. You said yourself it was dark when he went out."

"Just coming up light."

"Well, that's too early to be out looking for somebody."

"I might have heard him fall in. He probably called for help."

"Could he swim?"

"Of course."

"Was the sliding door open?"

"Yes."

"Then you would have heard him if he was struggling."

Cody listened to Anna ease the woman's anxiety as he washed his hands with the bar of Lava soap in the dish by the sink. He dried them with a damp dishtowel and joined them at the table. "I'm sorry. I don't know what else to say."

Maybelle's voice choked. "You don't have to say anything, Sheriff. There's nothing that'll make it better."

"We'll find out what happened. He coulda had a stroke, or a heart attack. You can't blame yourself for any of this."

John knocked on the sliding glass door. He stayed outside when Cody slid it open. "Buck's on his way, but I can't stay. I need to get to Hollis'. Just came through on the radio he's been shotgunned. The family's gathering and there's already talk about some of 'em going over to settle up with some Clays."

"He dead?"

"That's what they say."

Cody's stomach sank. He rubbed the back of his neck as he studied on John's statement. "All right. Head on over there and let me know what you find out. I'll be there as quick as I can."

John shifted from one foot to the other for a minute. "I need to tell you something else. Cody, step out here for a minute, will you?"

Cody saw concern in the face of the legendary lawman. John led him around the corner to the shade of a tall pecan tree. When they were out of earshot, John leaned close. "I got something to say, I hope you'll listen to me."

"What's the matter?"

John rocked back and forth on his heels to bleed off nervous energy from the uncomfortable conversation. "You need to leave here right now and let Miss Anna handle this. I believe you ought to stay either in your office or better yet, at home for the next few days."

Shocked at the advice, Cody inclined his head. "Why?"

"I'm talkin' out of school here, but you need to listen. I'm pretty worried about what's happenin' with all this mess. Your pen with your initials on it was found where Merle was beat to death."

Cody's breath caught. John held out his hand and talked in fits and starts, proving he was clearly uncomfortable with the conversation. "That axe handle cain't be used as evidence because Mr. Ned had it in his car and Top killed a chicken with it. And now you was the last person 'cept his wife to see Joe Bill alive right there beside that pool."

"You don't know that."

"I do. Mr. Ned told me yesterday you was on your way over here when I's looking for you for something else."

Cody felt numb. "We don't know what killed him."

"That ain't all." As he continued, John's voice steadied. "If I's to investigate, I'd find out you was home the night Frank and Maggie died and only Miss Norma Faye could vouch for you. You stopped by to see Hollis yesterday evenin', and now here he is shotgunned. I know, 'cause Avon told me she saw your car in the yard from across the pasture."

"Sure did. I been trying to get your people used to seeing me around, so they'll come to the rest of us and not just you when things are bad. He was fine when I left."

"I 'magine he was. What I'm sayin' ain't what I think's happenin'. It's what I'm *hearin'*. You can't take ballistics on a shotgun, so some folks are sayin' that's why it was used, instead of a pistol." He glanced down at the 1911 on Cody's hip. "Some of my people saw you talking to Wes Clay at the courthouse yesterday and said you slapped him on the shoulder when you left. You see how all this looks?"

Speechless, Cody gaped for a minute. "I saw Wes Clay going in to visit one of his cousins who's in jail and told him to keep his act clean or I'd throw him under the jail if any of this came back to him. You know him and Royal's the most dangerous of the bunch. Hell, I should have slapped his stupid face."

"I wish you had, but no matter. None of it passes for right. See what I'm sayin'? Let me and Deputy Sloan and Mr. Ned take care of this. Something's wrong here, and I cain't put my finger on it. It's white and colored now, no matter how you look at it. Some of my people are mad, and they're lookin' at *you*. It'd be best if you stayed away 'til we figure out what's what."

Knowing his experienced deputy was right, Cody wilted. "Fine. I see how it looks. Y'all handle it, but let me know what's happening. Step by step. I'm still running things, but you're taking the point now…you and Anna."

"Sure 'nough." John looked sad. He raised a big hand toward Cody, but lowered it, as if he couldn't bear to touch him, or simple contact wasn't enough. Without another word, he left and Cody walked back inside.

Anna was alone at the table. She saw his raised eyebrow. "She went to the bathroom to wash her face. What do you want me to do next?"

Cody took her arm and guided her into the living room. Brand new furniture covered in plastic protectors made the room look like something from the house magazines Norma Faye read. The fresh look registered with him, knowing Norma Faye came from dirt-poor parents and lived in a tiny, drafty, two-room house after she married Calvin Williams. It proved to be a dismal life of violence and pain before she left him and found herself with Cody. She filed for divorce and married Cody soon after.

Norma Faye often talked about buying new furniture for their house in Center Springs, though what was in Joe Bill and Maybelle's house would be dramatically out of place in the small country home they'd inherited from Tom Bell.

He leaned in and spoke in a soft voice. "Hollis Mayfield's been murdered and he's on his way out there."

Her breath caught, but Cody went on. "There's more. John's concerned about what's going on." He told her what he'd learned outside under the pecan tree. "You see how it is?"

Anna shook her head. "But we know you had nothing to do with any of that. It's this stupid feud."

"No matter. It smells, so I'm gonna back off and leave it to you two and Ned to do the investigating. Here's what I need you to do. Get acquainted with the Clays. Start with Donald Ray, he's the most normal of the bunch that's old enough to make decisions now that Frank's gone. See what you can find out from him or his wife. Folks talk." He glanced through the plate glass window to see the justice of the peace pull to the curb. "Buck's here. Follow any trail you can find in this and let me know. I'll talk with Maybelle for a minute, and then I'm gone. When you finish, make sure Buck goes on out to Hollis' place. John'll be there waiting on him."

Maybelle was back in the kitchen, standing at the sink and staring out the window at nothing. Feeling heavy and dead inside, Cody gave her a hug and left, wondering about the right thing to do.

Chapter Twenty-five

The baby was asleep when he came out of their tiny bathroom. The baby's mama lit another cigarette in the breathlessly hot trailer and dropped the match into a full ashtray. At one time she was afraid of The Wraith, but not anymore. The bruises always healed and at least she had a roof over her head.

Deputy Anna Sloan pulled up in Donald Ray Clay's yard and killed her squad car's engine. She studied the house not far out of Center Springs that once stood proud, but could use a little paint. The front porch was solid and level, but the end of several porch planks were broken off above the steps where they received the most foot traffic, a testament to hard financial times.

The shadows were growing long and dusk brought out the crickets and croaking tree frogs. Cicadas still buzzed their monotonous rhythm from the trees. A quail called from the nearby pasture and was answered by the covey gathering for the night.

She tapped the horn twice and waited to see if any yard dogs showed up. A tired-looking woman stepped through the screen door. "Is something wrong?"

"Not a thing." Anna smiled and spoke through her open car window. "I'm here to talk to Donald Ray about his brother's death."

"Well, I'm Cheryl Lynn, Donald Ray's wife. He ain't here. He's at work, but he'll be home in a little bit for dinner. You drink coffee?"

"Sure do."

"Get out and come in the house."

Hat in hand, Anna followed Cheryl Lynn through the door and into her spotless kitchen, wondering why she'd been invited in so quickly. The windows were open, and a light breeze scrubbed the air, freshening the interior smelling faintly of onions and fried food. "I'm Deputy Anna Sloan."

Cheryl Lynn plugged in a percolator and put a sugar bowl on the wooden table covered by a lace tablecloth. She opened the Frigidaire and removed a pint jar of cream. "I don't believe I've ever seen a woman deputy sheriff."

Anna put her hat upside down on a nearby cupboard beside some dishes she recognized as the Cactus Flower pattern. She sat at the table in the middle of the kitchen. "There aren't many of us."

"I don't imagine." Cheryl Lynn wiped her hands on her apron and sat opposite Anna. She tucked a strand of brown hair behind her ear. "I know it's getting late in the afternoon for coffee, but I dearly love the stuff. You're not here to talk about coffee, though, are you? Did you find something out about Frank's death?"

"You're not calling it a murder?"

"*I'm* not. Some of the boys are." Behind Cheryl Lynn, the electric coffee pot started to bubble with a fat, rumbling sound. "What I heard sounds like it was an accident to me."

"We can't find any evidence of foul play. Maggie might have dodged to miss something, a deer or a dog, maybe."

"I swanny, it's a crying shame, that's what it is."

"Tell me about Frank's wife and kids."

"Why you want to know that?"

"Because I'm trying to get a picture of him in my mind. Sheriff Parker hired me a while back because I look at things most of his other deputies don't think about, or miss entirely. I'm looking for any details that might help us solve what happened on the dam so we can cool down this feud between y'all's families."

"I don't know much, 'cept I bet you don't do this for every car wreck you come across. You're looking for more'n that, but I'll help you if I can."

Anna cocked her head, appraising the slender, wavy-haired woman. "I'd appreciate anything you can tell me."

"I bet." Cheryl Lynn adjusted the salt and pepper shakers in the middle of the table, putting them right back in their same positions. "Let's see. They were married for about twelve, thirteen years. They was happy. I never saw them argue. Frank loved his kids, Lordy did he love 'em. He was always taking the boys huntin' and fishin'."

"Did Harriet go?"

"Lord, no. She didn't do nothin' but stay home."

"She was a good housewife?"

"She was a housewife. Good? That girl didn't even sweep. I don't think she ever made the bed, either. I swear, I've been over there at all times of the day, but the beds looked like they'd just got up. I don't even know why she bothered to buy bedspreads, they were always on the floor at the foot. Frank finally hired someone to do that."

"Who'd he hire?"

Cheryl Lynn grinned. "Rubye Mayfield."

"Well, there's a connection."

"Ain't it?"

"Why in the world would he hire a *Mayfield* to do housework for them?"

"'cause that was always Frank's way. Rubye did everything for them. She cooked and cleaned and washed their clothes, at least until Saturday when Frank was killed."

"Does she live with them?"

"No. She lives down the road a couple of miles. She walked to work every morning, and home ever evening."

"How old is she?"

"Forty-five or so."

"She's married to who?"

"Cass Mayfield. They started early, and her three kids are already grown and gone. You can put that eyebrow back down. She worked for 'em, but I never suspected her and Frank of doing anything together."

Anna felt a flush on her face and wondered what else her expressions gave away. "What does Cass do?"

"He's a handyman for folks who don't mind colored people being around. You use cream in your coffee?"

"A little bit."

"You ought to go talk to Rubye. She knows things I don't."

"I will. Tell me this, what does Donald Ray think happened?"

Cheryl Lynn couldn't find a place to rest her eyes. "He thinks they were murdered."

"I don't see how that could have happened."

"He says it did. Ask him."

"I really came to see you."

Cheryl Lynn was taken off balance. "I...I don't...coffee's ready."

She took two saucers and coffee cups from the cupboard and set them on the table. She wouldn't look at Anna as she unplugged the cord from the percolator and poured. She set the pot nearby and slid one of the sets toward Anna. "Cream's right there. Hope it's not too strong. Donald Ray likes it strong, and that's the way I'm used to making it."

Anna adjusted the cup and added cream. "Cheryl Lynn, have you ever played poker?"

"Why, lands no. Playing cards is a sin. Why'd you ask me that?"

"Because you don't have a poker face and you'd lose every hand you played. You know something you're not telling me."

The kitchen grew silent as they waited for the coffee to cool enough to drink.

"I can't say no more, Deputy."

"You haven't said anything."

"That's not what Donald Ray'll think."

Anna blew across the surface and sipped. "This is good. It's a lot better than what we have at work."

Cheryl Lynn added more cream without answering. "You're not here just about the accident, are you?"

"No, I'm trying to stop what's going on between your families."

"I know. It's awful."

"It is, that. Can you help me?"

The air in the kitchen seemed to thicken, and Anna wondered if she could have phrased it differently. It was too late, though. The question was out there.

"I don't think it's Wes doing it."

The answer was so unexpected that Anna sipped more than she intended and burned her tongue. She hissed, sucking in cool air. "I didn't say anything about Wes." She put the cup down.

"You'll hear his name called any day now, because if something bad happens and a Clay's involved, people point fingers at Wes. You need to know he don't *plan* things like that. He fights when he gets mad, and if was a woman he might slap her, even beat her I guess, but he don't sull up and steam about things for a long time. He acts without thinking and then goes on."

"Well, then, maybe Wes saw them together and tried to scare them or something and it went bad."

Cheryl Lynn unconsciously twisted her wedding ring. "It isn't *him*."

"How do you know for sure?"

"I know." Their eyes met, and Anna read the story before Cheryl Lynn could place her gaze back in her coffee cup.

"Uh oh." Taken aback, Anna studied her cup for a moment. "I know it's none of my business, but you're wading in dangerous waters."

"I live there."

"Oh, honey. Be careful." Anna paused. "I have to hear you say it, though. You know with all certainty, that Wes isn't doing it himself, or having it done?"

"Yes. He was with me."

Anna watched Cheryl Lynn's face, expecting tears or at the very least a quivering chin. She was completely composed.

"Wes is my bad boy, but it isn't him. He's a lot of things, and he has a cold side, colder than sin about most things, but he's no murderer."

"Then help me. *Someone* killed Merle and Hollis Mayfield, and burned a house, and in turn, from what I hear about y'alls families, someone will start doing the same to Clays. This has to stop."

"I know it. I want to help, but there's nothing I can do."

"You could be covering for Wes."

"I wouldn't cover for a murderer."

Anna traced the pattern in the tablecloth with a forefinger, confident Cheryl Lynn was telling the truth. "Why are you still in this house then?"

"Because I won't leave Donald Ray for Wes. I'm happy with my life."

Anna frowned. "But you're having…"

"That'll pass someday. It's fun and exciting and dangerous, and I need some of that right now. Living out here in this house….I'm missing something. I'm missing a lot and the only way to get any excitement is…by looking for something fun, you know? Donald Ray works all the time, and when he's home he's out hunting or fishing. I need a lot more than I'm getting. You're a woman, you know what I mean. Me and Wes are kinda, you know, pals, but when it's over, I'll still live here and I'll be older and what I'm feeling will be gone and then I'll be comfortable."

"Donald Ray's your age. He should be feeling the same. That should work in favor of the two of y'all."

"I'm sure he does, but not with me."

"Oh.

"Oh's right. He gets his ashes hauled somewheres else, like over at that hot sheet place outside of Hugo. He sure goes over there a lot for feed, he says, or to the sale barn, but the funny thing is, he don't never come back with anything except the smell of perfume on him."

The kitchen was silent except for the ticking of a black Kit-Cat clock on the wall.

Cheryl Lynn leaned forward. "You know there's girly shows out there at Frogtown, where they dance and they have what they call 'acts' with comedians and such on stage, but I know what they really are. He goes there, too, sometimes."

Anna knew about the scattering of rough buildings at the Oklahoma bend of the Red River, but she hadn't been over there. She made a note to ask Cody about them. "All right. Let me ask you this. How can I find Rubye tonight? Will she be home?"

Cheryl Lynn met her eyes. "No. She works at Saperstein's store now and if you go over there after they close, she'll be cleaning up."

"So I go see Rubye Mayfield for what…?"

"She can tell you about what's going on with her family. She also does things for other folks no one else does and she listens."

"How do you know all this?"

Cheryl Lynn wouldn't look at her. "I just do."

"All right. I'll talk to her as soon as I leave here."

Cheryl Lynn sat straighter, as if she'd made a decision. "How tough are you?"

"Not very."

"I heard you was shot here while back."

Anna licked her lips and took a tiny sip of coffee. She didn't like to talk about it. "You're right. I was shot, but that don't make me tough."

"Get someone to take with you and go see Royal Clay. It might take several of you, but put Royal in jail and it'll stop."

"Is Royal some kind of title?"

"No, that's his name. He's Donald Ray and Frank's first cousin. He's been in the pen a time or two, and there's always a story coming from the beer joints across the river of how he's fighting or cuttin' somebody. He don't like anyone who ain't white, and being over there in the Indian Nations gives him plenty of folks to tangle with."

"What do you want me to put him in jail for?"

"Breathing for one thing. You think Wes is bad, or tough. He don't hold a candle to *that* mean son of a bitch. He despises a badge and lives on a hill not far from the west tip of Lake Lamar. He never had a wife or kids, and spends most of his time dodging the law."

"I still can't just drive up to a man's house and arrest him because he's mean. What has he done in all this?"

"If he didn't beat Merle to death and shoot Hollis, he had it done. He's tight with Cecil Clay, but he usually gets others to do his dirty work for him. Cecil will do everything Royal tells him, and that's a fact. Everybody knows that."

She stood and flicked on the kitchen lights, startling Anna. "And you didn't hear none of that from me. Remember, I'm married in, and even then you're not a Clay until you're about a bajillion years old and most of the elders dies off. Right now, I'm just a wife and that's all." She placed the palms of both hands on the table, a clear signal she was finished talking. "You can't use my name, neither. I'll deny we had this conversation if you do."

Anna watched Cheryl Lynn refill their cups and wondered how to tell her there was no way to keep her out of it.

Chapter Twenty-six

The Wraith worked in the shade, wishing the sun would hurry up and go down. He had a lot to do. He'd stumbled on a great idea when Charlie Clay came by looking for a job. Seeing Charlie was like getting a surprise dessert, and his plan for him would be just as tasty.

Friday morning found Cody in his office and chomping at the bit. He never was much for paperwork, though the stack on his desk was considerably smaller than it had been before Anna arrived. She made a pretty good dent in the piles while her wounds healed.

She and John were already gone, digging deep into the investigation of the two Mayfield murders. For a small town, there was a lot of killing and Cody was afraid it would get worse before it got better.

He fidgeted behind the desk, barely glancing at a folder full of reports. Disinterested, he sharpened a few pencils, filled an ink pen, and turned on the radio to hear the news. A Pepsodent commercial was about as irritating as the flies that came through the screenless windows. He dialed it to a different station. "It's Such A Pretty World" came on and he snapped it off. Wynn Stewart's voice always irritated him, and it was especially worse at that moment.

Unused to being inactive, he pushed back in his chair and stood in the window to watch cars pass on Main Street. A few loafers laughed in the shade of the crepe myrtles lining the sidewalk. A blue jay scolded them, and the smell of frying food drifted up from Frenchie's café, half a block to the north.

He flicked on the radio to catch the news which was still filled with Martin Luther King's murder and the capture of James Earl Ray. The ag reports came on and he flicked it off. Sighing, he went to see Judge O.C. Rains.

Mr. Jules, the frail old elevator man, slid the double doors closed, followed by the scissoring safety gate. "Where to, Sheriff?"

"You used to call me Cody."

Born a former slave's son, Old Jules nodded at Cody's feet. "Thass right, but now you's the high sheriff and it ain't right to call you by your first name no more."

"Everyone calls you Jules and you're older than anyone I know. That's not respectful."

"They's a lot both right and wrong 'bout this ol' worl', Sheriff. Where to?"

"Oh." Cody realized he hadn't told him what floor he wanted. "Going to see Judge O.C."

Jules ran gnarly fingers over the buttons, as if playing a musical instrument. "He ain't in his office. Had to travel to Dallas for some kind of meetin'."

Indecisive, Cody waited in the silent elevator.

"Sheriff?"

"Huh?"

"It'll be all right."

"What?"

"I know why you ain't on the street this mornin'."

Cody studied Jules' white hair cut close to the scalp and his rheumy eyes. "You hear a lot in this elevator, don't you?"

"Yassir. White folks forget I'm here, or don't think I'm listenin', so they talk free."

"You heard enough to help clean up that case with the Skinner a few years ago. You know anything on this feud?"

"Heered lots, both here and up at the barbershop."

"You talking about Tom Hubbard's place?" It was a house in the "colored" section of Chisum, south of the tracks. Tom cut hair on the porch when the weather was tolerable, and inside when it wasn't."

"Yassir."

"Anything that'll help us settle all this down?"

"'nough to know it ain't over yet. Blood's thick and when it rises, it's slow to cool. It'll be a while 'fore the families have shed enough of it."

"This ain't the Hatfields and McCoys. We're living in modern times."

"I ain't met none of *them* folks, they must be from down south in the county, but if they families got crossways too, I 'magine it took a while to settle down. The right ones got to settle down first, then the rest of 'em'll tag along behind. I'm afraid it's gonna grow some before it's through."

"You know of any way to take the fire out of it?"

"There's lots of ways to damp a fire, Sheriff. I'd start with the little things, if I could, and that might help some. Just the opposite of what it is. You know, a match sho' is small, but it can make a big flame."

"You're talking in circles to me now."

"I'm awful sorry. It ain't my place to tell you what to do, Sheriff, 'cept that I need to start this elevator. Mind ridin' down to the first floor?"

"Go on."

Cody chewed his lip as they descended with creaks and rattles of the cables above. Jules stopped the elevator and opened the doors. He held out a hand to keep Cody back and adjusted the elevator even with the floor.

"I got one mo' thing to say, if you don't mind."

Cody waited. "Go ahead."

"There's only one thing in this world that's real, son, and that's the here and now. You and me a-talkin'. The past is nothin' but memories, some bad, some good, and the future is what you do after this minute, what you want it to be, or think it might could be, but you cain't touch that yet. The things you do now, and the things you say changes the future, and the future of them around us…maybe not right away, but it does."

Jules glanced out the door to make sure no one was within hearing distance. "I heered 'bout that high-yeller gal gettin' killed with Mr. Clay. He was a good man, and she was all sunshine, from what I hear. I got no business noodlin' around with what they was doin', 'cause we don't know what goes on in other folks' minds. We all got demons, and dreams, and lives that others don't know about. That makes us who we are, if you know what I mean. Whatever they was doin' together in that car was they business, and folks don't need to go havin' a killin' over it. It was between them, and that's all."

"You think they were…together?"

"Didn't say that. I heered she was givin' him a ride. Thass all, and you know what? What difference does it make now? They both gone."

Cody chewed the inside of his lip, wishing he had a cigarette, but he'd quit once again. "I agree with that. Maybe your people will come to understand it, and I hope I can get the Clays to let things alone."

"Folks won't. That's human. They won't leave nothin' alone."

Two men in business suits and carrying briefcases came through the brass and glass front doors and headed for the elevator. Cody stepped off and they passed, nodding hello. Jules didn't say another word to Cody. He addressed the men while looking at their belts. "What floor, gentlemen?"

"Third."

The elevator closed, leaving Cody to think. The lobby was empty, except for Albert Shames sitting on the stool in front of his shoeshine stand.

The black man lowered *The Chisum News*. "Shine, Sheriff?"

"May as well." Cody climbed onto the stand, the chair a good four feet off the ground.

Albert stuffed Cody's pants into the tops of his boots to keep from getting polish on the cuffs and buffed the dust off with a long rag, snapping it a couple of times. He opened a drawer full of jars and cans.

The elevator returned and Jules stepped out. "Albert, I need to go outdoors while there ain't nobody around."

He nodded and selected a can of black polish. "Go ahead on. I'll tell folks you'll be right back."

While he blacked Cody's boots, the sheriff watched Jules pass the men's restroom. A small sign reading "colored restroom" pointed to an outside door. Beyond that were the water fountains designated "whites only" and "colored only."

Cody thought of the little matches Jules talked about only moments before, and Jules' "here and now" opinion. He thought of King's recent murder and came to a decision. "Hold it a minute, Mr. Albert."

The black shoeshine man raised his eyebrows. "Mr. Cody, you all right? Did I do something wrong?"

"Nope."

Khakis still tucked in the top of his boots, Cody stepped down off the shine stand and walked across the black and white penny-tile floor to the water fountains. The signs attached to the wall had been there since he was a child, but he'd barely noticed them. He stood there a good two or three minutes while Albert waited with the brush in his hand.

Squaring his shoulders, Cody grabbed the "Colored Only" sign with both hands and yanked. The old screws pulled loose surprisingly easy.

Jules came back inside and stopped beside Albert. Shocked into statues, they watched Cody yank the "Whites Only" sign off and return to the shine stand.

He leaned the signs against the wall and climbed back into the seat and met Jules' wide eyes. "Matches, Mr. Jules. Matches."

The old elevator operator exchanged glances with a confused shoeshine man as two secretaries came through the lobby. Jules shook his head. "I don't know if you blowed one out, or lit it, Sheriff."

His step was lighter, though, as he ushered the ladies into the elevator.

Chapter Twenty-seven

Miss Becky had already been to the garden by the time we got ready for school. Grandpa was gone, busy with law work. He hadn't been to the field at all since Friday and I knew it was worrying him.

I pushed back my empty breakfast plate. I wasn't too interested in finishing my milk, because it was fresh from the cow that morning and a little too warm for my taste.

Miss Becky gave me her mock frown. "Y'all rolled out early for a school day."

Mark wiped up the last of the honey on his plate with half a biscuit. "We're gonna go feed."

She finished her own eggs. "That'll be sweet of y'all. Grandpa'll be proud of you for it." She picked up our breakfast plates and dropped them into the dishpan full of water. "What a time for the phones to be out."

We lost electricity pretty regular and the phones were just as likely to go out as well. That was one more problem with our party lines. Her comment made me think. "I dreamed about lights last night, colored lights and sparks. Think there's a line down?"

"No. I think somebody didn't hang up and the line's open." Miss Becky fussed around the kitchen, getting it cleaned up so she could start dinner. It seemed like she was constantly cooking one meal after the other. "I was listenin', and it sounded like somebody moving around in a house. Miss Whitney, most likely. I think I can hear her whistling in the background. My lands. I never did like to hear anybody whistle. Your Aunt Lucy whistled all the time when we were kids and it always set my teeth on edge."

I gave Mark a big grin. Even though they'd see each other in class, Pepper'd called the last three mornings and jabbered at one another until the bus came down the road. I listened a couple of times at first, but they didn't talk about anything other than rock 'n' roll that interested me. Half the time Mark said "uh huh" and "yep" while Pepper did most of the talking. They wouldn't be at it this morning, though.

Miss Becky started to peel a potato, but put it down and dug around a drawer for her whetstone. "I despise a dull knife." She sat down at the table with us and worked on the knife's edge. She slowed down for a moment, thinking. "Was your dream last night from the Poisoned Gift?"

"No ma'am. I don't think so, but you never know."

I figured it was her way of worrying things out and it probably had to do with the dead man we saw at the fair. She never did act like most women who needed to talk through everything that happened around them. She just waited until the time was right and never asked too many questions. "You two all right this morning?"

What with dreaming of colored lights, flickering and flashing in the air like fireflies, I felt a little tired. I knew Mark tossed and turned, too, because I roused up several times to hear him on the other side of the room. I knew he was probably having a hard time of settling in since he'd been living in another world only the week before.

Mark shrugged and kept his head lowered.

Miss Becky's eyes softened and she stopped sharpening her Old Hickory. She rubbed the back of my neck. "Boys, we can talk if you want to."

I could tell she had something on *her* mind. I shook my head. I was glad Pepper wasn't there, too. "We're fine. I just dreamed all night, and I guess I'm tired."

The living room clock ticked in time with the rhythmic circular grinding against the stone as she worked the edge of the blade. "Top, I'm-a-gonna tell you something that might help you with them dreams, but you boys have to promise me and God that you'll never breathe a word of it to no one. I believe you're old enough, though I don't even want Pepper to know. It's about your Grandpa Ned. Can y'all keep it?"

I 'magine we both sat there with dumb looks on our faces, because I'd never heard Miss Becky talk about Grandpa at all. Mark blinked at me, and I realized he was as shocked as I was. We nodded.

"I know this is asking a lot of you, Mark, right now with you barely getting here and all, but you boys need to know this about your Grandpa."

"Yessum. I'm afraid I'm gonna feel bad about keeping it from Pepper, though."

"I know, hon. But it's not one of them secrets that's bad, it's one to help Top."

"Okay."

"Good." She kept working the knife on the whetstone, not making eye contact with us. "There's something in the Parker blood that I've called the Poisoned Gift ever since I met your Grandpa. The thing is, the Gift skips generations. Your Grandpa Ned had it when he was younger, when we first married, and it almost tore him to pieces.

"Now, I'm not gonna tell you everything, because I think the ol' Devil has a finger in that Gift, and some of the things that happened back then is best left alone. Your Grandpa had something different, though, a Gift that was both beautiful and terrible at the same time."

Neither me or Mark made a sound. The ticking of the clock, the circular grinding, and her voice were almost hypnotizing.

"It skipped your Uncle James and your daddy, for some reason or 'nother, but you've dreamed them dreams and have gone through a lot over the last four years or so. I think you're a lot stronger'n you think. You stand tall in the rain, if you know what I mean."

I didn't but I felt about ten times bigger just listening to her.

"The Poisoned Gift's different in every Parker male. Your great-great-granddaddy Will Parker knew when folks were about to die, if they were sick. He could tell 'em to change their ways, or what they were doing, and sometimes it worked.

"Your Grandpa Ned had something else. He told me about it when we was going together and I prayed about it might near every day after." Her grinding slowed. "See, he could help folks pass over."

I guess she noticed my frown and her sharpening sped back up. "When folks were bad off, if they were dying and making a hard time of it, he could hold 'em and they'd go easy, praise the Lord."

I watched her eyes fill.

"Sometimes he'd sit by their bed and hold a person's hand. Other times when they were trying to die and it was really hard, he had to gather 'em up in his arms." A tear welled and rolled down her wrinkled cheek. She didn't bother to wipe it away. "I've seen him help people get to Glory when they were too bad off to keep living. *Hallelujah*."

That last word was soft, almost to herself. She almost stopped moving the blade on the whetstone.

Mark cleared his throat, and his voice was low and wavery. "It sounds like he was just killing them."

"Oh no, hon. Ned just opened his arms and gathered 'em in. I believe that opened a way to Heaven's gates for them folks. But it was hard on him, and each time he'd be so wore out he couldn't do nothing for a day or so after."

"He doesn't do it anymore."

"That's right. We'd only been married for a couple of years, and he helped folks pass whenever someone could talk him into it. Then one day a little gal named Pickles came to him with her family and her bigger sister who was so bad off she wasn't nothin' but a bag of bones in her daddy's arms when he brought her into the house."

"Pickles is a funny name for a girl."

A tear rolled down Miss Becky's cheek. "She was a little colored gal, and I doubt that was her real name. But she was a corker, that one, only about seven or so." Now both eyes flooded and tears dripped from Miss Becky's cheeks as she remembered.

"I'm not going into all of this right now, because you boys need to be a little older for the whole story, but he helped Pickles' sister cross over by just holding her. He cried over it and after that, things got bad in town and there was some people wanted your Grandpa to go to prison for it. Well, O.C. finally cleared it up, but Ned stopped helping people after that and a while later he lost that Poisoned Gift and it never came back."

I blinked away my own tears. "I wish that would happen to me...that it would go away."

"I don't believe it's the right time for it to go, hon. I believe the good Lord gave you something you need to learn to use. Maybe you can do something good with it when you get older and understand what it is."

"How did Grandpa learn about it?"

She drew a deep, shuddering breath. "We was in a flivver, driving into Chisum one day and there was a bad wreck between a buggy and another car like the one we were in. The horse that was pulling the buggy was hurt bad, and it got loose from the harness when someone cut it free.

"We were just sitting there in the front seat, when that young gelding limped over to Ned and rested his head against Ned's shoulder, like he could help it. You know them old cars was open, so it was nothin' for that horse to do it, but Ned said when it leaned against him a-quivering and a-hurtin', something passed between them and that's how he knew he had it."

I thought about Grandpa's own Poisoned Gift and understood why he let it go. "Maybe if I just quit using mine it'll go away." It was a dumb thing to say, because I had no control when it came or went.

"I don't believe it works that way. The Lord will let you know what to do down the road." She stopped grinding the blade and tested the edge with her thumb. Satisfied that it was sharp enough, she laid it on the table. "Now, that's all I'm going to tell you right now. You get the rest of it when you're grown, I reckon. And remember boys, you promised to keep this secret."

We nodded the same time.

"Good. Now, don't even bring it up to your Grandpa. He'd be mad if he knew I told you." A weight seemed to be gone from her shoulders and she straightened. "Norma Faye's coming by to get me in a few minutes. We're going over to Wanda Leah's house to quilt. Y'all don't miss that bus."

She forgot about the knife and wrung out a washrag and wiped the table. "Top, put out the alfalfa when you feed so you won't go to wheezing. Give 'em some extra cubes. They didn't get fed yesterday, neither. Y'all stop and gather the eggs on the way back. My buckets were full when I came back from the garden."

A horn honked down on the highway as a car went past. Folks who knew us always honked howdy. Miss Becky glanced out the kitchen window. "That was Ralston's car. I believe I saw Miss Sweet in there with him."

Miss Sweet was one of John Washington's old twin aunts. She was the local healer for the coloreds and poor white folks who couldn't afford a doctor. Most of the white folks didn't admit that she came by when she did, but she didn't care who she helped. In fact, she kept me from dying a few years earlier from a bad asthma attack.

The kitchen door was open and we saw the car turn down the oil road past the Assembly church. It made the bend at Uncle Mason's house and kept going.

Miss Becky turned back to us. "They're heading down to the bottoms. There's a family living in that old house down on the slash. I heard their baby had the croup."

Mark knew the place. "The shack just down from Mr. Benson's place?"

"You remember that house?"

"Yeah. One of the Clotworthy boys lived there." He pulled

his hair back out of his eyes. "You remember, that set of twins was in our class before I had to go to Oklahoma."

I remembered. "They wore tennis shoes so worn out that they flapped when they walked."

"Bless their hearts." Miss Becky picked up the sharp knife and went to peeling potatoes. "Well, I'm gonna make this potato salad and Grandpa can take some of it over there if they're having troubles."

"I thought you were going quilting."

"I'll let these soak 'til I get back. You boys be careful and watch for snakes. I killed a copperhead over by the propane tank this morning. The lake coming up is running them out of the bottoms."

◇◇◇

It was warm for so early in the day, and I figured it'd be a hot one. The bitterweeds were already giving off their sharp smell in the warm sun. We followed the trail Grandpa mowed through the pasture from the gate to the barn. While we walked, Mark tied his hair back with a leather band Pepper had given him.

I watched him fiddle with the knot. "You know Grandpa or Uncle Cody's gonna make you get a haircut before long."

"Yeah. Mr. Stevens told me I needed to get it cut. He said I looked like a girl and school rules say it needs to be short."

Principal Stevens was our dough-faced principal who didn't take much off any kid for any reason. I opened the barn's pipe gate. "When you gonna do it?"

"When somebody makes me."

We exchanged grins. I climbed on top of the stacked hay and dropped a bale down to Mark. He grabbed the wires and used his leg to bump it along to the gate. I knocked another one to the barn floor and climbed down. Alfalfa bales are heavier than Johnson grass, and it was all I could do to half drag, half carry it out.

Mark broke up his bale and scattered the sections. The cows drifted up from the plum thicket, mooing and throwing their heads. They tore into the hay, snuffing and snorting each other out of the way. He handed me the pair of dikes Grandpa kept on the feed barrel and I clipped the bailing wire and scattered my bale. The cows were already gathered when we shook out two buckets full of range cubes.

Norma Faye turned in the drive and saw us. She tapped the horn twice and waved through the windshield. Miss Becky came out with her train case full of sewing stuff. At least that's what she called it. Mama'd called it an overnight bag and that stuck with me. Miss Becky got in Norma Faye's front seat and they left.

By the time we replaced the lids on the barrels full of nuggets and creep feed, the back of Mark's shirt was wet and I was dripping sweat. We headed for the chicken house. The grass in that part of the pasture was thick and tall. I figured that after school I'd start Grandpa's old push mower clean up the trail for him.

A twist of bailing wire held the warped door closed. It didn't fit flush, so Miss Becky used a piece of old board to brace it closed. I reached down to pick it up.

"Look out!"

Mark startled me and I heard the buzz of a rattlesnake. Let me tell you, that sound is completely different than that dead snake's rattle on the road. This one was hot and dusty and deadly.

That's when I saw a big old diamondback coiled beside the door.

I danced back and jumped to the side into the tall grass growing up against the chicken house. A sharp pain in my left foot told me I was bit. Someone screamed, and I realized it was me.

Chapter Twenty-eight

The Wraith walked away with both hands in his pockets, feeling two large pressure washers he'd removed from the equipment towering overhead. The spur-of-the-moment sabotage wouldn't do anything but provide entertainment at some point in his last couple of nights in Lamar County. But who knew? Maybe it would spark a different kind of fire that would stir things up even more.

Cody dropped by his office for only a few minutes when Judge O.C. Rains came in. "Boy, you done stirred up a hornet's nest."

"I've been waiting for you."

"By-dog, don't you think you shoulda asked me first, maybe gone about it a different way?"

"You talking about those signs?"

"I am."

Cody's eyes crinkled at the corners. Their conversation was a different version of the same one Ned and O.C. had been repeating for years. "They needed to come down, O.C."

"So you took the bull by the horns."

"Yep. In case you didn't notice, they're gone from the bathrooms, too. We don't have colored and white sections anymore."

"Signs don't matter. Folks'll keep using the ones they're used to, or think they're supposed to."

"They will for a while, but eventually someone'll forget, or new folks will come through and they'll drink from either one."

"Things are pretty tense around here right now. Don't you think you should have waited until this war is over with?"

"There's more than one war going on in this world right now. There's never a good time, O.C. You know that as well as I do. Reverend King's dead, folks are fighting in the streets and burning their own neighborhoods down, there's Vietnam, kids marching, and mark my words, one of these days somebody's gonna shoot some of them for doing it. I can't do anything about all that, but I can damn sure make a few small changes here."

Judge Rains sighed. "Son, I know you got beaucoup problems right now. You don't need to borrow trouble."

"Ain't borrowing it. It's already here. I fought in Vietnam with colored men. They did the same jobs as me, and we didn't have black and white latrines, or hooches, or tables in the chow hall, when we had one. I knew a full-blood Cherokee over there, too.

"It was just men who looked a little different on the outside, but were the same when we bled and I saw more than a few of 'em die for this country, and this town, and this courthouse where they couldn't get a drink of water but from a certain fountain. That ain't right."

"Well, I know things are changing, but sometimes they change a little too fast."

"It'll get better."

"Fine then." His eyes roamed over the office. "You making any headway on this clan feud of yours?"

Cody went with the change in conversation. "Not as much as I'd like. Anna's working on it with John."

"'cause you need to separate yourself from it all."

"We figured that'd be best. Something's going on and we're trying to get to the bottom of it."

"What have you found out?"

Cody shrugged. "Not a lot. I don't understand everything I know about it, yet. The trouble started with the wreck, but the first killing started the night the fair set up. There's no way to know why Merle Mayfield was killed, but I believe it has something to do with Frank and Maggie going off the dam."

"You reckon there's something else involved? Whiskeymaking, or a dispute over territory, maybe?"

"I thought of that, but the Clays haven't made any whiskey since before the war. The Mayfields never did, as far as I know. I talked to Bill Snow who checked the car out." Cody rocked back in his chair. "He couldn't find hide nor hair of anything wrong with the steering or the brakes."

"We couldn't-a picked two worse people to put in a car and die together." O.C. crossed his legs and thought for a moment. "Let me ask you a question."

"Go ahead."

"You're behind that desk because a lot of circumstantial evidence points to you. You don't think that's a coincidence, do you?"

Cody leaned back in his chair, thinking. "Of course not. Somebody's intentionally trying to tie me into it, but I don't know no more than you do. I'm just picking at it."

"What?"

"Like Ned would do. Pick at it until something happens."

"You can't do it from right there."

"I'm already doing it. I got John, Anna, and Ned out there scratching around. They'll turn something up."

"Well, I hope they plow straight and fast."

Chapter Twenty-nine

The snake's fangs bit deep and pain shrieked up my leg. I screamed and ran for the house, hearing that big ol' diamondback still rattling long and loud behind me. Mark shot around me before I reached the gate and grabbed a hoe that was leaning against the smokehouse. He spun and the last I saw of him was headed back to the chicken house.

I kept going to the porch and dropped onto the edge, my heart beating so hard that I could hear it in my ears. My asthma rose up and I started gasping for breath. My foot throbbed and I pulled off my tennis shoe without untying the laces.

I was already swimmy-headed. My stomach rose at the thought of that nasty thing's mouth and those fangs it'd buried in my flesh. I laid back on the boards and imagined the poison running through my veins. My stomach rolled at the thought.

Panic rose. There was no one in the house to help me. I knew what was going to happen, because I'd seen snakebit dogs. Their heads swole up the size of #5 washtubs and they sometimes died, all bloated up and moaning at the end.

Mark appeared beside me and dropped the hoe by the porch. "Bad?"

"Bad enough."

"Lemme look at it."

"We don't have time. I can feel the poison. It's already got to my head. Go call for help."

He charged into the house, letting the screen door slap behind him. He started hollering like he was getting help. It seemed like I waited for an hour before he came back out. "Phone's still not working."

"Oh no."

"I hollered into the receiver, to see if whoever left it off the hook could hear me, but no one answered. I'll take your bike up to the store."

"It has a flat."

"All right. I'll run and get help. You stay right where you are. They say you're not supposed to do anything but lay still if you've been snakebit."

"I should have remembered that back at the chicken house. You're gonna have to cut Xs in the fang marks and suck out the poison."

"That don't work except on television and in the movies."

"How do you know that?"

"My Uncle Bart told me. He was bit by a water moccasin and they had to take him to Hugo. His leg swelled up and the flesh around the bites sloughed off and…" he drifted off, realizing what he was saying. "You're wheezing. Is it the snakebite already?"

"No. The asthma."

"Stay right there and don't move."

He ran back inside and came out with my puffer. "Here. Use this. What else do you want me to do?"

I stuck the plastic nozzle in my mouth and squeezed the gray bulb, taking two deep breaths full of vaporized medicine. My lungs tickled. "Run for help, but first, get one of those evidence jars of whiskey out of the smokehouse. My foot's killing me, and I need something. Grandpa always said a dose of whiskey is as good as anything the doctor can give you."

There was a line of dusty mason jars full of white lightning on the top shelf in the smokehouse that smelled of dirt dauber nests and dust. Under that was a rancid odor of old grease drippings from when they cured meat in there. Each evidence jar was labeled with a date and name from the man who ran the still.

Mark jumped off the porch, long hair flying. His footsteps crunched across the driveway, heading toward the smokehouse. Still flat on my back, I pumped the bulb and sucked in a second dose of medicine. My lungs eased, but the hand holding the light plastic atomizer felt heavy.

Hootie came out from under the porch and laid down beside me, whimpering. He knew I was bit. It reminded me that Carlo, Grandpa's old yard dog, was bit by a snake once. He lived, but didn't look good for a long time.

Mark was back. He grunted as he unscrewed the lid. "Shouldn't have got the oldest jar, but I didn't want Grandpa to get mad if I got one of the newest ones." The rusty ring finally turned. "Them others might not be through the courts yet."

I was aggravated by all the talking and the fact that he was more worried about the evidence than me. Mark tossed the ring away and used his fingernails under the lid to pry it off. He knelt down. "Here, take a big drink."

I raised up on one elbow and took the full jar. The oily, acrid smell of pure grain alcohol cut through my sinuses. I took a little sip and fire shot down my goozle.

"Hold your nose and take a big old swaller. You need to drink more'n that little bitty ol' sip."

Mark wasn't the one snakebit and drinking pure, uncut moonshine, but he was probably right. I held my nose and took a big swallow, then another and another, like I was drinking ice water. The fumes raced back up my sinuses again when I turned my nose loose. I breathed out and took to coughing like I had the croup.

Mark frowned, watching me. "How'd it taste?"

I coughed again. "Like coal oil."

"Better take another dose. It'll help while I'm gone. I'll be back as soon as I can."

He vanished and I took one more drink that went down a lot easier than the first, then laid back again. I thought about what he'd said about his uncle and hoped my leg wouldn't swell up the size of a foot log. I wanted to raise up and look, but my head was really heavy and it felt like a boat anchor.

I went swimmy-headed again and tried to raise a hand, but nothing worked right.

The poison was working its way through me.

Someone laughed. My eyes grew heavy. When I was little, I liked to rub 'em until bright lights flickered and shot in all directions. Sometimes when I was dozing off for a nap, or at night, faces appeared and disappeared in the darkness behind my lids, floating around like planets.

This time something different happened. Instead of lights, or interesting faces, I saw smiles. Bright, painted, ghastly smiles. Some large, some small. Smiles painted like clown mouths floated past. Sometimes the big red lips separated to show straight white teeth, but one of them had fangs like that diamondback.

Bales of hay ricocheted through the smiles, bumping them softly, and sending them running spinning into space. My face was clammy with sweat.

Mirrors.

Mirrors reflecting my face.

Screams of laughter.

Manes of long red hair.

A dark man floated behind my eyelids like a scuba diver in dark water. An Indian with wheels for feet pushed him away and grinned wide.

He's a wraith.

A wraith.

The wraith floated downward, holding a giant crescent wrench that bloomed into a bouquet of bright, colorful lights.

I smelled popcorn, cotton candy, and rotting carcasses.

Everything around me swirled downward, like someone pulled the plug in a bathtub. I was sucked into the hole of spinning colors before darkness took me and insane laughter filled my ears.

Chapter Thirty

The Wraith stepped outside, rubbing his knuckles. He glared back over his shoulder at the crying woman curled on the floor. Absolutely no one questioned his whereabouts. It had been a long, busy night and now he had to work at his new job. He adjusted his loose clothes, pulled on a pair of thin white gloves, and smiled at a passing stranger.

Mark ran as fast as his legs could pump. He hadn't been back in Miss Becky's house but a few days and already bad things were happening. Now Top was dying from snakebite. The sorry-assed Grover was right, he wasn't half worth nothin' at all because he'd brought bad medicine to the Parkers.

He ran as hard as he could to Uncle Mason's house, because that's how he already thought of them, him and Aunt Wanda, but when he beat on their locked door there was nobody home. Farther down was Top's Uncle Cliff's house, but they didn't have a phone, and he was probably up at the store anyway.

That's when he remembered Miss Sweet passing in Ralston's car on their way to doctor that poor family down on the slough. They hadn't come back by, so he figured she'd still be there. He had a choice, run the rest of the way to the store, or cut through the pasture behind Uncle Mason's house and catch the dirt road to the bottoms that led to the slough.

He wondered if he was doing wrong by heading out to find Miss Sweet. He could just as easily run down the highway to the store, but then someone would have to call for help, or they'd insist on driving to the house to look at Top, and by the time they decided to get him to the hospital, he'd be dead.

Mark's mind shifted gears as he ran, one part worrying about Top, the other studying on the fact that he was back living with Miss Becky, but now they'd have to bury his friend. He was useless, nothing more than a stray that Aunt Tillie and Grover should have pulled over down at the creek bridge to dump out like a dog. They'd done something similar to his second cousin when she was sick all the time. They got tired of spending money they didn't have on her and the next thing Mark knew she was gone. He never knew for sure what they did with her, but she never came back and neither of the adults ever talked about it afterwards.

Now, here he was back with the greatest family in the world and he'd let Top get bit by a big old rattlesnake. It was him who should've opened the door to that chicken house. Feeding the cows was his idea, thinking he needed to do more to earn his keep, but since Top was their real blood, Mark figured he needed to hang back and let him be the leader.

Top needed that anyway, to not be a follower all the time but to be in charge.

Damn it!

He sprinted across the pasture, running like a house afire. Cows laying in the shade of an oak bellered and scattered. An old bull grunted to his feet and pawed the dirt, warning him away.

The pasture led downhill and the grass was close cropped from the cattle. Mark had enough speed and angle to leap a five-strand barbed-wire fence. The grass on that side was thicker, and slowed him down.

He pounded down a cow trail. Any other time it would have felt good, running with the wind in his face. His mama once told him their people were runners and could go all day if they needed to, but that was long ago back in the Olden Days. Running to run and running for help was altogether different because Mark was terrified that Top was dying.

He came to a line of trees and ducked under a low limb. Vines grabbed at his clothes slowing him even more. A thorn slashed his face, but he broke through in no time. The next barbed-wire fence was growed up, and he had to climb over using the sagging wires as rungs, cutting his palm with one of the rusty barbs. Two steps later, he stumbled onto the packed gravel and dirt road and took off running again free and easy now that he was warmed up.

It wasn't far to the shack, and Ralston's car was parked out in their dirt yard beside a tire swing. Miss Sweet was sitting on the porch like she was tired. Ralston slouched in the front seat of their car with the door open and one foot on the ground.

"Miss Sweet! Ralston! Help!"

Miss Sweet straightened and set down jar of what looked like tea. "My lands, what's wrong, honey?"

Ralston jumped out of the car as Mark slid to a stop. He grabbed the boy's shoulders. "You're Mark, right?"

"Yeah."

"Where you coming from?"

Over his shoulder, Miss Sweet made her way off the edge of the porch and waddled toward them on short, bowed legs. She was a big woman and her hair was grayer than the last time Mark saw her. "Tell us, baby. What's the matter?"

His chest filled with deep shudders at her soft, sincere voice full of concern. His legs suddenly lost their strength and he had to hold himself upright against their dented car. "Top's been snakebit by a big old rattler and nobody's home."

The old healer threw both hands in the air. "Sweet Jesus! Where'd it bite him?"

"On the foot."

"How long's it been?"

"Long enough to run down here and a few minutes besides."

A baby's cough carried across the porch.

She was already opening the car door. "Ralston, get my bag from out the house."

"Yessum." He darted around the car, but the young man who lived there came outside with the bag in his hand first. Ralston grabbed it and turned to leave.

The toddler's daddy held out a 'toesack. "Wait. I ain't got no money, but here's our pay."

Without a word, Ralston grabbed it and shot off the porch. Mark was already in the backseat when Ralston poked the sack and her bag through the open back glass and dropped them on the floorboard. Seconds later, they were throwing up a roostertail of dust on the way back to the house.

Mark leaned back, hoping they'd get there in time. A Dominicker hen stuck her head out of a hole in the 'toesack on the floorboard and clucked at him, and it seemed almost normal.

Chapter Thirty-one

The Wraith bided his time sharpening a long knife in the shade of a pecan tree. Distracted by the past, he hissed as the blade missed and cut deep. He studied the blood dripping onto the sand between his feet and knew it was sharp enough.

Ned pulled into Oak Peterson's lot and stared down the road leading to the dam, studying on the accident when Ike Reader's GMC pickup popped into view. Usually a slow driver, Ike had his foot in it this time and the old truck was flying. Seeing the only red Fury in the county, he braked and slid to a stop beside Ned's window in a cloud of dust.

Knowing something was up, Ned started the engine. "What's wrong?"

"Listen, listen Ned, I'm glad to see you! Wes Clay's killin' Olan Mayfield!"

"Where?"

"Reid's store."

Ned punched the accelerator. The big engine growled and the Plymouth rocketed toward Reid's store only five miles from Center Springs. It was another country stop in the middle of nowhere, offering staples to the rural families living and working the land.

Three agitated men in worn overalls were standing outside of the wooden clapboard store when Ned skidded to a stop on the bottle-cap parking lot. He was out before the engine quit knocking and died.

The oldest of the trio, Cash Wick, pointed. "They's around back, Ned!"

"Did Wes shoot him?"

Horse Nichols shook his head, eyes wide with fear. "Nope. It was a fistfight 'til a knife came out. When Wes started cuttin' on Olan, we got out of there. You know how he is."

Instead of going around the outside, Ned pushed on the Coca Cola screen protector and in through the store. The interior was cool from a slight breeze sucking through the open back door where Harvey Reid was watching through the screen.

He sensed someone behind them and glanced over his shoulder. Ned shushed him and stepped outside to find Olan Mayfield curled up on the sandy ground beside a stack of wooden soft drink cases full of empties. His back was to Ned, but blood was bright on his overalls and blue shirt.

Wes Clay squatted several feet away, watching Olan from the shade of a chinaberry tree. He leaned against a pile of weathered lumber and the bloody knife in his hand dripped blood. Keeping an eye on Wes, Ned closed the distance and edged around Olan to see how bad he was hurt. A thick pool of blood was already skimming in the heat.

"How you doin', Wes?"

His eyes were shaded by the brim of his straw hat and the man didn't look up. "Better'n him."

Ned watched Olan for a second. Sand and grass was caught in his short, thick hair. One gallus on his overalls was down and blood bubbled through a hole in his shirt. Moving slow as molasses, Ned eased closer. He couldn't see any evidence of a second weapon. Flies buzzed, drawn by the coppery odor of blood. "What happened?"

"Aw hell, Ned. I was inside and this son of a bitch come up to the back door. I recognized him as a Mayfield. He's probably the one killed Frank."

"I doubt it."

"I believe he is. I told him to scat on out of here, but he called me white trash and said he could do whatever he wanted, and he was gonna get him a cold strawberry drink whether I liked it or not. He was wrong."

"About doing what he wanted?"

"About getting that strawberry."

Ned started forward to check on Olan. Wes came out of his squat quick as a panther and stepped forward, holding the well-used butcher knife sharp edge up. "Leave him be."

Ned drew and cocked his .38 in one smooth move. Wes stopped at the sight of the gaping barrel aiming at his chest. Ned's mouth was suddenly dry. "I need to check on him."

"No you don't."

"Lower that knife. He needs help."

Fresh drops fell from the fingertips of Wes' empty left hand. A deep slash in his forearm gaped wide showing pink tendons that should have been covered. "No he don't, and he cut me bad with it."

"Back up and do it now before I by-god pull this trigger and you know I'll do it. He's gonna die if we don't get that bleeding stopped."

Wes spread his hands and dropped the knife. "He cut me first with this butcher knife."

"Back up like I said." Ned knelt beside the dying man and peeked into the hole. A pink bubble rose and fell. "How come all this got started?"

"He smart-talked me. I asked him if he knew something about Frank getting killed and he said no, but he didn't care if he was dead or not." He shrugged. "We got to arguin' and before you know it, we went to fightin'. He was gettin' the worst of it and come out with this knife. I took it away from him and he got cut. That's why he's layin' there."

"There's a lot of blood. How much did you cut him?"

"Enough to make him stop. He wouldn't quit." Wes held out his arm so Ned could see the long, bloody wound across a faded hula girl. "I only did what I had to."

"You ain't done nothin' to help him, then."

"I ain't done nothin' else to hurt him, neither."

A long death rattle emptied Olan's lungs.

Wes dropped his arms. "I reckon we're done, now."

"I guess we are." They heard a distant siren. "Sit back down in the shade right there. You're under arrest."

"It was self-defense, Ned." Harvey Reid stood just inside the store, holding the door wide. "We all seen it. They was just fighting 'til Olan pulled out that Old Hickory."

Ned sighed. "It ain't my job to say whether anybody's guilty or innocent. That's what the courts are for. Turn around, Wes. I got to cuff you."

"I'm bleedin'."

"I'll tie if off with the bandana in my pocket after I'm done."

Harvey spoke from the door. "You heard what I said, Ned?"

"I heard you. Get back inside and close the door. You're lettin' flies in."

"All right" Harvey let it slam and spoke through the rusty screen. "Wes, I'm still gonna need a dime for that Coke you drank, too, before you go to jail. I don't reckon you'll want to keep the bottle, so you can forget the deposit."

Chapter Thirty-two

Heat never bothered The Wraith, but the added humidity reminded him of when he hauled hay to make a living. It would be much nicer in Alaska, with a remedied past and a bright future ahead.

Top was laying flat of his back on the porch when Ralston skidded up the drive and slid to a stop beside the porch. He was out in a flash, rushing to Top's side before Mark could get out of the backseat.

Miss Sweet opened the passenger door and struggled with gravity. "Laws, if I only had my legs back. Mark, you get my bag for me."

"Your chicken's getting out."

"Don't' matter none, hon. We'll catch her later. Sweet Jesus, lay your hands on that po' baby 'fore I get there. Hon, I'm a-comin. Ralston!" She shouted his name as if he were a mile away. She finally made it out of the sprung seat. "Is he breathin'? He's so white and still, the poison's probably got to his heart if it was a big snake."

Ralston knelt over the boy's still body. "He's white as a sheet, but he's breathin'. Smells like a whiskey still, though."

"What from?"

Ralston fought down a chuckle, turning it into a cough. "Probably this jar of shine sittin' here beside him."

Miss Sweet frowned and shot Mark a sharp look. "I thought you said he was snakebit. If you boys was drinkin' and got me over here for sinnin', me and Miss Becky both are gonna wear your little white rears plumb out."

"He *is* snakebit." Mark stayed beside the car, unconsciously crossing his heart staring at a huge pool of vomit beside Top's head. "It was the biggest rattler I've ever seen. I chopped it in pieces over yonder if one of y'all wants to look. Me and him thought it would be a good idea to give him a drink of whiskey for the pain. We always heard it was."

She sat on the edge of the porch and blew through her lips. "Get his sock off and let's see the bite."

Ralston raised Top's leg. "Blood's a-running out on the ground. I ain't never see a snake bite bleed so much."

"Well, that ain't right." She leaned forward to see. "Snakebites don't hardly bleed and that's a fact."

Ralston pulled off Top's sock. She twisted the boy around and took his foot. "I don't see no marks." She twisted his calf one way and the other, looking for the bite.

It was Ralston who saw where the blood was coming from. "Bottom of his foot. There's a hole bleeding pretty good."

She twisted Top's whole leg to see his foot. "Why lands. This ain't no snakebite! Praise the Lord! He's done stepped on a nail. Look it went plumb through his shoe. Must have hit a vein to bleed like that."

She started to laugh. "Praise the Lawd. It ain't the poison that's got him, he's feelin' that whiskey."

Ralston joined in. Mark didn't know whether to laugh or cry. He was relieved Top wasn't going to die from the snake bite, but then again, it was him who got the whiskey.

Norma Faye's car turned in the drive and Mark saw Miss Becky's terrified face through the open passenger glass. He figured he'd just as well go inside and pack his sack so they could go ahead and kick him out.

Chapter Thirty-three

I woke up on the couch with my right foot soaking in a bucket. An empty galvanized bucket rested on the floor beside me. My head spun like a cyclone and I leaned over and puked in the pail.

Miss Becky and Miss Sweet came in through the kitchen door and I fell back on the couch and closed my eyes.

"Careful with that foot, baby boy. Don't slosh that coal oil all over your Grandma's linoleum." It was Miss Sweet's old crackly voice.

Someone put a cold washrag on my head and I cracked an eye to see Miss Becky. I started to say something, but my stomach rolled and I puked again.

"Lay back."

I swallowed. "How bad off am I?"

"Not as bad as you'd think." That was Uncle Cody's voice. I twisted my head to see him sitting in Grandpa's black wooden rocker. "Your foot's gonna be sore from stepping on that nail. Your butt's liable to be worse, though, when Ned gets home and finds out you've been into the shine he put back for evidence."

That time everyone laughed, even Miss Becky, and the sound plowed through my head. "I'm not gonna die?"

"No." Miss Sweet gave a pat to the Bible in her lap. "You was lucky. When you jumped away from that snake you stepped on a nail sticking through a piece of trim that blew off the front of the chicken house."

I finally saw Mark standing beside the hall door, looking uncomfortable.

The chair creaked as Uncle Cody rocked. "One question, kiddo. Did y'all get into the whiskey before or *after* you stepped on the nail?"

"I thought I'd been snakebit. I told Mark to get some because my foot was hurting and I figured it might help until he got back." My stomach rolled and clenched again at the thought of the oily moonshine. I choked it down because I didn't want to see the inside of that bucket again.

Uncle Cody chuckled. "All right, then. Y'all are off the hook with me, but Ned's gonna be a different story when he gets home."

When the nausea faded, I twisted around to see Uncle Cody. "I had visions. I thought it was the poison."

"I saw that contraption beside your head. It was most likely a panic attack and an asthma attack at the same time." Miss Sweet whistled through her false teeth. It aggravated her, so she bit them back into place. "You only drank enough whiskey get sick at your stomach. What in the world made you think that was a good idea for snakebite?"

"TV."

"Um hum." Uncle Cody rocked. "That idiot box is gonna be the ruin of us all. I'm taking you to Doc Townsend tomorrow to get you a tetanus shot."

"What's that?"

"Something so you don't get lockjaw from that rusty nail."

I closed my eyes and heat flushed through my body causing them to snap back open. "Uncle Cody..."

"Yeah?"

"I need to tell you what I saw."

"Mark showed me. It was the biggest rattler I've ever seen. Every bit of six feet, and as big around as my arm. Twelve rattles and three buttons. Mark chopped that snake into two dozen pieces for you." He chuckled and everyone laughed with him. "It's a good thing it didn't bite you, cause you'd-a died sure enough."

"No. Not the snake." I told him about my vision, while Miss Becky and Miss Sweet prayed for me and everyone else in Lamar County.

◇◇◇

All the old-timers around Center Springs always said that if you soak a wound in coal oil, it won't hurt as bad later. I believed them, because they've been right about a few other home remedies I'd used.

One was spirits of camphor for burns. It also took the sting of summer out of my skin every time and I barely peeled. The other was turpentine for small cuts. I tore my finger open a year earlier on a barbed-wire fence and Miss Becky wrapped a turpentine-soaked bandage on it for the day. It never did get sore.

I was thinking about that and already feeling better from some kind of awful-tasting tea Miss Sweet dosed me with. She was gone and Grandpa hadn't been home but for a few minutes. He heard our story and didn't do nothing but shake his head. He took off his pistol and laid it beside his hat on the TV set and went into the bathroom to wash up.

Mark went outside to sit on the porch, probably to get away from the butt chewing I was sure to get. The phone rang. Miss Becky answered and listened for a minute. The television was off and the house was so quiet I could hear the man's voice on the other end, asking for Grandpa.

"It's for you, Daddy."

The door was open and he was washing his face and throwing water like a duck taking a bath. "Who is it?"

"He called his name, but I didn't get it. Says he's the medical examiner in Dallas and he has news about that killin' at the fair."

I started to tell her the man's name, but decided not to. If Grandpa knew I could hear, he might hold the phone so I couldn't listen.

He dried his face and replaced his glasses. "That was fast." He took the phone and stood to talk, instead of sitting at the telephone table. "This's Ned."

As I hoped, he didn't put the receiver close to his ear. He never could get past the habit of pushing the receiver too hard and the arm of his glasses hurt his ear.

The voice on the other end came through loud and clear in the quiet house. "Sheriff Parker, this is Dr. Greg Miller. I'm the chief medical examiner here in Dallas. We have the body of Merle Mayfield, who was beaten…" he paused, and I imagined him holding a clipboard and squinting at the writing. "…at a carnival a few nights ago."

"That's right. Y'all must be all caught up. I haven't heard of you getting finished with an autopsy this fast in a long while, but I ain't Sheriff Parker. I'm *Constable* Ned Parker and he was killed in my precinct."

"Well, we're far from caught up, but I found something that you might like to know to aid in your investigation. Your name and number is on this report, but I wonder, should I call the other number here with this information?"

"You can, but it's on my plate, so Sheriff Parker'll tell me as soon as y'all hang up."

"I thought *you* were the sheriff."

"I guess you didn't hear me. We're kinfolk and like I said, I'm constable of Precinct Three."

"Maybe I should call Sheriff Parker first."

Grandpa sighed like he does when he's getting frustrated. He rubbed his head and I knew I was right. "You can if y'ont to, but let's cut out the middle man here. What do you have?"

There was a long pause on the other end of the line. "Well, we were evaluating the body of Merle Mayfield before putting it in storage when we discovered a wound that might change the course of your investigation."

"What's that?"

"The initial report states that the victim was beaten to death with a blunt object, possibly an axe handle found at the scene."

"Yep."

"He was beaten all right. The bludgeon wounds are most obvious, of course, but they weren't the true cause of his death.

During my examination, I found a knife wound high up on the back of his neck in the hairline. Someone knew what he was doing. A sharp, thick blade entered the base of the skull and severed the spinal cord where it meets the brain stem."

"How soon can you get me a full report?"

"Weeks. I only called this soon because I thought you should know about a different cause of death than you expected."

"All right then. Thanks."

"I'm not through"

Grandpa paused. "Go ahead on."

"There's another body here, one Joe Bill Haynes."

"He's the mayor…was, pro-tem, I mean."

"We were asked by Sheriff Parker to expedite this autopsy, due to the fact that he's an elected official. Well, the whole thing was too interesting to pass up, being it was from the same county. In the course of the procedure, I found Mr. Mayfield also died of a severed spinal column. It's my assumption that the two deaths are related. In all my years performing autopsies, I've never seen this before, and since they come from your county and happened close to the same time…"

Grandpa stiffened like somebody shot him. He looked into the big picture-print of a desert landscape above the couch that had been there for years. I don't think he was looking at the picture as much as looking *into* it.

"Hey, wait!"

"Sir?"

"You have two other bodies there. Frank Clay and Maggie Mayfield."

There was a long pause. "Another Mayfield. I didn't make the connection earlier. What about them?"

"Have you finished working on them?"

"Not yet. There's been a lot of business coming our way from y'all. It was a run-of-the-mill automobile accident, so they took a backseat." He chuckled. "Backseat. Car wreck. You get it?"

"Um, hum. See if you can get to them pretty quick. I think all this might be connected."

"I have a lot of other work from other places."

"Yep. I'm sure you do. I'll be waitin' on your call."

Grandpa set the phone in the cradle and stared into the desert for a long time. He was thinking hard with his back to me. He finally turned to face me. "How's your foot?"

"It ain't real good yet."

"I bet. You able to walk?"

"Yessir. It didn't go deep and I've been to the bathroom and back a couple of times. I'll be all right if I don't put any weight on it. It really don't hurt much."

"Good. Now about that whiskey. The next time you kids get into any of that, you won't be able to sit down for a week. Some of that stuff in there was run through radiator coils, and it'll make you go blind, if it don't kill you."

I'd never heard that. "Yessir."

"But I know why you did it." He picked up his hat to leave and stopped. "Don't you say nothin' about what you heard here, neither. That ain't none of your business."

I simply nodded and turned my attention to the trees beyond the screen door and wondered how he knew so much at his advanced age.

Chapter Thirty-four

The Wraith sat in the musty darkness, chewing a tasteless sandwich and hoping no one would come in to check on him. Sometimes he needed to be alone, to calm himself. If he didn't, bad things happened that he couldn't control. He finished and dropped the wax paper at his feet. Testing his work, he stepped on the wooden floor that fell out from under him like a gallows' trap door.

Cody was sitting on the porch, chuckling at Top's adventure and watching birds flitter around the house they'd inherited from Tom Bell. It was rare for him to be home to enjoy such a quiet afternoon. Norma Faye was in the kitchen and could tell something was bothering him because he didn't go back to the office after leaving Ned's house.

She finished the dishes and left them in an aluminum pan to drain. All the windows were open to catch the breeze and because it was still warm, she chipped ice into a glass and filled it with sweet tea.

Cody leaned back against the wall, boots propped on the top rail. The sad look in his eyes disappeared when she stepped through the screen door with the sweating glass. "That looks good and cool."

She grinned and handed it to him. "I figured you'd be warm out here and thought this might help."

He took the glass and she wiped the sheen of sweat on his forehead with her slim hand. She sat on the porch rail with her back against the post so she could see both the yard and Cody. "You know, babe, we've pretty well got it made here."

He drained half the glass and sat it beside her. "You're right about that. Who'da thunk it?"

"Neither one of us four years ago." She laughed. "I'm glad it worked out and you got me."

"Me too."

"I'm glad you're home this afternoon."

"It sure is quiet out here, away from town. I wish I could work out a way to sheriff from this chair. Maybe I need to get a radio out here and then I might not have to go in."

Norma Faye cocked her head. "You gonna tell me what's bothering you?"

"What makes you think anything's wrong?"

"Because you're talking foolish, and you're here now instead of working just like last night. That's not like you. What's wrong?"

He hesitated. "Well, John and Anna think I need to stay away from these murder investigations and let them handle it."

"I think that's a good idea. Your job is to oversee the whole department, not go out investigating."

"It is, but there's another reason."

Her eyebrow arched.

"Somebody may be trying to tie me to these murders."

"How could that happen?"

He told her about his missing pen, and his proximity to the crimes.

She was silent for a long while. "Well, we both know *you're* not killing people."

"Sure, but it don't pass the smell test. Whoever's trying to pin all this on me has to be either a Clay or a Mayfield."

"But why?"

"Well, I've arrested a few Mayfields, and maybe the Clays just want a scapegoat, someone to take all the attention away from them."

"I know what a scapegoat is, but that's a lot of trouble. They can kill each other without taking the trouble to drag you into it. That seems like a stretch."

"I agree, but John and Anna says there's some talk in town. So I'm going into the office to handle the usual, while they stay out and investigate."

"That's the way it should be anyhow. A sheriff has people to investigate for him."

"I feel like I need to poke around some myself."

"Let them do it and you sit back and think. You have plenty of other sheriff stuff on your plate."

"That's the truth."

"What does Ned think about these coincidences?"

Cody shifted his feet on the rail, alternating them to rest one on top of the other. "He didn't say much. You know how he is, but he agreed the best thing is for me to stay here or in the office. I think that's because he can say that if anything else happens, I was in the office, or he knew exactly where I was."

A comfortable silence stretched between them as Cody studied the shadows under the trees. His eyes roamed over the yard to the green circle of grass where Tom Bell had burned lumber scraps while he repaired and updated the house.

A hot lump rose in Cody's throat. The old Texas Ranger appeared out of nowhere one morning to pull Cody out of a bad car wreck. They soon found he was a family member and embraced Tom Bell as he bought the house and renovated it one board at a time. When Cody trailed a gang of drug runners down into Mexico, it was Tom who once again pulled him out of the fire. Shot and dying on a dusty street, the old Ranger fought a cover action as Ned and Cody escaped. One last act came weeks later, when a packet arrived with Tom's name on it. Inside were documents providing for Top and Pepper's education, the deed to the house, and a packet of other sealed envelopes with strict directions on when to open them.

"You know, Old Tom did a good job on this house."

Norma Faye raised her hair to cool her neck. "He did that. This is the nicest place I've ever lived and I can't believe he left it to us."

"That was a surprise to me and Ned, too."

"Why do you think he did that?"

"Because he was a good man, and family."

Norma Faye left the rail and snuggled into Cody's lap. He grunted in fun and she popped his shoulder. "You know what, buddy?"

"What?"

"I'm so glad that I have a good family to be part of."

"We're crazy and seem to attract trouble."

"It keeps things interesting."

He grunted. "Interesting. That's a fact."

She bit his ear. "I know somewhere we can get more comfortable than this old straight chair."

"I'm not finished with my tea."

"Yes you are, and if I'm put under oath later, I can vouch for you that you were right here at home, in the bedroom."

"Tart."

Chapter Thirty-five

The air was so still Friday night that even the top leaves in the trees weren't moving. I went out on the porch about dusk, hoping the humidity wasn't as bad out there as it was in the house. My foot wasn't hurting much, and cabin fever was already setting in.

It didn't help. Pepper and Mark came out with me and sat in the porch light, eating ice she'd chipped off the block in the water bucket. Pepper turned on her transistor radio and we caught the last half of the Beatles singing "Strawberry Fields Forever." She got up and went behind Mark and braided his hair. "You'll look like your ancestors when I'm done."

"I'm not sure they braided their hair much. The movies aren't the best place to learn history."

"It'll look good to *me*."

Grandpa came out and started his car. The motor barely fired over before he slammed in into reverse and backed around. He popped it into gear and rolled down the drive. He waved over his shoulder, slowed at the highway, and when he saw it was clear, steered left toward Arthur City.

Uncle Cody and Norma Faye had been in the kitchen, talking. He came outside and leaned against a porch post. "What're you outlaws up to?"

"Nothing." Pepper kept working on Mark's braids.

"I might have to take you to get that cut pretty soon."

Mark didn't turn around. "If that's what you want."

Pepper bristled. "Why do adults always want to cut boys' hair? You had hair down on your collar just a few years ago, before you were a lawman."

"You're right. But I was shaggy. That's long."

"It don't mean anything."

"It does to some of the folks around here."

She grunted. "That's one of the things I hate about this place. People yap and yap about things that ain't none of their business. You can't squat to pee without somebody knowing about it and telling someone else."

"That's the truth. Top, you sure are quiet this evening."

I'd been listening and thinking after my last dose of the Poisoned Gift. "Uncle Cody, I've been thinking about those ghosts you saw at the Ordway place." I didn't want to talk about seeing Mama by the footlog, but it had been weighing on my mind. "You know I've seen some. Do you believe in 'em?"

He studied on that question for a minute. "Well, there's something to it. I saw spirits that night when I was a kid sure enough, and it makes me think that folks sometimes hang around after they die, but they won't hurt you none. They may even try to help in some way. I worry more about live, crazy people."

He chuckled. "Now, you're Mama's daddy got spooked easy, by ghosts and his imagination both. They say when he lived across the creek there, he'd get scared at night if he heard something outside, especially if he'd been drinking whiskey. He'd get that old twelve-gauge double barrel in there in the closet and crack the door open and holler that if anybody was out there, they'd better get gone. For some reason, one old cedar post always made him think it was somebody that wouldn't run. So he'd holler again, telling them he'd shoot, then after a second, he'd cut loose with one of the barrels because it wouldn't move."

Uncle Cody started laughing, and that was the first time I'd heard him that way in a long time. "I swear, you'd think he'd remember after a time or two, but he scared easy. I heard that post was shot to pieces after a few years and you could get twenty pounds of lead out of it."

It didn't seem as funny to us, but we laughed anyway. Pepper finished with Mark's hair and sat back in her shell-back chair, Indian style. "I'm afraid of ghosts, and that old Ordway place, too. I don't want to live there."

"I believe you. We had ghost stories when I was a kid. Ghosts near the old spring, one in Forest Chapel by a water well. You know there's a story about the hanging tree not far from Uncle Henry's house."

"I haven't heard that one."

He pointed down the highway. "There's a big oak just before you get to Uncle Henry's place. They call it the hanging tree. They used it back in the eighteen hundreds, when Center Springs was a good-sized town. Remember, Neal Box's store was the courthouse, and the old judge who sat in there sentenced more than one man to hang. They took 'em out to that big tree in Uncle Henry's pasture to do it."

He jerked his head to the west. "Them old men hung folks from the big wide limb that's lowest to the ground. You can still see ghosts there by the light of the moon."

That perked us up. "You just go up there and look?"

"No. There's a certain way you have to do it. You know, that limb grows straight out to the west. So the story goes that at midnight on a full moon, you come up from the east in single file so's the tree's between you and the limb. Then one at a time, while the others stand still, you close your eyes, put your hand on the trunk and back around it three times, real slow. Each time you have to recite some lines. Halfway around on the fourth time, you lean your back against the tree and open your eyes while them on the other side touch the tree. If it's the right night, the one who does the backing will see the ghost of a horse thief hanging there named, Shotgun Bob Goodell."

Mark laughed. "That's a load of horse manure."

Uncle Cody joined him. "I thought so too, but I saw the ghost when I was about y'all's age."

"Let's do it!" Pepper jumped up.

"When?"

"Tonight." She turned to Mark. "How about it?"

"I'm in. It's Friday night and it's a full moon. Uncle Cody, you come go with us, like you did that time you took Pepper and Top hog hunting. I've heard all about..." He stopped all of a sudden and I knew why. Even though we had fun, it happened the night all of Mark's family was murdered.

I didn't want him to feel bad, now that those old memories had come up, so I piped up. "Let's do it. You haven't been able to take us camping or nothing for a long time."

Uncle Cody thought about it for a minute and grinned. "You know, I've been taking some time away from the office, so that'll be good for me too. Can you walk on that bad foot, Top?"

"If we go slow."

"Well, let's do it then." He went back inside to clear the way, and we stayed there on the porch and watched the moon come up.

All three of us were tickled to death to go on another adventure with Uncle Cody, just like it was when he was single and not a sheriff.

Chapter Thirty-six

Done for the night with one particular job, The Wraith drove down the dirt road and killed his truck in front of the house. He should have been at work, but figured he'd make one more stop before he got there. No one would notice his absence, because he was filling in for a friend and that job made him invisible to his boss.

Everyone has a mama, even someone who called himself The Wraith. He hadn't seen her in years and figured it was time to drop by for a visit. The dew was wet on the grass when he pulled up in the yard and killed the engine on his worn out truck.

He waited for old Rock to come barking out from under the porch. Instead, there was nothing but an owl hooting down on the creek and the chickens in the brooder house settling in for the night. The cicadas were silent, building strength for another long, hot day of singing.

The Wraith stopped at the bottom porch step as childhood memories flooded in, breathing the good country smells of cattle and grass. The porch light came on to reveal his gray-haired mother behind the screen in a faded house dress.

She held the door open with one shoulder, wiping her hands on a damp dishtowel. "Well, I declare. Look what the cat dragged in."

He ran grease-stained fingers through his hair. "Howdy Mama."

She pointed with a gnarled finger. "You look poor as a snake. Are all you hippies that skinny all the time?"

"I work hard. Not much time to eat, and I ain't no hippie. Where's Rock?"

"Dead. Buried over yonder." She waved the dishtowel toward a bois'd arc tree.

"What killed him?"

"Sump'in bigger'n him. You been to supper yet?"

"Nope."

"Well, come on in and I'll fix you a bite. I can fry you up some bacon and eggs."

He followed her inside. The kitchen hadn't changed since he was a kid. The same battered tin pans hung on the walls. Limp gingham curtains over the window did little to improve the looks of a chipped enamel sink. He pulled out a wooden chair that creaked on the scrubbed wooden floor.

She lit the stove with a wooden match and laid a rasher of bacon in a cast-iron skillet. "Where you been living?"

"On the road."

"They don't have razors on the road?"

He rubbed his caved in cheek, hollow on one side from several teeth knocked out in a fight four years earlier. "Saving money on razors by shaving once a day, and that was 'bout noon yesterday. It gives us a little extra to feed the baby."

She paused without looking at him. "You get a baby?"

"I'm living with a gal who has one."

"You're not married?"

"Nope."

"Is it yours?"

"I done told you, the baby's hers."

"It's a sin to live with a woman without being married to her."

He hadn't wanted to get on that subject, and here they were in the middle of it not five minutes after coming through the door. "Well, the first time I stood in front of a preacher didn't work out, did it?"

She turned the frying bacon over. "How long you here for?"

"A day or two."

"You smell like grease. You working on cars?"

He examined his caked fingernails and picked at a white matter caked at the edges of his nails. "I work with machinery when I'm not doing other things."

"There's a dishpan full of soapy water right there."

He stepped up to the warped plywood counter and dipped his hands in the lukewarm water, knowing it wouldn't help cut all the grease out from under his nails. He dried them with a damp dishtowel and sat back down.

The kitchen was quiet except for the sizzling bacon. She pushed the strips aside and cracked three eggs into the pan. "You don't need to go over there."

He knew what she was talking about. "I just wanted to come see you."

"When'd you say you got in?"

"Didn't for sure. A while back."

"And you're just now coming in to see me? Ain't had a letter or a word nor a phone call in four years. I's thinkin' maybe you was gonna be like your old man and just disappear for the rest of my life." She flipped the eggs over and reached for a clean plate from the drain pan on the counter.

He sat back out of the way for her to slip the plate onto the table. She remembered. The fried eggs were just as he liked them, crunchy on the edges, the yolk still runny.

"She's married now."

"I know it, Betsy."

"You call me Mama." She poured a glass of milk and thumped it on the table. She sat opposite him and tucked a stray strand of gray-blond hair behind her ear. "It's done. Go on and live your life."

Anger rose in his face. "When someone steals a part of you, you can't help take it back."

"You done said yourself you got another woman and a baby. That should be enough for any man."

"They ain't mine." His eyes burned as he forked eggs into his mouth and chewed on the left side.

"Neither was she. Then or now. Never was. She won't go with you, even if you was to talk to her, and you for sure ain't *taking* her back."

"Don't care. I'll make my point."

"You said you wasn't going over there."

Trapped, he saucered his coffee to think. "Let's talk about something else."

She laced her fingers and sighed. The conversation stalled and she looked around the kitchen that had been her domain for forty years, searching for something to discuss with a son who had never been close. Her eyes flicked to the screen door, out past the porch light, and into the darkness beyond. "I hear tell there's a traveling carnival set up north of Powderly."

The Wraith swallowed and cut another bite of leathery eggs. "Do tell."

Chapter Thirty-seven

It was full dark and we were buzzing with excitement about seeing ghosts. Uncle Cody and Norma Faye drove us to their house and we piled out in the yard. She laughed because for the first time in a long while, Uncle Cody seemed like his old self. "I didn't know I was married to a big kid."

"Yes you did." He pulled her close and gave her a kiss right there in the yard with us watching. "I bet you want to go, too."

I wanted to turn away, but watching them was fun at the same time. She pushed him away and grinned. Even in the full moonlight, her red hair glowed. "You'd lose that bet, mister. You kids go play and try not to wake me up when you come home."

He slapped her on the butt. "I might just do the opposite." She raised an eyebrow and he laughed again. "See, that's what happens when you make them bedroom eyes at me."

"Shush!" She punched him in the chest. "Behave yourself and y'all get out of here."

Pepper saw me frowning and leaned close. "They're feeling sexy."

"Huh?"

"They're talking about making whoopee."

I knew what she meant, because I watched *The Dating Game* on TV. That embarrassed me something awful, and I was glad it was full dark, because my ears got hot and I knew Pepper would make fun of me for not understanding at first. Mark stood off to the side, staring into the darkness like he was looking for something.

Uncle Cody saved me. "Let's go see a ghost."

"Norma Faye's not going with us?"

"Nope. She's gonna go back and visit with Miss Becky for a while and then go home. C'mon you outlaws."

He led the way with a flashlight in one hand and a pump shotgun in the other. The light was off because the moon was so bright we could see just fine without it.

Pepper was right behind him, complaining. "I got sweat running in my eye and the skeeters are driving me nuts. Ain't there a better way?"

We cut across the yard and over a barbed-wire fence. "We could walk down the highway I guess, but then we'd come up on the wrong side of the tree. Remember, you can't see the limb first or it won't work."

"It don't matter." Mark's voice came from behind, as we walked in single file. "I like the woods at night."

Uncle Cody followed a cow path that led across the small pasture. Deer used those paths too, and I limped along hoping we'd jump one and it'd scare Pepper. The trail wound around a thick locust bush and through a big patch of bull nettles until it led into the woods. The moonlight wasn't as bright under the trees, but we could still see just fine. Moldy leaves rustled underfoot and the smell of dampness rose in the air.

Something flew off a limb with a great, soft flapping of wings. "Owl," Uncle Cody said.

He stopped at the bottom of a small gully. "Y'all feel that cold air?"

It was warm one minute, and then I walked through a pocket of cool air. "I did."

"Me too." Pepper's voice was loud in the still night. "What was it?"

"A ghost. They wander around, lost. Their spirits turn the air chilly, and you always know when you walk through one."

I knew good and well he was trying to scare us, but I felt goosebumps prickle on my arms and neck just the same.

Mark cupped both hands around his mouth. "*Woooo.*"

Uncle Cody pointed in the silver moonlight. "Careful kids. It's a little boggy there, so watch when you jump across that little trickle." He hopped to the other side and started back uphill.

We came out in another pasture and it was bright as day. The path wound around bushes and whatever the cows didn't want to walk over, or through. We made good time to the next line of trees. This time there wasn't a gully, but we had to cross another barbed-wire fence.

A truck went by on the highway, its headlights flickering through the trees. A cottontail bounced up to the right and ran away. It scared Pepper. "*Eek!* I've had about enough of this."

Mark and I laughed to bleed off our own nervousness. The next pasture rose steep on the other side of the fencerow. Uncle Cody walked along with the shotgun on his shoulder like he was hunting quail. A whippoorwill called and other night birds peeped all around us.

He finally slowed when we reached the last barbed-wire fence. "All right guys, we cross this and the tree is right out there in the middle of the pasture."

"I hope nothing don't get us," I said in an eerie voice like Gorgon, the spooky guy that hosted *Nightmare* theater out of Dallas on Saturday nights. My foot ached a little and the bottom of my sock felt damp. I was afraid the hole was leaking blood, but it wasn't enough to stop me. I was having fun.

"Shut up. You're not spooking me." Pepper's voice was strong, but it had a little waver to it and I realized she was nervous. She yelped when Mark goosed her from behind. "*Yeep!* Shit!" She slapped his shoulder. "Mark, dammit. I'd expect that out of Top."

Uncle Cody slipped around me and grabbed her around the waist, snarling like a wolf. She jumped a good foot and fell into Mark, who almost went down with her. She caught her balance and thinking it was me, swelled up to give me a good butt chewing.

"Top, dammit!" She stopped all of a sudden when she saw it was Uncle Cody and gave him a push, laughing.

He stopped and spoke softly, like someone was close by and might hear him. "All right. Now listen, you have to do this the right way or it won't work. I saw a ghost hanging there when I did it. It was all pale, and bloated, and its tongue was sticking out."

"What did you do?" I think Pepper was hoping he'd say he ran.

"Nothing at first. I saw it as clear as day, but then when its eyes opened, I ran like a turpentined cat."

Her mouth opened in shock. "It *looked* at you?"

"Just like this." Uncle Cody leaned close to her. When he figured he was close enough, he opened his eyes wide and dropped his jaw.

Pepper jumped back with a squeal. I swear I could see goose-bumps on her bare arms.

Mark grabbed her and she hollered again. "Dammit. Y'all *stop*."

Uncle Cody laughed. "All right. Who wants to see the ghost first?"

I almost raised my hand like I was in class. "Don't we all get to?"

"You might, if the first person stays right there and is really quiet and don't scream or holler or nothing."

Pepper came up with an idea. "Rock, paper, scissors."

Mark shrugged. "Sounds good to me. Top, call it."

We gathered close and made fists. "Okay, one, two, three!"

We slapped our fists in our palms, and on three, each one of us made a shape.

Two rocks and a scissors. Mark was out.

Pepper and I did it again. This time I was paper and Pepper was scissors.

"You win." Uncle Cody took her arm and positioned her in front of him. "All right. Forget the trail now. Walk straight through the grass and stop when you get to the tree. Don't peek around and then we'll perform the ceremony.

She led through the bitterweeds and tickle grass. The green smell of crushed weeds rose as we crossed the pasture. Pepper walked with both arms straight down at her sides like she was tied up or something. I think it was because she was scared, but she'd never admit it.

The tree stretched out overhead. It was one of the oldest on our part of the river. An image of angry men and wagons and horses came to mind as I thought about the hangings that had occurred right there in the past.

Heat lightning flickered and backlit the tree and made the scene even creepier. Uncle Cody winked at me in the cold moonlight. His voice was even softer so that only I could hear. "Let's have some fun with Pepper."

I knew he had something up his sleeve and felt better. "Okay."

"All right, girl. Put your hand against the tree." She did, and he waved us forward. "Straight line. Boys, stay here. Pepper, close your eyes and back around the tree counterclockwise and slow so you won't fall, and recite, "*Oh living Tree of Death, help me see. Spirit show yourself, spirit come to me!*"

"I can't remember all that shit."

"Watch your language. I'll lead and y'all follow. Three times. One time each as you back around. Guys, close your eyes too."

Uncle Cody stepped behind me and put his hand on my shoulder. "Pepper, keep your hand on the tree. Recite with me boys."

We joined him, about half a beat behind. "*Oh living Tree of Death, help me see. Spirit show yourself, spirit come to me!*"

She made the first revolution slow, to be sure she didn't trip over any branches. "Shit!" she whispered.

"Pepper, dang it. Watch your mouth."

"I stepped in cowshit, *again!*"

We laughed and Uncle Cody urged her on. "It ain't the first or the last time. Now, do it again."

This time our voices were stronger, drowning Pepper's. She was concentrating more on not falling than saying the words.

"*Oh living Tree of Death, help me see. Spirit show yourself, spirit come to me!*"

I peeked and saw a slight breeze catch the eagle feather in her hair and flick up and out. *She made the second time just fine.*

"*Oh living Tree of Death, help me see. Spirit show yourself, spirit come to me!*"

Uncle Cody was holding Pepper's shoulder to keep her still. "That's the third. Now, back around to the other side and stop when I tell you and look up at that big old limb above you. One more time, boys, to get her there."

Oh living Tree of Death, help me see. Spirit show yourself, spirit come to me!

Pepper stopped and we waited.

The night was still and I heard her breathing hard, like I do when I have asthma, but she was making a sound like "*huh, huh, huh.*"

Before we could ask if she could see the ghost, she cut loose with a piercing shriek that I thought at first was fake to give us a thrill, but then realized it was the sound of sheer terror. Uncle Cody charged around me in a rush.

Mark and I followed and stopped to see Pepper with her back against the giant trunk, pointing at a still figure hanging from the limb. The hair on the back of my neck rose and I shivered. Me and Mark laughed for a second, thinking Uncle Cody had hung up a dummy.

Three long seconds passed.

The heat lightning flickered again, outlining the figure. Uncle Cody grabbed Pepper's arm and drug her toward him, burying her face in his chest. "Boys! Turn around now!"

We didn't move. It wasn't a dummy.

"Do it!"

It was a real person.

Pepper was sobbing in his chest and I got a look at Uncle Cody's face in the pale moonlight. It was something I never wanted to see again, just like the sight of that man hanging from the tree limb, his neck crooked, and his swollen tongue sticking out.

I heard Mark's shuddering breath and I puked on my shoes.

Chapter Thirty-eight

This was more entertaining than a carnival Funhouse. The Wraith checked the bindings on the terrified man and chuckled when he groaned. The poor guy had been in the wrong place at the wrong time with the right last name. His death would mean nothing in the long run, but it just might be the spark The Wraith was looking for. He was running out of time.

The headlights of half a dozen vehicles lit the area around the hanging tree.

The Parker lawmen, Deputy John Washington, and Justice of the Peace Buck Johnson watched two men cut the body down into the bed of a pickup backed under the great oak. They gently lowered the corpse onto a sheet and Buck climbed into the back with a hissing Coleman lantern.

Ned studied the darkness around their circle of light, absently rubbing the healed bullet wound in his ample stomach, and sick at the thought of still another murder. He worried about the effect on his kids who were back home. Fifteen years old and they'd seen more violence and killing than most men who'd been in the army.

A cluster of onlookers stood on the highway beside John's car. Its flashing lights were bright and sharp in the night. Ned realized the Wilson boys weren't there. That was unusual for the brothers, because they usually showed up at the first sign of trouble, especially on a bright night when they were most likely running the bottoms.

A voice cut through the knot of men. "Sheriff, y'all better come look at this."

"Uh uh. There's been enough tramping around here. Pull the truck back to the gap and we'll talk there." Ned waved toward the road. The pickup carefully backed from under the limb, following its tracks to disturb as little of the area as possible. The driver parked it on the shoulder.

After a cursory exam, Buck went through the dead man's pockets and came back to the cluster of lawmen. "John, would you hold this lantern so I can see?"

"Sure 'nough." John took the wire handle and raised it high. The man's face was so swollen it was unrecognizeable.

Buck opened the wallet. An accordion of photographs flipped out as he located a driver's license. "It's Charlie Clay."

"Ol' Charlie." Ned's voice wavered. "He never done nothin' to nobody."

"He was born a Clay." Buck slipped the wallet into his back pocket.

Ned studied the gap in the fence where Cody had cut the wires to allow the vehicles into the pasture. John's car parked on the highway in front of the gate protected the soft dirt so they could take plaster casts of the tracks, if there were any. "How long do you figure he was hangin' there?"

"Not long after dark."

Several farmers gathered around the lowered tailgate. The ambulance driver pointed with the beam of his flashlight. "Look, y'all. Somebody knocked him in the head first."

"That explains how he got him out here in the pasture. His hands ain't even tied."

Cody leaned forward. "You think he was dead when they hung him?"

"Naw. See, his tongue is sticking out and his face is swelled. A feller has to be alive for that to happen." Buck lifted one arm. "He was tied at one time, though. His wrists are raw."

"What's that?" Cody leaned close to the length of cut rope nearly two feet from the noose buried in the man's grotesquely swollen neck. He reached out a finger and touched a smear of white. Some stuck to his index finger and he rubbed it against his thumb. "Buck, is this some kind of grease?"

Cody held his hand out and Buck sniffed. "I don't know what it is."

John shook his head. "I ain't never seen nothin' like it. You know much about him?"

Ned frowned. "Naw. As far as I know, he goes to work and comes home."

"What does he do?"

"Machine shop."

"Well, that might explain that grease, then. He married?"

"Yep. Couple of kids." Ned pursed his lips. "Cody, you want to call his wife, or me?"

"It don't make no difference."

They drifted toward John's car and heard Martha Wells over the Motorola. "Cody?"

John dropped into the seat and keyed the microphone. "This is Washington."

She came back. "John. Glad you answered. Tell Ned there's a house afire in Arthur City."

John looked up at Cody. "You get that?"

"Yep."

"Martha, where's the house? Who's is it?"

"Don't know. It's about ten miles off 1499."

"That'll take a while to get to." Cody straightened to see Ned. He waved him over.

John keyed the mike. "Is the fire department on the way?"

"Yep, but you know how long it takes those boys to get together and go."

Even in the best of circumstances, volunteer fire departments took a long time to arrive at the scene of fire. Those living at the ends of dirt roads could expect to wait even longer.

The radio squawked again. Deputy Anna Sloan's voice came through. "John, is Cody there with you?"

"Sure is. Right here with Ned."

"Cody, Martha just got a report of another house fire four miles from the one I just told you about. It's Charlie Clay's. Hang on."

"Goddamn it!" Ned started for his car. He stopped, realizing it wouldn't make any difference to Charlie, who was covered in a sheet in the back of the pickup. He rocked from side to side, anxious to do something, but no matter where he went, he'd most likely wind up standing around while houses burned and people lost everything they had.

The lawmen waited for a long moment. Ned's stomach sank in his chest at the next transmission. It was Martha again. "Y'all. Matt Clay was found cut up in the parking lot at the bowling alley."

John rose. "It's gonna get worse. Cody, you realize this body is right here beside your house, don't you?"

"Yeah, and the dead man's house is burning down." Ned shuffled from one foot to the other like a sprinter at the start of a race.

Cody lifted the microphone in John's car. "I'm gonna send some deputies to those houses and get some more people out on the roads."

The back doors of the Travers and Williams Funeral Home ambulance slammed. Those nearby spoke softly, and their conversations faded out as the station wagon made a U-turn on the highway and accelerated.

Ned watched the taillights disappear into the darkness. John's radio squawked with information about the fire and murders. "All right. I'm going to them house fires."

Cody hung the microphone on its bracket. "I got deputies hitting the road. We're gonna be all over this part of the county until this calms down."

"I hope that's enough."

Cody stood. "This feud's gotten out of hand."

Ned shook his head. "Make no mistake about it. This ain't no feud. This is a war."

◇◇◇

Deputy Anna Sloan pulled off on the side of the dark road, careful not to get too far into the ditch. Several trucks were parked in the light from the burning house that was completely engulfed.

She met Jimmy Dale Warner, one of the first locals to come across Frank and Maggie's wreck. He was one of several volunteer firemen working the blaze. "We can't do nothing for thissun. It's too far gone."

"Who does it belong to?"

"Charlie and Loretta Clay."

"She in there?"

"Nope. It's empty. Someone said she's visiting their boy, Kenneth, in Sulphur Springs, but nobody knows where Charlie is."

Standing in the middle of the road, Anna watched the men rolling the hose as they retreated from the heat. "I do."

"Well, that's good that he ain't in there."

She didn't pursue the conversation any further. "Are you going to the other fire?"

"There's another'n?"

"Heard it on the radio. It's about four or five miles down the road."

Jimmy Dale thought for a moment. "There's only one house that close, and it belongs to some niggers."

"So?"

"They're Mayfields to boot. We'd have to go back and fill up the pump truck. There ain't nothing we can do."

Anna's chest hurt at the helplessness of it all. "These are people's houses. It's all they have."

"Well, I know it. We can stand out here and watch them burn, or we can go get some more water and maybe help the next 'uns that ain't so far gone when we get there."

She backed a couple of steps from the rising heat. "What do you mean?"

"This one was set, it looks like to me, and if a Mayfield house is afire too, it means there's likely to be more."

The roof collapsed, sending a great cloud of sparks into the sky like fireworks. Shouts from the men filled the air as they rushed to back their trucks out of danger. Jimmy Dale and Anna retreated to her car and her stomach clenched at the thought that she could do nothing that night but patrol in the vain hope of catching the arsonists at work.

Her Motorola came alive. "Anna?"

She reached through the open door for the microphone. "Go ahead, Martha."

"John and Cody are heading to town to see about Matt Clay. They don't think he's gonna make it. Ned's still tied up with the hanging. Cody said you need to go go back to 271 and look for any suspicious activity. Said y'all aren't doing any good going where trouble's already been."

"On my way." Her back tires spun on the warm oil road as she rushed toward still another murder scene with little hope of catching the killer. The thought kept running through her mind that Cody was right. Most law enforcement officials responded to incidents and did little to *prevent* the crimes from happening.

It wasn't the way she wanted to serve the people of Lamar County.

Chapter Thirty-nine

It's funny, but after everything we'd seen in the past few years, the sight of a dead man hanging from a tree limb didn't affect us the way you'd expect, other than me puking my guts out for the fourth time that day. Oh it was bad, that's for sure, and any other kids than us might have troubles down the road, but it seemed at the time that we lived in a swarm of bad stuff and we'd grown calluses to handle it.

Uncle James came to carry Pepper home. She bucked and snorted about it, but he got that new look in his eye that Grandpa said came from their troubles in Arizona. Pepper saw it and settled down right quick.

Grandpa left after he dropped us off at the house. Mark and I talked after we went to bed. The lights were out and we kept it low so Miss Becky wouldn't hear.

His voice was low in the darkness. "I wish Pepper hadn't seen that."

"I wish none of us had."

"I feel like I've brought bad spirits to this house again."

"Hey, Tonto. Don't start feeling that way. It seems like we always live in a cyclone. Since you left there've been gangsters and everything else."

His voice made me think he was grinning. "Watch that Lone Ranger crap. I'll get a medicine man after you."

"Pepper'll be fine. She's tougher than either one of us."

"She was crying pretty hard."

"Yep, but she wasn't cussin' like she used to. She's changed since she run off to California."

"She seems the same to me."

"Well, she's not. Her cussin' ain't as bad, and she don't get mad like she did, neither. Now she pretty much takes things as they come and goes on about her business."

"That might not be good. She's packing it down instead of dealing with it."

I started to answer, but didn't. I knew about packing things down. It was easier than talking about what plagued us. I needed to change the channel pretty quick, or the pain welling up in my chest might get free. I didn't want that right then.

"Hey, talkin' about Tonto, did you hear the one about the Lone Ranger who went in the saloon?"

Mark was quiet for a minute. "No. I guess you're gonna tell me."

"*Yep*. The Lone Ranger and Tonto were at the bar when a cowboy runs in and hollers, 'Whose white horse it that outside?'"

"The Lone Ranger says, 'It's mine. Why?'

"The cowboy says, 'Well, it's hot out there and he don't look too good.'

"They run outside and Silver's in bad shape in the sun. The Lone Ranger hollers at Tonto to get his turkey wing fan and cool Silver down. Tonto gets it out of his saddlebag and starts fanning. The Lone Ranger sees it might be doing some good and tells Tonto to run in circles around the horse and fan while he goes back in the saloon to get a bucket for water. Tonto starts running and fanning as fast as he can. While the Ranger's inside, another cowboy walks in and wants to know who owns the white horse. The Lone Ranger says, 'That's mine,' and the cowboy says 'Well, did you know you left your Injun running?'

"Get it. Engine running. Injun?"

Mark threw his pillow at me and dove over to get me in a headlock. We rasseled for a minute until Miss Becky hollered at us to stop and go to sleep.

We laid there in the dark, giggling and then it got quiet. A whippoorwill called in the dark and it sounded peaceful.

Mark's quiet voice came from the other bed. "Hey."

"What?"

"I know you're half Indian, but full-blood Choctaw is different. Our people were one of the Five Civilized Tribes. We had a written language, and a Bible, and lived in houses and had land." He was quiet for a long minute. "Sometimes those jokes like that hit a little too close to home. You know what I mean?"

I felt bad. "I didn't mean nothing."

We laid there quiet for a minute until his voice came again. "Hey."

"What?"

"You know why Kennedy is so hot to get to the moon?"

"No. Why?"

"'cause he thinks Indians have land up there."

I had to think about that a minute, and then got tickled. I knew it was his way of saying I'd hurt his feelings, but everything was all right. I decided then and there I wouldn't tell Indian jokes anymore.

I finally dropped off and dreamed all that night about running from a dark man who was bathed in colored lights and there were people screaming and laughing and then he chased me into a house and the halls were long and chopped up into a maze and I couldn't get away and something was making a cawing noise that finally woke me up. When I opened my eyes, it was nothing but crows greeting the day outside my window.

Chapter Forty

After a breakfast of three cold boiled eggs, The Wraith grunted, braced his feet and applied so much pressure with both scarred and powerful hands that his spine popped. The rusted nut screeched loose. He quickly disassembled the big engine, his mind not on the task at hand, but the coming night's work. By now, he should have pushed enough Clay and Mayfield buttons to start World War III, but it hadn't exploded the way he wanted, and Cody Parker was still above suspicion for the most part. He wanted more. He wanted them all to pay.

The sun was up when Deputy Anna Sloan and Constable Ned Parker left the smoldering remains of the house fire in Tigertown and drove to Powderly to find Royal Clay. He'd heard the leader of the clan had been seen loafing with his cousins out front of the Powderly school and Ned intended to have words with him.

The Wilson boys showed up earlier that night and though they weren't volunteers with the local fire department, they threw in to help. Ned arranged for Jimmy Foxx to drive his car to the house when they finished so he could ride with Anna.

She steered down the winding country road. "We don't have anything to arrest Royal for. We can't prove he had anything to do with any of this."

"You're right about that, but every time anything happens from now on, I'm gonna be right there in his face. Either he'll back down, or get mad enough to try and do something about it. I believe he's the spark on the Clay side and I intend to put him out, or cause him to flare up at me. Royal has a short fuse, and when he goes off, I'll slap the cuffs on his ass and take him to jail."

"Neither one of us is in any kind of shape to get into an altercation with him."

"By that I reckon you mean get in a fight. If I thought that was gonna happen, I'd-a brought John with me."

She stifled a grin. "You don't think I can handle myself."

His eyes cut sideways. "You do all right, but these boys are mean and they're apt to get meaner."

"Why?"

"Because I'm gonna be a tick where the sun don't shine. Every time they look up, they're gonna see me. I'll be there when they go to the outhouse, and in the churchyard every time they come out from services."

"Not by yourself. I'll be there with you."

"Good. John's doing the same thing with some of the Mayfields. We're gonna shake something loose."

Deputy Sloan turned on the highway and accelerated to the north. "So this is our next move?"

"For the time being. After we finish here, we're going home to get some sleep. Then this afternoon we're gonna find some Clays and start all over."

"He'll claim we're harassing them."

"What does that mean?"

Her eyes crinkled in amusement. "That's what the kids say if they think somebody's picking on them."

"They'll be right."

Anna tapped the wheel with her fingertips. "And John's doing the same thing?"

"Yep. These people are going to see us in their sleep before it's over with."

They came in sight of the WPA gym and saw three vehicles clustered in the dirt parking lot. Deputy Sloan hit her lights and slowed to a stop.

Nine men were gathered around Royal Clay who was sitting on his open tailgate. They included the kinfolk Ned and John saw when they were fishing the rat from Wes' well. Andy, Martin, Wilbur, and the youngest, Cecil, looked as if they wanted to bolt when Anna killed her engine.

Royal was in jeans and a dingy white tee shirt with a pack of cigarettes rolled up in the left sleeve. His brow furrowed when Ned stepped out of the car. "What's the matter, constable?"

"Got a report of loiterin'."

"Here in the school yard? Somebody called you on *that?*"

Instead of answering the question, Ned closed the distance, watching the men and their hands. He noted they all needed a shave, something unusual in a community that leaned toward a razor every morning. They also smelled like smoke, which was often the case out in the country. "What're you boys doing out here so early? Y'all been up all night?"

Royal puffed up like a banty rooster at the question. "We're fixin' to go fishing."

"Why're you *here?*"

"This was the best place to meet up."

"I don't see no fishing poles."

Anna craned her neck to look in the bed of the nearest truck. "None in here, neither."

Royal grinned and flipped the pack from his sleeve. He shook one loose and lipped it out. "Well, now that you're here, sweetheart, I might have another suggestion that sounds better'n fishin'."

She grinned back, stuck out her chest even more, and closed the distance until she was almost standing between his spread knees. "I have one, too." Her voice was low, sultry.

Royal removed the unlit cigarette from his lips and leaned closer, resting his right hand on the swell of her hip below her gunbelt. "Do tell."

He was unable to speak for the next few moments when the sap that had been in her back pocket cracked against the inside his knee. When Royal yelped, Anna snatched his collar, yanking him off the tailgate and face-first into the dirt. The others snapped to attention.

"Easy boys." Ned's voice was soft and steady. "That gal didn't get much sleep last night and she's feelin' fretful."

Royal spat grit from his teeth and groaned into the dirt. Ned addressed Andy, who was standing closest. "Where were y'all going fishin' before Royal fell off the tailgate and hurt his knee?"

"Uh, the river."

"Whereabouts on the river?"

"Uh, well, he, uh, ain't told us yet."

"Don't you boys need poles and bait?"

"That's what we was talkin' about when y'all rolled up."

Anna knelt to help Royal to his feet. "That hurts, I know. I've fell and hurt my knee the same way. It's liable to swell up, so if I was you, I'd stay off it for a day or two." She picked up his cigarette and stuck it behind his ear.

Gritting his teeth, Royal Clay stood and propped himself against the tailgate. "Y'all ain't got no call to come around here doing that."

"Royal, you boys need to listen to me." Ned spoke to them as if they were visiting at the store. "I believe one or more of y'all were involved in a lynching and a few incidents of arson last night."

"You can't prove nothing." Wilbur said.

"That's mighty interesting."

"What?"

"You didn't act surprised, ner asked who it was. All you want to do is argue about proof. Most people'd say they didn't do it."

Wilbur shrugged. "Well, like I said, you can't prove nothing one way or another."

"Might be able to. We got some plaster casts of the tread on the truck they used to drive him out to the tree and other evidence I'm not inclined to tell you about right now. Now y'all listen to me. This bullshit with the Mayfields is gonna stop."

"No one here knows nothin' about that." Royal doubled over the tailgate, supporting the weight on his stomach. He rubbed his knee as if that would take away the pain. "For all you know, we was camped out, or up at the hospital to set with Matt."

"He wasn't talking to you, Royal honey." Anna squeezed his shoulder as if he was a little kid who'd fallen and scratched his knee. "You need to be quiet."

Ned watched Cecil. He'd been looking everywhere but at nothing. "Nobody has to tell me right now. You can call the house with the information if you want, or come see me."

Cecil Clay chewed a lip. His tie-dyed shirt was faded, and the big bell bottoms on his jeans were frayed at the heels from being walked on. "We don't know a thing. You pigs ought to be working on how Uncle Matt got cut up last night instead of harassing us."

Cecil was the youngest, and spent a lot of time hanging out with radical college kids who were marching against the war, the police, and anything else that took their fancy.

Genuinely surprised, Ned relied on Anna for an explanation. "Pigs?"

"That's a new city term the hippies are using for policemen."

Disgusted, Ned drew a deep sigh. "That's the second time in fifteen minutes I heard that word, harassment. And now I'm a pig? Son, you better learn some manners before your elders take you out behind the barn."

"Look, get off of that." Cecil moved slightly closer to Andy Clay, as if for protection. "We heard Uncle Matt's guts was stickin' through his shirt."

"But nobody saw a Mayfield do it?"

Andy rubbed the stubble on his chin. "No. The guy slashed him between parked cars. You can bet it was a Mayfield, though, blending in the dark and all."

"I need proof."

"You won't do anything nohow."

"I'm-a doin' something now, Andy."

"Yeah, I call it harassment, and we don't need that from the local pigs." Cecil seemed to like spouting off memorized rhetoric.

"Call it what you want, Cecil. Give me whoever's causing from your side and I'll be gone."

"Them niggers is the ones squared off with *us*."

"I don't want to hear that word no more. I want the name of them that burned down Curtis Mayfield's house last night, too."

The exchange of glances told Ned there were a lot more folks involved than he thought. "We need to end this thing before some women or kids get killed. The truth of the matter is that if I had my druthers, y'all could kill one another all you want, if you was out of my county. But I don't. And you're in my pocket and I have to do something about it."

Anna spoke up. "Royal, honey. You like what you see when you look at me?"

He frowned, but kept both eyes on his knee.

"Well, you don't have to answer, but know this. From now on, every time you walk outside, you're gonna see me within an hour, or Ned. I hope you enjoy our company."

Ned tilted his hat back. "Well, that's about it, boys. C'mon, Anna. Let's go get some breakfast, and then we'll drop by one of these boys' houses after we eat."

She gave them a brilliant smile. "Sounds like a good idea. Y'all better hope I get in a little nap before we come back, though. I'm starting to get the cramps and none of y'all want to irritate me after that."

"We won't be there." Andy set his jaw. "We're going fishing, like we said."

"Well then, you'll have a mess of fish to fry when we show up. Tell your wives that we'll stay for dinner, too, if we's to be asked." Ned turned on his heel and went back to the car. Anna held back, moving slower so he could get to the door first. "Bye."

Ned watched her walk to the driver's side as the sullen group glared in silence. Royal glowered from under bushy eyebrows but remained rooted to his spot. Ned slammed his door as she started the engine. "Good job with that sap. Now, let's go get some breakfast."

"I need to make some stops this evening, then I can make a couple of calls on a Clay or two."

Ned gave her a quick pat on the shoulder and rested his arm on the seat back. "I believe you're gonna work out just fine and dandy."

The corners of Anna's mouth twitched. "Are we really going to their houses?"

"Yep. One at a time. All day long. They're gonna think we're traveling preachers looking for someplace to eat before this is over."

She threw her head back and laughed, then steered toward Chisum and Frenchie's café.

Chapter Forty-one

The Wraith got still another ass-chewing from his boss for being gone so much, but he didn't care. He let a job slip his mind because he'd been arguing with his girlfriend when it got out of hand. He couldn't remember how many times he hit her, but it was enough to shut her up for a while. The fury at his girlfriend and boss was so intense he saw red once again. He picked up a two-pound pipe wrench and headed back to work. He'd show them what a man of his talents and intellect could do.

"I ain't never seen no white woman deputy."

Anna laced her fingers and leaned across the rough wooden table in the rear of Saperstein's grocery. The small store barely forty feet wide and twice that deep was closed, but the back door remained unlocked until Rubye finished cleaning up the rough dining area that two generations earlier was a storeroom. Six scarred picnic tables formed two lines along one side away from a pair of stark, open-burner stoves.

Anna took it all in. "It's about time, isn't it?"

"For what?" The black woman lit a cigarette and dropped the half-full pack into her apron pocket. She blew smoke from her nose, settled on the bench opposite Anna, and rested her elbows on the table. Behind her, a brick oven reaching to the ceiling radiated heat as it smoked strings of thumb-size hot links. "Time to try these hot links, or the truth about them Mayfields?"

"Both. Tell me what you know about the car wreck that took Maggie."

"You hungry?"

"It's late and I haven't had anything but coffee since lunch."

Rubye carefully placed her burning cigarette on the table with the cherry hanging off the edge. She stood and opened the oven's cast iron doors. Strings of hot links hung from the walls in greasy brown strands. She cut half a dozen off with a pair of scissors and caught them with a paper plate.

The storeroom-cum-restaurant in the back of the small grocery store on Main Street served hot links, fried chicken, and chicken fried steak to anyone, as long as colored folks used the back door. The No Colored sign hanging in the front window only applied to the grocery store itself.

"I didn't see the wreck." Rubye put the plate on the table along with a stick of saltine crackers and a recycled RC bottle full of thin red hot sauce.

Anna smiled. "You know what I'm talking about."

"Why you got any interest in us Mayfields?" Rubye talked while she opened a fresh stick of saltines. "Why don't you just chalk it up to Mayor Frank Clay's death by the poor colored woman who drove him off the dam?"

"This is all one big tangle and I'm trying to get it unraveled." Anna poked at the links with a fork.

Rubye shook her head, picked up a knife, and cut the hot links into pieces. She drowned them with the hot sauce. "There. Now, get you some ketchup on that plate and drag a bite through and eat it with one of them crackers."

"I think that if I find out what happened that morning we can put an end to this trouble between y'all's families." Anna shook a dollop of ketchup onto the plate. "That's how us girls work, you know. The men go thrashing around and we look a little more carefully."

She took her first bite and chewed carefully. Her mouth exploded with a burst of flavor she'd never experienced. Then came the aftershock of heat from the Tabasco-like sauce. Sweat immediately broke out on her forehead.

Rubye took a long drag and blew smoke from both nostrils. She watched Anna swallow. "I do believe you care."

"I do. Can I get something to drink?"

Rubye laughed and got up. She crossed to a metal cooler and plucked an RC Cola from the ice and water. She pulled the cap and put the bottle on the table. "Don't grab the wrong one later." She laughed again. "So why you here with me? There's others know more."

"Maybe, but I can't get anyone to talk with me."

"How come you to be *here*? Who gave you my name?"

Anna shrugged. "That doesn't matter. From what I hear, you worked for Frank, but I just found out that you and Maggie were close growing up. You know her better than anyone."

"That don't tote no water." Her eyes narrowed. "Somebody called my name."

"Does it matter who?"

"Maybe. I don't want my name spread around."

"It's someone who wants this all to end."

Rubye thought for a moment. "You been talkin' to Cheryl Lynn."

Anna stopped chewing and Rubye laughed out loud. "Honey chil', you oughta stay away from the poker tables."

"She called you."

"Sure did!" Rubye laughed again. "Don't worry. I know you wasn't gonna say."

"I didn't want to."

"You done good, but Cheryl Lynn done tol' me I can trust you before you got here. What do you want to know?"

"Tell me about Maggie and Tylee."

Rubye snorted. "That sorry son of a bitch. She took up with him 'cause he promised her the moon."

"And she didn't get it. That's the same promise all men make."

"Ain't it the truth?" Rubye picked up Anna's fork and took a bite of the hot link. Anna took the opportunity to draw two big swallows from the chilly bottle. Rubye chewed for a moment and laid the fork down. "She believed him, though. They married and the next night he was at Sugar Bear's juke joint, messin' round with any tramp that looked at his raggedy ass. The last one might near got him killed."

"You know that how?" Anna took the fork back and speared another bite. They might have been sisters eating together, and Rubye loosened even more. Anna had passed her tests.

"Why, I's there and saw it. Everbody know what happen then. That sorry gal's husband came in with a butcher knife and told Tylee he'd run it into his heart if he ever saw them together again. Maggie heard about it. That ain't no way to start a marriage.

"Maggie, she's a good gal. Always wanting to make sumpin' of herself. She had a better chance than most of us, 'cause she's half white. She had no intention to being a field hand, or a house nigger neither. She told me she wasn't gonna clean houses for a living. She wanted more. I told her she had to leave Chisum for that, but she said she didn't need to.

"She wanted to make changes here. Said it was her duty to our people. So she got a job right here for a while, stocking shelves at night when there weren't no white folks around, and doing the books for Mr. Saperstein.

"She was good at numbers. It wasn't long 'fore she started keeping books for other stores here in town. Then she got a job at the bank."

"Sounds like she was successful."

"She was. Said she'd work her way up to a real position at the bank, but that's where it stopped. See, nobody's gonna put a colored gal up front these days, no matter if she's light. She told me one day after she heard a man say he thought she was pretty 'til he saw her eyes. Said, 'No nigger gal with yaller eyes was gonna wait on *him*.' See what I mean?" Rubye took another bite.

Without her fork, Anna used a fingertip to absently trace a name carved in the tabletop. He'd been meticulous about his letters. "So she decided to look somewhere else?"

"She did. See, Frank Clay was on his way up, and Frank was colorblind, if you know what I mean. He made a good mayor and hired her about six months or so ago. Then when he said he was going to Austin, Maggie thought it was the perfect way to make a difference. She said she'd move up there to the capital and come back here once she made her bones."

"When was the last time you saw her?"

"Oh, last week. She came by here for dinner, but she didn't stay long as she usually does. Said she wasn't feelin' good."

"Did she say anything out of the ordinary?"

"No. She didn't have time. I had a few minutes to talk and all of a sudden she said the smell of them links was turning her stomach, so she left."

It was Anna's turn to chew. "They're good, all right."

"They's nothing but greaseballs made mostly out of hog cheek and tongue, but they're a little piece of heaven."

"They're not the most healthy things I've ever eaten."

Rubye threw back her head and laughed. "You gonna crave 'em now, honey chil'."

"I'm perfectly healthy and all that grease should turn my stomach…" Anna paused.

Rubye tilted her head, watching. She lit another cigarette with a wooden kitchen match. "Maggie loved 'em 'til then."

Their eyes met. Rubye's eyebrow twitched.

Anna figured it out.

"That's why she and Frank were together that night. She told me she was going over there and they were gonna run off to be together." Rubye blew smoke through her nose. "You might need to talk to Miss Sweet, but I 'magine you know enough now.

"Oh, and one more thing. I'm tired of all this trouble and worry." Though the doors were locked, she spoke so softly Anna could barely hear. "Go pick up Willie and Bryce Mayfield."

"For what?"

"They was delivering firewood the other night and I heard Willie tell Bryce to run by the bowling alley where Matt Clay was ever Friday night and cut him low, then hurry over to the carnival and meet him there so's he'd have an alibi."

Anna thought back to Cheryl Lynn's reluctance to get her name involved. "I'd need a sworn statement, and eventually you'd have to testify."

Rubye blew two more streams of smoke from her nostrils and stubbed out her cigarette. "Honey chil'. I already knew that the minute I opened my mouth. It's time for all this foolishness to be over."

"Willie might come after you if I can't make it stick."

"I ain't afraid of my sorry-ass brother. Never was."

Chapter Forty-two

The three of us were in the yard Saturday evening when Grandpa pulled up. Jim Morrison was singing about getting his fire lit and it felt like we were right beside it with the sun going down and the air thick and hot.

My foot ached some and still seeped a little blood, but I was getting around just fine.

Grandpa killed the engine and got out. "What are you outlaws up to?"

"Nothing." Pepper held up her radio and turned down the volume before he could tell her to do it. "Just listening to music."

"Miss Becky run y'all out with that longhair crap?"

"Yessir."

He studied Pepper for a long minute. "What?"

"How do you know I wanted something?"

"You have that look in your eye, and y'all are out here waiting on me."

I wondered how he knew, but before I could say anything Pepper piped up. "Can we ask you a favor?"

He sighed. "What?"

"We want to go back to the carnival one more time before they're gone."

"No." He started up the steps. "Top probably can't hardly walk nohow."

"My foot's fine." I stood up from the shellback chair so he could see. I knew better than to walk, though, because it hurt like the devil if I came down on it wrong. "The coal oil did its job." I saw an opening and figured I'd better make my argument before Pepper threw in again and made him mad. "We didn't get to do everything the other night after y'all found that dead guy."

He frowned for a minute, then looked at Mark. "How come y'all want to go back so bad?"

"We didn't get to go through the Funhouse, or the carousel, or…"

Pepper cut in. "The Scrambler."

"I'm not riding that."

"Me and Mark will."

Grandpa ignored Pepper. "Which one did you want to ride?"

Mark started to pull the hair out of his eyes, but stopped, probably to keep from drawing attention to it. "I don't know. I've never been to a big carnival like that one, so I barely had time to look around. We rode the Ferris wheel, and that was all."

That's all it took. I saw Grandpa's face soften. "You've never been to a fair?"

"Nossir."

"Ever had cotton candy, or one of them candy apples?"

"Nossir. Never had any money for those things. Went to that powwow where I saw Cody and Aunt Norma Faye, remember, Top? I had some grease-bread with sugar on it. Like I said, we didn't get to do any of them things the other night."

Grandpa looked toward the dam and thought for a minute. "Y'all get in here and get cleaned up before we go."

I tried not to limp too bad on the way into the house and made a note to ask Mark what else he'd never done. It looked like for a while, we'd get free admission to a lot of places.

Chapter Forty-three

It was time to let folks know what was what. The Wraith paused, thinking. There were a lot of things he'd like to do that last night. Things he'd dreamed about over and over. His hands itched at the thought of touching those that passed so close he could smell them. He went inside his trailer and while the baby cried itself to sleep, shaved his face and thought of those girls who made his skin prickle in the darkness.

John Washington caught up with Willie Mayfield cutting firewood in the bottoms. Willie sold the wood to folks in Chisum who didn't have any land or way to cut their own.

Willie and his son, Bryce, were working both ends of a crosscut saw on the county road, cutting a fallen pin oak to length. Both were soaked with sweat, their shirts dark and sticking to them when John pulled up and stopped.

"We ain't stealin' this wood, Mr. John."

John slammed the car door. "I'm not here about y'all cuttin' wood, Willie, but you sure it's all right to take this one?"

"Yessir." Willie wiped sweat from his face with a pale blue bandanna. "It was growin' up in Mr. Dan Jacob's fence here and he was afraid it'd fall and take the fence down with it. He told me it was all right."

"Well, you be careful. It's liable to be on county property, and somebody might call in."

Willie studied the fresh stump. "Didn't think of that."

"It don't matter none."

"You need me for anything?"

Bryce remained silent while he opened their pickup door and took a quart fruit jar from the floorboard. He leaned against the fender, unscrewed the cap, and took several long gulps.

John watched his Adam's apple bob. "Well, not particularly. "I'm looking into the car wreck that killed Maggie, and this fight between your family and the Clays."

"God love her, John." Willie picked at the saw blade with a thumbnail. "We didn't start no fight with the Clays."

"Wes Clay had one with Olan Mayfield."

"That's a fact, but it wasn't full family business. Him and Olan got into it with each other half a dozen times over the years. They just never liked one another and it was bound to come sometime. The rest of us, we just wanna be left alone."

Sweat trickled down John's cheek. He drew a handkerchief from his back pocket and took his straw hat off to dry his face and neck. "And you're sayin' y'all ain't fighting?"

Willie shrugged. "I'm saying we ain't *fighting*, it's a reckoning. Some of them Clays is after something, but it ain't nothin' *we* done. There's lots of us in these two families, but the trouble's only between a few. If somebody'd get Royal or Wes Clay out of the way, we could rest easy."

"You ain't afraid?"

Willie patted the right front pocket of his overalls. "I got six reasons in here not to be."

John replaced his hat. "You think this trouble is because the Clays blame Maggie for the accident?"

"Could be. But see here, she married in, so it ain't like she was blood kin. Here's something I bet you don't know."

"What's that?"

"Maggie's white grandma was a Clay."

John paused. "I never heard that. You sure?"

"Yep, I heard tell of that before my mama died. It was one of them family secrets nobody liked to talk about. They weren't married and it was covered up where they came from. I doubt anybody wrote it in a Bible anywhere."

Bryce set the Mason jar on the shady running board to keep the water cool. "That's where Maggie got her wild side, but she was a good gal, too, if you know what I mean."

John wasn't sure how he meant that, or the earlier reference of a reckoning, but he nodded just the same. "She didn't like to be tied down."

"Well, the fact is, I believe she wanted to be." Willie glanced up at a buzzard circling overhead. "You know, Tylee didn't draw the knot too tight between 'em. He was always off chasing poon, and when he wasn't with Maggie, he was with his woods children in Dallas."

"I don't imagine she liked that too much. It's the reason she worked all the time. Only problem was she got all high and mighty and wanted to be white and worked herself into that job with Frank Clay. She was making money hand over fist, but look where it got her."

"She ever say that?"

"What?" Bryce's brow went up.

"That she was moving up and wanted to be white?"

"Naw, acted like it, though."

"Well, since she didn't have kids, I guess a career didn't hold her back."

"She kept kids sometimes, even after she started making money with Frank Clay. She was always partial to 'em. When me and her was runnin' together in high school, we talked about having a *passel* of kids."

John felt a little niggle in the back of his mind, but he couldn't nail it down. He wiped the sweat from the back of his neck. "You know how come her to be with Frank Clay that day?"

"Naw. Ain't got no idee." A crease formed in Willie's forehead and Bryce shut up. "None of this makes any sense, John. They're folks dyin' and getting' burned out, and we're all wondering who's gonna get hurt next. We're bein' careful, and watchin' out for one another, best we can, but there's still things happening to them Clays that we ain't responsible fer."

"You know that for the truth?"

"I do."

Bryce looked at the ground. "I ain't saying it's the truth, but more'n one person's told me Maggie's been seen in places she shouldn't be."

"Tell me."

"You know that joint up in Frogtown?"

John nodded. Most of the honky-tonks they dealt with were on Highway 271 across the river from Arthur City. But County Road 109 intersected the highway about five miles further north in Oklahoma. The narrow blacktop road stretched eastward for ten miles before turning north just before it hit a northern bend in the Red River called Frogtown.

A cinderblock joint called Ed's Place backed into the deep woods there. It was what local folks called a gun and knife club, one so rough that if you didn't have a weapon when you arrived, someone handed you one to equal things up. Dilapidated shacks were scattered behind like abandoned shoeboxes. Gap-tooth girls earned a living in a couple of them, and rough poor folks barely survived in the others, doing whatever jobs came by, no matter how unspeakable.

Bryce continued, even though Willie's expression said he didn't want him to talk. "Well, Sofie Bolton saw her car out front. Sounds like she was sneakin' off over there because that kind of place didn't care if she was high-yeller. All they care about's the color of money. I bet the white in her was drawed to that honky-tonk music they play. I saw her here while back and told her it wasn't a good idea to be messin' with them kind of folks. I told her she either belongs to us, or them."

"She said she was done with clubs in general, 'cause she couldn't stand all that smoke and drinkin' anymore. Said she was done honky-tonkin' now that she was working for Frank Clay. Said things were about to change. Not sure I believed her, though."

"Why's that?" John's eyes flicked between the two men, trying to read their expressions.

"A friend of mine he told me he saw Maggie in the car last week with Ralston, coming back from Oklahoma. It was on the road from Frogtown and he thought they was runnin' around."

"What'd he see 'em do?"

"Nothin', just ridin' back. He was on his way out to Ed's Place and was disappointed that Maggie was leavin'. What aggravated him the most was Maggie in the car with Ralston."

"There ain't no law about two folks riding together, married or not." John drew a deep breath as the dominos in his mind began to fall. "Pass the word for me. It's gonna stop now, Bryce. This feud between all-y'all and the Clays is over."

"Say it is?"

The smirk on his face flew all over John and made him want to shake the young man until his eyeballs rattled. "I'm not gonna stop 'til this is over. Y'all pass the word to all them you know."

The creases in Bryce's forehead deepened. "I can't stop other folks."

"You know the words. Tell 'em I'll shoot the first one I find killing white folks. There won't be no arrests."

Willie's mouth opened in shock. "Mr. John, you cain't say that."

"I did. Some of your folks is bringing trouble down on the rest of our people, and we don't need that right now."

"You oughta be out over to the Clays and arrest them that's doin' it."

"You tell me who they are and I will."

"I don't know for sure. I just want to stay out of it."

They stood in silence for a long moment. The shrill call of a blue jay echoed through the woods. A pickup rattled down the dirt road and slowed. Ike Reader didn't stop, but he took a good, long look. John waved. Ike waved back and sped up once he was past, making sure to put enough distance between them so as not to dust the men standing beside the road.

John studied his black boots. "Well, then. I'll let y'all get back to your sawin'. Whatever you do, be careful and let me know if you hear anything. Don't let me catch y'all trying to pay anyone back for anything."

"Yessir." Willie checked the set of his saw's teeth and returned to their job.

"Fine, then." John left them to their wood-cutting, and drove to town.

Chapter Forty-four

Grandpa radioed Mr. John on the way to fair. "John, you working tonight?"

The Motorola was the only light in the car, glowing bright enough to see his leather sap on the seat between us. His .38 was in the worn holster on his belt. I was sitting with my leg cocked up on the seat because my foot was throbbing.

Mr. John's voice cut through the static. "Yessir. I'll be out for a little bit, after I make one more stop. I need to keep an eye on that carnival, too."

"That's where we're headed. I got the kids with me. I need to run out to Tigertown after while. You want to go?"

"Sure. I'll see you there and we can take my car to save you the gas. You oughta let the county pay for more trips like that."

Grandpa keyed the mike again. "Good. I'll take 'em to the house after a little bit and then we'll go from there."

He hung the microphone on the bracket screwed into the dash and joined the line of vehicles turning in to the parking lot. Grandpa stopped at the far end of a ragged line of cars and killed the engine. He hung his elbow over the seat to see Pepper and Mark in the back. "Now y'all listen to me. I'm gonna give you money for rides and something to eat, but I don't want you to spend one dime of it on them crooked games."

Pepper had that look in her eye and I figured I'd have to rein her in at some point.

Grandpa handed me a few bills. "You're in charge of the money." He glanced over his shoulder at Pepper. "I'd put Mark in charge since he's never been to a fair before, but I got a good suspicion that Pepper'd talk him into doing something with it he shouldn't."

She rolled her eyes and I tried not to grin.

"And I don't want y'all leaving the grounds. If you get tired or your foot gets to hurtin', come wait by the gate. I'll drift around by there ever now and then to look for you, and we're going home at ten." Grandpa opened his door. "All right. Let's go."

The grass underfoot was dead and beaten into the damp ground. I figured half of those footsteps pointed toward the gate, all excited and full of energy. The other half most likely came back slow and sore-footed, and probably a little lighter in the billfold after the games and greasy food soaked up the money in their pockets.

We were used to grease. Most of what we ate was fried, and if it wasn't, it was cooked in bacon grease. Even a salad Miss Becky liked to make was nothing but leaf lettuce with hot bacon grease poured over it. She called it wilted lettuce. Come to think of it, bacon grease was in just about everything from biscuits to popcorn.

The grease at the carnival smelled delicious on the humid night air. The crushed grass mixed with the odor of damp dirt, frying food, and sweet caramel apples and cotton candy made my mouth water.

The lady at the ticket booth saw us walk up with Grandpa and waved us on through. Once inside, Pepper gave him a little tootles flip with her fingers and we split off. I followed her and Mark, limping a little because no matter how good I said it felt when Grandpa asked me, my foot was starting to hurt something fierce.

As soon as we were out of sight, Pepper took Mark's hand. "What do you want to do first? There's a Tunnel of Love over there."

His eyes were bright. "Get some cotton candy."

She snorted and I figured she wanted to ride in the dark with him and hold hands, and maybe even give him some sugar, but he had other ideas. I grinned and her eyes flashed at me, but Mark pulled her toward the line of food wagons in the middle of the midway.

We joined a group of kids waiting for the woman running the cotton candy machine to sweep the long paper cone around and around until it made what looked like a beehive hairdo. It was our turn when I saw Mr. Ike Reader.

A clown carrying a bouquet of bright balloons came by and Mr. Ike stopped like somebody jerked him back with a rope. He ducked behind a big woman buying a corny dog and waited until the clown was gone, then Mr. Ike disappeared into the crowd.

I started to laugh, but then felt bad about it, because everyone in Center Springs knew he was deathly afraid of clowns. I didn't want to make fun of anybody, because I was afraid of enough things to fill a book.

Chapter Forty-five

Unusually fidgety, The Wraith went back inside to get ready for work. He stared into the mirror and frowned at the sunken side of his jaw where Cody Parker once knocked out several teeth. There'd be payback for that tonight, one way or another.

Miss Sweet shared a small but neat frame house with her twin sister in Chisum. Neither she nor Miss Sugar ever married, but were aunts to most everybody who knew them. Miss Sugar was more of a homebody, and took care of the house while helping kinfolk and people who lived within walking distance because she couldn't abide riding in cars.

It was already dark when John turned into the two-track dirt driveway south of the tracks and killed the engine. The windows were open to catch the late evening breeze and Miss Sweet heard his door slam. She pushed the screen door open and limped out onto the porch.

"Law Pete! Look who's here. You bend down here and hug my neck!"

He stepped into her outstretched arms and folded nearly double to hug the short woman. "Miss Sweet, you're as purty as ever."

She squeezed him tighter, then pushed him away and slapped his shoulder. "You mind your manners around an old woman. I don't need no more lyin' in this old world than what I've already heard."

He laughed. "Where's Miss Sugar?"

She reached into the pocket of her house dress and fished around. A second later she popped her teeth into place. "She goes to bed with the chickens, and me, I don't hardly seem to sleep no mo'. Set down in that chair right there. The sun's down low enough it's kindly cool."

Sweat rolled off John's face and he bit his lip to keep from chuckling at her "thin blood."

"Where's your car?"

"Ralston took it for the night."

"Don't he have no job no more?"

"Sure 'nough. He's 'bout off probation and mechanicin' on cars over't Dale's station." She grunted as she dropped heavily in a cane-bottom chair. "Set down I said."

John took the chair beside her. "How does he get off to run y'all around?"

She adjusted her blue house dress to make a pouch in her lap and reached into a bucket of purple-hull peas sitting beside the chair. Her crooked fingers shelled the peas while they talked. "Dale's always been good to us."

John leaned back against the wall and plucked a hull from the bucket. He flicked it back and forth. "You been doing all right?"

"Fair to middlin'. Arthritis is bad and these old knees don't bend like they ought to."

"Mine are giving me trouble, too."

"You're filling out some. Looks like Rachel's feedin' you good."

John laughed. "Well, my britches are a little tight these days. I don't need no more to carry around, though."

"Your frame'll handle it."

John broke the hull open and used his thumbnail to shuck a pea into his mouth. He chewed for a minute, savoring the fresh taste. "Miss Sweet. I got something to ask you."

"I know it. You're here about all this fightin' and killin'."

Nothing about the old woman surprised John. "For one thing. How'd you know?"

"That's all they're talkin' 'bout at church, and I can't call the last time you set on this porch with me."

He flushed with embarrassment. "I know it. Miss Sweet, I ain't gonna ask you if you know who's to blame, but I need to ask you to see if you can settle these folks down."

"You don't think I'm-a doin' that already?"

"Well, I figured, but if you was to say I'd talked to you, it might help."

Peas rattled into the pan. "I'll do what I can, but it ain't much."

"I know that. But there's been some push back from the Mayfield side, too. Houses burned and such."

"Houses will burn."

"Yessum. Now I got another question and I don't like asking it."

"Go ahead on." She threw a handful of hulls off the side of the porch and took some more from the bucket.

"Maggie Mayfield."

Miss Sweet's gnarly hands slowed for a minute and a pea popped out onto the porch. "What about her?"

"All this started with her and Frank Clay, but somebody said they saw her and Ralston coming back from Frogtown not too long ago. I know she wasn't no angel, but is there some connection between them that I oughta know about?"

"I can tell you this for a fact. Ralston weren't messin' with that gal."

John didn't respond.

"None of this he'n and she'n is any of my business, and it goes on all the time, but Ralston's done straightened up. He's got him a little girlfriend out towards Honey Grove."

"That a fact?"

"It is. He don't say much about it, 'cause Honey Grove's in Fannin County and he ain't supposed to be leaving thissun', and John Washington, don't you go to gettin' on to that boy on my say-so, you hear?"

He stifled a grin. "Yessum."

"Well." She paused and allowed her arthritic hands to fall limp in her lap. "I sent Ralston out to Frogtown to get her."

"You did?"

"I did." She bit her dentures back into place. "See, she didn't have no business over there."

"You're raising everybody around here?"

Miss Sweet smiled, added another acre's worth of wrinkles in her face. "She ain't mine to raise. She was done growed and that was part of it." She threw another handful of hulls off the porch and stopped. She sighed. "John, I don't know if I should be talkin' 'bout this."

"Well, I'm asking as a lawman, not somebody that's nosey." He watched the profile of the old woman he loved as much as his own mother. He also knew the secrets she kept for those folks she treated. "Miss Sweet?"

She worked her lips as if trying to sound out the right words. "You know about such things they do out behind them places out in Frogtown?"

"Gambling and prostitution."

"Lawd, no. I'm talkin' 'bout worse, but not in back rooms of that joint, I'm'a talkin' about them shacks futher back, where the po'est folks lives and the nasty things they do for money."

John frowned. He could tell she was struggling for the right way to describe what she knew, but there were stumbling stones in the way and she was picking her way through.

"Hon, I do my healin' for good. I work for the Lord and for them that ain't got no money for any of those fancy medicines or expensive doctors, though they do the Lord's work too. There's some things I won't do, though. What I'm talking about is the things that are done there that ain't legal ner right with the Lord."

"You ain't talking about juju or clay men, are you?"

"Naw, bless your heart, hon. You ain't seen what I have. The dirty side of doctorin' on tables where they take them poor little babies before they ever draw a breath."

Her old eyes filled, and she salted the raw peas in her lap while she spoke of a secret she'd sworn to carry to her grave. "She couldn't do it. She couldn't do it, praise the Lord. But she told the baby's daddy, and he was glad. See, Frank was a good man and lost in the love that had died with one woman, and was set afire with another."

"Maggie."

"You're a-hearin' me."

"That's why they were in the car together on the dam?"

Miss Sweet nodded. "I 'spect. It weren't right, ner wrong. It just was."

Chapter Forty-six

Cody and Norma Faye sat in his El Camino parked where he could see both the fair and the parking lot. Crickets and frogs sang a melody as dusk gathered. Cody didn't want to drive the sheriff's car; it attracted too much attention and he was still trying to lay as low as possible.

She cut her eyes across the cab. "This reminds me of when we used to go out at night and have fun. But sometimes I feel like my mother, washing, ironing and cleaning day after day."

"I know what you mean." He gave her hand a pat and rested it there, feeling the small wedding ring on her finger. "Four years ago we were dancing on Saturday nights, now we spend most of them at home, when I can get off and be there."

"You think this is better than going to the movies?"

He'd checked the paper before they left to see what was showing. "We don't have much choice. The Plaza's showing that Disney movie *Monkeys, Go Home!*, and the Grand has a documentary about that horrible singer, what's his name? Bob Dylan."

She grinned at her husband who only listened to country music. "Now how do you know about him?"

"Your niece. Pepper listens to his music, but I couldn't tell you why to save my life."

"*My* niece."

"You bought in, so it's share and share alike."

"I gotcha. I love that girl, but sometimes I want to ring her neck."

"Because she reminds you of you."

She glanced at the lights. "That, and other things. So Mr. Big Spender, you brought me to this cheesy carnival instead of a happy Disney movie."

"Right." His attention wavered as a cluster of Mayfields stopped at the ticket gate. He'd already seen at least one Clay and his wife in the parking lot. He hoped those who ran into each other would let it go and simply enjoy the carnival.

Norma Faye noticed where his attention was focused. "You're not here to work, are you?"

Cody brought himself back with a mental yank. "Nope. We're here for a little safe excitement and to have a good time." He watched the Tilt-a-Whirl spin screaming customers in a blurred circle as the lights flashed by in streaks of color. "Hey, how about next weekend we go to the Sportsman and do a little dancing? What's the fun of owning a honky-tonk if you can't enjoy it?"

"Well, it'd be fun if we went and you didn't work. You promise not to talk business?"

He realized she'd seen through the idea. He wanted to spend some time with the customers he recognized, looking for information, because he still couldn't get his mind off the accident. "All right. We can go once all this is wrapped up. But we're here tonight. I promise you a lot of fun, how about that?"

"Rides?"

"None that'll make me sick."

"Well then, we'll probably wind up on the carousel or one of those little kid rides that move plywood boats or cars in a circle."

"Any of that'd make me dizzy for sure. We can fool around in the Tunnel of Love, or I'll grab your butt in the Funhouse."

"All right, you can have your way with me in a cheesy little cart, but you have to buy me a hotdog and some cotton candy first."

"Deal."

Norma Faye gathered her purse and didn't notice Cody's frown as he saw Royal and Cecil Clay loafing near the entrance gate, looking like they were waiting for someone.

His stomach tightened when Royal spat a stream a tobacco juice in the direction of Bryce Mayfield who ignored the challenge and stopped at the first game at the entrance, to lose some of his hard-earned money at the Bottle Toss.

Chapter Forty-seven

The Wraith studied the face in the mirror. It wasn't his and he ached for the times past when he could simply be himself. It wouldn't be long now.

The Skydiver reminded Cody of a small, vicious twirler's baton with caged passengers pivoting on the ends of the spinning arm. Cody shook his head, knowing he'd lose his supper if he ever let someone lock him into one of the tiny metal chicken coops.

Norma Faye eyes glittered. "I would have *loved* that when I was a kid."

"Not me. I like having both feet on the ground."

The redhead laughed and bumped him with a hip. "I bet Pepper'd like it."

"Go home and get her then, if you want to ride that thing. It looks dangerous to me."

"I don't have to." Norma Faye pointed.

Cody followed her finger and spotted their urchins in the moving crowd. Knowing Ned had to be close, he scanned the people until he found him near the ticket booth.

Screams of pretend terror filled the air and Cody turned back to the ride. The cages spun on their axis and he watched for another minute in the middle of a steady stream of people jostling past. Some ignored the badge and sheriff's patch on Cody's shirt. Others nodded hello and stopped to visit for a moment.

A flicker caught Cody's attention and he looked past the strings of light bulbs outlining the carnival's perimeter. Heat lightning to the north fractured a distant line of clouds. It was obviously psychological, but Cody thought he immediately smelled damp ground and rain, thinking the old-timers always said if you smelled rain, it wouldn't fall.

A local farmer gave Cody's arm a pat as he passed. He caught sight of a familiar figure and let go of Norma Faye's hand. He laughed. "Ike Reader! What are you doing here again? I thought you might've got enough of this fair last weekend."

Obviously embarrassed, Ike stopped. "Listen. Howdy Cody. Norma Faye."

She reached out and hugged Ike's neck. "How are you this evening?"

He hugged her back, but he looked as if he'd bitten into a green persimmon.

Cody noticed Ike couldn't take his eyes off the badge pinned to his shirt. "Something wrong, Ike?"

"What?" He backed up. "Nothin'. Listen, I'm fine.."

"You're acting like a cat in a doghouse."

"Well, there ain't nothing."

Ike stiffened and Cody followed his gaze. A clown passed, selling brightly colored helium balloons.

Cody grinned. "I figured you'd fight shy of this place, what with all the clowns everwhere."

Ike drug his eyes off the clown. "Listen, listen. I came to see what I missed the other night. What with the murder and all, I didn't get back in to get my money's worth."

"Anything special?" Norma Faye's expression was as mischievous as an imp.

Ike looked as if he wanted to melt into the ground. "Not that I can think of."

Cody let him off the hook. "I'm not here working tonight. You go ahead on and see your show."

"Well then." Ike shuffled his feet a couple of times and left. "I'll be seein' y'all."

Norma Faye jabbed Cody with her elbow. "You're mean. You know good and well he's here to see that girly show."

"Yeah, but he needed to pay twice. This was the second time."

"It'll be four, big boy. Twice there at the gate, and once here with you and then they ask for even more money to get in that hot tent."

A deep metallic boom sounded as if an artillery shell had exploded nearby. They felt it in their chests and it rolled over the fairgrounds, banging harsh and painful over the music and carnival noise. At first Cody thought someone had set off a stick of dynamite. He hadn't heard anything like that since he left Vietnam.

A second slam of steel against steel echoed the first. He whirled to see a car on the Skydiver had come loose just as it passed the loading gate, catching the steel railings and throwing it halfway into the midway. The massive arm spun one last squealing revolution before grinding to a stop with one of the twin cages twisted between the pivot's forks at the two-o'clock position high above the ground. It appeared to be held into place by only a pin on the side.

Cody pushed through the retreating crowd. "Get out of the way! Get away!"

The line waiting for their turn dissolved as people of all ages scattered and ran from the accident. Sure the car was about to fall, Norma Faye raced behind, grabbing gawkers by blouses and sleeves and jerking them away from the accident. She snatched two stunned youngsters away from the damaged loading ramp.

The Skydiver operator barely out of high school slapped the red kill switch and backed away, neck craned upward. The straining motor grew quiet. In the aftermath, those on other rides continued to spin and shriek in glee while the music blared as if all were normal.

Instead of screams from happy riders, cries of horror created an entirely different sound that came from Hell itself. Cody looked up to see fingers wiggling through the cage's mesh, looking for a way out. Cupping both hands around his mouth, he shouted at the frightened passengers. "Stay still!" He turned toward the operator. "Do you have any chain?"

"Chain? Naw." The young man shrugged. "What do you need that for?"

"Give me your belt. Now!"

The operator responded as if surrendering his belt was an everyday order. Cody snatched it from his hand, pushed the prong through the first hole, and dropped the loop over his head in a bizarre necklace. He pointed at another man's waist and he too slipped his belt free of the loops and passed it over.

Cody unbuckled his gun belt and handed it to Norma Faye. "Hang on to this." He collected two more belts, added his own, and dropped the loops over his head. "Hold on girls!" He grabbed a strut and climbed up onto the bent handrail.

Ignoring the questions and warnings that followed, he scaled the wheel's superstructure. Forcing himself not to look down, he kept an eye on the wedged cage high above. "Hang on up there! Be still so you won't fall."

Customers trapped in the other undamaged cage near the ground screamed and beat on the mesh as he climbed. "Y'all quit! Be still! You're fine, but I need to get up to the top. There's people hurt up there."

He didn't know for sure, but he wanted to appeal to their sympathies. If no one was hurt, it was okay for a rescuer to move past for the moment.

It didn't take long to reach the damaged car. The tear-streaked faces of two pale young women appeared in the darkness and pressed against the interwoven mesh sides. From his position below, the car was angled above his head and the girls were forced against the side of the woven steel. Already battered and bruised, they strained to keep from pressing their bare arms further into the mesh.

Cody's hands were oily and he took care in wiping one after the other on his khakis. "Don't move. Y'all hurt?"

The tiny voice of a college-age girl barely reached his ears. "I think my arm's broke."

"You'll be fine then. Now, don't move at all. I don't know how tight this thing's wedged, but it might come loose if y'all don't listen. Who's in there?"

"Belinda's arm's broke for sure. I'm Sandy." Her voice trembled. "What are you gonna do?" She pressed the palms of her hands against the sides as if they were made of glass.

"I haven't decided yet, but it won't be right this minute." He inspected the forked superstructure and noticed one side of the pivot pin was completely free from the bushing. It meant the entire cage was held into place by friction and a single bolt. He swallowed a lump in his throat. "I intend to use these belts to strap this thing tight until the fire department gets here with a ladder, but y'all lay still." He gave them a grin. "It's a good thing neither one of you's no bigger'n a minute. You're gonna be fine."

Belinda shivered as if she were cold, rattling a loose piece of metal. "You promise?"

Cody winked at the girl, wondering if she was already going into shock. "Sure 'nough."

It wasn't easy. Standing on one foot, Cody wrapped his other leg around an exterior spoke and held on. He looped an arm around the same spoke and hugged it as tight as possible. Slipping one belt at a time over his head, he uncoupled them and wrapped them around the outside rim of the wheel and the cage's brace. The first one took longer than he expected and his leg supporting most of the weight started to quiver.

Cody almost fell off when a voice spoke beside him. "Hold on honey."

His head snapped around. "Norma Faye! Get the hell off here. You're gonna fall."

"Nope." She picked her way up behind him. "And you aren't either." In the next instant, she reached both arms around him and grabbed onto the nearest supports. Pulling tight, she pressed against his back, securing her husband against the strut. "I'll hold you against here until you get those belts tight."

He felt surprisingly safe. "Let me know when you get tired."

"I will."

"You know what?"

"What?"

"It's a good thing you didn't wear a dress tonight."

He felt her stomach muscles contract in laughter at the thought of the show she might have provided to those watching from below.

Cody chuckled and went back to the job at hand. "This won't take a minute. Girls, stay still." Both hands free, he quickly wrapped the belts around the brackets and tightened them down.

The third one was in place when still another body appeared on the opposite side. "Be still girls." The carnival's owner, Delmar Hopkins, scrambled higher as if he'd spent his whole life crawling high above the ground. Chains rattled in his hands and he threw one loose end over a second strut farther up. "Hold onto that end, Sheriff."

Using one hand, Cody held the chain in place as Delmar slung the other end around the cage's main support and through a brace. He slipped a padlock through the links and snapped it shut. "That should do it for now." Delmar gave the cage a pat, feeling the girl's fingertips extended beyond the mesh. "Fire department's on the way."

Sandy shook her head. "Don't go."

Cody felt Norma Faye work her way out from behind him and glanced down to see her moving slowly toward the ground. "You gals hang tight. You're not gonna fall now. This whole thing is steady and my legs are getting tired. We're climbing down, but the fire trucks are on the way to get you down with a ladder and believe it or not, they're just gonna open this door and you'll be able to leave the way you came in."

Belinda was silent as he started down. He winked up at the girls. "Y'all done good."

Norma Faye was already on the ground by the time Cody joined her. Smeared in dirt and grease, they trembled against each other on weak legs.

Sirens wailed in the distance. Cody pressed his forehead against hers. "Girl, you're something else."

"Great date, buster. You should be glad we're married, because this kind of thing could make a girl reconsider."

Ned appeared in the dusk and squinted up at the ride. "It don't look like you can go to the fair without getting in trouble, neither."

Norma Faye threw her head back and laughed. "We came here looking for some excitement."

"Well, you dern sure found it."

Chapter Forty-eight

We hardly made it halfway down the midway when we heard the Skydiver'd gone haywire. Pepper grabbed Mark's hand and they cleared a path back through the crowd. I limped along behind, trying not to get my cotton candy on everyone who was jostling along in the same direction.

The crowd was packed tight like boys do when someone gets into a fight on the schoolyard. We didn't need to get close, though, because I saw Uncle Cody climbing his way up the wheel. The Skydiver wasn't but half as tall as the Ferris wheel and it was a good thing, because when Uncle Cody reached the cage that was broke, he had to wrap one leg around a support strut.

It was hard to tell what he was doing up there, but I knew him well enough to know that whatever it was, it needed to be done.

Pepper gasped a second later when she saw Norma Faye shinnying her way up behind Uncle Cody. "Why, I've never seen anything like it."

Mark's blue-black hair shimmered in the lights as he shook his head back and forth. "I can't believe this family." Since they were in front of me, I saw their fingers twined together while we watched the rescue. "She's something else."

Pepper gave his hand a jerk while people around me jabbered to one another, carrying on like their own people were up there in trouble. A white-haired feller joined Uncle Cody and Norma Faye, and pretty soon they were finished with what they needed to do. They came scampering down quick as you please.

I had no doubt Grandpa was in the middle of it too and I suddenly had an idea. The people up there were safe, and nothing would happen until a fire truck out of Chisum showed up. It'd take them a while to get those folks down, and all the while Uncle Cody and Grandpa would be tied up right where they were.

I'd been thinking about the girly shows Mr. Floyd Cass was talking about up at the store and decided right then and there I wanted to see what was in that tent at the far end of the midway. I didn't for sure know what was *in* a girly show, but it sounded like something I needed to see. Pepper and Mark were sure to spend the rest of the night making goo-goo eyes at one another, and I didn't want to be the third wheel through all of it.

It was a suddenly delicious feeling that swarmed over me. I was doing something I wanted, without Pepper leading, and it was a bona fide sin to boot. I was darned near grown.

Maybe I'd see some lady with tattoos shimmying up on a stage, her hair all wild and dancing like that skinny little Goldie Hawn on *Laugh In* that came on television every Monday night. There were girls in California dancing at a place called the Whiskey a Go-Go I'd read about in *The Police Gazette* and I figured they'd be something to see. The girls in the canvas tent not far away might even be topless and I wanted to be able to tell Mark I'd seen a pair of yabbos, something I figured *he* hadn't even seen yet.

I knew for sure and for certain I wasn't gonna get through the front flap, but all I needed was to sneak under the tent and get a peek at what was going on inside. Then I could find them again later.

I backed up and limped away quick as I could. Neither Pepper or Mark knew I was gone. The Midway was as empty as I'd ever seen one, what with everyone at the gate end watching the excitement. Even the game barkers were standing on their counters, trying to see through the lights and over the crowd.

I handed a surprised little girl my cotton candy and made good time going opposite the flow. No one was paying me any mind, because a kid on the midway was nothing more than an ant on a red ant bed.

Since we left early the first night we were there, none of us made it to the far end of the midway. Little kids' rides and some of the flashiest attractions were behind me. The line of games on both sides petered out and at the Funhouse on my left. I stopped for a minute to watch two girls feeling their way through the glass and mirror maze right there in the middle and up front for everyone to see. One of them bumped her nose and squealed so loud I heard it through the glass. Her friend laughed and used both hands to feel her way inside and out of sight.

It looked like fun, and I was tempted to go in myself, but I decided to wait for Pepper and Mark. It'd be better with the three of us wartin' one another. Once past the Funhouse everything was a little darker and seedy. It was louder, too, with the rattle of gas generators overpowering the music.

Colored tents lined both sides with men in rumpled suits standing on knocked-together stages made of raw lumber. Some of the tents had painted canvas banners with strange-looking people on them. One was a fat lady, another a strongman. To my right was a tired-looking tent behind a sign that said I could see the world's smallest horse.

I stopped and turned in a slow circle.

Freaks!

Oddities!

World's Strangest!

Two-headed Lamb!

World's Most Tattooed People!

No Bones in Her Body!

Double-sex Person!

The whole thing almost made me swimmy-headed and my being there suddenly seemed like a bad idea. I started to leave when I saw the sign I was looking for.

Girls! Exotic Dancers! Illegal in Most States!

A barker stood on a high stage in front of the tent. Despite what was going on down the midway, there was a crowd of men in overalls and khakis watching him point at a woman in a skimpy outfit that looked like one of them bikinis I'd seen in those beach movies, only this one was so tiny it barely covered that old gal's important parts.

The barker's suit was worn plumb out and his white shirt was as dingy as one of Miss Becky's dish towels. The cuffs of his pants were walked down and dried mud caked the material around his ankles. "This is what you wanted to see, ladies and gentlemen! The most exotic show in the southern United States! These aren't your wives, girlfriends, sisters, or mothers. These women know what a man wants and this show is guaranteed to excite and amaze!"

The woman beside him shimmied and shook. I'd never seen anything like that before, and I felt my face flush. Her boobs moved by themselves and seemed to be made of jelly.

A stranger came up behind me and laid his hand on my shoulder. He wasn't looking at me. Instead, he was watching the woman. "Boy, you better get on out of here 'fore your grand-daddy finds out where you are."

I looked up at that redheaded guy, but he didn't look familiar. He knew who Grandpa was, though, and that blew my cover. He turned me with one hand on that shoulder and I slipped out of the crowd with my whole head on fire with embarrassment.

Instead of going back to the rides, I checked to make sure he wasn't watching me before I ducked around a sign to sneak between the tents. There weren't any lights on and after being on the midway, it seemed dark and gloomy. Thick cables like giant snakes ran through the grass in all different directions. There was enough light to pick my way over them and I rounded the girly tent.

It was a whole new world back there. Raggedy trailers were scattered everywhere in the gloom and it looked like somebody was having a rummage sale. Tubs, tables, clotheslines, brooms, spare tent poles, spare tires, and chairs were scattered in front of the trailers. They'd been there a little over a week and all the grass was beaten down to the dirt.

People were walking every which-a-way through the darkness, coming and going. I could tell some of them probably worked for the carnival, but a couple looked like farmers. One man came out of a trailer, ran fingers through his hair, and slunk back toward the midway like a worried dog.

The trailers themselves weren't interesting at all, so I checked around to see if anybody was looking at me. When I was sure it was clear, I dropped to my knees beside the girly tent and ducked my head under the bottom. I knew how to do that because I'd seen the Little Rascals do the same thing on television one time.

It took a few seconds for my eyes to adjust. All I could see were folding chairs stretching out to my left. There was no floor, just more trampled grass.

Music fired up from a portable record player and on the right I caught a glimpse of a woman in a glittery bathing suit walking out on a stage that looked like it had seen better days. Somewhere off to my left a spotlight winked to life and flooded the stage with harsh light. The woman smiled at the hooting crowd of men who rose from their chairs and started clapping.

She wriggled around for a minute and then reached both hands back to undo her top. She winked at the crowd and the next thing I saw was the ground rushing by as someone grabbed my ankles and jerked me back out from under the tent. I dug three furrows in the dirt, two with my hands. My chin made the last.

Chapter Forty-nine

The Wraith stopped outside his trailer to light a cigarette. He was fidgety as all get-out and couldn't settle down. A slender man stepped out of Lola's hot trailer several yards away after leaving his sweat on her sheets and twenty dollars on a small table beside the bed. The man turned his head, but The Wraith saw him anyway and recognized Ben Taylor, a cotton farmer who lived out toward Lake Crook. Ben had a wife and three kids, and The Wraith wondered how he was gonna explain the problem Lola'd most likely shared with him in about seven days.

The Wraith had to get back to his shift in the Kid's Amusement Tent, but he wasn't in any hurry. He wanted to finish the night so he could slip away one last time before the carnival packed up the rides to leave. He'd done all he could do to create as much chaos as possible and needed one last visit to settle that last wrong from his past life.

His stomach clenched with a pain that was more than familiar. It was both the ache of loss, and excitement that he was finally getting the payback he deserved. He was confident he'd started a war between the Clays and Mayfields that would go on for years. Maybe it would settle the bad blood he had for both families. The bonus was the coming culmination that night of four years of planning and a week's work in Lamar County. He couldn't wait to get started.

His girlfriend's baby started crying and The Wraith decided to wait a few minutes before finishing his makeup. Crying babies drove him nuts and he had to get outside before he lost his mind again and did something he'd regret. The nearby midway was noisy, but it was a different kind of racket. He lit his umpteenth cigarette of the day and squinted at a movement between the strip show and the freak show tents. It was darker there, and he barely registered the slight movement on the ground. He finally made out the shape of a kid lying on his stomach with the upper half of his body under the canvas.

Damn kids, always trying for a peek to get their cheap thrills.

He crossed the distance in a few long strides, grabbed the boy's ankles just above his U.S. Keds, and yanked him back into the open. "Hey kid, get your ass back where you belong!"

Top Parker rolled over, his eyes wide. The Wraith straightened in surprise and turned his head so the boy wouldn't recognize him, forgetting that the partially finished makeup job hid most of his features.

"I'm sorry, mister."

"Get the hell outta here."

"Yessir!"

The kid jumped to his feet and hurried back toward the lights. The Wraith watched him go and wondered if he should have done more.

His question was answered when Top stopped at the edge of the tent and stared back, mouth agape. He pointed. "Hey, I know you."

The Wraith jerked as if he'd been hit with a jolt of electricity. "Come here." His voice was hoarse and came from deep inside his chest.

Top dropped his arm and took a step backward. "Why?"

"Because I said so." He advanced.

The boy stiffened. "You."

"I said come here!"

"It's been you all the time." The boy hesitated and The Wraith saw him working on something in his mind. "That makeup don't hide your meanness or all your features. It's glowing nasty all around you. I know what you did, what you've done!"

The Wraith knew about Top Parker's gift for getting into places he didn't belong, and especially about his visions. His whole plan was in danger of dissolving if the kid went to his granddad and told him The Wraith under a different name was back in Lamar County. A scream of frustration rose in his throat. Instead of succumbing to the familiar rage, he spread his hands wide and forced a smile.

"You're right kid. It's me." He moved forward a step. "I bet you didn't think you'd ever see me again."

Another step, and his voice lowered. "You know, I always liked you."

Step.

"I didn't mean to scare you."

Step.

The Wraith tilted his head toward the tent, completely misreading Top's curiosity about the girly tent. "How about I sneak you in the back of this titty show and let you get a good long look, huh?"

Top looked like a rabbit ready to bolt.

The Wraith stopped only five feet away. "Hey, if you're interested in what's going on in there, let me tell you a secret. Your Aunt Norma Faye has a little birthmark I bet you'd like to know about."

Top went white as a sheet and The Wraith realized his mistake. "Shit!" He lunged, but Top was just as scared as that rabbit and twice as fast. He turned and shot into the crowd of men pouring from the strip show.

The Wraith followed, jogging into the open to see where the boy was headed. Several patrons laughed and pointed at his half-painted face.

"Wow, I think that's creepier than it should be."

"Hey Bozo! You're missing something!"

Barely registering their comments, The Wraith kept an eye on the kid who was alternately jogging and limping as he worked his way through the crowd. The Wraith didn't remember Top having a limp, and wondered if he'd turned an ankle. No matter, it would work to his advantage.

A couple of people gave him an inquisitive look, but The Wraith grinned as they passed. "Late for my shift." He saw Top duck under the restraining rope and skip into the Funhouse.

It was perfect. He had the little shit for sure.

He hurried back toward his trailer.

Chapter Fifty

I flipped over as soon as the guy let go of my feet. "I'm sorry, mister."

The face floating above me against the night sky wasn't a clown, really, but someone in regular work clothes with a most of a clown face and big red lips.

"Get the hell out of here."

"Yessir!"

His clown eyes were big and white and outlined with arching black eyebrows. His mouth was drawn in bright red and he was even scarier that he would have been. I was lucky, because if he'd been all painted up with a red ball nose and one of them orange wigs on, I wouldn't have recognized him as Calvin Williams. The last time I saw him was four years earlier on the day Uncle Cody whipped Calvin to a frazzle in front of Neal Box's store and sent his friends to the hospital.

Calvin was married to Norma Faye back then, though she'd already left him and was seeing Uncle Cody after he came back from his year in Vietnam. Calvin wasn't a clown then, just a no-account from Center Springs, hauling hay to make a few bucks that he mostly spent across the river.

That was the first time I'd ever seen a real fight that wasn't on television, or one in our school yard. It was bloody and mean and didn't seem to ever end. Uncle Cody even tried to drag Calvin out from under a hay truck where he crawled after he was whupped, to beat on him some more.

It turned my stomach and Uncle Cody had to talk to me for a long while to get it through my head that fights had to be won. When you fought, there was nothing fair about any of it.

Calvin Williams disappeared soon after that and no one ever saw him again. But here the man was and I knew what would happen if he got his hands on me. The truth behind the Poisoned Gift came alive in the brightly colored carnival lights, the laughing clown faces, the huge red mouths full of teeth.

It all made sense. The word "Indian" popped up over his head like in a cartoon and a shotgun blasted it away. The scream of Maggie's tires squalled in my head over the shrieks and music coming from a dozen rides. I saw the hanging tree and the image melted into Calvin smearing greasepaint on his face and then drawing on bright red lips.

Suddenly my feet wouldn't work and my breath disappeared. I backed all the way to the edge of the tent and stared with my mouth open wide enough for flies to get in. "Hey, I know you."

"Come here."

"Why?" I stepped back with my right foot and came down on a stake sticking about an inch out of the ground. It twisted and the nail-hole hurt so bad I felt my face prickle. I stiffened with the pain and remembered several nights earlier when I saw him from the Ferris wheel. It was Calvin with the axe handle that disappeared from the midway only to beat a man to death a few minutes later. "Why?"

"Because I said so."

"You!"

His face swelled to the size of a #5 washtub. Words came out of my mouth that I didn't think on. "I said come *here!*" His voice was hoarse, like he'd been screaming for hours.

"It's been you all the time. That makeup don't hide your meanness or all your features. It's glowing nasty all around you. I know what you've done."

He spread his hands wide and smiled. "You're right kid. It's me."

He moved forward a step and I held out a hand to make him stop. I wanted to run, but my feet stuck to the ground.

"I bet you didn't think you'd ever see me again." His voice lowered. "You know, I always liked you."

My knees trembled and everything around us disappeared and shrank down until it was just the two of us separated by only a few feet. The humidity was gone, the people vanished, and we were alone in a swirl of lights.

"I didn't mean to scare you."

Calvin Williams tilted his head and smiled mean like the Grinch in that cartoon Christmas show. The paint around his mouth spread out wider and wider until it like to near split his face in two. "How about I sneak you in the back of this titty show and let you get a good long look, huh?"

My whole body was trembling, vibrating like a guitar string.

He stopped. "Hey, if you're interested in what's going on in there, let me tell you a secret. Your Aunt Norma Faye has a little birthmark I bet you'd like to know about."

I didn't want to hear nothin' about Aunt Norma Faye! I'd only come to sneak a peek under a tent to find out what the men up at the store'd been talking about, to prove to myself that I was growing up, not a little baby like Pepper said. And besides, Aunt Norma Faye was family. What he was talking about sounded nasty.

Calvin Williams was only five feet away when the world snapped back crystal clear.

He must have seen something in my face. "Shit!"

He lunged at me, but I was faster. I twisted away and planted my foot to duck around a stream of men flowing from the girly tent.

Another hot jolt of pain shot up my leg and the wound woke with a vengeance. The next step on my damaged foot made tears well. I felt Williams behind me, but I figured I had enough of a lead to disappear into the crowd.

Twenty steps later, I knew it was impossible to run away. It felt like I was stepping on that nail again every time my foot hit the ground. A blind panic muddied my thinking and it never occurred to me to just stand there and holler for help. A terrifying *clown* was after me and he'd already scared me spitless, so bad my mind wasn't working right.

I glanced over my shoulder to make sure he wasn't gaining and saw him bearing down on me and the word *wraith* popped into my mind, pouring gasoline on my terror.

Blood squished in my shoe as I skipped and hopped past game booths and exhibits until I saw the entrance of the Funhouse on my right. I'd been in them before, weaving and winding through the maze and dark corridors that seemed to stretch forever.

It was the perfect place to hide, because even if Calvin Williams did see me duck inside, he'd never be able to find me in the giant trailer. If he didn't see me go in, he'd pass and then despite my bleeding foot, I could slip out the other side and find Grandpa.

Chapter Fifty-one

Norma Faye delicately plucked off tiny bits of cotton candy and let them melt in her mouth as Cody finished up with the fire department. The girls who'd been trapped in the dislodged cage were on the ground, telling their story over and over again to anyone who would listen. Belinda's arm wasn't broken, only bruised and strapped down in a makeshift sling.

Cody slapped one of the volunteer firemen on the shoulder. "Good job. I'm glad you boys got here when you did."

The man grinned and held out a roll of coiled leather. "I reckon you'll want your belt back."

"It'd look bad if I lost my britches." Cody hitched up his now-dirty khakis and threaded it through the loops. Norma Faye took his tooled leather gun belt from a friend who'd held it for them when she climbed the wheel. He strapped the 1911 on and waved at Ned and Delmar Hopkins in a heated conversation beside the ticket booth.

They joined Cody with Delmar still talking. "Honest, Mr. Ned. We've never had trouble like that before."

"Does that kid running it know what he's doing?"

"He's been here a couple of weeks. Cal's been showing him the ropes and he lets the boy run it when he clowns up."

"And what does that mean, clowns up? Your men ought not be kidding around with things as serious as these big machines."

"No, clowning up is when they put on makeup and become clowns. See?" He pointed to one walking away with a cluster of balloons. "A lot of the guys work two or three other jobs to make ends meet."

Ned removed his hat to rub his bald head. "All right. Where's this Cal feller now?"

Delmar shrugged. "Damned if I know. He's in and out so much lately I don't know for sure when he's working and when he ain't. Cal's a good mechanic, but he's not a very good clown. He scares more kids than he can make laugh and I can't keep him on the job, especially in this town. I'm gonna let him go when we break down because I spend half my time looking for his ass."

"You done broke down."

"I mean when we break down for the next town."

"Is he your only mechanic?"

"Nope, but he's the best. He's good with his hands, but most of these rides are owned by individuals who maintain 'em. Cal's part owner in the Skydiver, so the maintenance is exclusive on this one."

"Why don't you find this feller and tell him to meet me right 'chere in about half an hour? I believe I need to talk to him. Either me or the sheriff might have to report this, if we can find out who to report it to. This kind of stuff's dangerous."

Delmar shook his head. "We haven't had anybody hurt in years. I'm gonna get one of my other mechanics to take a look at it. Cal should have been inspecting it pretty regular, so we'll check the log to see when the last time was."

"You do that, and bring me that log. I need to look at it. What's this feller's name? Cal how much?"

"Cal Willis."

"All right. I'll be right here."

"I'll be here with him," Cody said. "I need to talk to him myself."

Delmar held out his hand to Cody. "Thanks, Sheriff. That was fast thinking on your part."

"I didn't do much, just held it tight until you got up there with the chain."

"Good work. I'll be back in a little bit."

Delmar disappeared into the swirl of people and Ned shook his head at Cody. "I don't believe I've ever seen anything like that, the two of you climbing around on that thing like a couple of monkeys."

Cody dusted his hands off. "Seemed like the thing to do."

"I reckon it was, but I never. You should've let these carnival folks handle it."

"They weren't moving fast enough to suit me, so I figured I'd better get busy. You'd have done the same."

"I doubt it. My climbing days are over."

Norma Faye grinned and offered Ned a bite of her cotton candy. "You'll feel like a kid again if you eat some of this."

"Naw, I don't believe I'd care for any. That stuff's too sweet, but thanks anyway. You know, I saw a feller with a camera from the paper. You'll likely wind up on the front page."

Cody chewed the inside of his lip, thinking. "That could be good or bad, depending on how you look at it. Right now I probably need to stay away from that kind of thing."

"Naw, it won't hurt you none."

Norma Faye took another bite of cotton candy. "What are you doing here, Mr. Ned? You keeping an eye on things this last night?"

He grinned. "Nope. I found out a little while ago that Mark ain't never been to a carnival or fair, only a couple of powwows in Oklahoma, so I brought 'em out. They didn't get to finish their fun the other night, and that wasn't right."

Cody raised an eyebrow and tilted his hat back. "I'm surprised they aren't right here underfoot, after all this excitement."

Norma Faye scanned the crowd. "You're right. I bet they're up to something." She looked around, snapped her fingers, and gave Cody that grin he loved. "Tunnel of Love."

"If they have one, but not if Top's with them. We'd better go look."

Ned waved a hand. "Let's give 'em a few more minutes. I told 'em to meet me right 'chere. If they ain't back in five minutes, then we'll go walk 'em up. I'm sure they're fine. There ain't much more trouble they can get into here."

He rubbed the back of his neck. "You two're beginning to remind me of Top and Pepper, though, gettin' into more and more ever year."

Chapter Fifty-two

I felt safer the minute the Funhouse darkness wrapped around me. I'd given Calvin Williams the slip and now all I had to do was wait for him to pass. Wheezing, I leaned against a wall to catch my breath. The hole in my foot had opened and blood soaked my sock.

My atomizer was on the dresser in my room and the only thing I could do was concentrate on drawing long, slow breaths in and then forcing the air back out. Getting it all out was tougher, but I was able to straighten back up a couple of minutes later.

I heard the entrance door slam open. The corridor I was in kept all the light out, so there wasn't even a glow.

Two chatty, squealing girls came in. "Where do we go?"

Giggles. "I don't know. Jesus! It's dark in here."

"I sure hope nothin' gone reach out and grab me."

"C'mon. There's only one way."

The rustle of their clothes told me they were coming my way. I slid my hand along the wall to stay ahead of them. I felt around it and found an alcove of some kind. I backed into it and they passed close enough for me to smell their shampoo.

They went on and I followed. A loud thump caused one of the girls to scream, and at first I thought Calvin had come in from the other side when I realized they were just having fun in a carnival attraction.

I felt my way a little farther until the corridor bent and there was a dim yellow light over a door. The girls were gone, but I heard screaming somewhere ahead. I needed to get out pretty fast and get help.

My mistake was that I didn't go back to the entrance and wait for somebody to open it up. Then I could have simply dodged the attendant, and bugged out.

Instead, I thought it was a good idea to walk through the whole Funhouse to the exit. I headed for the door under the weak light and the floor dropped out from under me.

Chapter Fifty-three

Pepper and Mark stepped out of a dented boat aluminum cart with flaking paint and left the musty Tunnel of Love behind. Pepper was mad as a hornet. "You didn't even *try* to kiss me!"

Mark grinned. "I held your hand."

"After I grabbed *yours*. You could have put your arm around me, like that couple in front of us."

"I could have, but the people in the cart behind us would have seen that, just like we did. I didn't really like watching them rassle around, did you?"

Instead of answering, she took another tack. "You didn't seem too embarrassed to snuggle up to me in there."

"I didn't have any choice. That little ol' cart wasn't hardly big enough for the both of us. I don't see how two adults could ride that thing without making babies."

Pepper's mad dissolved into a fit of laughter. "I can't believe you said that!"

"Why?"

"Because you've never said anything like that since we met."

"Well, maybe you're getting to know me."

She studied his face and the features that defined him as Choctaw. Even though they weren't kinfolk, he favored Miss Becky, something she hadn't noticed before. "Maybe I am, but I don't think I'll ever really know you, Mr. Mark Lightfoot."

"Nope. Don't know myself."

They passed the Funhouse and stopped to watch two kids feel their way through the glass and mirror maze. "Let's do that."

Mark shrugged. "It'll be more fun if there's three of us. Let's find Top."

"I don't have any idea where he might be."

"He was headed this way…" Mark stopped and grinned. "I bet I know where he went."

"Where?"

He pointed toward a sign at the end of the midway. "The boob show."

"They won't let him in, and besides, he ain't interested in half-nekked girls."

Mark threw back his head and laughed. "Girl, sometimes you don't think straight."

"Why?"

"Just 'cause." Mark leaned over and kissed her cheek, brushing the eagle feather and making it tickle her neck. Pepper jumped and he laughed. "There. You feel better now?"

She frowned and hit his shoulder with a fist. "That's not cool!"

"What? You were mad five minutes ago because I *didn't* kiss you."

"Yeah," she looked around. "But that was in the dark and nobody could see. Everybody and their uncle saw *that*."

Mark sighed. "Jeeze."

They strolled past carnies waving their arms and calling for the next suckers to lay down their money. Pepper glared at them. "So what makes you think he'll be in the girly tent?"

"Just some things he mentioned yesterday."

She took his hand to lead the way, but turned her head so he couldn't see the grin on her face.

Chapter Fifty-four

Deputy Anna Sloan thought she had the Lamar County Accident all figured out, except for one part, and that was why Frank and Maggie were on the dam in the first place. She used her Motorola to call Deputy Washington. "John?"

He came back after only a moment. "Yessum?"

"Where are you?"

"Nearly to the carnival. They had some trouble, but it'll all be over 'time I get there, Why, you need me?"

"I need to talk to you. How about I meet you there in the parking lot."

"Come ahead on. I'll find a spot close to the gate."

"See you in a minute. Oh, do you know where Ned is tonight?"

"Yessum. He's at the carnival now, and so's Cody."

"Good. We all need to talk. And John, you don't have to call me ma'am, or say yes ma'am. Call me Anna."

"Yessum."

"Anna."

"Yessum, Miss Anna."

Chapter Fifty-five

The Wraith, now once again Calvin Williams, aka Cal Willis the mechanic, aka Clocko the Clown, stopped the moment he saw Top duck into the Funhouse. Calvin cut between two rides and jogged back to his trailer.

Connie and the baby were asleep in their one chair when he stepped inside the stifling interior. She blinked away the cobwebs and adjusted the sleeping toddler in her lap when the door slammed. "Aren't you late? You didn't go out looking like that, did you? Delmar'd have a fit if he saw you half made up."

He paused. "I went out to have a cigarette. I meant to tell you, Delmar wants me to, well, he has a new job for me."

"That don't explain why you're outside with half your makeup on." She waved a finger toward three overflowing ashtrays. "And since when did you change your mind about smoking in the house."

Heat prickled his face. "This ain't no house. It's a goddamned trailer, and I can smoke anywhere I want to. I'm clowning up because I was thinking about skinning some extra money from the rubes with the after-catch over at the titty tent. I needed some air and some time away from that squalling baby and forgot I hadn't finished."

She ignored his comment. "That don't make no sense. You're lying to me again. Them gals'll skin you alive back behind that curtain if you get between them and their business. What'n hell you got to show or sell the rubes back there anyway?"

Rage again boiled in his chest. "You better watch your mouth or you'll be back up on the stage with 'em again, shaking them little things and showing what you got for fifty cents."

Connie's face closed up and he knew he'd hurt her again, but he didn't care. It was time to go anyway and her being mad made it that much easier.

Ignoring her, Calvin dropped into a chair in front of a battered lamp table he used as a makeup dresser. He switched on a light and finished lining the white greasepaint on his face. He only had a few minutes, ten at the most. "Anyway, Delmar wants to send me out tomorrow as his new advance-man, so I'll be gone for a little while."

The advance-man arrived in the next town before the carnival finished its current run, handling details such as licenses and sponsors. In the more stubborn towns, the ones with highly religious sheriffs or mayors, they sometimes passed bribes to the local officials before a carnival arrived in town.

She frowned at still *another* obvious lie and shifted the baby's sweaty head lying on her arm, watching him pull on his wig and add the nose. She was young, but experienced beyond her years. "Since when are you doing that? What happened to Ray Marco?"

"Nothing. He's still working." Calvin couldn't come up with a story fast enough to answer her question. "Now, let me alone."

Instead of continuing the argument, she lit her own cigarette and concentrated on smoothing the baby's cowlick. Five minutes later, Clocko the Clown left the trailer for the last time and headed toward the Funhouse.

When he was gone, Connie looked around the empty trailer and relaxed. It was better when he wasn't there.

Chapter Fifty-six

Deputy Anna Sloan joined John in the passenger seat of his car and closed the door. He immediately opened the driver's door and put one foot on the ground, keeping the dome light on so anyone looking inside could see the two deputies talking.

"Miss Anna, looks like we missed some excitement."

The volunteer fire truck was back outside the gate, along with an ambulance and several cars parked haphazardly at the entrance. None of their emergency lights were on and the small crowd of men beside the truck seemed to be loafing rather than working.

"I was away from the radio, talking to someone about Maggie and Frank's wreck. I think I've found out what's going on, and who's doing it, and how this feud is still burning."

John grunted. "Well, I hope you have."

"But I still can't figure out why they were on the dam that morning. That road didn't lead to anyone's house or anywhere they needed to go." She paused. A mental itch needed scratching, but she wasn't sure how to do it.

"Maybe they's just driving around."

"Talking!" Anna sat forward in excitement. "You're right! They were talking, or arguing, but they weren't just driving around." It all came to her in an instant. "They'd parked on the overlook, back up against the trees. You can't see inside the car from there, no matter what direction you're traveling."

John watched a couple walk past, holding hands. "They was doin' this, 'cept not with the light on."

"They'd probably been doing more, but I'm sure they were talking it out. But before I can tell you what I suspect, we need to visit your aunt, Miss Sweet."

"I already have."

"You're kidding."

"No'm. I just visited with Miss Sweet this evenin' and she said some things that made sense then told me to go talk to Rubye who worked for Frank."

"That's where I was."

"At Saperstein's grocery store."

"Right! You know her?"

John laughed again, delighted with the young woman. She'd been there less than a year and had gained the respect of every deputy in Lamar County. "Sure do. Took her out a few times when we was younger."

Anna cut her eyes across the car. "Miss Sweet told you the same thing I heard from Rubye."

"Yep."

"A baby." She sighed, as if a great weight had been lifted off her shoulders. They'd solved part of the Lamar County Accident. "Rubye told me something else, too. She said Bryce and Willie Mayfield is for sure two of 'em we're after. They've been setting fires and were the ones who cut up Alfred Clay last night. You know them?"

"Sure do. She know that for a fact?"

"Overheard Willie tell Bryce where to find Alfred and then to meet him here for an alibi."

"This is a good place to be seen all right."

"I'll get a warrant tomorrow…"

John cut her off. "Don't need to."

"Why not?"

"I just saw 'em go in. Will Rubye testify to what she heard?"

"Said she would."

John set his hat. "Let's go pick 'em up for suspicion."

They were finally getting a handle on things.

Chapter Fifty-seven

Pepper pointed. "There he goes sneakin' into the Funhouse without paying when the ticket man was talking to that clown with the balloons."

"I can't see him doing that." Mark led her toward the big, two-story attraction with different size boxes protruding from odd places. "I bet he'd already paid and had to leave for some reason and went back in."

"I swear, you sound just like Miss Becky. He's not as little and innocent as y'all think."

"You're right about that." Mark dug in his pocket when they reached the ticket taker. "I don't think nothin', though." He held the money out to the ticket taker. "Three."

The man in a faded shirt took the money and dropped the change into the money apron tied around his waist. "There's only two of you."

"My cousin just went in and I'm ashamed to tell you he didn't pay." Mark met the man's eyes and looked apologetic.

The carney's head snapped toward the entrance ramp. "I didn't see nobody."

"You was talking. I just wanted to make things right."

The man dug in his apron and tried to give Mark his money back. "Here, kid. Y'all go in for free. I don't run across very many kids as honest as you."

Pepper's mouth fell open as Mark refused the offer. "Nossir. Go ahead and keep it. You don't have to do that for us."

The carney held the change out to Pepper. "Well, you take it then, missy, if your boyfriend won't. Y'all use it later." He winked. "But stay away from the games."

Pepper took the money, stuck it in her pocket, and pushed Mark forward. They stepped inside and the door closed, leaving them in total darkness. She slugged him in the back. "You knothead. Why didn't you take the money? He was just *giving* it away."

"Because it wasn't right." She heard Mark laugh and he vanished into pitch black.

She reached for him and found nothing but the thick odor of stuffy, stale mildew. Pepper held out both hands and felt her way forward. "Where'd you go?"

Someone pushed her shoulder from behind and she shrieked. Mark laughed and grabbed her around the waist. "It's me."

"How'd you get around me?"

"I felt a gap in the wall here. You just stepped right past."

"Well, it's so damned dark I can't see a thing." She advanced, holding both hands out and feeling her way in the walk-through. Mark stepped close, wrapped his arms around her waist, lockstepped behind her, and they went to find Top.

Chapter Fifty-eight

Ned rubbed his head in frustration. He blew out his lips and replaced his hat.

Willie Mayfield passed, wearing new overalls and gnawing on an ear of corn. His son Bryce followed. The muscular young man was counting a wad of folding money and not paying any attention to the barkers trying to entice him closer. Someone called his name and Willie smiled and waved.

Cody suddenly ran out of energy knowing full well it was the letdown from the adrenaline dump. At the same time, he registered the Clays and Mayfields mixed in all around them. There were suddenly way too many clan members in close proximity. Cecil and Martin Clay seemed to be following Willie and Bryce down the midway, though it could have been only his imagination.

Cody picked up on Ned's unease. "What's wrong with you? All these feuding people making you nervous?"

"Partly. I don't like 'em all in the same place at the same time. If things come unraveled here, we'll be blowed up. But right now I'm mad as a wet hen. Them kids were supposed to be back by now."

Norma Faye laughed. "I'm not surprised. They're probably having a great time, something *we* should be doing instead of standing here worrying."

"It don't matter none. I done told 'em what to do, and it's partly because there could be trouble. Now it looks like somebody let the gate down. This place is filling up like nobody's business. I never thought about these two families all deciding to come at the same time."

Cody shoved off the post where he'd been leaning. "Well, let's go look for 'em again. If we make ourselves seen, it might take some of the fire out of these idiots if they're thinking about starting something."

"Then the kids'll show up here and we'll be gone."

A woman with tight curls and deep dimples peeled out of a crowd around the Ring Toss game and saw Norma Faye. She rushed forward and they hugged. "Why girl, I haven't seen you in years."

"Christine Rankin!" They squealed like school girls as Norma Faye slid her arm around the woman's thick waist. "Not since I moved into *this* life. Do you know my husband, Cody Parker?"

"I've heard of you, Sheriff, though we've never met."

They shook and Norma Faye gave Ned a pat on the arm. "This is Constable Ned Parker. Me and Christine went to school together. Ned, why don't y'all go find the kids and I'll wait here for them? We can catch up while you're gone."

Relieved, Ned shook Christine's hand. "That sounds good. A pleasure to meet you, ma'am."

Cody paused. "I'm in the El Camino and don't have a radio. Did you come in yours, Ned? If you did, we can call John and maybe Anna to come out tonight. It won't hurt to have two more uniforms out here with all these people who don't want to get along."

"We came in the car, but I'm worried about them kids. You can go call on the Motorola while I look for 'em, if you want."

Cody saw Ned was more worried than he let on. "I'll wait 'til we get ahold of those knotheads. We can split up and find them faster than just one."

"Fine then."

Chapter Fifty-nine

Ned and Cody made their way to the darker end of the midway. They paused beside a pair of clowns joking around and selling balloons.

"Well, that's about it." Ned jerked a thumb toward the exhibit tents. "You don't think them little shits went back there, do you?"

"I doubt it. The attractions in those tents cost more money than the rides, and I figure the kids would rather ride than look at a two-headed calf."

"Well, you never know." Ned tilted his head back and scanned the crowd and the lines. "They might have been on one of these rides when we passed them."

"You're right about that. Let's stand here a few minutes to give them time to get off and make a sweep back toward the gate. I imagine they're with Norma Faye already."

Ned frowned at a group of men leaving the girly tent. "There goes Royal Clay."

"He ain't the only Clay I've seen here tonight."

"Yeah, but he's the meanest behind Wes." Ned scanned the crowd. "There's a bunch of 'em all right."

Cecil Clay hurried up to Royal and waved his arms while he talked. Seconds later, they rushed back down the midway toward the gate.

A white-faced clown pulled a little girl's pigtails and acted surprised they wouldn't come off. Cody watched her giggle when he plucked a balloon from the other clown's bouquet.

Cody met the first clown's gaze and received a big wink. Cody smiled back before a boy and girl making their way through the glass maze of the Funhouse caught his attention. For a moment he thought it was Pepper and the boys, but when she turned her head to find a way out, the wavy glass distorted her image and disappeared.

"You know, we better keep moving so these Clays and May-fields don't bunch up."

Ned sighed. "Good idea."

A different kind of shriek reached them and Ned stopped. "What now?"

A shout floated over the crowd. "Fight!"

The crowd surged back toward the entrance.

Chapter Sixty

The floor didn't really fall out from under me, but it sure felt that way. The false panel only dropped a couple of inches, making me think I was going all the way through and into a basement. I guess if that'd happened, I'd've died right then and there.

Instead, I hollered and jumped back. Somebody grabbed me around the waist and I screamed like a little girl.

"Damn! And all this time I thought you were a boy!"

I turned to fight, and saw Pepper falling back in the dim yellow light and into Mark's arms, laughing. "Dammit girl!" The shock on her face was funny, but I couldn't enjoy it.

"I can't believe you cussed!"

I looked past Mark, and into the darkness. "Did anyone come in behind you?"

I could barely see them in the feeble light, but it was enough to tell they were frowning.

"Why?"

My knees went shaky and I wanted to cry. "There's somebody after me."

Mark spun. "Where?"

Pepper saw the look on my face and grabbed my arm. "Who? Are you all right?"

"No. My foot's bleeding like a stuck hog and Calvin Williams is here."

"Who?"

"Aunt Norma Faye's ex-husband."

"So what?"

"He's after me."

"Why?" She grinned like she does when she's up to something she don't want the adults to know. "What'd you say to him?"

"I'll tell you later. C'mon!"

We heard the entrance door open and a voice came through. "Where you going, Cal?"

"Just want to give the kids a little extra thrill." The door slammed shut. That was all we needed.

Chapter Sixty-one

Norma Faye and Christine were laughing and acting like school girls out for the night when Anna and John Washington came through the gate. Norma Faye called them over.

John stopped at a distance. "Howdy, Miss Norma Faye."

"John, I wish you'd leave out the Miss part."

Anna rolled her eyes. "He won't listen."

"Cain't." John glanced around. "Least not in public. That all right?"

"As long as you promise to drop it when it's just us."

"Deal. You seen Mr. Ned?"

All three women laughed, surprising John before he realized what was so funny.

"He was just here with Cody. They left to go find the kids."

"That'll take a while, I 'spect."

Anna positioned herself to keep an eye on the patrons passing in all directions and watched the carnival workers beside the Skydiver. "Anyone hurt bad?"

"Nope." Norma Faye raised her thick red hair to cool the back of her neck. "A couple of girls banged up, but that's all. One of them was a Clay."

"Good." Anna raised an eyebrow at the name and watched John intercept a group of black teenagers who squealed in delight when they saw him.

He wrapped a couple in his big arms and launched into an animated conversation with the kids. "Sharonda Mayfield! When'd you get out of jail?"

The others around her screamed and laughed at the joke that was old as the hills.

Running out of conversation in the loud midway, Christine gave Norma Faye a squeeze. "I want to come see that house of yours."

Norma Faye laughed. "Any time. It's a lot better than that shack where we lived and you stayed with me that week Calvin went hunting in Oklahoma."

"It was too bad he came back, hungover and stinkin' to high heaven. Honey, you sure picked a loser in that one. He never was worth half of nothing, and that house! I don't believe I ever saw a rat come running out of an oven before!" They laughed and Christine left after more promises to get together.

When she was gone, Anna sidestepped closer to Norma Faye. "Did you ride over here with Cody?"

Norma Faye rolled her eyes. "Yep. We're on a date."

Anna hadn't been on a date since she moved to Chisum. Recuperating from the shotgun blast and working nearly eighteen hours a day didn't lend much chance at finding anyone. It was a vicious cycle, no dates and no social life meant she could work harder and longer hours.

"At least you're on one." Anna passed both hands up and down her uniform. "I haven't had too many guys ask *me* lately. That's one reason I'm working tonight."

"I might know someone…"

"No. That's not what I meant. Cody brought you here for a night out and here you stand, talking to me."

"That's okay. It's his job, and besides, this is the life I chose."

Anna studied Norma Faye's face. Her mass of red hair was even brighter in the colored lights. "Cody told me how y'all got together. You're both lucky."

"We sure are. It didn't happen the way I would have liked, and there was a lot of talk. I believe I heard the word 'hussy' about once a day for a year, but I didn't care. We were supposed to be together."

"Why don't I find him and send him back? Y'all need to enjoy your time together."

"He'll be back in a little while with Ned and the kids."

"Well girl, I love your spirit." Anna paused, watching two men glare at each other in the middle of the midway. "Uh oh. I better get over there."

Norma Faye followed her gaze. "One of those guys is Cecil Clay. The other two with him are kinfolk. The other'n over there is a Mayfield, but I don't know his name."

"All the more reason."

Chapter Sixty-two

Anna left Norma Faye and headed directly toward Cecil Clay. She caught John's attention as she passed and pointed. The warmth in his eyes vanished and he left the youngsters to make a bee-line toward Bryce Mayfield, who wouldn't break eye contact with Cecil.

If seen from above, a viewer would have witnessed a stunning sight. Cecil Clay and Bryce became human magnets, their posture drawing people toward them from up and down the midway. With the hive-instinct of insects, family members left what they were doing and headed toward the building confrontation.

Rage radiated from young men tight as fiddle strings and the air crackled with electricity. Clay's cousins Andy, Martin, and Wilbur formed a line facing the gathering Mayfield clan.

Bryce Mayfield slipped one hand into his overalls and met Cecil's gaze. It was as challenging as two fighting dogs in a pit, and just as effective. Almost as if it were orchestrated, more Clays pressed within feet of their adversaries. Neither advancing line was intimidated by the other.

Sensing the coming storm, onlookers stopped to watch the action, packing people into the leftover spaces in front of the games. Even the barkers quieted down, straining to see the conflict.

John stepped between them, holding out a hand to warn his people back. "Hold on now. You Mayfields settle down!"

Anna rested one hand on the butt of her pistol. "You men cool off! We're not having this here tonight!"

"Shut up little girl!" Royal Clay's unwashed hair was combed back behind his ears and his blue work shirt needed to visit the inside of a washing machine. "My people don't have to take no shit off a woman deputy at any time."

Her voice was calm and steady, not reflecting how she felt inside. "How's that knee, tough guy?"

The man put his hand in the middle of Anna's chest. "You was lucky this mornin'. Now, go on home and scrub a commode or something and let the men settle things...."

He pushed and Anna's leather sap once again came out of nowhere, this time cracking against Royal's head. His eyes rolled back and he collapsed in a heap, blood gushing from a split in his scalp. She stepped back, ready for another swing at the next target that was Cecil. "Give me a reason, young man. Just one."

"There's too many innocent people here for this." John hadn't taken his eyes off the collection of opponents pressing close. "Bryce! You better get that hand out of that pocket."

The men wavered and shrank back. Willis wriggled his fingers into a set of brass knuckles. "John, go on and get gone. This needs to end here."

"Nothin's happenin'." John drew his own sap that looked tiny in his big hand. "Y'all back off or I'm fixin' to hurt somebody."

Chapter Sixty-three

No one had ever seen Clocko the Clown in the Funhouse, but that didn't make any difference. Clowns were known for doing whatever came to mind, and Calvin had an idea. If he caught the kid inside, he could have enough to time to finish up before he left.

He knew the layout of the Funhouse as well as the owner, Fredrick Bellows. Calvin Williams was the best mechanic they had at the carnival, and spent his days helping to maintain and repair the rides and exhibits. He even repaired some of the oddities and illusions such as the corpse of the Outlaw Ben Steele. Supposedly gunned down during a bank robbery in the 1880s, the corpse was nothing more than a mannequin body with a dried leather face made from deteriorating deerskin.

Calvin had fixed the Funhouse's false drop only two days before and he almost laughed that Top was trying to hide inside a place he knew as well as the back of his hand.

Kyle Philips, the kid taking money at the door, was surprised when Calvin jumped the rail. "Where you going, Cal?"

Aggravated, he held the door open for a moment. He didn't need anyone to question what he was doing. Calvin had an agreement with Delmar that he clowned when he wanted to, and could come and go as he pleased.

He spoke softly so only Kyle could hear. "Clocko, you dumbass. When I'm in paint, it's Clocko." He widened his eyes, spread his hands and fingers and rocked back and forth. "Just want to give the kids a little extra thrill." He paused. Well, hell, he didn't have to follow the kid through the maze. He spun and Kyle backed out of the way.

"Cal...Clocko." Kyle held up both hands in a startled defensive move. "What'n hell you doing now?"

"Shut up, kid. It's none of your business, but I changed my mind." He pushed the young man out of the way and shoved through a half dozen teenagers lined up for their turn.

They laughed and pointed at Clocko the Clown, but one of the boys puffed up. "Hey clown, don't push my girlfriend! What's that all about?"

Clocko turned dead eyes on the kid who quickly found something more interesting further down. The boy took his frightened girlfriend's hand and they left, dodging another clown coming from the opposite direction with a spray of bright balloons.

Clocko held out a hand. "Hey, Dale."

Instead of reacting the same way as Calvin when Kyle called his real name, Baggy the Clown paused. "What?"

"Loan me a couple of them balloons."

Baggy peeled two away from the strings in his hand and passed them over. "You better do something before Delmar sees you standing around like you got good sense. You're supposed to be in character."

Clocko's eyes widened and he held both hands wide again, this time speaking in falsetto. "Well I needed a *balloon!*"

Two teenagers laughed as they passed, reaching for the balloons in Clocko's hand. He leaned in, showing his yellow teeth and the frightened kids hurried away.

Baggy skipped in a circle. "Balloons for sale! Balloooooooon-nnnsssss!"

"Hang around with me for a few minutes," Clocko said.

Baggy shrugged. "Sure."

In a complete reversal of personality, Clocko lightly pulled a little girl's pigtails and handed her one of his balloons. She let go of her smiling father's hand, took it, presented the clown with her own smile. Patting her on the head, Clocko turned to a tall teenage boy. "Hey, smell this flower and tell me if you like it."

When the youngster leaned in for a sniff, Clocko squeezed a bulb in his pants pocket, sending a squirt of water into his face. The boy's friends laughed and the teenager good-naturedly wiped it away, grinning from ear to ear for being taken.

Clocko's smile was painted on, but his real lips buried in a thick layer of red paint were pursed in concern. His multiple personalities struggled to get free. To hold them steady, he gave another little boy a pat on the head and positioned himself to watch the Funhouse exit door, using Baggy and his balloons as a shield.

Chapter Sixty-four

The Funhouse would've been great if we'd been in there to enjoy it. Instead, I needed to find Grandpa. Pepper and Mark led the way faster than I wanted. My foot hurt like sin and blood squished in my tennis shoe.

I limped along as we went through the spinning Barrel of Fun tunnel and I might near fell over twice because it made me dizzy. My foot wasn't helping my balance neither. We left and stumbled across the dancing bridge that tilted ever which-a-way when we stepped on it. The place was full of noise and organ music. We went through a room with lights popping like flashbulbs while our eyes were trying to readjust. The next hall led into a room full of distorted mirrors.

Pepper held Mark's hand and they bulled on ahead, pushing past a gaggle of girls laughing at their wavy images. We turned a corner behind some boys and girls about our age and found ourselves in the glass house. There was no way to hurry, because the lights were set so's you couldn't see well and every little cubicle had only one way out.

I was feeling each pane of glass when I realized Mark and Pepper had gotten ahead of me, and it wasn't all because of my limp. "Hey!"

They were only a few feet away, but when I reached out, my hand cracked against the glass. I hollered again, but they couldn't hear me over the noise and screams of other kids. The music was so loud that it hurt my ears. My head pounded so full of pressure I thought it'd pop.

Mark stopped about two cubicles over and pointed at his feet. I looked, but couldn't figure out what he wanted me to see. He mouthed something and I frowned at the dirty floor that looked like it hadn't be cleaned in a hundred years. There was something…oh! The wooden frames on the floor were the giveaway. You couldn't find your way very fast by patting the glass, but when you looked at the frames on the floor, you could real quick tell that some had glass in them, and the empty frames told me the way out.

From there it was only a few seconds until I caught up with them.

Pepper acted as frustrated as I was scared. "Stay with us!"

"My foot hurts! That's why I'm in here in the first place, because I couldn't outrun Calvin."

"No talking!" Mark sounded like Uncle Cody when he was mad. He checked over his shoulder to be sure Calvin wasn't behind us and led the way again. "Come on!"

We came to steps that bounced and jiggled, but using the pipe handrails, we climbed to a landing where a spinning barrel revolved around a slide. Pepper dropped down on her butt and slid out of sight. When she hit, we heard her scream, and it wasn't one of fun.

"Pepper!" Mark jumped onto the long slide and shot out of sight and I went in right behind him.

I knew it. Calvin had come in from the other side.

Chapter Sixty-five

Clocko watched Ned and Cody drift to a stop only feet away. His stomach clenched when Ned looked his way, but then Clocko remembered they wouldn't recognize him under the greasepaint and wig. Even though Ned had known him from the time he was a kid in Center Springs, Calvin was as camouflaged as a quail squatting in tall grass.

It was suddenly a glorious situation and he threw his head back and laughed. Baggy the Clown took it as a cue, and they laughed together, one a real guffaw, the other stage acting. Clocko's attention flicked to Cody's empty shirt pocket and another thrill ran up his spine when he remembered taking the sheriff's silver Cross pen from the kitchen table that night in his house. Cody needed to suffer and worry just like him, only the pen didn't throw enough suspicion his way.

It was a spur-of-the-moment souvenir after he spent five minutes standing in their bedroom door, watching Cody and Norma Faye's sleeping shapes in the moonlight. Breathing through his mouth, he thought about killing them both right then with the razor sharp knife riding in the homemade shoulder rig under his oversize clothes, imagining Norma Faye's scream at the sight of Cody's spurting blood, but he wanted them to suffer first, just like he did.

Instead, he decided that he could sneak in any time before the carnival left and do it then.

Calvin only took up the carney life to come back and get even with the man stole his wife and destroyed his future.

Standing on the midway, Calvin frowned and pressed the knife against his chest with one hand. He never went anywhere without it and now he wanted payback. He wanted Cody to recognize him in the last seconds of his life, to watch his eyes widen in fear.

Then he'd make Norma Faye beg as he cut her throat for leaving him when he needed her the most. He was weaker then, and confused about what he should do. But not anymore.

He had the chance to bring it all to a head this night.

He laughed again. It was exciting. Stir up a little trouble and the long-festering resentment between the families boiled over. It was beautiful to play those fools one against the other, burning houses and killing both Clays and Mayfields as if hunting season had opened, while the laws were running around like chickens with their heads cut off.

Ned and Cody looked as if they were waiting on someone, or maybe looking *for* somebody. It took a moment to realize it was probably Top. The kid recognizing him might change things, good or bad, one way or another, but Calvin knew as sure as he'd ever known anything before that the time had come for all of them.

Cody's eyes drifted over the balloons, Baggy, and then came to rest on Clocko.

Calvin's chest swelled when Cody didn't register any recognition at all. Clocko's painted smile widened, emphasized by the red lips and black outline. He danced a little jig, a shave-and-a-haircut move with his feet and then slapped the pavement with his shoe to finish.

He gave Cody a wide wink.

The sheriff responded with a curious grin which immediately faded when shouts came from the far end of the midway. "Fight!" was repeated back down the line of tents, rides, and games.

Ned and Cody took off and Clocko's smile became even wider. Tonight his knife was going to slice Cody Parker's throat, as soon as he finished his business with that damned kid in the Funhouse. He waited for Top to come out and shuddered in ecstasy at how it would feel when the edge cut through Cody's living flesh, arteries, and the crunchy cartilage of his throat.

Chapter Sixty-six

Pepper was standing up in the flickering lights, wagging her finger in the face of a guy dressed in black. She had him against a wall and was giving him a good cussin' when I hit the bottom of the slide and saw that it wasn't Calvin after all.

Mark grabbed her arm. "What's wrong?"

"This son of a bitch grabbed me."

The guy held out his hands when I was close. "Honest. That's my job, to step out of the dark and grab you. I'm *supposed* to scare you."

"Well you damn sure grabbed something that you shouldn't…"

"Them little skeeter bites of yours ain't enough to tell…"

Pepper drew back her fist to punch the sneering teenager when Mark hooked her elbow and pushed on the exit door. "Cool it. We're out of here." He drug her across the threshold and out into the thick humidity at the same time a jet of air shot up from the floor with a loud whoosh.

"Shit!" Pepper turned to charge back inside away from that startling burst, but Mark shoved her the rest of the way outside and followed. The jet caught him too, then me as I pushed outside and we stumbled down the metal steps to the ground.

A clown with a bunch of balloons watched us. I gave him a good, long look to make sure it wasn't Calvin Williams behind all that paint, but that guy had a wide red frown instead of Calvin's half-finished smile.

Another clown beside him reached out to rub a little boy on his bare head.

Pepper and Mark led the way, and I limped along behind them. We hadn't no more than stepped into the throng of people than we heard someone shouting there was a fight going on.

It looked like our school yard when boys tangled up. More'n half the people close by us took off to see what they could see. I thought I saw Grandpa and Uncle Cody's hats in the crowd. So many men wore straw Stetsons that I couldn't tell for sure.

Mark and Pepper disappeared into the crowd and I limped along behind, my bleeding foot killing me. "Hey, y'all. I can't walk that fast."

Chapter Sixty-seven

Clocko nudged Baggy when Top and two others boiled out of the Funhouse. He immediately recognized Pepper. "Did you see what those three kids did?"

The clown who was once a gas station attendant followed Clocko's finger. "Cal, I see dozens of kids."

Clocko took a deep breath to calm himself, wishing he could slide his knife into the base of the dumbass's skull like he did that idiot Joe Bill Haynes, just before he pushed him into his dirty swimming pool. Joe Bill was another of those who had to pay with his life, because right out of high school he'd asked Maybelle Simpson out on a date only a day before Calvin planned to express his own feelings to her. After that, he'd lost the battle as she and Joe Bill quickly became engaged and married.

Maybelle didn't have him now, though, that was for sure.

Clocko grabbed Baggy's oversize shirt and tugged. "Look. That long-haired Indian kid and the girl with the feather in her hair. I think they've been picking pockets all night. I saw him slip something out of that woman's purse and he passed it to the girl and she stuffed it into that hobo bag on her shoulder."

Baggy squinted, shaping his makeup into a ghastly frown. "Oh, yeah."

"See that crippled kid limping along behind them?"

"Yeah."

"He's the shill. I saw him limp in front of the lady to get her attention and the other two snatched her billfold."

"There ain't no pros like that out here in the country. Maybe in Dallas, or Houston, but not here in the sticks."

The guy was driving Calvin nuts. Baggy was slower than most other people when it came to thinking, but he wasn't getting the idea at all. "Look, they're some of them hippie kids that travel all around the country. I bet they follow us and make a living stealing from these honest folks." He took Baggy's elbow. "C'mon. We're gonna grab them when they pass the freak show tent. Help me drag the Indian kid and the girl out of sight and I bet the crippled kid'll follow, and then we'll get 'em all. One of us'll hold them while the other'n goes and gets Delmar."

Baggy thought for a moment. "Why don't we follow 'em 'til we come across somebody to help us?"

The Wraith was fast taking over Clocko the Clown. His hand twitched, aching to feel the knife's bone handle. "Because we might lose them. Look, they're getting away. Come on!" He grabbed the remaining balloons from Baggy and handed them to a group of black kids who squealed with delight.

Baggy followed and they broke into a jog, much to the amusement of the carnival's patrons who expected a show. Clocko and Baggy grabbed the long-haired Indian boy and his girlfriend in painful arm locks and quickly ushered them between the tents.

The boy with the limp shouted. "Help! It's Calvin Williams!" He followed them out of sight. The crowd moved on. No one wanted to get involved.

Chapter Sixty-eight

Cody moved faster than Ned, bulling through the gathering crowd that packed tighter the closer he came to the confrontation near the ticket booth. Most of the gawkers stepped aside, but those sympathetic to either family intentionally held him back.

Ahead, one rumbling voice rose above the others. There was anger radiating like waves of heat from Deputy John Washington, the giant of a man who rarely spoke above a normal tone. "Enough!"

Ned trailed behind, shoving people aside before the wake behind Cody closed up. "Move! Laws coming through!"

Cody's subconscious heard Ned at the same time he broke into the circle of men and absorbed the terrifying picture of an imaginary fuse hissing toward several sticks of human dynamite. The tension was palpable in the garish flashing lights. Both deputies were squared off like dogs in a pit against two families who hated each other as much as the Devil himself.

The sheen of John's tight face came not from the humidity, but from the rising temperature of the confrontation. His right hand rested on the holstered revolver hanging from his dress belt. His left held a sap.

Deputy Anna Sloan's eyes were glassy with anger and pressure. Royal Clay lay bleeding at her feet and she faced Cecil with her own sap held ready.

Cody's relief that they hadn't drawn their weapons was short-lived. The appearance of only one firearm in the crowd would trigger a slaughter. Too many people crowded in around them. If anyone were to fire, there was a hundred percent chance that onlookers would be soaking up lead.

The feuding families knew it too. Outnumbering the deputies at least twenty to one, they closed in on each other until they were within spitting distance. It took a moment for Cody to hear them through the chaos and shouts.

"You killed Hollis!"

"One of you bastards burned down my house!"

Cecil laughed. "I sure did and I'll light another'n if you don't get out of this county!"

"Go ahead. Swing and see what happens."

"I ain't startin' nothin'!"

"It's done started you son of a bitch!"

John held out the sap in his left hand like a dagger. The portion of the crowd closest to him shrank back as if it was sharp and dangerous. He hadn't yet acknowledged Cody's arrival. The big man pushed into the middle of the confrontation. "Bryce! You better get your hand out of that pocket."

Cody finally registered the entire scene. Bryce Mayfield's hand was in the pocket of his overalls, where it shouldn't be in the last few seconds before a fight. Behind him, relatives assumed rigid stances, ready to launch themselves at the Clays...

...who mirrored their readiness. Royal Clay was on the ground, holding his bloody head and struggling to rise while others of his clan moved between him and the Mayfields to protect their own while he was down...

...and Anna reached for Cecil's collar when a voice rang out and Cody realized it came from Willie Mayfield...

...who said, "John, go on and get gone. This needs to end here," and...

...John raised the sap for a blow saying..."Nothin's happenin'," and...

...Ned placed one hand on Cody's shoulder as he shoved past saying, "Oh, shit," and drew his own sap, and immediately swung at Bryce's head where it connected in a spray of blood as...

...Bryce's hand came out of his pocket and a snub-nosed .38 fell to the ground one second before Bryce landed beside it and...

...seconds later the world exploded as men clashed like charging armies.

Chapter Sixty-nine

One of the clowns pushed Pepper to the ground and knelt with his knee on her neck. "Stay right there, miss!"

She grimaced with her face in the beaten-down grass. "Get your knee off me you son of a bitch! You ain't got no right to drag us back here!"

Mark kicked back like a mule, trying to catch the other clown's knee. He missed and I launched myself at the guy to make him turn Mark loose. Adults knew more about fighting and he didn't do nothing but duck. I went over his shoulder at the same time Mark hollered because of the pressure on his shoulder from the hold that feller had on him.

They both went down. I stumbled over them. I couldn't believe this was happening right in the open behind the tents. Carnivals were supposed to be fun, but here we were in the middle of a nightmare.

The snarling clown holding Mark reached out and grabbed my shirt and slung me down. "Let me go!" I tried to twist out of his fist, but he held solid.

The other one wasn't as mean. "You kids settle down and we'll work this out!"

Pepper screamed anyway, but it was lost in the noise from the midway. I rolled and fought and my shirt came up around my arms. I twisted some more and suddenly the clown was holding nothing but cloth. I was standing there without a stitch on from the waist up.

All that fighting and wrestling had messed up the talking clown's paint. It smeared down one eye past his mouth, making it all droop like he'd had a stroke. I looked around for something to hit him with when the light caught him just right and clear as day I saw it was Calvin Williams.

He dropped my shirt. Someone screamed like a little girl. It was me. A farmer in overalls shot into the light a second later, swinging something long and hard. It cracked across the side of Calvin's head with a clang and his red nose popped off. Blood spurted and he hollered and fell back in a roll.

The farmer swung again, squalling like an old tomcat, screaming and jabbering in what sounded like the tongues I'd heard in Miss Becky's little Assembly of God church more than once. Babbling like a terrified lunatic, he took another two-handed swing and hit Calvin across the ribs with a bildukey shovel. It smacked against something solid. I hoped it was the sound of a breaking rib.

The other clown let go of Pepper and stood up, hollering. "Hey! It ain't us. These kids are thieves. They're pickpockets! We're holding them for the laws."

The farmer was still squalling and babbling. He juked to the side and took a swing at that talking clown, who squealed and ran away. By that time Calvin struggled to his knees where the farmer whacked him on the back of the head. His red wig flew away as he staggered to his feet and stumbled after the other clown.

They disappeared into the crowd on the midway. I turned to see the wide-eyed features of Mr. Ike Reader who stood there trembling, waving the shovel. "Clowns! Listen, listen. I hate clowns!" He swallowed and I saw his big Adam's apple bounce up and down. "Now, why was they after y'all?"

Pepper laid on the ground and laughed herself sick. Mark, and I were shaking, but we managed to explain what was happening.

Chapter Seventy

A bright and shiny flash cut through the sparkling lights. Ned recognized it for a knife blade. He swung his sap again, missing the head he was aiming at. Cody surged forward, straining to get his hands on a Clay he recognized only by his features.

Anna's size put her at a disadvantage in the fight that blew up like a hand grenade. A short man caught a savage blow to his face and dropped at her feet, nearly knocking her down. She backhanded a Clay and lunged through the crowd, trying to get her back to John. Someone grabbed her leg and she stumbled, nearly falling. When she looked down, Royal Clay was bleeding from his nose but holding on to her like a toddler. He waved a pistol in the air, but he was so dazed it could have been a pickle.

A fist flew before her eyes, barely missing her chin. She did the only thing possible to stop Royal's threat, kicking his chin with her steel-toed boot. He fell as limp as a dishrag. One of the younger Mayfields stumbled over the unconscious man and struck a blow that numbed Anna's shoulder. Her sap snapped out, dropping the combatant beside Royal.

Divided along both racial lines and blood lineage at the outset, the altercation dissolved into a gang fight. Big John quickly found himself in the middle of furious white men who used the opportunity to strike the black deputy. In that brief instant, there was no law but that of survival. He grabbed Cecil Clay by the shirt and whipped around, using the slender man's body as a weapon. Cecil gasped and came off his feet kicking, but John pivoted using his massive upper body to sling Cecil outward like a child spinning in the yard. His legs cut people down as smooth as a scythe through a wheatfield.

Getting a better grip under Cecil's arms and around his neck, John whipped the limp man in the opposite direction. Men dodged Cecil's flailing legs and still battered each other in desperate individual fights using everything from teeth to nails to knives. Cousins Martin and Wilbur Clay leaped into the fray. John slung Cecil again. The heel of his boot smacked Wilbur on the jaw, dropping him like a rock.

Cody took a fist to the jaw that he felt all the way to the soles of his boots. He grabbed the guy's wrist and forced his arm up between the man's own shoulder blades. Holding one Clay was ineffective in such a fray. Cody shoved him between two combatants and grabbed a Mayfield arm, jerking the man off his feet and spinning him into the crowd of onlookers.

Too old to fight with his fists, Ned furiously laid about with his sap. "That's enough! Back off!" He saw a knife glint and swung at the man's wrist, snapping it like a twig. Without losing momentum, he turned the blow into a backswing, collapsing the assailant with a vicious whack to the temple.

A fist hard as a brick hit him hard in the ribs. Another blow landed behind the ear, exactly where Ned liked to pop drunks with his sap. Sure enough, the punch nearly bashed the old constable to his knees.

John threw Cecil into a knot of fighters, grabbing Ned under the arm to hold him upright as black and white fists rained against his body. The big man roared again, jamming his elbow into a Mayfield temple and knocking him unconscious. Ned grunted from a glancing punch.

No one touched Mr. Ned. The dark monster Big John kept buried deep inside broke free and clawed to the surface. A sea of frenzied faces blurred and the banshee in the deputy went to work. The crowd of fighters closed in, black and white against the mountain of a man who fought back with solitary, awesome power.

Enemies of the badge swept over John like a wave. He stepped back under the onslaught, keeping himself between them and Ned, to stem the charge both black and white. His rage exploded in close hand-to-hand battle until unseen fingers struggled to unsnap the revolver on his belt.

Knowing the devastation that a pistol would unleash, John pressed his own elbow against the man's hand, trapping it against his side. He reached around and grabbed a fistful of hair, yanking the man off balance. John thrust his forearm under his assailant's armpit, twisting up and back until he felt ligaments tear. The man screamed and dove toward the ground. When the big deputy let go, he side-kicked a knee that snapped, forcing another shriek of pain.

The sharp, deep crump of a single gunshot stopped the brawl. The distinctive threat of a shotgun shucking another shell into the chamber was crisp over the carnival noises.

Ned's heart sank at the shot, thinking the worst had happened. His head snapped around to see Delmar Hopkins pointing a twelve-gauge pump toward the pitch black sky. He pulled the trigger again and the crowd recoiled.

Sliding a third round into the chamber, he leveled the shotgun. "That is *enough*! The plug's out of this shotgun and I have three more shells waiting. The next man who swings at another'n's gonna get a full load of buckshot and I don't give a *damn* if there's people standing beside or behind him. Y'all understand? This fight's over and the carnival's closed."

The white-haired carny took two steps toward Royal Clay who lay unconscious on the ground. Delmar put the muzzle of his shotgun against Royal's chest. "This thing's got a hair trigger. If any of y'all make me jump, it's liable to go off. Constable Parker, y'all do your business."

Ned grabbed Milton Clay by the collar and jerked him toward Delmar. "Go over there and sit down by Royal."

"He, he said that gun's liable…"

"Move slow then."

Cody pointed. "John, round up everybody that was fighting and sit them right there."

The big deputy looked down at the man who'd been trying to take his pistol, recognizing Cecil Clay. Surprised at how much fight the man had despite his damaged legs, he nudged him with one foot. "Oh, yeah, and you're under arrest for arson."

On the ground, Cecil pulled his good arm under his body as if to hide the nonexistent coal oil stains on his fingers.

"You don't have to do that. We know it was you, and Royal had you do his dirty work for him."

Instead of answering, the young man dropped his head on the dirt and closed his eyes. Anna knelt on Cecil's back and snapped a cuff on his good wrist, then clicked the other onto Royal who was starting to come around.

Ned's voice rose. "Me'n John know ever one of you, so don't be trying to slip out. Y'all sit down right where you stand. Sit!"

Bleeding, with one eye swelling shut, Willie Mayfield dropped to his knees beside his son. "Mr. Ned, Bryce's been stabbed."

John looked down and saw blood pouring from Bryce's side.

Cody knelt beside him and pointed at the brass knuckles on Willie's hand. "Here." Cody covered the wound with his palm. "Drop them knuckles and put pressure on the wound like this and hold it."

Willie shook the weapon free of his fingers and held both hands against his son's side just under his ribs. "How's that gonna help? He's bleedin' inside."

"Because that's what I was taught and I don't know nothing else." Cody rose. "Anna, run out to the car and call for help. We're gonna need every car and ambulance we can get."

Delmar waved one of his people over. "Junior, pass the word down the line. We're shut down for the night. Wrap this up."

"Yessir."

Ned swiveled in a slow circle, moving toward Delmar. He leaned in close. "Thanks."

"I hate trouble in my carnival."

Ned met his eyes and Delmar explained.

"This kind of shit costs me money."

Aggravated that Cody sent her away from the action and out to the car to make the call, Anna pushed through the throng leaving the carnival. Someone grabbed her arm and she spun around, amped up from the fight and almost swinging the sap still in her hand.

Pepper raised a hand to ward off the blow. "Whoa, Anna! Hold it! It's me."

The deputy relaxed and kept walking. "Oh, honey. Where are the others?"

"That's why I'm here." Pepper followed, almost running. "We was attacked by a couple of damn clowns."

Anna rubbed her face. "Hon, I don't have time for this. Y'all need to go wait in your granddaddy's car."

"No! Listen! I mean it! Mark's arm is hurt and Mr. Ike Reader saved us. He stayed back with Mark and Top and said tell Grandpa the bad clown is Calvin Williams."

"I don't know who that is."

Jumping in frustration, Pepper flapped her hands. "Listen! Top says Calvin Williams who was married to Norma Faye has been doing these bad things around here. He tried to kidnap us tonight because Top recognized him from bad dreams, his Poisoned Gift. You know about that, don't you? Mr. Ike Reader saved us."

Anna paused. She'd heard about his dreams. "Where are the boys now?"

"They're not far from the Funhouse. Top's foot is bleeding and Mark's staying there with him and Mr. Ike. I saw Mr. John and Grandpa over there, but they have their hands full. *Do something!*"

"As if I wasn't doing something already." Anna led Pepper to her cruiser and called for help, then they hurried back inside the grounds to find the boys. "Come with me."

Chapter Seventy-one

I was shaking like a leaf when Miss Anna showed up with Pepper. The midway was emptying out and the only people moving around were the folks that worked there. They kept glancing over at me and Mark sitting on the ground with our backs to a sharpshooter booth.

Mr. Ike stood over us, leaning on the shovel like he was resting in the field. He started talking to Miss Anna long before she got close enough to hear. "Listen, listen. There's trouble here."

She kept coming, all the time checking around like somebody was gonna jump out at her.

He repeated himself when she got to us. "Listen. There was clown trouble with these kids."

"I know that Mr. Reader. Pepper told me. There's lots of trouble here tonight." She didn't waste any time. Instead of kneeling down beside me like anyone else would, she stayed upright, her eyes moving all the while. "Tell me what happened."

It aggravated me that she asked him first, but that's how adults always were. Mr. Ike rested the shovel against the game counter and waved his hands. "Did Pepper tell you who he was?"

"Yes. Norma Faye's first husband."

Mr. Ike laid out what happened when he showed up. "I was coming from back there." He jerked a thumb over his shoulder and I saw Miss Anna's eyes widen when she saw the girly tent only a few yards past the Funhouse. "I's coming out of that exhibition tent when I saw a couple of clowns and you know, I don't like clowns. They was in the way, and I didn't want to pass close, so I ducked around this Funhouse ride to come out past 'em, when I looked up and here come them same two clowns pushing a couple of kids into the dark back there.

"Listen, you know how I don't like clowns, don'cha, Top? Well, I's afraid they was gonna kidnap these kids and brainwash 'em to run off and make more clowns, but I didn't know who they were at the time. Then when they pushed 'em to the ground I got scared and saw this shovel and the next thing I knew I was whuppin' on 'em with it and they run off."

Miss Anna nodded and scanned around us again. "Top, tell me about this Calvin Williams."

"I can't tell you anything else for sure, but he came after me when I recognized him. He's been the reason for all the meanness that's going on right now."

"I can't arrest a man based on what you've dreamed."

"I know that."

"Bust him!" Pepper couldn't be still. "Him and that other clown attacked all three of us. You can at least get the son of a bitch for *kidnapping*, can't you?"

"I can get him for assault, if we can prove it was Williams, but how do you know *who* was under all that makeup."

Mark rose to his feet and ran both hands through his hair. "Clowns, man. We were attacked by clowns. That's just downright *creepy*."

"Them things are awful." Mr. Ike twisted around to look over one shoulder like one was sneaking up on him. "You don't know who or what's under all that greasy paint."

"All right." Miss Anna patted Mr. Ike's arm. "I know. We're gonna find out who they were. Top, are you hurt?"

"He didn't hurt me. My nail-hole's bleeding pretty good, though. They grabbed Mark and Pepper."

"They stabbed you with a *nail*?"

"Naw, stepped on one yesterday."

"All right. You stay off of it for the time being." Still not understanding, she eyed Pepper. "Well, I know *you're* all right. Mark, how about you?"

He rotated his shoulder. "That'un had me in an arm lock and I believe he near twisted my elbow behind my head, but I'll be all right."

She turned back to me. "Do you need some help to walk?"

"I'll help him." Mr. Ike took up his shovel. "They'll stay with me."

"Fine. Y'all head for the gate and I'll go look for Calvin Williams."

Chapter Seventy-two

Anna left the kids with Ike Reader and headed in the direction Mark had pointed. She stopped at the first game booth she came to. The owner of the Basketball Throw was already taking it apart and packing up the prizes. "Hey, buddy. Do you know someone named Calvin Williams who's a clown?"

The greasy-haired young man stopped and glanced at her badge, but it took a moment for him to lift his eyes. She could tell he didn't want to answer any questions from the law and was more interested in her chest than anything else. "Why?"

"Don't matter why. Hey, my eyes are up here. Do…you… know…Calvin Williams?"

The man raised his gaze. "No."

"Try again."

"I don't know no Calvin Williams."

She grinned. "So what does he go by, then?"

The carney forgot the stuffed elephant in his hand. This time his eyes went directly to the tent. "There's a guy named Cal who mechanics here. Clowns sometimes."

"That's the one. Cal how much?"

He immediately understood her request for a last name. "Willis."

"And that doesn't make you think of Calvin Williams?"

"Well, maybe."

"Do you know where he is?"

He suddenly acted like the stuffed elephant was too heavy to hold and sat it on the counter. "He might be in his trailer."

"Where is it?"

"Turn before that titty tent, uh, the girls sideshow over yonder. His is the one with the green awning. Lives with a little hippie gal named Connie."

Without another word, Anna drew her revolver and followed his directions, stepping between the tents and dodging the stakes and guy ropes. The dilapidated trailer was dark. Holding the pistol down beside her leg, Anna checked the area, then stood to the side and knocked on the trailer door.

She heard shuffling on the other side. The door cracked open and a young woman's face appeared. "Shhh. The baby's asleep."

"Connie?"

The long-haired girl's expression was quizzical. "Yes."

"Does Calvin Williams live with you?"

"No. Cal Willis does."

"Is he here?"

Connie opened the door wider, but kept her voice low. Her black eye and bruised face spoke volumes to the deputy. "Just left. Cleaned up and took off. He's the new advance man." She finally noticed Anna's uniform and posture. "Why? Is something wrong?"

"I need to find him."

"Well, like I said. He's gone."

Anna took in the puffy eye and noticed even more bruising on her neck and ear. "Are you all right?"

"I'm fine. Cal took his Indian and left."

"Who's that?" She had a brief image of him with Tonto.

"His Indian motorcycle. He couldn't take the truck because I need it to pull the trailer tomorrow, so he took the bike."

"How long ago?"

"Ten, fifteen minutes. He was in a hurry. He left so fast I don't even think he got all the paint off his face."

Paint. Top had mentioned greasepaint a moment earlier and a wisp at the edge of her mind told her it was important. "Can I come in and look around?"

"I done told you the truth."

"I know, but I need to make sure."

The girl stepped back. "Just don't wake the baby."

Connie held the door for her and gently took Anna's arm. "I got a lot to tell you about him."

Chapter Seventy-three

It was daylight by the time they got everything sorted out. Though no one was killed in the melee, half a dozen Mayfields and Clays had been transported to the hospital in funeral home ambulances. Bryce was hurt the worst, but expected to live. After being used as a battering ram, Cecil Clay had a broken arm and leg, and two dislocated knees. Royal didn't regain consciousness until he was strapped down on the stretcher. They would all eventually go to trial.

Half a dozen deputies and highway patrol officers hauled more than two dozen combatants from both sides to jail for a laundry list of charges. The midway was finally stilled. Knives, saps, and a dropped pair of brass knuckles littered the churned ground like a medieval battleground.

Ned, Cody, and John finally joined Anna beside Calvin Williams' trailer after getting the kids' and Ike's statement before sending them home. Norma Faye reluctantly rode with them, almost in shock at the thought that her ex-husband was the devil behind everything that had happened the past week.

Ned slid both hands into his pants pockets and watched the carneys break down the rest of the rides and exhibits. Some were packed and ready to go, while other rides were more complicated. They'd been inside with Connie, gathering as much information as they could about Calvin, who was long gone.

Cody scratched the stubble on his chin. "I can't believe Calvin Williams is behind all this. I never thought he had sense enough to pour piss out of a boot and here he was, a clown right under our noses."

"I need to get my hands on 'im." Ned lifted his hat to wipe the band. The humidity was still thick and heavy. The back of his ear was throbbing and he was feeling mean as an old sore-tailed tomcat.

John tilted his head toward the sound of the baby crying inside the trailer. "Do you think he got after Top just 'cause the boy recognized him?"

Replacing his hat, Ned grunted. "We'll find out once we catch him."

Cody cross his arms and studied his boots, thinking. "Well, we got an APB out for him. He won't get far riding a motorcycle without somebody seeing him."

Anna leaned against Calvin's truck. "Connie told me all about this guy. He's been going out at all hours and coming back smelling like smoke. She says she figures he's hurt some folks, but doesn't know for sure."

Thinking hard, Cody glanced into the truck bed and raised an eyebrow. It was odd in that part of the country to see a bed so devoid of farming litter. Most every truck he'd ever seen was littered with hay, bailing wire, and feed sacks. The boards in the Ford's bed were clean except for coiled ropes they used to stake tents and a few muddy footprints.

He reached in and picked up one of the coils. "Well."

Ned leaned in to look. "Well, what?"

John understood at once. He walked around and dropped the tailgate with a bang. "Looky here."

Anna came around. "What? Rope, stakes, and footprints."

"This is red clay."

"So?"

"Red clay that looks like what might have come from under a hanging tree. This is the same kind of rope somebody used to hang Charlie Clay."

Anna cleared her throat. "That's what's been bothering me. Connie said he left so fast he didn't get all of it off and that's what was on the hanging rope that we thought was grease or paint. It was grease*paint*. The kind clowns use to make themselves up."

"We got him." Cody patted his pocket to celebrate with a cigarette. There wasn't even a stick of gum in there.

Chapter Seventy-four

We were sitting around the laminate and chrome table in Miss Becky's kitchen the next morning. Instead of bustling around, she was in her usual place, sipping her second cup of coffee, something she rarely had. I'd never seen her so still.

"This old world's gettin' so rough, I believe I'm afraid to let any of y'all go anywhere. We just need to stay at home from now on."

Pepper frowned at her plate. "That won't be any better, now that Mama and Daddy's bought the Ordway place. It's just as dangerous as eating dinner in the middle of the highway."

Mark grinned and picked at a piece of toast. "It wasn't nothing but the wrong place at the wrong time."

Miss Becky studied me. "You poor kids. Y'all've been through more'n kids your age ought to have ever seen. I hate it, and I know it's hard on you. It was Calvin you been dreaming about, ain't it, hon?"

"I believe so. Everything fit. The lights, the giant lips...all of it."

"Do you think it's over?"

"My dreams? No."

"Why not?"

"He got away."

Norma Faye came in from the bathroom where she'd washed her face. Her eyes were red and puffy from crying. Uncle Cody dropped her off and promised to be back as quick as he could. "Miss Becky, I'm so sorry."

"Hush, hon. This ain't nothing you done."

"But I was married to him…and…you know, that brought this trouble."

Miss Becky's eyes cut over at us. "Well, that was then and this is now. This ain't your doin'. You're family now, so that's it. Me and you'll talk later, but you quit frettin' about it."

Pepper glanced at the wooden kitchen door that was propped open to air the house out. There was nothing between us and the outside but wire screen held closed with an eyehook latch. "He could come walking right in here like nobody's business if he had a mind to."

Norma Faye nearly dropped her coffee cup. She looked as scared as if she'd picked up a snake.

Miss Becky sipped again. "No he won't. Hootie's outside and I'm not afraid with that shotgun leaning in the corner."

"One of them clowns didn't have you down on the ground."

"Well Pepper, I don't expect to see any clowns coming up the driveway this morning."

Mark grinned. "That's the truth. It's so hot his makeup would run off his face like ice cream."

Still trembling, Norma Faye leaned a hip against the cabinet counter and took a long, shuddering breath. "I'm so sorry."

"Hush, I said." Miss Becky reached out a hand and Norma Faye took it.

Pepper gave Mark a good-natured nudge and twirled her long hair. "Well, it's too hot to do anything today. I just want to go in the living room and listen to the radio."

"All right." Miss Becky stood to clear the table. "Y'all get out from underfoot, but don't turn it up too loud."

We left the table and Pepper dialed a station in until it was clear. "Take the Last Train to Clarksville" was on and Pepper made a face. "I hope they play something good after this shit."

I limped over to the couch and laid down where I could see the south door. I didn't want anybody to come sneaking in from that way. Mark laid down on his stomach and opened *The Chisum News* on the rag rug covering the floor. He turned to the Sunday comics and I watched a fly bump the screen while Miss Becky and Norma Faye talked in the kitchen.

Chapter Seventy-five

Ed's Tourist Cabins in Hugo, Oklahoma, was the perfect place to lay low for a couple of days. Reclined in a sagging bed in cabin number five, Calvin lit another cigarette and thought back over the past week. There was no longer any use in stirring up trouble between the Clays and Mayfields. They were already mad enough to kill each other for the next ten years. His idea of framing Cody for all of it had failed, but his string of successes was like a tonic.

He'd killed and burned out some of those who wronged him, and that was enough for now. He could even come back and finish up tomorrow, next month, or next year.

He was patient, and smarter than any lawman he ever ran into. He chuckled. Even if he had to wait another year or two, it would be sheer hell for them every time they opened their eyes in the morning, wondering if this was the day, or if he'd come tomorrow.

With the makeup gone, Clocko the Clown ceased to exist. Cal Willis was also gone. He didn't think of himself as Calvin Williams, either. He was now The Wraith, and he had business to finish.

The Wraith drew a deep breath, smelling the gas from his Indian that had barely fit through the door.

He lay there with both hands behind his head, listening to Hank Williams on the radio and remembering how he'd cut Hollis Mayfield in two with a shotgun because Hollis once dusted Calvin's back and ass with a load of rock salt one night when he and his running buddy Ron Preston snuck into Hollis' watermelon patch. The teenagers were headed for the woods carrying a melon apiece when the dim of a flashlight beam caught them two rows away from the barbed-wire fence.

Hollis hollered and cut loose with one barrel that hissed through the air behind them. Ron dropped his watermelon and ducked to the left. Calvin made the mistake of hanging onto a big melon and running straight for the fence. When they didn't stop, Hollis fired again and the load of salt had time to spread out, cutting through his clothes and setting him on fire.

Calvin remembered how he screamed at the impact, thinking he'd been shot for real. It was only after the wounds began to burn with an ungodly fire that he realized what had happened. He ran through the woods in an inferno of pain. They met up at the car parked on the other side of a strip of woods and Ron drove across the river to his uncle's house while Calvin shrieked and writhed in the backseat.

The uncle he never saw again used the point of a knife and tweezers to pick the salt from the seeping, burning wounds in his back, ass, and legs. The scars were still there, and from time to time Calvin found himself rubbing his fingertips across the thick skin, remembering.

The worst was when women asked him about them. He could never come up with a good story, instead telling the truth and waiting in embarrassment for them to laugh, which they always did.

Now he'd settled all but one of the scores that had plagued him all his life. He grinned at the stained ceiling, thinking about how he'd finish the job that night and be gone. Something up there caught his attention, and he stood to turn on all the lights. A laugh bubbled in his chest when he recognized the stain as blood splatter. He followed the dried drops from the ceiling down the wall to where it had been wiped away.

It looked as if someone had taken a baseball bat to whoever'd been sleeping in his bed. That, or the guy had blown his own brains out.

The Wraith dropped back on the bed and laughed loud and long at the irony.

Wouldn't Norma Faye and Cody be surprised when they woke up dead in *their* bed the next morning?

Chapter Seventy-six

The lawmen's cars were positioned the next morning to temporarily block the lanes crossing the Lake Lamar Dam. Ned's shirt was already sticking to his back, telling him it was going to be another miserable day. Despite the heat and humidity, he felt better after catching a few hours of sleep.

John, Anna, and Cody joined him at the twisted guardrail to hear Anna's theory about the car crash and resulting clash between the two families. She pointed at the highway only twenty feet away from the damaged rail. "See that tire mark?"

Cody used his foot to point. "This curved one here?"

"Right. Those short skidmarks from Maggie's car are back there, and there are two of them. This is where someone peeled out on a motorcycle."

Ned studied the scars on the slope below and then looked up to see his house a mile in the distance. He unconsciously scanned the horizon and stopped when he saw the roof of Cody's house.

"My Lord."

John heard the tension in his voice. "What, Mr. Ned?"

"It's as plain as the nose on my face." Ned pointed. "John, that there's the roof of Cody's house in them trees and there's mine on the hill over yonder."

"So?"

Anna agreed. "That's my point. Calvin Williams was sitting here in the dark on his bike, watching y'all's houses. It was late. Maggie and Frank came around at a high rate of speed. She instinctively tried to dodge him and instead of taking to a ditch, they went through the rail. That mark's from where he peeled out and was gone."

Ned's voice was soft, as if he were trying to sneak up on the answer that he already knew. "She's right, but that still don't explain what *they* were doing together."

She pointed to the wooded overlook. "You can park against the trees and nobody can see you. My guess is they spent most of the night right there, talking. They could have been having sex, or arguing, or both for all I know, but from what I've heard, they'd probably decided to be together because Maggie was pregnant."

Anna spoke softly, eyes almost closed as if she could see that night. The dam was silent. A hawk rode the thermals above the woods lining the creek. "She started to have an abortion in Frogtown, but changed her mind." She saw Ned's eyebrow rise. "Miss Sweet sent Ralston to bring her back. Miss Sweet told John, and I talked to some other women, so I know it's true."

Cody faced the west in the direction the car was traveling. "So Frank and Maggie's accident was just that, an accident that came at the worst possible time. But I'm still wondering why his car was at a joint across the river. No one there saw them."

"'cause that's a good place to leave one." John thought aloud. "Maybe they just pulled up out there at the edge of the lot and he got in with her."

Anna thought about it. "It fits. I doubt people recognized a car from Chisum sitting out there in the dark. They were probably going to go back and get it before daylight, but almost ran into Calvin instead. Good Lord. He had no idea who they were at first, but when he found out, he used the wreck to restart this feud and tried to put the blame on Cody. At the same time *we* got locked into who they were. It led us to concentrate on the wrong set of events."

She watched their reactions. "It was brilliant. Once we get all this sorted out, I think we'll find that he was behind some of the fires, in addition to the murders of Merle Mayfield, Joe Bill, and if I'm right, Hollis Mayfield."

Ned rubbed the back of his neck, digesting her theory. The puzzle pieces fell into place and they all fit when he realized why Calvin had been on the dam in the first place. "He was settin' here, Cody, stewing on you and Norma Faye, I 'magine. Y'all might have been next, or if he hadn't got caught here that night, first."

Cody's eyes roamed over the house and woods. "If y'all are right, Calvin'll might try to come to the house."

John shook his head. "That guy's most likely gone for good."

"But we don't know that. If Maggie'd hit him, none of the rest of this would have happened." Cody hooked both thumbs behind his gunbelt. "But she didn't and he got away. Anna, you done good. This explains almost everything."

"Except where Calvin Williams is now," Ned said.

Cody drew a long breath. "All right. Let's get back to what we were doing and see if we can't run him down. We need to find him now more than ever."

They started back to the cars when John pointed. "Sheriff, your car's leaking oil."

Cody squatted and looked underneath. Oil dripped like water. "Dammit. Looks like the oil pan's got a hole in it. Look at the size of that puddle."

Ned's stomach rumbled, reminding him he'd only had coffee for breakfast. "You think you got enough to get back to town?"

"Maybe. You follow me, though, just in case."

"You bet. I'll bring you back to the house." Ned faced the creek bottom and the house he'd called home for the past forty years. "Mama'll have dinner ready by then."

Chapter Seventy-seven

The Wraith couldn't take lying around the Oklahoma motel room any longer. His head throbbed all night from where Ike Reader split his scalp with the shovel and he added Reader to his now short list of people to settle up with.

The urge to do something, anything, took over. No one would be looking for him in Center Springs. Anyone with any sense would think he was long gone from the state. Right *now* was the time to finish his business and go.

He worked the handlebars of his 1949 Indian through the cabin door. Once outside, he tied a red bandanna around his head and put on a pair of sunglasses, figuring it was enough of a disguise to do what he wanted.

He kicked the engine alive and grinned. He had a new plan. Like everyone else in his old community, Ned's family most likely gathered at his house for Sunday dinner. The Wraith decided to ride his bike back into Texas to the Sanders Creek bridge and park it underneath. Then he could follow Center Springs Branch, just like he did the night he slipped into Norma Faye's house, only this time it would be broad daylight.

No one would be there and he could wait for the couple to come home, full of fried chicken and sleepy, and not expecting what they were due. The Wraith pressed his left arm against his chest, feeling the knife under his shirt.

It would be quick and silent. Then he could simply walk

back down the stream and ride away. It would all be happy trails after that.

He gunned the engine and rode south, singing the Roy Rogers song. "Happy trails to you..."

The Wraith crossed the Red River bridge twenty minutes later and into Texas. He turned right onto 197 and glanced into his rearview mirror. A red Plymouth Fury popped up right behind him and he recognized the men in the front seat. "Oh, shit!"

In the passenger seat, Sheriff Cody Parker slapped a red light onto the roof and it came to life.

The Wraith gunned the engine.

His plan had just come unraveled.

Chapter Seventy-eight

The motorcycle accelerated as soon as Ned turned in behind him. He mashed the accelerator and the Plymouth's big engine roared.

"I don't believe it!" Cody slapped a light on the roof and snatched the microphone off the dash. "John! Anna!"

Deputy John Washington came back first. "Cody, what's wrong?"

"We're coming back from dropping my car off and Ned just turned in behind Calvin Williams on that Indian motorcycle. He's on 197 from Arthur City and heading for Center Springs. Where are you?"

"I was nearly to my house." The sounds of squalling tires came through the Motorola's speaker telling Cody the deputy was making a U-turn. "I'm on the way."

"Ned!"

"Go ahead, Anna!"

"I'm coming, too."

"Where are you?"

"Just west of Powderly."

Ned leaned forward over the wheel and squinted into the distance. "Tell her to come back down the new road across the dam."

Cody saw the wisdom in the move that would close off all three routes. Williams would have only one option to escape and that would be to take the dirt roads through the bottoms that led nowhere. They'd have him trapped.

Ned grunted. "She shuts that road off, and we'll have him."

"Did you get that, Anna? Come through Powderly and cut him off at the dam."

"Got it."

Chapter Seventy-nine

The Wraith twisted the accelerator, leaning into the curves as he pulled away from Ned's Plymouth. The white Indian jumped forward and roared down the road. He couldn't believe his bad luck! It was the same luck he'd had all his life and he was *tired* of it. He was smarter than everybody else, but John Law was always picking on him, or showing up at the wrong time, or trying to bust him for things that were out of his control. Now here they were again, right on his ass and it just wasn't *right!*

After one quick glance over his shoulder, he leaned over the handlebars. He blew around a lumbering truck full of hay. The Wraith shot past the startled farmer and hit the straightaway leading to the creek bridge. He gained distance on the one mile straightaway to the curve around Ned's house.

Past it, the turnoff over the dam was only another mile farther on.

He could take it, cross the lake, and then cut back down Highway 271 for just a minute and disappear into the backroads on the east side. From there he had a dozen options. His best bet was to head for Red River County and cross back into southeast Oklahoma. If he could make it to the gravel and dirt roads in the rugged, undeveloped Kiamichi Mountains, they'd never find him.

Chapter Eighty

The hay truck slowed Ned and he chewed his lip for a few seconds until he could see the oncoming lane. It was clear and he pushed the pedal to the floor.

Cody braced himself with one hand on the dash and the other gripping the door. He knew the old constable was a good driver, but when he glanced at the speedometer as they hit the Sanders Creek straightaway, the needle was pegged at 120 miles per hour. "Careful, Ned."

"You want to drive?"

"Yes."

"Well, we don't have time to switch."

"Then why'd you *ask* me?"

"'cause you wanted me to."

Ahead, the motorcycle's taillight flickered as he slowed to round the curve past Ned's house.

Cody keyed the microphone. "He passed Ned's house. If he don't take the oil road to the bottoms, he'll be in Center Springs in half a minute. John, cut him off."

"Nearly there."

Chapter Eighty-one

The thick air was so still that I could hear a motorcycle coming over the creek bridge. It was whining loud and coming fast. A car was winding out behind it and I thought some teenagers were racing. I limped across the living room and went out on the front porch. Pepper and Mark followed me.

From the edge, we could see down the straightaway from the bridge. Mark whistled. "Man! That bike's *moving!*"

Pepper grabbed a porch post and leaned out to see better. "I hope he knows this curve's coming up." Her hair hung down as she tilted her head to see around the brushy Bois d' Arc tree at the bottom of the curve. "If he don't, he's gonna wind up in that bodark or Gary Halpin's raggedy-assed barbed-wire fence."

Mark pointed. "Look! That's Grandpa's Plymouth chasing that guy! Look at him go! Whooee! He's a driving son-of-a-gun. I never woulda thought it."

The pitch of the motorcycle's engine changed as he slowed to take the bend. We lost him for a second at the bottom of the hill and then he shot out past the house, leaning into the S-curve and accelerating even faster toward Center Springs.

"Son of a bitch!"

I heard a crack and turned to see Miss Becky'd whacked Pepper on the back of the head. "You watch your language on the Sabbath, young lady."

She mouthed "shit" and rubbed her head as Grandpa came around the curve, tires squalling. "Mark said son-of-a-gun."

"Well, that ain't really cussin'. You keep a civil tongue."

The back end almost broke on the Plymouth below the house and the tires squealed, but he steered into it and his engine roared again as the road straightened. He shot past and we had time to see Uncle Cody in the passenger seat, talking into the Motorola's microphone.

Mark turned to look at me. "Man! Someday I'm gonna be a lawman."

I liked the idea. "We can be partners, deputies."

Pepper rolled her eyes. "Oh, puhleeze."

Movement caught my attention behind Pepper and I saw Norma Faye's eyes were watery again. "That's Calvin. They said he got away on an Indian motorcycle." Her voice broke into deep sobs when she turned from the door and went back inside with Miss Becky behind her.

The three of us stayed on the porch to listen as the car's tires whined away toward Center Springs on the hot concrete.

Chapter Eighty-two

Cody keyed the mike again. "He's past the cutoffs to the bottoms and headed your way, John. Can you catch him before he gets to Oak Peterson's store?"

"I ain't there yet. Got behind Ike Reader and a trailer full of cows. If Williams gets to Center Springs before me, he might take to that oil road past the Ordway place. If I miss him, it'll take him around behind me and I won't even know it 'til I get there."

"Do your best. Anna, where are you?"

"Off the highway and almost to the dam. I have him cut off on this side."

There weren't any roads branching off that one. "Don't let him get around you, gal."

"Don't worry about that."

John's voice came back through the speaker. "Coming into Center Springs. I don't see him. He might have cut off before the post office and headed to the bottoms that way."

Cody started to tell him that didn't happen, because they could see the bike ahead when John came back through. "There he is!"

The radio was silent for a moment, and the two lawmen held their breath as wooden fenceposts flashed past in a blur. John's voice came through. "He turned toward the lake. He damn near lost it when he saw me. Anna, he's heading your way. Ned, look out!"

Chapter Eighty-three

The Wraith was thinking of only one thing.

Getting across Highway 271.

He saw John's oncoming deputy sheriff's car at the last moment. For just a second, he considered shooting off on the oil road behind Neal Box's store, but decided on hard concrete instead of an oil road so he could ride faster.

He nearly laid the bike down, drastically cutting his speed and dropping his left foot to the pavement. The sole of his boot smoked as the rear tire skidded, caught some traction, and then he was back up, leaning over the handlebars and accelerating past the Baptist church.

The Wraith threw a look back over his shoulder and laughed when Ned almost skidded into John's car. They stopped in a cloud of white smoke.

The Wraith ducked to reduce the wind resistance and shot toward the dam.

One minute. That's all he needed. One more minute to gain enough distance to get clear.

He was gonna make it.

Then he'd come back in a couple of years and kill every *god-damned* one of those Parkers.

Chapter Eighty-four

"Look out, Ned!" Cody stiff-armed the dash, his eyes wide.

"Shit!"

He'd already committed to the turn at the same time John whipped his car to the right. Ned's brakes shrieked as he fought the wheel. For a moment, Cody saw the terrified look on John's face as they slid toward the deputy's car.

John jerked the steering wheel to the left toward Oak's store. Ned spun *his* wheel left and their rear bumpers kissed as the cars skidded past in a boil of burned rubber and dust. Without missing a beat, the old constable stomped the accelerator again. The back tires white-smoked on the pavement until they caught traction and shot forward. John spun a full 360 degrees on the gravel and bottle-top lot and roared down the highway behind them.

Holding the dash with one hand, Cody keyed the mike. "Anna. He's yours. He's coming across the dam with us and John right behind."

"I see the lookout. I'm stopping in the middle of the dam and blocking it with the car. He won't have anywhere to go."

"He might try to get around. Use your shotgun. Shoot the son of a bitch off the bike if you need to. Don't let him get by."

"You want me to shoot a man for fleeing?"

"Fine then. Shoot the tires."

"That's the same thing on a motorcycle."

"I know it."

Ned shook his head and spoke to Cody. "Some folks just need killin'."

Chapter Eighty-five

A bug exploded against The Wraith's face, stinging like he'd been slapped. "Dammit!" He hit the dam and accelerated to make time. Another bug hit him above the eyebrow as he punched through a thick swarm of bees. Their soft bodies felt like BBs against his face. He ducked his head, terrified that one would hit him in the eye. He didn't have time to slow down. He needed all the distance he could get between himself and his pursuers.

The curve in the middle of the dam approached and he let off the accelerator. Coasting into the bend, he hit the gas. The next thing he knew the tires felt like they were on ice. The bike slammed to the pavement. The Wraith's head smacked the concrete with the sound of a dropped melon. He heard a sharp crack and then nothing.

The bike skidded across the oncoming lane with his leg trapped beneath, sanding through his jeans and then flesh. The Indian shot through the hole in the railing. What was left of the man now known only as Calvin hit one of the splintered support posts with his shattered head before the limp body flew off the edge and rolled down the already scarred dam.

Chapter Eighty-six

Ned rolled onto the bridge the same moment he saw Calvin's bike hit the ground and disappear off the edge. "Son of a bitch!"

Cody brought the mike to his lips. "Anna?"

"I didn't do it. I didn't shoot. He lost control on the curve and went over the backside."

Ned slowed and stopped before he reached the twisted guardrails. He and Cody were out of the car as John pulled up behind them. Anna arrived moments later and they met beside the twisted rails opening to the north.

There was no movement down below. John took the shotgun from Anna's hands and started down the slope. "I'll check him out."

"I've already called an ambulance." Anna stopped with her knees against the railing.

Cody nudged Ned and pointed. "Look. He hit that oil from my car. It must have felt like ice."

"An oil slick'll do the same thing." Ned wiped the sweat off his face with a shaking hand. "That proves what I've always said."

"What's that?"

"Folks always get what they deserve."

Chapter Eighty-seven

We heard rather than saw the wreck that killed Calvin Williams. The three of us were still standing on the porch when the whine of Grandpa's big engine reached us from the dam. I was squinting that direction when I heard the distant crash and saw something shoot off the road up there.

"Dude!" Mark's voice was almost a whisper. "That bike went off the side. One minute he passes here alive and the next he's probably dead right there."

Miss Becky was in the living room and heard us. "My sweet Lord. Norma Faye, thank the Lord it's over and our people are safe."

Norma Faye spoke quietly to herself, and I believe she didn't think anyone could hear her, but she was wrong. I was close to the screen door and her voice came through crystal clear. "Thank God. I hope it killed him."

She turned away and didn't say anything else.

Her comment froze my brain for a second and I stood there, gaping like a fish. Pepper stepped off the porch. I watched her. She started across the yard and I found my voice again. "What are you doing?"

"Going to see the wreck."

Mark stopped at the edge of the porch. "What?"

I pointed toward the dam, past the trees on the opposite side of the highway. "There's a trail that leads to right where he went off. We used it last weekend when Frank and Maggie died in that same place." I paused and swallowed a lump in my throat. "That was only a little over a week ago."

Pepper was already going down the hill. Mark dropped off the porch and followed her. "You coming?"

I thought about it. "I'll be behind y'all. I can't walk as fast as you, and besides, I've done seen enough over there."

He threw me a wave and disappeared down the hill. They reappeared across the highway and ducked into the woods. I didn't want to go, but then I remembered the Kleenex I'd picked up when we went to see Frank and Maggie's wreck. It was wrapped around something, but I'd forgotten all about it.

I slapped my empty pocket like it would be there and waited a beat, thinking.

I figured I'd lost it somewhere between here and there, and all of a sudden I wanted that lump of tissue really bad. I stepped off the porch on my good foot and limped along behind them.

Sweat broke out on my face in no time, but it was cooler in the woods. It felt like it took a week to break out the other side, then cross the meadow to the trees lining Center Springs Branch. Mark and Pepper weren't anywhere in sight when I came to the foot log. I stopped to rest, feeling my nail-hole throb. That log looked as skinny as a straw and I wondered if I'd be able to limp across.

I didn't have to, though.

A wisp of smoke formed at the edge of the deep draw and while I watched, it became a woman, then Mama. She stood there as real as anything, holding a chubby baby with curly black hair. Tears sprang into my eyes and I couldn't move. She smiled at me. The worried look I'd seen on her face the last time was gone, replaced by something different. She was younger this time, like she looked in those old black-and-white pictures Miss Becky kept in a shoebox in the closet.

Her hair was soft and wavy, and the worry lines in her forehead were gone. She was wearing a skirt and blouse I'd seen in old pictures of her and Daddy. She bounced that baby for a second as it grabbed for her chin, and then pointed to the ground.

There wasn't anything there, so I looked back up and she nodded her head in the same direction.

"Mama?" There was nobody else around, and I desperately needed to hear her voice one more time.

It didn't come. She pointed again and waved and turned and walked into the space over the deep gully. I could see that baby's face looking back over her shoulder at me. It was one of them mixed babies, white and black.

Then they were gone.

I limped over to the base of the footlog and looked down where she pointed into the gully to see the tissue that had fallen out of my pocket. It was caught on a root poking out from the side, about two feet down.

I got down on my stomach and stretched as far as I could. My fingertips barely touched the Kleenex and I was afraid I'd knock it loose and it'd fall all the way to the bottom, but I caught it between my index and middle fingers.

I sat up and twisted around with my feet over the edge. Using my thumb, I tore the tissue open and shook two rings into my palm. One was a band big enough to fit a man's hand. The other was a woman's wedding ring.

I studied on them for a second and realized they belonged to Frank and Maggie who'd died in that wreck, and what those two little bands of gold meant. Mama's mixed baby came suddenly clear and the rings burned hot in my palm. A deep pool down below told me what to do. I pitched them into the water where they disappeared in two tiny splashes. A squirrel ran out on a limb, probably the same one that scolded me a week earlier, and told me off, but I barely heard him.

I waited until the water stilled. Thinking I'd kept their secret, I struggled to my feet and went back to the house.

To receive a free catalog of Poisoned Pen Press titles, please provide your name, address, and e-mail address in one of the following ways:

Phone: 1-800-421-3976
Facsimile: 1-480-949-1707
Email: info@poisonedpenpress.com
Website: www.poisonedpenpress.com

Poisoned Pen Press
6962 E. First Ave. Ste 103
Scottsdale, AZ 85251